FIDELI

Fidelis Morgan is an actor and an ~~~ ~~~
comedy. Acclaimed for her stage plays, ~~~
Hangover Square, she also collaborated with Lynd~~~
Plante on Channel 4's tense psychological thriller *Killer Net*. She has written non-fiction studies of charismatic female figures from the seventeenth and eighteenth centuries, and edited the bestselling Virago anthology, *Wicked*.

Forune's Slave is the fourth novel to feature the Countess and Alpiew – dubbed 'Cagney and Lacey in corsets' by one admiring critic.

Up-to-date news of personal appearances and future publications can be found at www.fidelismorgan.com

By the same author

FICTION

The Rival Queens
Unnatural Fire
The Ambitious Stepmother

NON-FICTION

The Well-Known Troublemaker
A Woman of No Character
The Female Wits
A Misogynist's Source Book
Bluffer's Guide to Theatre

PLAYS & ADAPTATIONS

Pamela
Hangover Square

Fortune's Slave

A Countess Ashby de la Zouche Mystery

FIDELIS MORGAN

HarperCollinsPublishers

HarperCollins*Publishers*
77–85 Fulham Palace Road,
London W6 8JB

www.harpercollins.co.uk

This paperback edition 2005

1 3 5 7 9 8 6 4 2

First published in Great Britain by
HarperCollins*Publishers* 2004

ISBN 0 00 713428 2

Typeset in Meridien
by Palimpsest Book Production Limited, Polmont, Stirlingshire

Printed in Great Britain by
Clays Ltd, St Ives plc

ONE

Tear — one or more bubbles deliberately introduced into glass by pricking it and letting the resultant bubble expand in the heat

'What was that noise?' The Countess sat bolt upright in bed, leaving her wig on the pillow. 'Listen! We're being burgled!'

Anastasia, Lady Ashby de la Zouche, Countess of Clapham, Baroness Penge, etc . . . was not accustomed to worrying about burglars. She never usually had anything worth stealing, but, for once, she was sitting upon a fortune: one hundred guineas in bright shiny coins. 'Someone is upstairs. Don't you hear?'

A body in an adjacent bed shifted, groaning, and a blanket fell to the stone-flagged floor.

'Burglars, inside the house!' repeated the Countess. 'Listen! Hear the boards creaking.'

A series of dull squeaks and the muffled sounds of padding feet seemed to pass across the ceiling above.

'Shut your row!' growled Godfrey, the Countess's ancient steward, letting another blanket slip to the floor. 'Some folk are trying to sleep.'

'Criminy, I hear it!' In a flash of white linen, Alpiew, the

Countess's quondam maid, leaped out of the third bed and stood with her ear pressed to the door, a raised poker in her hand. 'He's coming down the stairs!' She snatched the carving knife from a nearby shelf. 'Watch out for me, milady. I'm going to check.'

The Countess held up her hand, signalling Alpiew to wait while she gave Godfrey a wallop and pulled his bedclothes right back. 'Come on, you lazy slubberdegullion,' she hissed. 'You're meant to be the man of the house. Get out there with Alpiew.'

Baring his gums in an ineffectual snarl, Godfrey got up and took a position behind Alpiew while the Countess lit a candle from the dying embers of the fire.

'Wait till I have light.' The Countess shielded the flame and moved towards the door. 'Let's get him.' She gave Alpiew a nod.

Alpiew inched the kitchen door open. 'Go!' she shouted, dashing into the hallway just as the front door slammed shut. 'I'm going after him.' She loped the length of the hall, pulled the door open and stood on the step, looking left and right along German Street.

But she could see no one running into the moonless night.

'Where the devil? Help ho! Watch!' cried Alpiew from the doorstep. 'Where is the night-watch?' In her night-gown, still clutching the poker and knife, she ran along the cobbled street to the small box which housed the night-watch Charlie, and hammered upon the side.

An elderly man kicked the door open and lifted his head. 'What an almighty noise,' he grunted, pulling his coat around him. 'What are you waking me up for? I was asleep.'

'So I see, you bone-idle bugger. Might I remind you, you dribbling dotard, that you are paid to stay *awake* at night,' yelled Alpiew. 'Someone was just now inside our house and made their escape by running right past you while you snored away your hours of duty . . .'

'That's a nice pair you've got . . .' The old man was focused upon Alpiew's enormous bosom and quite lost to all reasonable thought. 'Can I 'ave a feel . . . ?'

'No, you cannot.' Alpiew pulled her night-gown up almost to her chin. 'You'd better fetch the constable, and fast.'

'But I'm a war veteran . . .'

'I don't care if you're the ghost of the Great Protector himself. Get on with it!' Alpiew slammed the door on his foot and ran back towards the house.

The Countess, who had been lingering on the doorstep, waving the candle about and peering into the dark, turned and went back inside. She started to mount the staircase.

'Wait for me, madam.' Alpiew ran past her into the kitchen, where she replaced the carving knife with a gimlet and small hammer. 'Who knows what else you might find up there.'

'You mean . . . ?' The Countess, who was already half-way up the first flight, stopped where she stood and placed a chubby hand on her heaving bosom. 'Of course! He may have an accomplice.' She leaned over the banister and shouted down. 'Godfrey! Come upstairs. We need you.'

'Hold the light aloft, madam.' Alpiew handed the poker to the Countess as she overtook her, and, squinting into the dark, climbed the stairs to the first floor.

The candle guttered. The draught from their movement threw leaping shadows on to the decaying white walls as they reached the first landing.

The two women stood still and listened. Silence. Huddling together, the poker held out before them, the hammer high in the air, they tiptoed towards the first room. The Countess gripped on to Alpiew and nodded. Alpiew lurched forward and flung wide the door, revealing a dusty, dilapidated, small empty chamber. Pressing themselves tight against the landing wall they edged along to the next door. Again Alpiew held up the hammer, the Countess the candle.

Alpiew kicked the door. It slammed back, hitting the wall, revealing another larger rundown room. A lump of plaster fell from the ceiling and landed with a thud on the bare floorboards.

A sudden crash from the floor above made them leap up and shriek. Wax from the candle spilled down on to the Countess's hand, burning her skin.

'Godfrey! Godfrey!' Alpiew called down as she ran up the next flight of stairs. 'Go into the street and raise the hue and cry!'

'But I'm half-way up now . . .'

'Do it!' ordered the Countess.

Alpiew had already thrown open the door to the back top room and was now at the doorway of the front attic. She took a deep breath as she entered. She watched the casement fly open, bounce against its hinge, and slam shut with a thud. In the dark she crossed the room, pushed the window open again and looked out across the adjacent empty roofs.

''Tis nothing, madam,' she yelled back in the direction of the puffing Countess. 'The wind blowing the window, making it bang in its frame.'

'These stairs!' squawked the Countess. 'I'm sixty years old. Too old for mountaineering.'

As the Countess reached the top landing a hollering from below heralded the arrival of the constable and his headboroughs. Waving their lanterns and clutching smoking links, a band of men in night-gowns, boots and coats thumped upstairs.

'False alarm!' The Countess leaned over the banister and called to them. 'The window had come loose.'

'Are you sure no one is here?' A burly fellow, bearing the painted staff of constabulary authority, bounded up the stairs three by three. 'No intruder? No murderous malcontent with malice on his mind?' He shoved into the attic room, holding his staff before him in both hands, ready to use it as a weapon. His colleagues poured in behind him, sweeping Alpiew along in their wake.

'Someone made his exit through the front door a few minutes ago.' Alpiew did not like looking a fool, especially while standing in dishabillé in a room full of men. 'But I suspect he may have come into the house this way.'

The headboroughs ambled over to the window. They gathered in a huddle, scratching their stubbly chins, taking it in turns to glance out of the window. One after another they swung open the casement then shut it, examined the catch and the hinges, looked out into the night and then back into the room. All the while they nodded and grunted to each other.

'If a felon *was* here,' said the swarthy constable, handing his staff to a junior while brushing down his military coat. 'And if they used this particular window as a method of entry, I would suggest that the said intruder was a child of no more than ten years of age.' He stared out across the roofs. 'Definitely a child. A man's weight would have broken something out there, a tile perhaps, and a man would have been hard pressed to squeeze himself through this little frame.' He pulled the window shut. 'Not only that, I wonder if you were right in your assumption that there was an intruder at all.' He looked around the room, at the holed ceiling, the peeling walls, the lack of any furniture or adornment. 'What would a burglar be after? This place looks singularly uninviting for a thief. I'd venture a guess that no one has entered this room in months.'

'If it's any of your business,' snapped the Countess. She did not like people to know she had run into hard times and sold up all the furnishings and let the rest go to ruin, except for two rooms – the kitchen and the front parlour. 'We prefer the lower floors.'

'Wait!' said Alpiew. 'Someone has been in here.' She stooped in the corner and picked up a piece of nutshell. 'What is this?'

'You think someone came into your house to leave you a nutshell?' inquired the constable, looking at Alpiew as though she was an escapee from Bedlam.

Alpiew lurched towards him, fists raised.

'I didn't mean to offend, madam. But you should go to a locksmith and get this window seen to in case of a repeat visit. There is a good man in the Hay Market, I believe.' He stood to attention and saluted. 'I am John Shaw, by the way, your new constable.' He thrust out a sturdy hand. 'Formerly a captain in His Royal Highness's army, but now that the late strifes are ended, the wars in Europe resolved, and we proud English are supposed to pretend to be friends with the idiotic Dutch, the stinking French, the stupid Irish, the dirty Scots, the smug Spanish and all the other nasty foreign shagamuffins, I am engaged to serve my time instead hereabouts, on the streets of London, protecting the individual English citizen from locally bred miscreants.'

The Countess gave a wan smile, wondering if he had finished his speech.

After a few seconds' silence, when it became clear that he had, she thanked him and ushered him and his colleagues down the stairs and back out into the street.

'If the dirty little diver bothers you again, madam, know that, if I am not on the prowl keeping the streets safe, you can always rouse me at the green door next to The Feathers.' John Shaw lifted his coat to show a pistol tucked into his wide leather belt. 'Mesdames, witness! My weapon stands idle waiting upon your call.' He leaned close to the Countess and whispered into her ear. 'I have no doubt in my mind that if a child *was* employed to get in, there are other villains working in league with him.' He tapped his nose. 'Be alert!'

The Countess smiled and patted her nose by way of reply, leaving a grey dusty smudge.

'I shall watch while you secure your front door.' Captain Shaw saluted, then folded his arms and with a stern expression stood in the centre of the street, his legs planted firmly apart. 'Good night to you, ladies.'

'Come on, Alpiew,' whispered the Countess. 'We'd better check that the you-know-what is still under the you-know-where.' She ushered Alpiew in and closed the door behind them.

'Godfrey!' The Countess shouted, although Godfrey was standing only a few feet away. 'Balance a chair under the handle. Let's make sure we have no further nocturnal visitors.'

'Much good that'll do,' muttered Godfrey, slouching off to fetch a chair from the kitchen, 'when all the windows are rotten and all the catches broken.'

'The catches work perfectly, but first, Godfrey, they must be applied,' the Countess called after him. 'Some male member of the household should make it his business to go round each night and check.'

While Godfrey shoved a chair under the door handle, the Countess and Alpiew ran up the stairs to check on their stash of money, which was hidden in small amounts all around the house.

Alpiew stuck the gimlet down into the floor of the front

attic room, used the hammer to prise up a board and plunged her hand down into the rafter void. She pulled out the sheet-wrapped parcel. 'It's still here, and it's heavy enough.' She unravelled the fabric, revealing the dull glint of coins.

'I was worried.' The Countess took hold of the money-bag and cradled it as though it was a swaddled baby. 'The rest of tonight this precious cargo will stay under my pillow, and tomorrow morning I suggest we find some way to dispose of it.'

With cups of hot spiced beer and milk posset, the Countess, Alpiew and Godfrey sat up for hours discussing the problem.

'We could entrust it to a goldsmith for safe-keeping.' The Countess stroked the sheet-wrapped parcel on her lap.

'Milady, how often have you heard the tales of goldsmiths who absconded with their clients' funds, or went bankrupt, having secretly spent all the money that they were paid to keep safe? We would never know it was gone till it was too late. At least we trust each other and while we hold on to it can keep checking to make sure it is all here.'

'We could buy lots of valuable jewellery or paintings,' said Godfrey. 'Some folk do that.'

'Yes – and a burglar could still run off with them.' Alpiew had never understood the world's fascination with precious stones or art-works. 'We'd be a sitting target.'

'We could try putting it into one of these new-fangled banks. They are springing up everywhere.' The Countess counted on her fingers. 'Why, there is Coutt's at the Three Crowns in the Strand, Child's at the Marigold by Temple Bar . . .'

'How comes it, milady, that you suddenly know all these establishments by their addresses?' Alpiew gave a sidelong glance. What was the Countess about?

'To tell you truly, Alpiew,' – the Countess blushed and picked up her cup – 'I have been living in constant fear that something like this would happen. So I have made a few inquiries.'

'Me too!' Alpiew laughed. She had rarely been able to hold on to money for long, and was terrified that it would somehow vanish.

The Countess too knew the vicissitudes of wealth. Her fortune had whipped up and down since she was a child, and the last ten years had proved the most difficult financially.

And here they both were with a fortune to protect: one hundred guineas earned on an escapade in France which had paid them well.

'It is a worry, madam, sitting on all this money. I go and check it every day.' As usual Alpiew did a mental audit of their hidden funds. 'I'd love to know who left that nut up there.'

'What nut?' Godfrey had a shifty look about him.

'The nut in the attic.'

'Have you been fiddling with my nuts?'

'No one likes even to think about your nuts, Godfrey.' The Countess held her cup out for a refill.

Alpiew faced Godfrey, her hands on her hips. 'You go up to the attic and eat nuts?'

'I go and check the money every now and then, and I might bring a bag o' nuts with me. What's wrong with that?'

'So, alas, the nut meant nought.' Alpiew swung the kettle back over the flame. 'Ah well, regarding the money problem, milady, tomorrow shall we take advice?'

'Do you know, I wonder whether having money is almost trickier than having none. I have owned valuable things before, jewellery and the like, but never a stash of coins like this.' The Countess sank into her easy chair. 'We need someone experienced to help us, a person who has always had lots of brass, someone with so much money it is mere air to them.' She rubbed her chin, leaving a grey imprint like a Spaniard's beard. 'I have hit it! Who could know better what to do than my darling friend Pigalle?'

'*Trou du cul de cochon!*' Olympe Athenée Montelimar, Duchesse de Pigalle, cracked a horse-whip, raising dust from the cobbles. '*Retournez dans votre banlieue de merde!*'

Further down the street a liveried man was running, clutching the seat of his breeches.

'Olympe, sweetheart!' cried the Countess, emerging from behind a row of coaches stuck in an early-morning jam outside the Duchesse's Arlington Street home. 'What on earth is going on? Wasn't that your coachman running off?'

'*Voleur!* In France we should have had him branded. *Zut!* He is never to be mentioned again, and zat is zat.' Pigalle threw the whip up on to the driver's seat, and stood with her hands on her hips. She was wearing a gentleman's riding suit in a particularly vivid green damask which clashed wildly with her upright clump of orange hair. She stepped forward and kissed the Countess on both cheeks, leaving a scarlet imprint on either side. '*Alors!* There is nothing else for it. I shall have to take ze reins myself. Are you coming? Now zat I am riding up top zere is room for one more inside.'

The Countess hesitated. She only wanted a quick word. But Pigalle was always impossible to pin down, so she thought maybe she should take up the offer of a ride.

She flapped her mouth open and shut again.

'You look like a sea-lion in ze menagerie, darling. *Bien sûr, chérie,* Alpiew can ride up with me.' Pigalle pulled the coach door open. '*Zut,* Ashby! Inside! Or we shall miss all ze fun.'

'But where are you taking me, Olympe?' cried the Countess, as Pigalle pushed her rotund backside into the coach and slammed the door behind her. 'I've only come to ask your advice.'

Alpiew clambered on to the driver's perch. Pigalle leaped up and grabbed the reins.

The Countess leaned out of the window and yelled, 'Where are you taking us?'

'Ashby, my darling, where else would we go today?' Pigalle flicked her whip and the coach lurched into motion. 'To Tyburn, of course, to see the hangings.'

Inside the coach the Countess introduced herself to Pigalle's guests, a ruddy middle-aged merchant, Edward Stark, his wife Cynthia and Robinson, her young nephew.

There was an uneasy atmosphere and the Countess wondered whether she had not come into the coach at the zenith of an almighty family row.

'Are you staying with Olympe?' asked the Countess, trying to ease the edgy silence.

'No,' said Robinson, a thin youth with pale eyelashes and a brown wig which must be much darker than his own hair.

'Pip! Pip! Pip! Buy my pippins!' An apple seller was strolling alongside the static carriages. 'Pip! Pip! Pip!'

A handful of leaflets was thrust through the open window.

'"Laura's Lace Emporium",' Cynthia read. '"Bruges, Bucks, Bobbin and Bedfordshire —"' Before she could continue, her husband had snatched the card from her hand and thrown it out of the window.

'That's enough of that,' he said.

'Husbands!' Cynthia rolled her eyes and turned conspiratorially to the Countess. 'He hates me spending money.'

'Better to spend it on lace than on the lottery,' said

Robinson. 'At least we know that lace is certain to appreciate in value.'

The Countess was amazed that people like this were in Pigalle's coach. The Duchesse usually spent her time with disinherited European princes, disgraced players, fairground freaks, cross-dressing vicars, and flamboyant members of the aristocracy, not strait-laced nonentities from the self-regarding merchant class. 'Have you known Pigalle long?' By asking this the Countess hoped she might find out what relationship they had with Pigalle and therefore know how civil she need be with them.

'I have an interest in today's proceedings at Tyburn, Countess,' said Edward Stark with a hearty grin. 'So when the Duchesse told me she was taking the coach we decided to make a party of it.'

Cynthia patted her gaping mouth with her hand and let out an audible yawn.

Phough! The Countess looked round at her companions, astonished. She had never attended a public execution any more than she had sailed single-handed round the Cape to the Indies. It was enough having to drive past the impaled heads on London Bridge, or the tarred bodies of traitors in iron cages at the City gates, without having to witness the grisly deed performed before your eyes.

'Have you ever witnessed the Hanging Fair at Tyburn?'

The Countess shook her head.

With a shudder the coach stopped. Cynthia sighed and glanced out of the window. 'Turnpike,' she stated. 'Wretched things.'

'*Merde!*' Pigalle jumped down and called into the carriage. 'Coins? Who has some coins to pay ze road charge?'

Everyone rooted about and presented Pigalle with an assortment of small change.

'What a thing, to charge us to drive upon our own roads

here in ze capital city,' cried the Duchesse de Pigalle, counting up. 'But, *alors*, who would expect any different in zis land where there is neither faith, law nor priest?' She pulled one coin out of the pool and spat. 'Augh! Zat one is more trouble zan it is worth.' She tossed the coin to the ground. 'Clipped.'

'There are still so many of them about, these clipped coins,' sighed the Countess. 'I thought the Royal Mint was putting a stop to it.'

'Never can stop a thing when it makes a profit,' said Robinson.

'Did you know,' Edward Stark jumped in to join the conversation, 'you are more like to hang for defrauding His Majesty's Exchequer than for highway robbery?'

'Here!' Cynthia plunged her hand into her pocket and passed Pigalle a coin to replace the clipped one. 'Pay up and let's move on.'

'*Merci*, madame.' Pigalle presented the fee to the turnpike operator. '*Voilà!* And now to ze fair.' With a howl of anticipation she leapt back up into the driver's seat.

'Turkey figs, apricocks and ripe black dates?' A woman with a basket of dried fruit popped her head into the carriage window. 'A feast of fruit for a shilling.'

'Yes, please.' This time Cynthia looked to her husband to provide the funds. 'I am half starved.'

'You've already got a belly on you,' snapped Edward Stark, pulling a shilling from his vest pocket. 'You eat too much pudding and drink too much chocolate.'

'Good!' Cynthia snatched the money and paid for a paper cone of dried fruit. 'So perhaps this fruit may act as a purge.'

In the corner Robinson sniggered.

The Countess took out her fan and flapped. ''Tis hot for May, don't you think? And so sunny! It seems more like August.'

Robinson laughed aloud and pulled out a handkerchief, feigning a sneeze to cover up.

Cynthia crammed a handful of apricots into her mouth and let out a contented sigh as she chewed.

'What have you there?' Edward Stark poked a finger into the cone. 'Five pieces of each fruit, if that.' He slumped back, jotting down figures in a notebook. 'The price of these commodities is fascinating, do you not think, Countess? At wholesale a tiny smidgen such as my wife has just now purchased would be worth a penny, if that. So, somewhere along the line, someone is clearing a handsome profit. Perhaps the market in dried fruit is worth an investment.'

'Holiday prices, dear husband!' Cynthia spoke through a mouthful of half-chewed fruit. 'Everyone knows at fairs and suchlike the prices shoot up. 'Tis the very nature of high days. You have a captive market. Something you'd know all about.'

The Countess gazed out of the window, wishing heartily that they would soon arrive at their destination so she might excuse herself from this kinship of discord.

Pigalle decided to abandon the coach under a tree at the corner of the park. They could walk the rest of the way. All around, parties of eager excited people were spilling out of carriages and chairs, making their way to the gate out of Hide Park.

'The procession must be well past St Giles,' said Cynthia, dropping down on to the grass. 'Listen to the roar! Now to find somewhere where we can see more than the flea-ridden perukes of the man standing in front of us.' Cynthia took Robinson's arm. 'You'll be a gentleman, won't you, Robinson dear, and get me a good spec.'

'Excellent situation, ladies and gents!' yelled a man at

the foot of a long ladder leaning on the tall wall which edged the park. 'Beautiful Prospect! Only five pennies a perch.'

The Countess turned and assessed the proposition. The top of the park wall was already precariously full of drunken spectators. One of them stopped swigging from a wine pouch and pointed along the Tyburn Road. 'Here they come!'

'Zut!' said Pigalle, thrusting herself into the festive crowd. 'Follow me!'

> 'A young man and a maid
> Together lately played . . .'

Nearby a fellow played a jaunty tune on a hurdy-gurdy. A woman stood beside him, hands on her hips, singing.

'What lovely music, Mr Stark!' cried the Countess. 'It makes you feel like dancing.'

The singer clapped her hands and continued her song with a fervour verging on wantonness.

'Put in all!' she sang.

> 'The maid she did protest
> She bid him do his best!
> Put in all! put in all!'

Rather embarrassed at having drawn Mr Stark's attention to such a lusty song, the Countess pressed on towards the sideshows. All around her pie sellers and cherry girls swung through the mob crying their wares.

Children were riding on their father's shoulders. Lovers kissed as they strolled along. Red-faced women tucked into juicy pies and sweetmeats, their faces raised to the warm sun. Gaggles of people stood before the row of sideshows hollering and laughing at the antics of clowns, singers and magicians.

'What a lovely day for a hanging,' said Edward Stark. 'I'm so glad. It's very depressing here when it rains.'

'I rather imagine if you were one of those going to be hanged the weather wouldn't matter quite so much.' The Countess smiled.

'Yes,' said Edward Stark. 'But sunshine makes it more fun for the kiddies.'

'Come along, Countess.' Cynthia looped the Countess in her free arm and yanked her away from her husband. 'We ladies are safer if we stick together.'

'. . . *her rolling eyes, Put in all! put in all!*' cried the singer with a suggestive wink.

> *'My skin is white, you see,*
> *My smock above my knee*
> *What would you more of me? Put* in *all! put* in *all!*
> *Put in all! Put in all!'*

A line of dusty children steamed through the crowd, marching in step like a squadron on manoeuvre, shoving the two women apart.

Staggering to regain her balance, the Countess found herself swept along in the thick of the mob, her face squashed into the filthy clothing of the sweaty revellers. After a moment's panic she was reassured by the sight of Pigalle's carrot-coloured hair bobbing a few yards ahead.

'My kerchief!' cried Cynthia, emerging somewhat ruffled and falling in step at the Countess's side. 'One of those little dusty bastards has stolen it. Best Flanders too. I always forget that public hangings are a hotbed of crime. Now my swine of a husband will *have* to let me buy another.'

She couldn't exactly say why, but the Countess suspected

Cynthia's histrionics were only acted, and that she was inventing this theft in order to get herself a jaunt to the milliners.

With a final shove the two women squeezed through a screeching bundle of Billingsgate fish-wives and arrived near the convent doors.

'Well, look at that!' said Cynthia, munching on a piece of dried fig and staring up.

The triple tree of Tyburn, a sturdy wooden triangle eighteen feet high, loomed before them. Men swung like monkeys from the tops of ladders, grabbing on to the crossbars, ready to tie the ropes which were soon to conduct the condemned criminals into the next world.

Nearby, a row of officials were beating back the crowd, making a path for the fated prisoners' wagon.

'I could murder a pie!' said Cynthia, gazing around, hoping to spot a pie seller.

'Olympe, I need your advice.' The Countess eased alongside Pigalle and Edward Stark. 'Alpiew and I have a little nest-egg. How would you recommend we invest our money?'

Edward Stark leaned forward, all ears.

''Ow should I know zat?' Pigalle glared at the Countess, threw her arms in the air and let out a squawk. 'I never had a penny of money to invest in all my life.'

'But, Olympe . . . !'

'Oh look, darling! How wonderful! A conjuror!' Pigalle grabbed the Countess's sleeve and tugged her away towards the sideshows. 'My favourite!' She gave a merry shriek and stood gaping up at a magician's stall as though in a trance.

The Countess was mystified. Her friend Pigalle was famously one of the richest people in Europe and had been so for fifty years, since her father, mother and uncles (some of the most prosperous and powerful people in France and Italy) had all died, bequeathing to her their vast fortunes.

Since then a number of lovers, mainly crowned monarchs of both genders, had also left her large legacies.

Nor had the Countess ever noticed her to be particularly interested in conjurors.

'I say blow by the high and abominable . . .' The magician, wearing a long gown of black and silver embroidered with stars and all sort of hieroglyphs, blew into his gloved hands. '. . . A ho-bee bo-pee! Jacko cracko! Felto!'

He clapped his hands together and flung them up above his head. A fine sparkling mist fell about the stage.

'Augh! Zere's no magic in zat,' said Pigalle. 'Ze gloves are full of glitter. It's a mere *trompe l'oeil*.'

In the thick of the crowd, Alpiew found herself crushed up against Robinson.

'Do you have a particular interest in today's hangings?' She lurched sideways to get out of the way of a mutton-pie seller whose tray was dripping rancid-smelling fat.

'I'm just tagging along.' Robinson grabbed his sword-knot and manoeuvred Alpiew away from a small gaggle of beady-looking ragged boys leaning against the convent wall. 'I imagine the pick-pockets will be making a good profit today.'

Alpiew thrust her hand into her pocket. She wrapped her fingers around the few coins she had brought with her. She had no intention of being a cully to some young strolling dubber.

'You know, Alpiew –' Robinson rubbed his forehead in thought – 'I feel certain there is a living to be made out of theft.'

'Of course there is,' said Alpiew. 'For the thieves.'

'No. A legal business. Something like gambling. I have this idea of taking money from a person every week, and if no one burgles them I keep the money. But if they do get burgled, then I must pay out to replace what they lose.'

'You think people would bet on that!' Alpiew wondered whether the boy might not be cracked.

'Why not? People are beginning to pay out in a like manner in case of fire. It's the new road to a fortune. It's called insurance. Lloyds coffee house has been insuring ships in this way for many years.' As he spoke they passed a fire-eater's stall. The moustachioed entertainer puffed a great orange cloud of fire above their heads. 'So why not houses?'

'You'd better not insure the house where he is a lodger,' said Alpiew.

Robinson looked up at the fire-eater and ignored Alpiew's comment. 'I even think it might be something,' he said, 'to insure a person against dying.'

'But we all die.' Alpiew took a step away from him. Presumably he had something to sell. She had met quacks before who tried to sell secret recipes for elixirs for eternal life, but never one so young, bright and good looking.

'Yes, but the policy would be against sudden death, and they'd have to pay all the while they were living.'

'Really,' said Alpiew. 'Sounds like a murderer's charter to me.'

'I don't know. But I am thinking about it as an idea. Ho!' he shouted, waving a hand high in the air. 'Look ahead! My aunt is up with the magician.'

Up on the conjuror's stage, Cynthia took a card, glimpsed at it and handed it back.

The magician threw the card into the air. 'Swift fly!' He stamped and glared down at Pigalle who stood with the Countess before the middle of the platform. His dark eyes lowered under his black brow. He caught the card and wrapped his fingers around it. 'Begone!' Bending forward he blew a thin coil of smoke from his lips. 'Quick, presto!

Passa largo mento. Hi cocolorum! The card is flown.' He spread his empty hands wide.

'Pigalle, darling, what is going on?' hissed the Countess into her friend's ear. She was not at all interested in the prestidigitator's capers. 'Why do you say you have no money? You have always had oodles.'

'I know zat!' Whispering, Pigalle peered over the Countess's shoulder. 'But Edward Stark and his nephew are both after it. So I am pretending to zem zat I lost it all investing in bad stock.'

'And why do they want your money?' the Countess asked, idly watching the magician as he stooped and swirled his hands in a dizzying pattern about a foot above Pigalle's hair.

'Ze boy Robinson is a broker and Edward Stark is a banker or something. Zey both want me to invest in them. But I already have invested where I please.'

'Invested?' said the Countess. 'In what?'

'Oh, Ashby, you are such an innocent. Ssssshh!' Pigalle slammed her finger to her mouth and glanced in Cynthia's direction. 'Never, ever tell other people where you have put your money.'

The magician clapped his hands and swerved round to the Countess.

'Open your mouth, madam.'

The Countess obliged. The magician appeared to pull the missing card from it. The crowd gave a dutiful round of applause.

A sudden drum roll and burst of trumpet at the far side of the ground were followed by a great roar.

The magician held his hands up. 'My presentation will now take an interval, for see – here comes the main event! The prisoners are even now arriving at the gallows.'

The Countess turned to see the four condemned riding

on a large wooden cart, loose nooses swinging freely from their necks. Another smaller cart behind carried four empty coffins.

'Let us see who is on ze menu for today's spectacle.' Pigalle tossed the programme vendor a shilling. 'Ze list of ze condemned, please. So what have we?'

Alpiew shuffled the papers and read the headings. 'A murderer, a female thief, a highwayman, and an old man for treason.'

'Treason? An old man?' Pigalle tapped some snuff on to the back of her hand and snorted it, leaving a stain like a black moustache. 'Ze elderly should behave with dignity. What has ze silly fool done?'

'Coining.' Alpiew ran her fingers down the broadsheet. 'He ran a mint. And did some forgery. Forged bills and official documents.'

'So, four birds dance ze Tyburn jig today.' Pigalle punctuated her speech with a number of little sneezes. 'Zis will be quite a show. Which is which?'

Alpiew ran her finger down the columns, glimpsing up at the prisoners in between reading. 'The highwayman is a fine-looking fellow, it says here.'

'Ze one in white,' said Pigalle, through another loud sneeze. 'Ze pretty lad with ze golden locks and ze delightful nosegay.' She sneezed again.

'The murderer is bald and fat . . .' Alpiew read. 'He killed a man as he slept. Hacked him to pieces with a meat cleaver. He has a scar on his face.'

'I cannot see any of them, let alone their scars.' The Countess bounced up and down, trying to get a glimpse of anything.

'Cherries-ripe-oh!' Cynthia came to join them. She cradled a cone of cherries which she popped into her mouth one by one. 'Anyone?' She held out the cone.

'Madam?' From the stage behind them the conjuror stooped and whispered in the Countess's ear. She in turn whispered to Alpiew, who handed the man two shillings. A few minutes later the entire party were happily sitting on a highly decorated trunk in the centre of the stage.

'How many are here would you say?' The Countess was taking in the magnitude of the crowd. 'A thousand?'

'I'd bet you two guineas that there are between three and four thousand,' said Edward Stark.

Three of the prisoners stood proudly on the cart waving and bowing like players in the theatre. The old coiner slumped alone in a corner.

As the cart pulled in at the gallows, the mob surged forward, cheering.

'That's the thing that makes you proud to be English,' said Edward Stark. 'We have humour, and irony. We laugh at the delicacy of other nations who make such a mighty matter of being hanged.'

Cynthia tutted.

The Countess and Alpiew exchanged a look. The Countess pursed her lips and gave a sly glance at Edward Stark. Oblivious to the frisson his remark had caused, he dug his plump fingers into his wife's cone of cherries, took a handful and crammed them into his smug mouth.

Ahead of them, the Newgate chaplain, sitting next to the old man, was shouting, reading a passage from the Bible as the cart shunted into place between the gallows' beams. When it came to a halt, the young blade in white stood. 'Mummy!' he cried. A lumbering fat woman was clambering up to him. She swung from his neck, showering his rosy cheeks with kisses. 'I knew you'd come.'

The mob bobbed up and down, shrieking with approval.

'I am proud to stand here today at Albion's triple tree.' The highwayman put one arm round his mother and flung his nosegay into the crowd. 'My soul is at peace and I am ready to make the great experiment.'

'John O'Hara, of Hounslow, aged twenty-nine,' read Alpiew. 'Terror of the roads around the Heath, from the village of Staynes as far as Tippett's Corner.'

'The hangman is drunk,' noted the Countess. 'Look at him wobbling about.'

The masked hangman balanced on the back of the cart, one hand gripping the head of the chaplain to steady himself, while with the other he handed the loose ends of the prisoners' nooses to the boys swinging from the crossbars.

The Countess couldn't understand how she and Alpiew had wound up here at a public hanging, when all they wanted was advice from Pigalle on where to put their money. The prospect of seeing four humans leap from a cart to their deaths, swinging from lengths of rope was not filling her with glee. 'Olympe darling, will we be here long? I have things to do.'

'*Zut*, Ashby, don't leave me now.' Pigalle squinted and then glared at the Countess. 'Stay here until it is polite for us to leave, and zen I will owe you a big favour.'

'I'm starved.' Cynthia grabbed a passing vendor and bought another cone of cherries, which she gobbled while reading over Alpiew's shoulder.

'I don't understand.' Alpiew's head bobbed up and down, taking a look at the prisoners. 'It says here there is a lady among the condemned. I only see men.'

'She is in breeches and a leather jerkin,' said Edward Stark, pointing. 'Dark hair, swarthy look.' The woman he indicated sat grimly in the corner of the cart. 'She is a house-breaker.'

'Kate Timony,' read Alpiew. 'Of Hounslow. Aged twenty-four.'

The woman stood proudly alone, head held high, while the other prisoners were being embraced by weeping friends and relatives.

'Make your last statements, if you will,' shouted the hangman. 'One at a time.'

He pointed his hand towards Kate Timony.

With a surly sneer, she rose and addressed the mob. 'I have only one thing to say.' She put her hands on her hips and glared at the crowd. 'Is there a midwife amongst ye?'

'Midwife?' The hangman swung round, still clutching the rope which was tied to her neck. 'What need have you of a midwife, you tawdry maux?'

'Because by law you cannot hang a woman who is with child.'

'You're not with child. To be with child you must first lie with a man, and what man would lie with you?'

'A midwife!' Kate Timony spat into the hangman's face. 'Please.'

Some men in the crowd hollered and threw their hats into the air.

Edward Stark bit his lower lip and leaned forward.

A couple of women pushed through to the prisoners' cart.

'*Two* midwives!' Edward Stark rubbed his hands. 'That's good. That's good!'

Kate Timony pulled open her leather jacket and unlaced her breeches. After a few minutes fumbling the midwives nodded at each other and one yelled to the crowd.

'She's knocked up all right!'

'Let her down,' shouted a young man and everyone else took up the cry, chanting rhythmically: 'Let her down. Down! Down!'

The executioner reached up for the rope, lost his footing and fell down into the jeering mob, who lifted him up to shoulder height and passed him along over their heads.

John O'Hara, the boy in white, released himself from his mother's embrace, climbed up on to the top of one of the cart wheels and sprang up to the crossbar of the scaffold where he worked frantically at untying Kate Timony's knot, until the rope slipped down and fell to the ground. 'All's fair in love and war,' he cried, and jumped back down on to the cart. He took a bow, his own noose still hanging loosely between him and the crossbar.

The sheriff's men were crowding round the prisoners. One picked up the loose end of Kate Timony's rope and yanked on it.

Kate Timony gave a gruff wave to the mob and climbed on to the back of the official's horse. She held her arms up in a triumphant gesture and yelled: 'Today, my friends, is not the day for me to dance the hempen jig from the branches of the deadly nevergreen. Adieu to you all.' She rubbed her belly. 'And pray, drink a toast to the child that saved my neck.'

'And to the brave blind man who put it there,' yelled a nearby wag, to an accompaniment of hoots and whistles.

'How can they know that the woman is with child?' The Countess leaned towards Cynthia and took one of her cherries. 'They only took a quick peek.'

'She'll have a belly on her,' said Robinson.

'My wife has a belly on her,' said Edward Stark. 'A belly can mean anything. Too much cherries and cakes and chocolate, for example. Midwives know how to recognise a baby. They have their secrets. Believe me.' He winked. 'These women are no strangers to mysteries of female anatomy.'

'Bellies!' Cynthia snorted into her hand as she fired a barrage of cherry stones into her palm. 'Much you'd know about female anatomy, husband dear.'

'Why don't you use your kerchief, wife? Your fingers are all sticky and messy.'

'Because my kerchief was just taken out of my pocket. One's Flanders can be filched anywhere.' Cynthia punctuated her sentence with a string of hiccoughs 'You are too quick to jump to conclusions. I shall have to replace it.'

'Enough!' snapped Edward Stark, holding up his palm to silence her.

'So, Olympe,' the Countess tried to whisper. 'I am asking you what would *you* do?'

'With a measly hundred guineas? How would I know? I only deal in vast amounts of money, tens of thousands, and as you know I use my money to buy land and houses.'

A sombre drum roll echoed against the park walls.

'And where do you keep any spare money? Where would you put it to keep it safe?'

The three remaining men were told to get to their feet.

The horseman in charge of the prisoners' cart looked back over his shoulder. 'Are you all set? Have you made peace with your maker?'

The hangman touched each of the ropes to make sure they were attached to the crossbar.

'*Spare* money?' Pigalle squinted down at her friend.

'Make your last farewells,' shouted the hangman, raising his gloved fist. 'For when I signal, the cart will move away and you will be left, as the law requires, to hang by your necks until you be dead, dead, dead!'

'Why, ze same place everyone keeps their spare money, of course. Under ze floorboards and in my pillow.'

The crowd gave another roar and the sheriff's men started pushing people clear of the cart.

'Hold up the paper, Alpiew.' The Countess grabbed hold of a corner of the broadsheet. 'I cannot bear to watch.'

The executioner slammed his fist down and the cart

lurched forwards, tipping the prisoners back, leaving them swinging in the air, suspended by the ropes round their necks.

'The caper begins!' cried the conjuror, rubbing his gloved hands together. 'Now we see the grim dance of death.'

All three prisoners writhed and kicked, spinning round on the ropes which were squeezing out their last breath. Their legs bobbed up and down, forward and back, knees jerking as though they were performing some macabre Irish jig.

The crowd pressed forward. The sheriff's men pushed them back with their pikes.

'Cut the coiner down now,' cried the executioner. 'He's a treason case.'

'What on earth is going on?' The Countess found that, against her own inclination, she was taking peeks over the top of the paper. 'Why is the old man to be cut down?'

'He clipped coins.' Edward Stark stared intently at the proceedings. 'Cheating His Royal Highness's Treasury is a treasonable offence. If he was a woman, he'd be taken off to Smithfield and burnt,' he added. 'But as he's a man he'll be disembowelled and quartered.'

'Please, Edward, let's talk about something else,' said Cynthia.

Stark did not take his eyes off the scaffold. 'I was only answering the Countess's query.'

Half dead, still twitching, the coiner was lifted on to the same cart he had a moment before been pulled from. The cart rumbled away.

'With male coiners they cut the body into four,' said Edward Stark. 'Then they dip the pieces in tar and hang them up at the City gates as a warning to others not to mess with the King's currency.'

'Remember zat *charognard* has cheated us all,' said Pigalle.

'It is *our* money zat he is corrupting and stealing. If you do not punish these people ze world goes into disarray.'

'You will see him cold-riveted, hanging in a gibbet, every time you go in or out of the City,' said Cynthia under her breath. 'Displayed to the north the east the south and the west.' She had gone very pale, and now looked down at her lap rather than watch the final indignities of the man on the gallows.

Meanwhile the hangman's assistant grabbed on to the murderer's jerking legs and pulled. There was a crack as his neck broke. His body hung limp, his eyes and mouth open, his tongue sticking out.

Edward Stark's knuckles were showing white on clenched fists. His lips tightened over his teeth. He stood up, staring intently at the scaffold, a wild grin spreading over his face.

Like Cynthia Stark, the Countess was intently studying her lap. 'Oh lord, Alpiew,' she hissed. 'Let us get away from this place.'

Alpiew held up the broadsheet and gulped in air.

The hangman grabbed the boy in white by his breeches and pulled.

But instead of the expected crack of neck, the boy fell down upon him. The rope which had suspended him slithered to the ground.

The crowd gasped, then surged forward, hollering.

'What is going on?' The Countess tried to get a better view now.

'The pretty boy!' Alpiew was on her tiptoes, scanning the mob. 'It's the pretty highwayman. He's made a break for it.'

Anxiously rubbing his lips, Edward Stark sank down on to the magician's chest. 'So there was an unexpected ending.'

As the hangman staggered to his feet he looked about, shouting to the sheriff's men.

In his hands he held the highwayman's white jacket. But the man himself was gone.

TWO

Founding – the initial heating of the batch so that it slowly becomes a workable glowing liquid

The Countess flapped her fan as she turned into St James's Market. 'Four o'clock, and the place stinks to heaven,' she cried.

A black cloud of flies flew up from a pile of rotting garbage on the roadside. 'Sometimes I think the night-soil men leave more mess than they cart away – look at the place.' The street was scattered with cabbage leaves and maggoty oyster shells, old torn newspaper and the droppings of horses, geese, sheep and dogs.

'Good lord, what a rabble!' The Countess's face was squashed against a tall man's back as a group of stallholders pressed past her, balancing baskets of fruit on their heads.

'Execution day. Apprentices' holiday, remember, so the world has gone shopping. Look, the place is crammed with boys and their sweethearts.'

Jostling along Six Bell Alley, past the stalls selling cheap pots and pans, cutlery, candles, candlesticks and snuffers, pewter and leather drinking vessels and other household items, the Countess and Alpiew reached the Hay Market, emerging behind a busy horse sale. The auctioneer stood on a bale of hay next to a roan colt. Tethered to a bar, six other horses waited in line for their turn.

'Four guineas? Army bred. A good dependable animal. Anyone four guineas the colt?'

A grey mare kicked her hind leg and scattered a bale of straw, making a soft clean path for the Countess. Alpiew squeezed herself up against the wall to get past a wagon laden with barrels parked outside the locksmith's shop.

'Cherries ripe, all ripe!' cried a girl with a basket of cherries on each arm who jostled through the crowd. 'Cherries, all ripe!'

The Countess reached for some coins from her pocket and veered off towards the cherry seller, but Alpiew grabbed her and pushed her towards the door under the sign of the crossed keys.

'We can buy as many cherries as you like *after* we have talked to the locksmith.'

The little workshop was dark and cool.

Tall narrow rows of shelves were crammed with metal parts of locks, cogs and great iron keys. A longcase clock ticked in the corner and on the counter a white cat quietly snored.

'Third break-in I've been told about today.' Bob Gaunt, the locksmith, dipped his pen, ready to make a note of the Countess's address. His grey quill scratched at the rough paper of his ledger, spraying black speckles of ink all over the cat. 'All through roof windows. Some ne'er-do-well had a busy night of it.'

'We were lucky.' The Countess could not take her eyes off his hairy hands. 'We chased him out before he had time to poke around. Did the other people lose much?'

'Smashed dishes and the like.' He pushed back his cuffs,

revealing even hairier forearms. 'The villain seems to have no knack for quietness. Fellow woke everyone with his racket.'

'Perhaps he is deaf.' Alpiew stroked the cat and got an ink-black palm for her pains.

'The constable seemed to think the felon was a child,' said the Countess. She liked to be in the know.

'When they can't catch the malefactors they always blame children.' The locksmith sniffed, and dipped his pen. 'Lazy buggers, the constables.'

'Clearly you supply a lot of locks around here.' The Countess had an idea to help them deal with the problem of finding a home for their stash of money. 'I suppose bankers have much use of your services, and men of means. Are there any bankers or suchlike nearby? I am seeking financial advice . . .'

'Round here? There are of course many rich people . . .' He gave an obsequious grin, baring a row of small yellow teeth. 'But in this area they are not mere merchant upstarts like you find in the City these days, but people more like yourself: respectable nobility.'

'No, no.' The Countess toyed with a large greasy cog which lay on the counter. 'I mean men who invest their money for a living. I am not looking for those types who were born with silver spoons in their mouths, I seek rather adventurers in the land of riches.'

'That limits your choice, for as you know those fellows tend not to buy houses round here. They prefer the new-built properties round the May Fair, or up St Martin's Lane.' The locksmith pursed his stringy purple lips and tickled them with the tip of his feather quill. 'I'd say Sir Richard Dainty was your only man nearby.' He wiped a bead of spittle from each corner of his mouth, bent over the counter and whispered. 'Sir Richard is worth a fortune.

Richer than any duke or earl, I'll swear. He lives down the way in Pall Mall Street, just round the corner from the Unicorn.'

'Really! What started him off?' asked the Countess. 'Did he inherit or work for it?'

'Investments!' hissed the locksmith. 'Sugar from Jamaica. Shipping. Spice and tea from China and the Indies, Africa, the usual stuff. But he has employed my services in the past few weeks. I have made him some locks which, being modest, I'd still have to say are masterworks of the art of lock-smithing. Apart from their superior workings, they have shuttered keyholes, blind keyholes, anything you like to foil a pick-lock, however artful.'

Alpiew, who prided herself on her skill as a pick-lock, longed to have a go at this alleged unassailable bastion of security. In her experience there was no such thing as an unpickable lock.

'Is he a pleasant gentleman, this Sir Richard?' The Countess had put the cog down and was now looking for somewhere to wipe a blob of black grease from her finger-tip. She stroked the cat.

'Oh, certainly. Though the fantastically rich are not famed for their good humour, I find.' The locksmith glanced at the Countess's worn and tired clothes and knew he was on safe ground to continue. 'But despite being as rich as Croesus, Sir Richard is as sweet-tempered a gentleman as you are ever like to find.' The locksmith gave a little cough as he finished writing out his order and put the quill back into its stand. 'I shall send someone round to see to your window as soon as I can.'

The Countess lifted the knocker and gave Sir Richard Dainty's door a hard bang.

The door opened a crack and the tip of a sword appeared.

'Yes? Yes? Are you come about Captain Caruso?' A piping voice spoke through the gap. 'Poor Lettice is at her wits' end.'

'I have come to ask some advice from Sir Richard Dainty,' said the Countess.

'Sir Richard Dainty?' The chain was pulled away, the door opened a further six inches, and a wiry little man in a shabby suit and a worn grey wig peered out at them. 'And who might you be, if I may inquire?'

'A near neighbour, from German Street.' The Countess glanced at the edge of a very sharp Toledo blade and raised her hands in surrender. 'I am Lady Anastasia Ashby de la Zouche, Countess of Clapham, Baroness Penge . . .'

'Really?' said the old man. The sword wavered slightly. 'You don't look like a countess. You could be anyone.'

'Do you mind lowering your sword, sirrah. We are not duelling on the Artillery Ground now.' The Countess looked the old man up and down. For a footman he had a lot of nerve. What a specimen of antiquated humanity! She knew her mantua was out of fashion, but *everything* about this man was old and dishevelled. It was clear that his clothes were almost as aged as he was. The lace of his cuffs and cravat was holed, the cloth of his frayed jacket was patched with shiny scraps. His toes peeped out from the scuffed ends of a pair of battered slippers. He was a picture of tattered privation. What could have possessed Sir Richard Dainty to put such a poorly dressed and impertinent fellow on his front door, let alone to issue him with such an impressive blade?

'A countess, eh? Well, you'd better come in, adod,' said the old man, reluctantly lowering the sword and opening the door just wide enough to let the Countess and Alpiew squeeze through the gap. He peered out at the street behind them. 'Look at the heat! You'll bake in this sun, like pieces of pottery. And imagine what kind of a doctor's bill you might run up if you got overheated. Women shouldn't go outdoors on such a day.' The old man slammed the door and hastily threw a number of bolts across. He shuffled along the hall. 'So what's your business?'

'We wish to consult Sir Richard on a private matter concerning money.' The Countess spoke with a condescending air. 'We have a sum to invest.'

'Money?' The old man stopped and squinted at them. 'You have money for me?'

'We have a question about money . . . for . . . Sir Richard.' With some astonishment, the Countess suddenly realised that this decaying specimen of manhood was no dilapidated footman but the master of the household himself. 'The locksmith recommended you as something of an expert on dealing with investments.'

'I have the safest strongbox in the country.' Sir Richard sucked his teeth for a moment, squinting first at the Countess and then at Alpiew. 'I'll not have thieves running off in the night with my cash.' He slid his sword into its scabbard and slouched into the large front room. 'Lettice,' he cried, addressing the prostrate form of a young lady who lay slumped over a sofa. 'Here are some ladies come to visit us. Adod, ladies, this is Lettice Dainty, my ward. We are to be married tomorrow.'

Lettice, a damp handkerchief applied to her tear-stained face, looked up from a mound of cushions covered in Indian silks and sateens. Through the tears the Countess could see that the girl was still a child, and a very pretty one too.

'They've not found Captain Caruso?' The girl glanced from the Countess to Alpiew, then, with a wail, plunged her face back into the heap of cushions. 'My darling boy! He is gone forever, isn't he, Pigsny? My handsome Caruso has left me, never to return. Oh, alas and alack!' She burst into another chorus of sobs. 'I loved him so much, so much.'

The Countess gave Alpiew a sly glance. What was this? Had the miserable old fellow seen off a young rival to his pretty ward's affections.

'Little Lettice loves her Captain, and I am particularly concerned that she finds her beloved boy *before* the wedding. I don't want her marching up the aisle in tears because she misses that rogue Caruso.'

What on earth was going on? The Countess turned warily to face Sir Richard.

He was beaming down on the girl with a beatific smile, a large tear welling in his eye.

'They were a perfect match, my little Lettice and the Captain,' said Sir Richard, fiddling with a row of primitive wooden statuettes on the mantel. 'The child is right to be upset. I have never seen anyone make her laugh quite as much. By running off and leaving her, I believe the naughty fellow has quite broken my poor darling sweety's heart.'

The Countess and Alpiew both found themselves grinning like death masks. What kind of a scenario were they witnessing here?

Sir Richard flopped down into a high-backed chair at the table as Lettice let out another strangled wail.

'I have had a worrying day – a shilling went missing. It was on the table here and then it was gone. I can only imagine some passing jackanapes saw it through the window, nipped in and prigged it.'

Lettice groaned.

'I was a little cross with Letty earlier as I thought that mischievous monkey might have run off with it . . .'

Lettice sobbed.

'And now the monkey has scampered off.' Sir Richard Dainty glanced at Lettice and winced. 'Now, Countess, would you care to sit? And your woman?' The old man shot Alpiew a gummy smile. 'What would she like to do?'

'I'll sit too, please.' Alpiew went to sit beside the Countess. She pulled at the chair but it appeared to be stuck. She gave it another yank.

'No point in trying to move it,' said Sir Richard. 'All the furniture is nailed to the floor. I find that a very satisfactory way of keeping it safe from thieves.' Sir Richard took a small crystal candlestick from the table and placed it on the mantelpiece.

Lettice wailed as he passed her.

'Alpiew and I work together as writers,' explained the Countess, grimacing at Alpiew while she lowered herself into the immovable seat. 'The money is equally ours.'

'Indeed!' Sir Richard tottered across the room and sat, leaning towards Alpiew, screwing up his eyes and peering at her décolletage. 'And what a comely woman she is too. Very well kitted out, adod.'

Alpiew pulled her bodice up an inch or two.

'We are here, Sir Richard, on a sensitive matter,' said the Countess in a low tone.

'You'll have to speak up!' Sir Richard leaned forward cupping his wrinkled hand to his ear. 'I'm blind in one eye.'

'We are here,' the Countess shouted, 'to take your advice on a financial matter. We have, through our joint labours, come into a nice bit of money.'

Sir Richard sat silently nodding, so the Countess continued.

'Would you recommend employing a banking company?'

Sir Richard was still gazing in the general direction of Alpiew's cleavage.

'Or something more speculative . . . ?' The Countess tapped the table-top with her fingernails. 'Sir Richard?'

'Yes?' The old man snapped back into reality. 'What?' He sighed and loosened his threadbare cravat. 'Adod, but it's hot today. What were you saying just now, Countess?'

'She wants to know where we should best put our money?'

'Into a strong-box, of course.'

'Within a banking company?'

'Egad, what was that?' A rapping on the door jolted him up on to his feet. 'Lord, but the door has never stopped a-knocking today. Let's hope it's someone with news of the Captain. Letty says the marriage cannot go ahead unless the fellow is there wrapping his arms about her and kissing her pretty rosebud lips.'

The old man tottered out of the room, still muttering to himself.

'This is a mistake,' whispered Alpiew. 'The old fool is addled in his brains. How can he help us?'

They could hear lowered voices from the front door.

In the far corner of the room Lettice emitted another low moan of misery. She raised her head and glanced towards the Countess. 'Oh no! Save me!' she whispered. 'Save me from him!'

'Lettice, deary!' Sir Richard came into the room. 'That was that troublesome boy, Robinson Stark, saying that he and his uncle and aunt will be pleased to come to the wedding tomorrow. He wanted a word with you, Letty, but I told him you were indisposed.'

Lettice's face sank again into the pillow.

'Fancy!' said the Countess. 'We met the Starks this morning, with my friend the Duchesse de Pigalle.'

'Edward Stark has done business with me. Bought a few things, you know. But that cheeky nephew of his has some sort of obsession with Letty. Sure he is a saucy, scurvy, scandalous fellow! He has hung about this place for years, trying to acquaint himself, sending her billet-doux. But I have fended him off. Have I not, my sweet?'

Lettice sniffed.

'Oh, 'tis a hard thing, pleasing a young bride-to-be,' said

Sir Richard, squinting over his shoulder at the limp Lettice. 'I am all at sea when she is upset like this.'

'She is very young,' said the Countess. 'Pretty, too. You are a lucky man.'

'Adod, I am!' Sir Richard giggled and sat, rubbing his wrinkled, bony hands together. 'Only one day to go – how I yearn to be at her.' He looked at Alpiew, then the Countess and scratched at the top of his wig. 'You ladies have come to ask me something, though lord knows if I can think what it was.'

'We wanted advice on what to do with a large sum of money.'

'Money?' He leaned back from the table and squinted at them. 'Why would you come to *me* about money? I am as poor as a church mouse. Poorer! They at least can eat little bits of free cheese people leave them, if they're clever enough to get it out of the traps. Even a rat can eat from the bins and the refuse of people's tables. Even beggars can make a free meal of the scraps dropped by the night-soil men. But as for me, I have to toil and sweat to pay for my victuals.' He pulled his pockets inside out. 'See! Not a penny to my name.'

'Let us put it this way, then, sirrah.' Alpiew was already standing, ready to leave. 'If you did *happen* to have any money, what would you suggest doing with it?'

'There are only two things to do with money. First you make it,' said Sir Richard, gripping the handle of his sword and looking about him as though some mysterious thieves might be listening, hidden behind the wainscot. 'Then you lock it up, ladies. You lock it up.'

'Take that!'

A large turnip flew through the air and bounced with a thwump from the bewigged head which protruded from one of four wooden pillories in the market square.

'You Hackney turnip!'

The Countess and Alpiew emerged from a side street into the Stocks Market just as an egg whizzed through the air and broke on the man's cheek.

'Poor fellow,' said the Countess. 'What has he done?'

'Who knows?' said a man in the crowd, pulling his hand back ready to lob an egg towards the stocks. 'Who cares? I'm trying to score a direct hit on that mole of his.'

'Probably sold someone some bad fish, or something,' yelled a woman tossing a rotten tomato, which splattered against the board and dripped to the ground.

'I feel sorry for the poor fellow. He has a kind face.' The Countess looked around. 'Besides, the stocks is such an absurd punishment for petty crime.'

The market they stood in was assembled in a large garden paved with pebble stones. As it was a holiday only a few traders had their stalls set up. A few women, clearly the worse for drink, sat slumped against the railings which protected a huge stone plinth that bore a huge statue of Charles II.

'Ah, look! My old darling, Charlie,' cooed the Countess, gazing up at the gilt figure of the late King, sitting in armour atop a horse. '*So* handsome, do you not think?'

'King Charles was nothing but a long, lazy, lascivious lecher,' shouted the man in the stocks. 'Pox upon his corpse, and damn his whorish ways!'

'I'm sorry, sir.' The Countess turned and addressed the pilloried man. 'But the King was a particular friend of mine. Would you care to repeat what you just said?'

'King Charles was a long, lazy, lascivious lecher,' he shouted, even louder. 'Pox upon his corpse, and damn his whorish ways!'

'Excuse me.' The Countess seized a half-eaten apple from

Alpiew's hand. 'Take that!' She hurled it at the man's head. 'Now, Alpiew, let us leave the Stocks Market, and make our way to the place where all the trading in money is done.'

They walked briskly along Cornhill.

The street was blocked ahead. A mob was gathered outside a small office building hunched up between two taverns.

'Why the throng? Are they giving away money?'

'It's the Plantation Office,' said Alpiew. 'Where people buy themselves a way to the New World.'

'America?' The Countess glanced at the people in the queue. A fine mix of poverty, threadbare clerks and men with the haunted look of having lost a fortune on stocks or cards.

'Well, if ever we need an escape route . . .'

'I've seen it at first hand, milady. These coves may look down and out now, but after the punishing work and conditions, toiling all day in the hot sun for little or no food, I tell you they are like walking cadavers.'

'We should warn them . . .'

'Oh, I tried that, when I first arrived back from America. No one listens. They think the place is all milk and honey. And for this lot, at least they are assured of their freedom. If they don't like it they can walk away. It's not the same for the blackamoors they ship in from Africa, or for the criminals who get sent there rather than swing, or for the poor Irish who Cromwell sent over.'

'Excuse me.' The Countess spat and put her hands over her ears. 'I cannot even abide to hear the name of that Puritan king-killer.'

'But for some America is a land of plenty – the Puritans are very successful.'

'No more talk of Puritans, Alpiew, please, or I shall disgorge.'

They arrived at the steep narrow flight of steps that led down to Exchange Alley.

'It seems awfully quiet down there.' The Countess teetered at the top, gripping the handrail. She knew all about the quiet alleys where thieves lurked to knock a person over the head and seize all they could gather from their pockets. 'Are you sure this is where they do it?'

'So they say.' Alpiew marched on down the steps. Still clutching the handrail, the Countess followed.

The alley was only two yards across, its walls plastered with posters so that the brickwork was quite covered. Quacks' bills, boasting cures for blindness, rheums, quinsies, agues, vishegoes, bloody flux, megrims and the pox, nestled alongside bills for concerts, plays and lectures, with smaller squares offering the services of wet-nurses, drivers, messengers, footmen, coachmen and chairmen.

'What a dank, dismal place.' The Countess followed as Alpiew turned abruptly into a tiny dark courtyard, on either side of which was a door. Over each door hung a swinging sign. At the end was a trough, a bench and a tethering post for four horses.

'Jonathan's . . .' The Countess looked up to her left. 'Garraway's . . . Hm! So which do we try first?'

'They're coffee houses, madam. Men only. Unless we take a serving job, we can't go in.'

'Why on earth not? We are offering ready money. Is women's money worth any less than men's?' She trotted over to Garraway's and peered through the fugged-up window. 'Oh Lord! Fire! Quickly, open the pipes! Summon a fire engine, Alpiew!' She flapped her arms and looked about for assistance. 'Help ho! Look at the smoke inside!'

'That's no fire, madam.' Alpiew laughed and pressed her face to the window. 'That is the monstrous use the men make of pipe tobacco. I once worked in one of these places

42

and every day returned home as well smoked as a kipper. My clothes stank as if I had been sitting on a bonfire.'

The door opened and a billow of smoke preceded the young man who stepped out. He put his feathered beaver hat on his head before bursting into a smile. 'Countess! Alpiew!' He proffered a hand. 'Robinson Stark. We met this morning.'

A huddle of men in fur coats and thrum caps shoved past and went into Garraway's.

'My lord! Who are those moustachioed fellows, so wrapped up on a lovely spring day?'

'Dutchmen!' said Robinson. 'They are hard dealers. In the Africa trade and diamonds mainly, and famed for building their own welfare upon the ruin of their neighbours.'

'Never did care for Flatlanders,' huffed the Countess. 'Now, might you introduce us to some traders? We have money and want to become part of this new world of stocks and shares and huge profits.'

'It's not an introduction you need, Countess. It is a broker or a jobber. And I can oblige you in that. Look no further.' He offered the Countess and Alpiew a seat on a bench by the tethering posts. 'I may be young, but I am good. I can double your money and more in no time.'

'So, what is the procedure?'

'Are you familiar, milady, with terms of interest and return with bonds, stocks and shares?'

'A little,' said the Countess, totally mystified.

'Would you wish to venture your capital in trust, accruing interest, or would you prefer to speculate on the market?'

'I'm sorry,' said the Countess, leaning forward, cupping a hand to her ear. 'Did you say you were Dutch? I am having a little trouble understanding the language.'

'Then you should not hazard your money quite yet. Might I suggest I give you a little private introductory session?'

'Why not?' The Countess smiled meekly. 'This evening, at my house in German Street, Anglesey House, opposite the church, with the blue door.'

'One hundred pounds at seven per cent over thirteen days . . .' Alpiew was sitting up on her bed, with a piece of paper and pencil resting on her knee. At her side lay an open book. She flicked on a few pages and made a mark in the margin.

'We could always spend the money,' said the Countess, lolling in an easy chair, imagining life with a carriage and equipage.

'Four shillings and eleven pence,' said Alpiew. 'For nineteen days, seven shillings and three pence. If we put it into a bank we could live on this money, madam.'

'What on earth is that book? And how does it know such things?'

'It is called *An Interest Book at 4, 5, 6, 7 etcetera per cent from one thousand pounds to a pound, for one day to ninety-two days, and for three, six, nine, and twelve months.*'

'Snappy title, Alpiew! What on earth prompted you to buy such a thing?'

'If we handle the money properly, we could double it in a few months.'

'I seen the old buggers who sit in the park doing that.' Godfrey was sitting at the table picking his few remaining teeth with a prong of the serving fork. 'They lay bets on how fast the ducks can cross Rosamund's Pond, and how many minutes go by before a cow moos. They double their money one day. And half it the next. Anyhows, it all ends up the same – in the innkeeper's pocket for all the small beer they consume to replace the nervous sweat while waitin' to see who wins.' He guffawed and a large gob of dribble swung from his lip and pooled on a stack of papers.

The Countess swung forward and pulled the papers clear. 'Thank you Godfrey!' She swiped the fork from his hand. 'I would be thankful if you avoided my papers when you drool. These are the important facts and figures there comparing our different investment ideas.'

A loud rap at the front door interrupted her.

Alpiew ushered Robinson into the kitchen.

'It is excellent timing.' The Countess made room for him at the table. 'We were just assessing what we could make in interest.'

'Phough! Pish to interest, madam! Interest is for timid creatures. What you need is to invest in stock or a project. That's where the serious profits lie.'

'Well, that's what we want. So, Robinson, tell us all.' The Countess relaxed. She was looking forward to being part of the new world of finance. 'Please explain to us the principles of investment.'

'Well, there are stocks, shares and bonds.' Robinson laid his pocketbook before him and pulled out a few sheets of paper. 'Which of them do you favour?'

'We are not yet decided.' The Countess gave a coy smile. She wanted him to lay out his shop before she let him know her thoughts. 'Perhaps you could give us a little guided tour of what you offer.'

'My pleasure,' said Robinson, doodling figures on the paper. 'Stock is either a capital sum, as distinguished from revenue, or principal, as distinguished from interest. There is common and preferred stock. Preferred stock – which is cumulative – having priority with respect to claims on assets in liquidation. Bonds are securities bought at a price which accrues dividends, but their interest is not held in principal. Shares are the fractional but volatile interests which divide the capital of a joint-stock –'

'Enough!' cried the Countess, taking a swig from her

cup. 'I am exhausted already. I tell you, young man, you may as well sit here speaking Tonkinese as bombard us with this barbarous gibberish.'

'What exactly is a project?' said Alpiew, disappointed to find that she was as confused as the Countess. 'And does its explanation come in the English language?'

'A project is just that. Some thing or service which somebody – an inventor, or a shopkeeper or whoever – hopes at some future date to accomplish. The investor gives the inventor the money to make their new invention – an engine or I know not what – and you then take a share of any profit it makes when it comes into being. Or it might be a new manufacturer, setting up their business. Whether linen-makers, glass-makers, copper mines, salt-petre works, they all need financing to get up and running. And then as they start selling their wares – hi-jingo, you get paid back with dividends, profits.'

'And where does the money come from to make us this profit?' Alpiew was scribbling in her book. 'Surely the manufacturers and inventors need to take that to live upon?'

'Ay, mesdames,' said Robinson, leaning forward earnestly. 'But if so many eggs are hatched, there will be so many chickens, and those chickens may lay so many eggs more and those eggs produce chickens more, and so on.'

'I ain't spending no money on eggs and chickens,' growled Godfrey. 'That yard is messy enough as it is without 'aving to wade through an ever-expanding mire of fowl droppings.'

'Of course, while some things go up in value, some go down. I can tell you for instance that a few years ago the price on glass eyes was booming, what with the wars and the number of soldiers and sailors coming back from their martial campaigns lacking in the ocular department. Well, you can imagine. The glass-eye works couldn't churn 'em out fast enough. Big money was invested in the glass-eye trade. But now, with the peace, glass eyes have bottomed out. But other types of glassware – mirrors and drinking glasses, for instance – look as though they may have a good future.'

'But surely, Robinson . . .' The Countess leant back in her chair till it emitted a crack. 'You may talk of "new" projects, but there is nothing new under the sun.'

'All right, Countess. I'll allow you that some ideas are pretty far-fetched. I met a man who thinks he will invent a carriage which can travel without the aid of a horse . . .'

'And what would he use to propel it?' snarled Godfrey. 'Flying pigs?'

'A horseless carriage indeed!' The Countess chuckled. 'Whatever next?'

'Madam, you may laugh, but there are many reasonable projects around. Look at Mr Dockwra and his idea for a Penny Post. What a success that has been. Though I hear there is talk of reducing the number of collections.'

'The penny post deliveries have been getting slack recently. I mean, sometimes you can put a letter in the post at ten in the morning and the recipient not even get it that same afternoon.'

'The service may not be all it was designed to be, but for a penny, madam, fifteen deliveries a day is not so bad! And how much cheaper than employing a servant to run about London with your letters.'

'Do you have any other examples of projects?'

'Think of the benefits that the City would have reaped had the new fire engines been invented *before*, rather than after, the Great Fire of Pudding Lane. And you can imagine the success of all the water houses which pipe water into the City in elm-wood pipes, right along your street, in fact. But to get any of these projects up and running, the projector will need to raise capital . . .'

'Capital?'

'Oh, that's an easy one. Capital is the stock of resources and material assets. There is the fluid intangible asset of money and the real or physical asset, made up of buildings, machinery, labour . . .'

'As long as it ain't the capital in capital punishment, I don't care,' said Godfrey, laughing himself into a coughing fit.

'Certainly not!' Robinson laughed too, out of politeness. 'I have the ear of a handful of projectors, all searching for financial assistance. Street lighting is one . . .'

'But surely that would entail a great loss of livelihood among the night-watchmen and link-boys?'

'It may well do that, madam, but think of the advantages – there would be less crime, the streets would be safer . . .'

'And so the constables and headboroughs, the justices and gaolers would lose their jobs into the bargain . . .'

Robinson could see street lighting was not perhaps the investment choice for this household. 'There are plenty of other paths to take. Let us talk, for instance, about the new banks: they look after your money and valuables and . . .'

'Put all the goldsmiths out of work, for up till now they were the ones who kept a person's money safe.' The Countess was beginning to wonder whether the so-called progress provided by all these new inventions would not simply lead to everyone losing their jobs, whereafter chaos would reign.

'Robinson!' Alpiew interrupted. She was very interested in the prospect of the new financial world and wanted the boy to continue. 'If you had to choose a project, what would it be, and what exactly would it entail financially?' She poised her pencil ready to jot down any figures.

'Well, there are any number of projects available for investment at any time . . .'

Another bang from the front door interrupted Robinson's sales pitch.

'It's busier in this kitchen,' growled Godfrey, 'than in a Covent Garden harlot's bed at midnight on a public holiday.'

'Godfrey!' The Countess shot him a stern look. 'We have no desire to hear about your grubby fantasies.'

'I'd invest in something of that nature.' Godfrey slouched down in his chair and sat glaring at her. 'Plenty of profit in harlots' beds, I'd say.'

'The door, Godfrey!'

With a grunt Godfrey slopped out. A few seconds later, Sir Richard Dainty burst into the kitchen.

'Adod, now I can catch you at it!' shrieked the old gentleman. 'I should have been more careful. I might as well have let a pair of rakehells or figging boys inside to ransack my house as a pair of impudent superannuated jades like you. Let me look! Let me look!' He turned on his heels and ran back into the hallway.

'What is going on?' Mystified, the Countess exchanged a look with Alpiew. 'Is the old fellow out of his seven senses?'

'I have heard that, for an old man, preparing to marry a young wife can bring on a sort of frenzy, madam.' Alpiew leapt from the bed to follow him. 'I'll fetch the old cove back here to explain himself.'

By the time she reached the hall, Sir Richard had clattered up the stairs. Wheezing as he reached the first landing, he flung open a door.

'Egad!' he cried, standing in the doorway to the bare empty room. 'What has happened here?' He staggered along to the next disused room, and spluttered again. 'What trick is this you are pulling, you vile old bawds? Where is your furniture hidden? Are you on the move in order to evade me? This is some den of thieves!'

Alpiew had caught up with him by now. The Countess stood at the foot of the staircase and called up.

'If you would tell us what you are come here for, we might be in a position to help you, Sir Richard. But 'tis most unmannerly to tear about a person's house without so much as a by-your-leave.'

'I will have justice, adod.' Sir Richard let out a shriek and scuttled up the next staircase. 'I know you! You have hid the goods some-whereabouts. But don't you worry yourselves, I will not be foxed by a pair of tawdry sluts such as you. I will retrieve it, and have you hanged for it, if necessary.'

Alpiew tore ahead and stood before the old man, blocking his way.

'If only you would tell us, sir, what it is you have lost, I am sure we can help you find it.'

'Ah! Ah!' He waved a gnarled finger in front of her. 'So you admit you know it is lost – how else would you know that, unless it was you had taken it? I have told no one of its existence.'

Alpiew was in no mood to banter with such a demented specimen of senility.

'What is going on in this house? Explain, wench! Where is all your stuff got to?' The old man peered about him. 'Is it not very strange to live in a great house and yet show no trappings of life?' He ducked under Alpiew's arm, sneaking looks through into the empty attic room. 'Something is afoot in this household and I will get to the bottom of it.' He pointed at the floor. 'That floorboard has been disturbed lately – that is your hiding place. I have hit it!' He struggled with Alpiew. 'If you'd like me to have you and your mistress locked up in Newgate on a writ of capias ad satisfaciendum I can accommodate your desire. So leave hold of me, you pert miss, or I shall have no qualms about having you all put behind bars and keeping you there till I am satisfied.'

'Put behind bars on what charge, Sir Richard?' Alpiew had hold of his wrists. ''Tis *you* has broken into our house.'

'I shall call up the debt.'

'What debt, sir? We owe you nothing.'

'You owe me twenty guineas, you saucy minx. Twenty guineas! And in a few months, with interest and gaol charges, that would shoot up. You'd owe me a hundred within six months, two hundred in . . .'

'Does Letty know where you are?' Robinson, come up to join the fracas, said from the doorway. 'Does she know you are out and about disturbing respectable folks in the privacy of their homes?'

'You! Here! Robinson Stark, you impertinent jackanapes! What business have you with my Letty?' Sir Richard advanced on the boy. 'I knew it! This house is the head-quarters of a conspiracy of lying poltroons and cheats set upon destroying my peace.'

'I suspect, Sir Richard,' said Robinson, 'that Lettice would not marry you if she knew the truth about you. Shall I go fetch her and tell her?'

Sir Richard froze.

Robinson turned and started marching down the stairs.

'What business have you with my pretty young bride to be, you idle coxcomb?' screeched Sir Richard over the banister. 'Have you been sneaking in and a-jigging it with my little Letty behind my back? Have you? Have you?' He clattered down after him, waving a withered fist in the air. 'Let me have at you, sir. I shall curry your jacket for you, you randy rogue.' Just as the old man reached the landing, he tripped and fell pell-mell down the remaining stairs. Robinson put out an arm to catch the tumbling old man as he staggered, but he stumbled again, and continued his painful downward trajectory until he landed, cushioned in the plump arms of the Countess. Whimpering, and with a thin line of blood oozing from a cut lip, Sir Richard grabbed on to her like a baby at his mother's breast.

'Now, the time has come to stop being silly, you old fool. Come along with me, sirrah.' The Countess led him slowly along the hallway to the kitchen. 'Godfrey will get you something warm and comforting to drink while you explain to us what it is you think we have of yours.'

'You were there in the room with me.' Sir Richard started jabbing his finger in the air. 'I only left it for a moment and when you were gone, so was it.'

'And what is "it" exactly?'

'Half a banknote. And the banknote is for forty guineas. Unendorsed.'

Once in the kitchen, the Countess pulled out a chair and helped the tousled old man to sit. She poured them both a drink then took a seat opposite.

'And you have the remaining half?'

'Oh yes.' He pushed his hand down into his breeches and pulled out a crumpled piece of white paper. 'That part is safely about my person. 'Tis the other half has gone missing. I cut it in two to stop it getting stolen, and yet it has still happened.'

'Ah, I see!' The Countess smoothed out the half-note on the table-top. 'And half a banknote is no use without the other half.'

Sir Richard wiped a tear away from his swollen cheek, where a bruise was already starting to show through the papery, sallow skin, and with the other hand grabbed the note and shoved it back whence it came.

'So tell me, sir –' the Countess took a sip of her drink – 'where did you last see the absconding half?'

'It was on the mantel in the room where we chatted.' He let out a sob. 'While the other was safe and close upon my person.' He patted his jacket pocket.

'Let's see it again.' The Countess nodded towards Sir Richard's jacket.

Sir Richard pulled out half a banknote.

'I think I have solved your mystery, sir.' The Countess rose and took a step away from the table. She had no intention of being accused of a cunning piece of legerdemain. 'Leave the note upon the table, beside your cup.'

Sir Richard smoothed out the note and laid it down.

'Leave your right hand upon it.'

'Is this a trick?' He looked warily about him. 'Are you a conjuror?'

'I assure you not, sir.' The Countess took another step back. 'Now, may I ask you to put your left hand inside your breeches pocket.'

Sir Richard thrust his hand into his breeches.

Alpiew and Robinson hovered at the door. The Countess put her fingers to her lips.

Silently Sir Richard pulled his hand out of his pocket and removed another half a banknote. He peered at it and then its companion on the table. He slid them together to make a perfect fit.

'There you are,' said the Countess. 'All is well.'

Hastily Sir Richard folded up the two pieces of banknote and slipped them into his jacket pocket.

'So that is all sorted.' The Countess went to the kettle and poured out a cup of warm posset. 'Now sit down and have a warming drink, Sir Richard.'

'I don't want one,' he snapped, heading for the door.

The Countess held the cup out to Robinson. 'Young man, perhaps you would like it?'

Sir Richard spun round and grabbed the cup before

Robinson had a chance to reach it. 'I'll have it, then.' He slurped hungrily, polishing off the drink.

'He doesn't want it himself,' Robinson sneered, 'but he can't stand anyone else to have it. Isn't that always the way!'

'Very tasty,' said Sir Richard, slamming the cup down on the table and looking warily out of the window. 'How am I going to get back home? It's dark out.'

'Usually is after the sun goes down.' Godfrey scowled at Sir Richard, who was sitting in his chair.

'I might be set upon by footpads.' The old man winced, and the Countess felt moved at the pitiful figure he cut. 'I am a feeble old man, an easy target. I could lose the lot. Oh, the worry!' His breathing was laboured and heavy. 'The night before my wedding, too. I have waited long enough for tomorrow. I hope I am not struck down by some vicious malefactors and left, beaten to a pulp in a dark alley, so that I cannot perform my lusty duties as a husband, as Letty will expect.'

'And what is it worth?' asked Alpiew. 'To help you?'

'She's right. How much? And what about the reward?' mumbled Godfrey. 'When a fellow loses a banknote 'tis customary to offer a reward to them as found it. You lost it; her ladyship found it.'

'I am indeed indebted to you, Countess,' said Sir Richard as Robinson helped him to his feet. 'Of course I would offer some reward for the lost note, but, as it was only mislaid and wasn't lost at all, I think I have no need.'

'And yet you thought nothing of screaming in here like a madman.' Alpiew tutted. She could see that this was how a person got to be rich – by never laying out. 'I think, sir, that if you believe no reward is necessary perhaps you might consider apologising for insulting us all earlier on.'

'No insult intended . . .'

'Fie, Alpiew, Sir Richard does not mean to insult us.'
The Countess steered the old man towards the kitchen door.
'He knows we have no need of his money. That is why he
has not offered it.' She smiled her ingratiating smile, trying
to make the old fellow feel guilty. 'Will the wedding be a
big affair, Sir Richard?'

'Oh good lord, no. Myself, my bride, the priest. A few
friends from the City . . .'

'No feast, dancing, music?'

'Music!' Sir Richard shrieked. 'Lord, madam, do you
think I am made of money? Do you know how much these
fiddling fellows charge for scraping their bows over a length
of taut cat-gut? At the end of it, all you get is a din of
caterwauling. 'Tis daylight robbery. No, no. Those who want
music can sing for it.'

'Wedding a young woman and not offering her any
perks. Tch, tch!' The Countess shook her head. 'How is she
to dance with no music?'

'We can clap in time . . .'

'Phough! You'll never hold on to a girl that way. Off you
go, Sir Richard.' The Countess held open the door. ''Tis
only a step or two from my house to yours. I am sure you
can get there unaided.'

'Oh, I see.' Sir Richard looked at her suspiciously. 'Some
sort of bargain is being struck, is it not? So what is it that
you want?'

'A mere gesture, sir.'

'All right, all right! Come to the wedding, and bring your
friends. Perhaps that is a good idea anyhow. I do want my
Letty to be in a good mood. After all, 'tis not every day an
old fellow like me gets to bed a pretty thing like Letty.'

Robinson groaned and lurched forward, teeth gritted,
fists clenched.

'And of course I will make every effort to get you home

55

safely,' said the Countess, giving the old boy a sharp look. 'But if I were you, and wanted to hold on to a young wife, I'd contemplate calling in a few fiddlers at least. Now, let's get someone to walk with you.'

'I ain't goin' nowhere . . .' Godfrey reclaimed his chair. 'I done me back in with all that palaver earlier.'

'Was anyone asking you, you lazy good-for-nothing? My lovely boy –' the Countess turned to Robinson – 'would you be so kind as to help the old gentleman back to his house in Pall Mall Street?'

'But . . .' Robinson lurched forward. 'Him?' He fell back, looking down. 'My projects . . .'

'Pshaw, Robinson, we can talk about them tomorrow. But tonight Godfrey, Alpiew and I need to discuss the whole matter of money between us.'

'But . . .' Sir Richard looked Robinson up and down with distaste. 'Ah well, you look strong enough to keep us from harm by footpads, and cheaper than a link-boy. But I'll not be inviting you in at my end to plague little Letty with your lusty intentions. I know what you're after, but it's me she wants.'

Alpiew held the front door open.

'Along with you both.' The Countess guided Sir Richard on to the step, where Robinson waited.

When the two men had gone the Countess sat at the table with Alpiew and Godfrey. They spread out pieces of paper and tried to work out what to do. After an hour's debate they decided to sleep on the ideas and make up their minds in the morning.

'Do you know, milady, I've had a thought. I think we should get all the money together and divide it equally between ourselves,' said Alpiew, sliding down under the covers of her bed. 'And then I think we should each do as we please with it and see who wins.'

'Mmm! Like the parable of the talents.' The Countess was gazing out of the open window into the yard. 'Godfrey, rouse yourself, man. Go fetch all the pieces of money from the hidey-holes and let's do it now.'

'Now? It's dark out there.' Godfrey grabbed a fork and a candle. 'I 'opes I can find it.'

The Countess was already emptying an earthenware pot on to the table, while Alpiew cleared a space.

'Equal snacks for all.' The Countess laid out three pieces of paper and started counting out coins. 'One for thee, one for me, one for . . .'

'Godfreeee,' said Alpiew, pulling the stopper out of another jar and pouring yet more golden guineas on to the pile.

'Twenty-three, two, three; twenty-four, two, three . . .' A cracking sound came from outside the window. 'What on earth was that? Godfrey!' The Countess looked out into the darkness. 'Are you all right out there?'

'Yes,' growled Godfrey. 'I'm a man, not a mouse.'

'Where was I?'

'Twenty-five, two, three . . .'

Godfrey slammed the back door and slouched in, wiping the dirt from the pot.

'Phough! What is that stink?'

'Don't look at me,' grouched Godfrey. 'It's the sludge. I planted this pot right by the privy. I reckoned as how no one would want to go messin' about in the foulings that dropped from our behinds.'

'Fie, Godfrey!' The Countess panted a little, fanning herself. 'You have a knack of quite turning a person's stomach. Please take the pot outside and clean it.'

'But it's dark out there.'

'Do it!'

Godfrey marched back into the yard, banging the door behind him.

The Countess flapped her fan around the room and lit a perfume burner, while Alpiew brushed the blobs of foul mud on to a piece of paper and threw them out of the window.

'I'll call in the night-soil men to clean out the privy tomorrow, madam. They're overdue. And with this hot spell . . .'

At the exact moment they both sat again there was an almighty crash from upstairs.

'What the . . . ?' Alpiew leaned out of the window. 'Godfrey! Intruder again. Come on.' Gathering up her skirts and grabbing the hammer, she ran out into the hall and up the stairs, while Godfrey lumbered in, depositing the pot by the back door.

Brandishing a poker in one hand and a chamber candle in the other, the Countess was only a short way behind.

As Alpiew reached the upper landing there was a second crash and a yelp.

'You're cornered, you thieving devil!' cried Alpiew, flinging open the door. She took a deep breath and marched in, wielding the hammer.

The Countess heard a scurry of footsteps and a leap as she rushed in behind Alpiew. But, as she raised the candle to illuminate the scene, the window slammed shut and the candle blew out.

There was a patter of footsteps on the tiles above them.

'The young fiend is on the roof!' Alpiew flung open the window and hauled herself up on to the ledge.

'No, Alpiew!' The Countess grabbed on to Alpiew's nightgown. 'You'll fall to your death.'

'I see him,' cried Alpiew. 'He's a dwarf!'

'A dwarf?' howled the Countess, letting go of Alpiew. 'Not a child? Who'd have thought it.'

'He has hairy hands.' Alpiew gripped on to the rotting wooden window frame to steady herself. 'A very agile dwarf in red satin pantaloons, a white shirt and a fez. He twinkles.' She strained her neck to get a better view. 'Curse this darkness! I cannot see him any more.'

'A burglar in satin pantaloons? Whoever heard of such a thing?' The Countess scratched at her wig. 'A fez, you say? That sounds a little exotic for a house-breaker. Do you think he's foreign?'

'And what would a foreigner want, breaking into this house?'

Godfrey and the night-watch Charlie staggered, breathless, into the attic chamber.

'Let me at him, missus!' Wheezing, and holding on to the door handle to maintain his equilibrium, the Charlie peered into the gloomy, empty room. 'Where is the scoundrel? Has he got away so fast?'

The Charlie waved a great club. Godfrey swung his lantern around the room.

'He ran off across the rooftops, sirrah,' said the Countess. 'The little fellow is probably just now back down in the street, strolling past your box.'

'Did you get a glimpse?' The watchman puffed, staggered over to the open window, and looked out. He reeled back, covering his eyes. 'By jingo, it's a long drop. I doubt but he'll suffer a broken bone or two in his descent.' He glanced around the empty dilapidated room. 'But Lord alone knows why anyone would want to burgle a place like this. What a dump!'

'Thank you, you miserable, lazy old bugger,' said Alpiew, moving him towards the landing. 'Let's get you back into your box so you can have a good snooze.'

Spluttering, the watchman turned back to the Countess. He fumbled inside his breeches and pulled out a cone full of boiled sweets.

'Like a lemon drop?'

The Countess shook her head. The Charlie popped a sweet into his mouth just as the church bell tolled the hour. 'Midnight!' The watchman ran past Alpiew, thrust his head out of the window and hollered. 'Twelve o'clock and all is well.'

'What are you bellowing about? It is not so well, is it?' Alpiew grabbed the lantern from Godfrey and shoved it into the watchman's hand. 'If you had not been asleep on duty, you'd have spied the little fellow coming in and there would have been no alarm.'

'It is my duty to call the hour.' He turned towards the window and yelled again. 'A lovely, clear peaceful night.'

'Oh, very peaceful!' exclaimed the Countess. 'What with bizarrely clad deaf dwarves breaking into people's houses and leaving them nutshells.'

'If he was short he could have slipped past me unawares. The May Fair is just finished, is it not?' The watchman tapped his forehead with a grimy finger. 'Where can such a fellow have come from, apart from the fairs?'

'The more important question at present, surely, sir, is where he has gone to.'

'Don't look at me,' said the night-watch Charlie, poking out his yellow tongue. 'Look at this! I spat out me sweet calling the hour.' He pulled out another lemon drop and sucked. 'Anyhow, I didn't see nothing.'

'*Nothing* is exactly what you saw. What you failed to see was a hairy foreign dwarf attired in a fantastical rig-up – twinkling, according to my friend Alpiew, in a pair of red pantaloons and a fez – strolling across our roof to break and enter my house with intent to burgle, and perhaps to murder us in our beds.'

'Have a lemon drop,' said the watchman. 'Go on. You're all safe. You ain't lost nothing. Life is sweet.'

*   *   *

The man behind the counter at the Bank of England kept the Countess waiting for over half an hour while he dealt with a line of male customers.

A separate queue waited at a grille at the far end of the counter to talk to a burdened-looking man in a heavy brown wig, who riffled through the pages of a great leather-bound ledger.

The Countess noticed how each customer pressed his face close to the grille and lowered their voice into an urgent whisper. 'My wife used the wretched banknote to wrap some butter, if you can believe it!' The mousey-looking fellow spoke in great anguish as though talking of a drowned child. 'A note for fifty-four pounds, thirteen shillings and one penny.'

The frazzled assistant flicked through his book. 'The note has endorsements . . .'

The Countess turned back to the main line and rapped on the counter. 'Is there an embargo upon women's money in this place, sirrah, that you will not serve me?'

'Absolutely not, madam.' The man wore a look of lugubrious indifference as he slouched over to her. 'I can assure you twelve per cent of all capital investors in the Bank of England are of the female gender.'

'Harrumph!' said the Countess, in fear of bringing forth another eruption of financial terms from the teller.

'So what can I do for you?'

'I have some money to spare and wondered if the Bank of England might be a suitable place to invest.'

'How much were you thinking of venturing?'

'One hundred guineas.'

'Indeed? And would that be investing in the Bank as a shareholder in the company, or do you wish to deposit?'

'What are your terms?' The Countess knew that this was a pretty safe reply to anything, financial or otherwise.

'I can put your name on the waiting list of people wishing

to become shareholders. Minor shares do come on the market from time to time. However, if you care to invest the money as a simple deposit, I could take your money now.'

'And what would I get in return?'

'Eight per cent per annum.'

'Anything else?'

'I would give you a receipt.'

'Yes? And what would that effect?'

'What do you think?' The man gave a long sigh. 'It would tell you how much money you have given me.'

'But I'd already know how much money I'd given you. What else would I get?'

'That depends on which of our investment options you chose. Or we could issue a running cash note.'

'Running cash?'

'A note which informs the recipient that we, the Bank of England, promise to pay the bearer the sum you have deposited, in coin of specie.'

'Whatever you like,' said the Countess, anxious for him to stop. She gave him her name and address anyhow.

'Your marital status?' The cashier peered over his spectacles as he dipped the pen, ready to fill in the details in a huge ledger.

'And what business is that of yours, sir?'

'If you are a spinster or a widow, your money is your own, madam. If you are married and your husband living, we should send the interest payments to him. Is he an English earl or a foreign count?' He pronounced the word count to rhyme with pint.

The Countess resisted the temptation to tell the man that her husband was an English count and rhyme the word with runt.

'The Earl of Clapham is under the sod,' said the Countess, crossing her fingers and praying her absentee husband wouldn't make a sudden reappearance. 'I am a widow.'

'As are most of our female investors, madam. Among women 'tis generally acknowledged that of all available marital situations, widowhood is the happiest.'

Pope's Head Alley and Poultry were hectic with people handing out leaflets. The Countess was busy reading one for the Royal Unparalleled Wash-Ball. '"Its admirable virtue for cleansing the skin from all discolour, as sunburn, freckles, swarthy, yellow, or tawny, makes it the greatest beautifier in nature . . ."' She muttered to herself and read on as she walked. '"By washing therewith it fortifies the head from cold . . ."'

She collided with someone, nodded an apology and walked on.

'Countess? Are you going to walk right past me?' It was Mrs Cue, the mighty force behind *The London Trumpet*, and the Countess's employer.

'Ah,' said the Countess, suddenly realising she and Alpiew hadn't even thought about delivering their piece for the next issue. They didn't have so much as a tiny scandal stuffed at the back of a drawer that they could offer. 'I am so glad I bumped into you, Mrs Cue. Look at this –'

The Countess thrust the advertisement at Mrs Cue.

'"It comforts the head, brain and nerves, also strengthens the memory, by supporting those tender parts by its noble scent and virtues,"' read Mrs Cue. '"Each ball sealed and with printed directions, outlining the virtues more at large." What is this to me?'

'Balls!' said the Countess. 'They think that their balls can strengthen the memory. Surely that claim is scandalous in itself? Alpiew and I were thinking of investigating the claims on these hand-outs.'

'But we don't want you to write investigatory stories about balls, Countess. We want scandal.'

'Yes. You're right. Scandal. In fact we are pursuing a great big juicy financial scandal this very morning.'

'But, Countess, we depend on you for sex.'

'But, Mrs Cue, money is the new sex. Believe me. Sex is passé. It's money everyone's chasing after nowadays. Sex went out with the ark.'

'If you say so.' Mrs Cue looked disappointed. 'It's lucky I bumped into you. I wanted to tell you about Mr Cue's new discovery.'

'Really?' The Countess could not imagine what the woman was twittering about. Was he too moving into the world of projects?

'We're going graphic!'

'Graphic?'

'My husband has discovered this wonderful new artist.' Mrs Cue beamed. 'An engraver. And now every week we will have a lovely picture to go with one of the stories. So we were wondering what you had up your sleeve for us so that we can tell the artist and he can get on with it.'

'Ah . . .' The Countess wracked her brains for anything she might have encountered in the week that could make a scandal story. 'It is about a . . . a . . . a wedding we are going to attend later this morning. The groom is very old. The bride is very young. And we suspect she has two other gay blades in hot pursuit. One is a Captain Caruso . . .'

'Oh, an Italian!' Mrs Cue flushed. 'Italian men always make a good story. An ex-army man?'

'Yes.' The Countess spoke in a tone which allowed no contradiction. 'He's in . . . ur . . . Princess Anne's Regiment of Dragoons.' The Countess was so pleased with herself for thinking up a regiment she stopped there.

'And the other fellow . . . ?'

'Other? Oh yes – and this is what I mean about money

being the new sex – the other rival for the girl's affections is a stock-broker.'

'A stock-broker! What on earth does one of those do?'

'Oh,' said the Countess with a brisk nonchalance. 'It's easy once you know. He plays with the preferred limitations of the capital sum, as distinguished from fractional dividends, and accrues revenue in liquidation.' The Countess cleared her throat in a knowing manner. 'You see – this money thing even has its own new language, understood only by the cognoscenti.' She glanced up at a clock set into the façade of the Royal Exchange. 'Ah, look at the time! Dear Mrs Cue, I would so love to stay and gossip, but thrilling stories will wait for no man . . .'

'No, nor women neither.' Mrs Cue chuckled. 'Run along, my dear.'

'And give our love to Mr Cue,' yelled the Countess as she trotted away into a throng of leaflet-givers.

By the time she met up with Alpiew at Exchange Alley, the Countess had a fistful of advertisements and fliers.

'I told Mrs Cue we were writing about Sir Richard's wedding, so now we'll have to go.'

Alpiew sighed. She wanted to get on with pursuing this money business, which she was beginning to find rather exciting. 'What news at the Bank of England?'

'Grocer's Hall! Lord, what a place!' cried the Countess. 'They should have left it to the grocers, for surely bankers live in a foreign land. I barely understood a word of what he said. You give them all your money and they simply issue you with a piece of paper declaring that they have it.'

'We shall need this –' Alpiew presented the Countess with a bandbox the size of a small book.

'What on earth is it, Alpiew?' The Countess opened the box and inspected its contents. 'It looks like six tiny mangles in a row.'

'Napier's rods. It is the very latest thing in the world of money. A gadget similar to the Arabic abacus!'

'Arabic abacus? What is that? Some sort of cabalistic gibberish? Have you turned conjuror?'

'Not abracadabra; Arabic abacus – a calculating machine of the Arabian variety.' Alpiew glanced towards Jonathan's. 'One of the girls behind the counter in there gave it to me. Some blade gave it to her, hoping to have a fondle by way of exchange.'

'You've been inside the coffee house?'

'Oh yes. I helped out behind the counter for a while. I can brew coffee as well as the next wench, and serve it with as comely an air. The wench within made me laugh. "Coffee," she declared, "would make a man as barren as the deserts in which it grew. And the offspring of coffee drinkers would dwindle into a succession of apes and pigmies."'

'And, apart from that pearl of wisdom, Alpiew, did you get any good tips?'

'A young ugly spark – I find the ugly ones are keener to part with their information – advised me that the safest companies at the moment are the New East India, the Hudson Bay and the Royal African.'

'Well and good, Miss Arabic abacus!' The Countess flicked through the leaflets in her hand.

'"*As Oyster Nan stood by her Tub,*
To shew her vicious Inclination;
She gave her noblest parts a rub,
And sigh'd for want of copulation."

Oh fie.' She handed it to Alpiew, who read on.

'"Anna Smythe. Available to sing at parties, weddings, funerals &c. Renowned for her public performances of the works of Finger."' Alpiew reeled back. 'Lor', madam, we all

66

have our private inclinations, but there's no need to shout about it.'

'I think she means Mr Godfrey Finger, the celebrated composer, Alpiew. But she certainly could have worded it better.' The Countess flicked her hand on the paper and read the next. 'Aha! "Laura's Lace Emporium! Best fine Chantilly and Flanders. Bodices, lappets, caps, frontanges, stomachers. Prickwork. Private fitting rooms." Advertising is a key factor in a successful business, I suppose. Perhaps we should look about for a project which advertises.'

'Let's see . . .' Alpiew glanced at one of the leaflets, and read: ' "The Navy Royal – or the Sea-Cook turned projector, proposals for manning out ships with the best of sailors, without violences, and with good tack . . ." I cannot see how one would make a profit from that.'

'"The Famed Elixir for the Wind,"' read the Countess, '". . . which expels it to admiration, whether sewer or windy belches from indigestion, etc. It removes the wind upon the spot. To be had only at Mr Spooner's new living, at the Golden Half-Moon in Lemon Street, Goodman's Fields, at two shillings and sixpence a bottle, with directions."' She gulped and continued, putting the advertisement down. 'On the other hand, Alpiew, perhaps the very successful businesses are the ones which have no need to advertise.'

'Advertising is the Devil's work!' A middle-sized man in a dark brown periwig growled from the bench. His head had been slumped forward, lolling on his lace cravat. The Countess had assumed he was asleep. As he spoke he seized a placard which lay at his side, and waved it before them. 'Advertising is a mere tool of this confederation of swindlers who have sold the whole British nation to usury!'

'I don't think he's a very nice man.' The Countess grabbed Alpiew's elbow and steered past him, trying to take a sneaky second look at his face. 'Oh no, look who it is!

I'd recognise that nasty big mole on his upper lip anywhere.'

'Ay, madam. 'Tis the unmannerly cove who insulted you as he stood in the stocks yesterday evening.'

'Beware of jobbers and brokers and dealers and all who ply their lies within that league of fiends,' hollered the man, clutching his placard and advancing on them. 'What tricking, what fraud, what laying plots as deep as hell, as far as the ends of the earth is therein?' He pointed towards Jonathan's. 'What cheating of fathers and mothers and brothers, what gulling of widows, orphans, cozening the most wary, plundering the unwary, takes place within those fatal doors?' He indicated Garraway's.

'Thank you so much for your advice, Mr . . . er . . . ?'

'Foe,' said the man. 'And when it comes to this system of knavery, my name is suited to the word. I am their sworn enemy, one who knows the filthy truth which lies within.'

'Thank you, Mr Foe, but my friend and I are in a particular hurry. We were just wandering through this alley by chance, and . . .'

'I heard you discussing investing in a project, otherwise known to the poor dupe who loses all as a cheat, a bubble, a swindle.' He gave a maniacal laugh. 'How many lesser robberies than these bring the friendless poor to the gallows every sessions?'

The bell of St Edmund, in nearby Lombard Street, tolled ten.

'Mr Foe. My dear. I would so love to stand and chat with you, but, alas, if we do, we will be late for a friend's wedding. Meanwhile, perhaps you would like a little light reading.' She handed him the verses on Oyster Nan, turned on her heels and scampered up the stairs leading back into bustling Corn Hill. 'Now, Alpiew,' she panted as she reached the top, 'let us hurry to the old fool's wedding. Who knows, when we are there, perhaps a fellow guest might give us some financial advice.'

Alpiew looked back. As she turned the corner she could have sworn she heard someone following them up the steps.

But the dark stairway was empty.

THREE

Fritting — preheating of some materials together to form a white amorphous mass, which is then cooled and broken up for reheating in the main batch

'Ay. Sugar stock is up today but mark my words, 'twill be down tomorrow.'

'I am told rates at the RAC have never been better . . .'

'Royal African? I heard that had levelled out.'

'A young broker told yesterday of some new secret project which he thinks will make thousands: a flushing privy!'

'. . . If the bubble don't burst . . .'

The Countess and Alpiew moved along a bench lined with old men talking money.

From the desultory atmosphere no one would have the vaguest idea a wedding party was in full swing. Needless to say, there was no fiddler.

All alone at the far end of the room, Lettice, the only other female in the place, sat gently flicking her fan open and shut, and gazing wistfully down at her lap.

The Countess marched over to her.

'Why so sad, young lady? Tell me, is it the loss of the young Captain or the prospect of wedding a miserable old man?'

Lettice raised her eyes.

'Or is there some secret young man in your life? That nice Robinson Spark, for instance?'

The look Lettice gave the Countess was full of panic.

'What did you mean yesterday when you asked me to save you? Save you from what, exactly?' The Countess plucked a non-existent piece of lint from her skirt. 'Or rather, from whom?'

Lettice looked down into her lap, and pushed a stray wisp of pale blonde hair out of her eyes.

'You don't *have* to marry Sir Richard, you know. You are very young. You can wait.'

'He wants it.' The girl looked coyly at the floor. 'I only . . . Oh!' She let out a long sigh.

'Listen, Lettice, 'tis not yet too late. But once you have echoed the preacher's vows, there will be no turning back. At least not till one or other of you dies.' She patted the back of the girl's hand. 'If you want to run away, do it now. I'm sure Robinson would take you.'

'It's Robinson I want to be saved from.'

'Robinson?'

'He wants me to run away with him. I hate him.'

'Captain Caruso, then?'

'Oh!' A tear welled in Lettice's eye. 'He made my life worth living, and now he is gone. Please talk of something else. Mention of the Captain upsets me too much. Tell me about yourself, your life, anything.'

The girl was very agitated, so the Countess decided to change the subject. 'I will tell you about the strange thing that happened to me last night. I was burgled by a dwarf. I say "burgled", for we surprised the diminutive fellow before he had a chance to take anything. Whenever have you heard of such a thing in St James's? A hairy dwarf in red satin pantaloons and a fez.'

'What?' Lettice reeled back. 'Do you rally me, madam? Why do you treat me like a fool? Do you hope to make me more miserable than I already am?'

'No.' The Countess was alarmed at the pallor which had drained Lettice's cheeks of all colour. 'It really happened. Ask the night-watch Charlie.'

Lettice gave the Countess a sharp look, crossed the room and peered out of the window.

Sir Richard was at the Countess's side. 'What did you say, madam, to brighten up little Letty? I have not seen her so animated for days, adod.'

A guffaw of laughter came from the hall. Edward Stark and his plump wife Cynthia entered the room.

'Oh no! Those miserable hangers-on have arrived. Hoping for a free drink, I surmise. They imagine I am made of money!' Sir Richard was inspecting the solitary candle on the mantelpiece as though he was about to light it. 'At least they haven't brought that impudent young fornicating rake, Robinson, with them. Come along, madam –' Sir Richard grabbed the Countess by the arm and lowered his voice. 'You wanted to know how to keep your money safe. I will show you.' He shuffled out of the room, the Countess close behind, and tottered up the stairs, leading her into the front bedchamber. Apart from a large tattered four-poster bed, the furnishing was as threadbare as its owner. The floorboards were bare but for a frayed rug. At the end of the bed was a chest. It was ornately painted in red, blue and gold, and ornamented with scores of keyholes and cast-iron crossbars. Sir Richard clambered upon it and sat, swinging his legs.

'Sometimes I am utterly happy, and that is when I am sitting upon my entire fortune.' He gave a toothless grin and patted the trunk. 'Bob Gaunt made this up for me. I believe it is impregnable, for by the time the rascal who wanted to rob me had worked out the score of different locks and puzzles and secret compartments, he'd surely have been caught.'

The Countess was unimpressed. Rich people had kept their money in such coffers for centuries. It seemed to her that a money chest was an open invitation to any burglar, as it pinpointed the exact spot the money was kept.

'What if a robber came here and ran off with the entire box?'

'I knew you would say that. Everyone does.' He leaped to his feet and grabbed the Countess's hand. 'Try to move it!'

The Countess gripped the handle and pulled with all her might.

'Nailed to the floor, I daresay,' said the Countess, stooping to look at the base of the box.

'Fixed to the floor, yes. But also lined with lead and iron. It would take a burly man indeed to carry it, even when it is empty. But once it is full of gold – it would defeat Hercules himself! Nay, even Atlas, who shouldered the earth upon his shoulders, would find it hard to move my precious box.' He sat again and patted the lid of the chest, inviting the Countess to sit beside him. 'I tell you another thing. I was thinking about your house. You have the right idea in keeping the place looking so sparse and dilapidated. Tradesmen and so on, who out of necessity have to come inside, will tell the world you have nothing worth taking. Adod, yes. I'd think that would be a very good place to keep your money – in one of those empty upstairs rooms.'

'I was wondering if you could give me some advice about investments.' Alpiew approached the row of gossiping money-men.

As one, they leaned back, sour-faced, refusing to meet her eye.

'Maybe you could suggest a good company or project?' They shrunk back even further.

'Ah well,' Alpiew sighed. 'No matter.'

The minute she turned her back on them they started babbling again. 'Ay, the Old East India stock has swung from three hundred per cent to thirty-seven per cent, with fluxes and refluxes.' 'This morning I heard that Bank was at one hundred and sixty, and South Sea dropped to one hundred and twenty'. A collective 'Mmmm!' of wonder, followed by a joint nodding or shaking of heads.

Alpiew looked back along the bench of prattling financiers. Their chatter ceased.

She turned away. They piped up again. What a shame, she thought, that money brought such bad manners in its wake.

Lettice was standing by the window, gazing out. On the other side of the room Edward Stark was deep in conversation with his wife, while nearby the priest had started pulling out vestments from a great black leather bag.

Alpiew stepped out of the front door and leaned against the house wall, watching the carts coming and going along Pall Mall Street.

'She must not do it!' Robinson was suddenly at her elbow.

Alpiew jumped. 'You surprised me!' She glanced back to the window. But Lettice had moved. Had she been signalling to this boy out here in the street?

'I'm sorry, Robinson. It's not my business who Lettice marries.' Alpiew edged back towards the door. 'If she wants to marry the old skinflint . . .'

'She doesn't know the truth – or doesn't believe it . . .'

'The truth?'

'Let's just say that the wedding must be stopped.'

'On what grounds?'

'I cannot speak about it.' Robinson suddenly darted past her into the house. 'Excuse me.'

Alpiew followed him in, ready to note down any emotional scene for the *Trumpet*.

'Here you are!' Cynthia Stark thrust a gilded sprig of rosemary into Alpiew's hand as she came into the front room. 'If the old tight-wad isn't going to provide the wedding trimmings, I will. Poor little girl. If she's doing such a mad thing she might as well have the usual rig-me-role.'

Alpiew fastened the herb posy into the lace that edged her bodice.

'Look at that,' exclaimed Cynthia. 'How depressing.' She strutted across to the fireplace and moved a pair of ugly wooden statues to one side, laying a few sprigs of gold-painted laurel and rosemary in the centre of the mantel around the candlestick. 'Do you have a tinder-box?'

Alpiew pulled one out of her pocket.

'Light the candle – a flame is so pretty with all this silver and gold.' Cynthia looked at the room full of gloomy chattering old men. 'Pity there's no music. That might liven up this affair. My nephew should have brought his fiddle.'

She nodded in Robinson's direction as she dived her hand into her bagful of trimmings and moved across to start adorning the bride.

While Cynthia bustled about the child, pinning her with the usual wedding accoutrements – a sprig of rosemary and some pieces of lace – Alpiew watched Robinson. He seemed very nervous, never taking his eyes off Lettice.

'Bridal knots,' said Cynthia, thrusting pieces of lace into Lettice's hand.

From a nearby chair Edward glared and grunted disapproval.

75

'I got them cheap in the market.' Cynthia beamed back. 'A job lot.'

During the marital spat, Alpiew noticed Lettice momentarily catch Robinson's eye. There was a determined look about her. She gave a bob of the head, which Alpiew would have read as 'it's all right'.

Once she noticed Alpiew watching, the girl looked demurely to the floorboards.

Before she could see anything else, the Countess bustled back into the room.

'The old fellow was showing me his strong-box!' the Countess whispered into Alpiew's ear. 'Anything here for the *Trumpet*?'

'Plenty!' Alpiew was tempted to leave now and write up the mysterious love rivalry she felt sure she had observed.

'Rosemary?' Cynthia addressed the Countess.

'Anastasia, actually, but . . . Oh!' The Countess realised her mistake and took a sprig of the gold-painted herb. 'How pretty.' She gave Alpiew a wink as she pulled at an immobilised seat. 'Pshaw, I had forgot these nailed-down chairs. Make a note of it, Alpiew, for the column.' She edged around and sat.

Sir Richard tottered in and moved across to the fireplace. 'Waste of tallow!' he muttered as he blew out the candle.

'Have you the two part-coins, Sir Richard?' Cynthia was rifling through her bag of wedding trimmings. 'The ceremony would not be complete without the exchange of half a silver coin, as you know.'

'How much?'

'How much what?' Cynthia held out a silver semi-circle.

'How much will you charge me for it?'

'Men!' Cynthia rolled her eyes. 'It's a gift, Sir Richard. For your wedding.'

'Ah well, adod.' He took the half-coin and popped it into a small pocket in his waistcoat. 'I was going to use a lead one I'd had painted up, but a real one would be so much better . . .'

'Rosemary or bay?' Cynthia thrust the choice of painted shoots at him. He grabbed the bay. As Cynthia turned to give the rosemary to her husband, Sir Richard's hand shot out and snatched it. 'I am the groom, after all. I would prefer to have one of each. For luck.'

Cynthia seemed slightly taken aback by the grasping gesture, but she merely inclined her head and walked away.

'I hope, Alpiew, that you are making mental notes.' The Countess sat back in her chair and glanced around the room. 'What a crew! How is little Lettice taking it?'

'A few minutes ago I'd have sworn she wanted nothing more than to be spirited away by Robinson,' whispered Alpiew. 'But look now. It's a sight to be seen.'

Leaning against the empty fireplace, toying with the bouquets of gilded rosemary and bay propped up by the reflecting candlestick, the child was gazing at Sir Richard with an expression verging on the ecstatic.

Cynthia was pressing the other half of the silver coin into the girl's palm.

'Canonicals, Sir Richard!' The priest, who had been waiting in the doorway, was now rubbing his hands together in impatience. 'Come along, sir! Canonicals. Shall we get on with the service? I have many more nuptials to perform before the hours are up.'

'Adod, Your Reverence, I wait upon you.' Sir Richard stood before the priest. 'Let us proceed.'

As Lettice took her place beside the withered old man, the priest started to read from his huge prayer book.

Robinson had taken up a position near Alpiew. 'No,' he muttered as the priest droned. 'No, no, no, no!'

'Have you the licence and so on?' The priest held out his hand and Sir Richard pulled some crumpled papers from his pocket and handed them over, carefully placing the half-coin back after he had done.

'So let's begin.' The priest laid the papers to one side, took a deep breath and was about to start chanting when the front door banged open and a commotion in the hall silenced him. 'There is a ceremony going on here.' He lowered his spectacles and groaned. 'Please can I have some quiet?'

A scraping sound came from the hallway. Then a tall chairman appeared, his hands gripping what appeared to be the front handles of a sedan chair. 'I'm sorry, everyone. We appear to be stuck.' He winced, tugging at the bars.

'Good lack, boy, what are you doing in here?' Sir Richard threw his arms up and stamped. 'Can't you see I am being wed? The street is that way.' Sir Richard turned back to the priest. 'Continue, sir.'

''Tis I, Sir Richard!' A muffled voice came from the hall. 'I am to witness de wedding, remember?'

'Hendrick?' Sir Richard held his hand up to silence the priest. 'Is that you?'

'Ay, sir, 'tis me, sir, but I cannot get out of de chair, as de door will not open.'

'Of course the door will not open, Hendrick. Your chair is in my hallway, which is too narrow for a chair. Leave it out in the street like everyone else.'

The priest gave another audible sigh.

With a rasping sound, the chairmen backed the chair out. A few moments later a very strange creature appeared in the doorway.

As old as Sir Richard, but considerably plumper, Hendrick Van Loon was wrapped up as though it was a particularly chilly winter night rather than a steamy morning in May. Apart from a heavy greatcoat, he wore innumerable scarves tightly wrapped round his neck, his hands were hidden inside fur-lined leather gauntlets, and atop his thick wig sat a winter beaver hat.

To wander about on such a beautiful hot day dressed for a blizzard might be considered eccentric, but the strange wooden plugs he had sticking out of his ears and his nostrils could only be described as bizarre. 'Carry on, sir, carry on with de ceremony! Pay no attention to me,' cried the Dutchman. He hugged his coat closer to him as he pushed himself into a seat 'Don't wait upon me. Continue de nuptials.' He hauled a large scented kerchief from his pocket and held it up against his mouth.

One of the chairmen clicked the hall door shut and tried to retrieve the long carrying handles which were jammed in the banisters. The resultant banging made it necessary for the priest to shout.

'Wilt thou, Richard Dainty, have this woman to thy wedded wife, to live together after God's ordinance in the holy estate of Matrimony?' he bellowed.

'Oh, yes.' Sir Richard nodded eagerly. 'I will.'

Beside Alpiew, Robinson was sniffing into his hands.

'Wilt thou love her, comfort her, honour, and keep her?'

The Countess watched Lettice, yesterday all tears, now standing beside this wizened and unattractive little man beaming from ear to ear, and wondered what on earth could have brought about such a transformation.

'. . . And wilt thou, Lettice Dainty, take this man . . .'

The Countess assumed that the girl must have traded in her maiden name some years previously when she became Sir Richard's ward.

The front door slammed. The chairmen had obviously got their handles and gone out into the street.

Beside the Countess, Cynthia wafted herself with a large brisée fan.

'This child is the strangest up-and-down creature, do you not think, Mrs Stark?'

'Oh, the old fellow is too.' Cynthia raised her fan in one hand and cupped her other to the Countess's ear. 'He is a strangely perverted kind of fellow. But needs must . . . The child has two choices: him or the gutter. It's a tough world out there.' She let out a long weary sigh. 'Poor girl. A lamb to the slaughter.'

Before Lettice had a chance to say 'I do', the front door slammed again, and a ragged, smut-faced urchin ran into the room, kneading his cap in his hands. 'Hendrick Van Loon! Sir Richard Dainty! Gentlemen! News from Lloyds Coffee House.' All heads turned to the child. 'The great ship *Cassandra*, bound for Southampton from Virginia, last spotted passing the Fastnet Rock, has gone down, with loss of all aboard.'

The gentlemen of the congregation rose and gasped.

'And de cargo, my boy?' called Hendrick, running his fat fingers between his scarves and his neck. 'What of de cargo?'

'Lost!' wailed the boy. 'Lost without a trace.'

'Enough!' cried Hendrick. 'My chair!'

The other gentlemen were busily grabbing their hats and making for the door.

Sir Richard hesitated, torn between completing his wedding ceremony and rushing to exploit the news.

'Come along, Sir Richard,' wheezed Hendrick Van Loon, clicking his fat gloved fingers to summon his chairmen to assist him. 'Why are you standing there dithering, you old fool? De ship is down. Think of de profits.'

'Profits? Oh yes, surely.' Sir Richard bit his lip, and looked towards his young bride.

'Adod, Pigsny, I will be back shortly. Just wait for me and we will still be married later.'

'Later?' Lettice wore an expression of utter dismay. 'Just complete the ceremony now, then go. It will only take a minute or two . . .'

'Enough time for me to win a fortune,' said Van Loon, limping out of the room and throwing his hands up. 'I am happy to get it, and you, Sir Richard, will be de loser.'

A look of total panic flooded Sir Richard's countenance. He gnawed at his lower lip and dived for his stick. 'Worry not, adod,' he whispered to Lettice while shoving on his hat. 'We will be married later, impatient little Letty. But I cannot lose this profit to all those others. I am right behind you, Hendrick.'

'Later?' The priest growled and glared at the clock. 'Canonicals!' he added with a grunt. 'Or it's another ten shillings.'

'Another ten shillings?' wailed Sir Richard, grabbing a stick. 'Have no fear, I will be back in time for your wretched canonicals!'

And with that he ran from the room.

'Me too,' said Robinson. He hung his head, but both Alpiew and the Countess noted that he darted a brisk look at Lettice as he followed the others out of the room.

The Countess could not be sure, but it seemed to her that Robinson's look was one of complicit panic.

'Now what?' The Countess stood up. 'Should we go and come back, or sit here and wait?'

No one replied.

Lettice still stood in a desolate rapture facing the priest, who was hastily repacking his black bag.

Next to the Countess, Cynthia, her face glazed in a fine sweat, slowly fanned herself. Alpiew seated herself in the corner and started scratching down numbers into a little notebook.

'I shall be off, then. Canonicals wait upon no man, you

know.' The priest removed his ecclesiastical cap and slammed on his outdoor hat. 'I will return.'

When the priest had gone, silence fell upon the four women. The only sound was of Cynthia's fan flapping.

'I am gasping for a brimmer!' Cynthia suddenly snapped her fan shut. 'Today has been too hot and bothersome by half. Let's go next door to the Unicorn and share a bottle of claret.'

Lettice moved slowly across to the window and sat staring out into the street. Her face was a picture of disappointment.

'Pshaw, 'tis the strangest thing for a bride on her wedding day to lose her husband to news of the gains that can be made from a shipping disaster,' the Countess whispered to Cynthia. 'Why, the man is not even her husband yet – they have not said the vows.' The Countess watched a tear of sweat dribble down the side of Cynthia's face. 'Perhaps rather than leave the house we should get the wine and bring it back here. The groom may yet return in time for the ceremony.'

'Not even tossed the stocking, poor girl,' said Cynthia, looking into her purse and pulling out a lacy handkerchief. 'Pity! I would have made good aim. It would surely have hit its mark, and I'd be next in line.'

'Tossed the stocking, Mrs Stark? But you are already married.'

'Ay, ay, that's true enough. I am married,' said Cynthia, thrusting the purse into her pocket. 'But who'd know it? I tell you, ladies, if you marry a City man you are as good as a widow from your wedding day – but without a widow's freedom.' She laughed. 'I shall buy a large jug of claret and we can all drink to widowhood.'

'I need some air,' said Lettice.

The Countess rose.

'I'd prefer to be alone for a few moments, please, Countess.' Lettice gave a sweet smile as she left the room.

'Shall I fetch in some other goodies to go with the wine?' Cynthia followed Lettice to the door. 'Sweetmeats? Nuts, fruit? Anybody?'

'Why not?' The Countess held out a handful of coins. 'There is no wedding feast, so let us provide it!'

'I'll get a bottle and glasses for four.' Cynthia beamed. 'Put up your money, madam. The drinks are on me. And for a snack I shall garner what I can from the higglers in the Hay Market.'

'Sixpence a day on four per cent,' muttered Alpiew, still hunched over the table, chewing her pencil. 'Hmmm. It would hardly be worth it.'

'Miss Numbers?' As the front door slammed the Countess clapped her hands and Alpiew looked up from her calculations. 'Alpiew, have you witnessed any of the events of this morning?'

'Of course I have.' Alpiew blinked and looked about her. 'Where is Lettice gone?'

'She's out there in the street. Talking earnestly with one of the old boys who make up the watch.'

Alpiew came to the window and looked out. Lettice was gesticulating and laughing.

'What a conundrum that little girl is.' The Countess brushed the dust from the window pane to get a clearer view. 'Yesterday all tears and now . . . Hey day, look at this!'

She pointed to the corner of the pane of glass, where someone had scratched four letters. '"ERIS" – I wonder what that means?'

'Perhaps it's the name of the glass-maker. Why is the girl so upon the grin?' Alpiew glanced up and down the street. 'Because the wedding was stopped? Because now she is free to wed another?'

Pall Mall Street was full of people coming away from the morning's market. Lettice was jumping up and down like a child with a rope as she talked to the old watchman.

'Captain Caruso . . .' sighed the Countess, who loved a romance. 'Or Mrs Stark's nephew, Robinson.'

A few yards away, Cynthia came out of the tavern door and strode off towards St James's. She was pulling coins from her purse.

Alpiew looked again at Lettice. The girl was biting her lip and rubbing her hands together, an excited flush on her cheek. The old watchman put his hand to his mouth and shouted down the street. A blackamoor came loping up to him.

'What the . . . ? Madam! Look who it is!' Alpiew gathered up her skirts and ran out into the street. 'Cupid!' she called, breaking into a run. 'Cupid!'

The Countess followed and stood on the doorstep. She looked up and down but could see no one like Cupid in the street. But then, the Cupid she remembered was a charming child of six who played upon her knee, decked out in gorgeous silks and satins, on his head a sweet striped turban pinned with a huge diamond brooch.

How many years ago must it have been that he left? Why, the little pretty darling must be a man of about thirty by now.

The Countess was tempted to follow Alpiew, but realised she was the only person left in Sir Richard's house. And surely if it *was* Cupid and Alpiew found him, she would bring him back.

Cupid! Her darling Moorish boy. How lovely it would be to find him again.

A cart-horse lumbered slowly towards St James's Market. Alpiew had lost sight of Cupid. But perhaps it wasn't him after all. She had shouted his name loud enough, and he seemed to glance back. He had even caught eyes with Alpiew, but then he had turned on his heels and run the other way, quickly disappearing into the crowd. Why would Cupid do that to her? They had always been close. She was like his big sister. And he and the Countess had adored one another.

Those were the days! When Cupid lived with them. Alpiew sighed. When the Countess had money and standing, and they all lived together in luxury.

She had half a mind to run after him, but if after all these years he thought fit to snub her, why should she pursue him?

'Good afternoon!' A hairy little man stood before her. Alpiew had to look twice to see it was Bob Gaunt, the locksmith. 'My boys have been a bit held up. I am hoping they will start work shortly.'

'Thank you. My mistress will be very happy about that.' Alpiew turned and strolled back towards Sir Richard's house in Pall Mall Street.

A few yards from the front door, pale as a ghost, stood Cynthia, buying sweetmeats from a street seller's tray.

As Alpiew watched, Cynthia put out her hand to steady herself on the higgler's basket then slid slowly to the ground in a faint. The bottle she was holding smashed on the cobbles, red wine running in rivulets along the gaps between the cobbles, soaking into the white lace of her cuffs in vivid red splashes.

Alpiew rushed to her side, kicking away the broken glass while she knelt to loosen the woman's stays. 'Shall I get someone to run to the Exchange and fetch Mr Stark?'

'No!' Cynthia grabbed at Alpiew and whispered. 'Not my husband. I am all right. It's only the heat, and the excitement.'

'Oh my, Mrs Stark!' Lettice stooped over the prostrate woman and fanned her gently. 'You do look pale.'

'Pale, yes. As alabaster! I've been told before.' Cynthia shut her eyes and gave a sardonic laugh. 'Pale as alabaster.'

It was past four when Edward Stark returned to Sir Richard's house to pick up his wife.

The priest had come back and waited for Sir Richard. On the last toll of the midday bell he exclaimed, 'End of Canonicals!' grabbed his bag and departed.

Cynthia had insisted that her husband was not told about her faint. And though she looked none too well, the Countess and Alpiew honoured her wishes. Then they sat patiently with Lettice till it grew dark.

The Countess tried to draw the girl on the subject of her marriage and the other men in her life. But Lettice only sighed, and glanced at the large clock ticking in the corner. 'If not today, then tomorrow,' she kept repeating at random times.

Paying no attention, Alpiew scribbled away in the corner, alternating with sums and jotting down points for the wedding story. When the light was almost gone she went to fetch a taper to light the wall sconces, only to discover that there were no candles in any of the holders.

'My pigsny prefers us to use only that one reflecting light for the house,' Lettice explained, pointing at the sole candlestick on the mantel. 'Then we won't accidentally leave a candle burning when we go out of a room.'

'He is scared of causing a fire?' asked the Countess, scrutinising the glass stick with its mirror and reflecting glass drops. 'That surely is one of a pair.'

'No.' Lettice ran over and fetched the candle. 'It is good husbandry, Sir Richard says, to have but one stick in the house. Not only do we cut out the chance of accidentally leaving a candle alight in an empty room, we save money on candles too.'

'Mmm, yes,' said the Countess. She couldn't believe it. That a person would stint on an essential like light. 'I suppose it would save money.'

In the dim flicker of a solitary beam the three women huddled round the table.

But as the night drew in and drunken youths staggered along the street outside, still Sir Richard did not return.

'Where can he be?' said Lettice with a gulp. 'Now I am really worried. What if he doesn't come home?'

'Would you like us to stay here with you?' The Countess was not over-keen to remain sitting in this murky house with its air of stinginess and nailed-down furniture. 'Or would you like to come with us and wait at our house?'

'Oh good!' Lettice jumped up and pulled on a wrapper. 'Thank you so much for inviting me. I thought you would never suggest we go there.'

'What of Sir Richard?'

'Yes. I am very worried that he is not back. But I suppose it must be important business that keeps him. I'll leave a note telling him I am gone to your house. When he gets home my little pigsny will come and fetch me. The business at the Exchange must have led him elsewhere.'

'Does he frequently stay out overnight?'

'Never.' Lettice glanced eagerly at the Countess then blew out the light. 'But I'm sure he would think it was lovely if I could stay with you for a while.'

The Countess noted a flush to the girl's cheeks. Whatever was going on, Lettice was clearly very excited by it.

Godfrey was slumped snoring in front of the fire when the Countess led Lettice in.

'You see how it is,' the Countess indicated the room, with its three beds. 'If you want to stay here you will have to share a bed with one of us.'

'I couldn't do that,' said Lettice, her eyes aflame. 'I will sleep in the attic room. The one where the little fellow in pantaloons came in . . .'

'But that is hardly wise. Besides, there is no bed . . . !'

Before the Countess could finish her sentence the girl had grabbed a chamber light, bounced out of the kitchen and was on her way up the stairs.

'Oh, leave her to it, madam.' Alpiew flopped down on her bed and unlaced her boots. 'It's so uncomfortable and draughty up there she'll be down again soon enough.'

'What a day!' The Countess wound back the events of the day and grimaced. The world of money-men was certainly like nothing she had ever encountered. She looked hopefully at the embers of the fire and peered into all the pots hanging up in the fireplace. There was nothing she wanted so much as a bowl of stew and a quiet evening reading. 'And this miserable old bugger hasn't even made us any supper.' She slammed the last iron lid down loudly, hoping to wake Godfrey, but he just shuddered, licked his wiry lips, turned in the chair and emitted a long, burbling fart.

'For goodness' sake, Godfrey.' The Countess applied her fan. 'There are ladies present.'

'You two?' Godfrey rubbed his stubbly chin with a knobbly hand. 'You ain't ladies.'

A thump came from upstairs.

'Oh no, not again.' Alpiew wondered if Godfrey had just spent the whole day asleep. 'Godfrey, did the man not come to fix the casement?'

'The man? Casement? Yes. I let him in, pointed to the stairs and told him to let himself out when it was finished.'

'Did you go upstairs and check the work, Godfrey, because I just heard the wretched thing banging again.' The Countess kicked the leg of his chair.

'Check it?' Godfrey got up and started busily poking at the remains of the fire. 'I don't know about that. I was busy. It was lunchtime.'

The Countess eyed Godfrey. By lunchtime he obviously meant he was asleep and hadn't a notion what time it was. 'Did he leave a bill?'

'I signed for it – yes. Then some strange hairy-looking fellow came in an hour or so after and . . .'

'The night-soil man?'

A louder crash above them interrupted Godfrey before he could reply.

'What is the girl at?' Thin-lipped, the Countess glared at Godfrey. 'I hope you have not paid out for a job not done.'

Godfrey thrust his hand into his britches, pulled out a receipt and read: '"I hereby accept . . ."'

'Accept?' The Countess snatched the note. 'What on earth . . . ?'

From the top room a scream interrupted her.

'I'll go up, madam.' Alpiew grabbed a poker. 'It's probably nothing.'

'Did you check the window was mended, Godfrey, before you accepted this invoice? "Divers items of carpentry . . ."' The Countess flicked the paper and read aloud. '"I hereby accept delivery . . ."' Delivery? It was a window he was fixing. '"Prepaid by sender. . ."' The Countess turned the note over. 'This is the strangest carpenter's invoice I ever saw.'

'There was a lot of banging up top so I know they did something. It's a long way up those ruddy stairs and me legs ain't . . .'

'Enough!' The Countess glared at him. 'Godfrey, you

have nothing to do all day but sit around snoring. Go on. You can go up now and check it.'

'But . . .'

The Countess glowered, an arm outstretched, pointing towards the hall. 'Out!'

Godfrey slouched into the hall, muttering under his breath.

What a day. The Countess grabbed a pen and paper and sat with a sigh. She smoothed out the invoice on her lap. 'Prepaid indeed!'

She was looking forward to writing up this non-wedding for the *Trumpet*. She sucked the end of the quill, ready to dip it. Her stomach rumbled. She put the writing things and the delivery note aside and got up, searching the kitchen tops for something to eat. She pulled open the larder and inspected the shelves. She twisted the stopper out of a blue-and-white jar and plunged her hand inside, pulling out a cinnamon biscuit. Popping the biscuit into her mouth she wandered back across the kitchen.

What was keeping them all? She went to the dark hall and called up.

'Alpiew? Don't help him. He can do it himself, the lazy sloven.' There was no reply. 'Alpiew?' The Countess raised her voice. 'Alpiew?'

No sound came from upstairs.

She looked to the front door. Had they gone out? But she had not heard the door go, and in any case why would they need to go out at this late hour?

'Alpiew? Godfrey?' She swung up the stairs. 'Is everything all right?'

As she reached the top landing she heard a strange muffled sound like giggling. Flickering light spilled under the door.

Were the three naughty things playing a joke on her? She tiptoed to the door and listened.

Silence.

Certainly they were up to something.

Fine. If that's how it was, she would play along. No one could accuse her of having no sense of humour.

'Alpiew?' She put on a timorous voice and walked into the room. 'Godfrey?'

Instantly she was thrown to the floor and felt a great weight upon her back.

When she looked up from the dusty boards where she sprawled face down, she could see a pair of smart gentleman's tan riding boots before her, illuminated by the glow from a single chamber light, the one Lettice had carried up. 'What is happening?'

'Shut up, you old cow,' said a rough female voice close behind her.

'Welcome, Countess!' The boots creaked and white britches came into view, then a white jacket and cravat, and finally the swarthy chin of a young man as he crouched to speak to her. 'What an age it took you to come upstairs and join us.' His voice was quiet, oily.

The Countess recognised John O'Hara, the young man in white who had made a run for it when strung up at the Tyburn gallows yesterday morning.

'Ease off a bit, Kate.' The boy smiled his icy smile. 'Let the poor Countess breathe. We don't want to hurt the old dear, now, do we?'

The woman climbed off the Countess's back.

With the foot on her back the Countess couldn't look around, but from the corner of her eye she could see Godfrey, Lettice and Alpiew in a row on the floor under the window, their hands and feet bound, mouths gagged.

Kate Timony, the woman who had also escaped a hanging,

in her case by a claim of pregnancy, loomed into the Countess's vision. In her gloved hands swung a pair of pistols.

Alpiew was squawking through her gag, wiggling about on the floor, fury in her eyes.

'Up!' Kate pointed the muzzles of the guns towards the Countess's head.

Alpiew squirmed further, fighting her bonds.

'It's all right, Alpiew. Stay still.' The Countess clambered to her feet. Once upright she held her hands up in surrender. 'What do you want? Money?'

John O'Hara stepped in front of Kate and pushed the barrels of the pistols towards the floor. 'For shame, Kate! The Countess is our friend and partner. We don't want to injure her now, do we?' He put his arm round the Countess and walked her across the room. 'We have no intention of hurting anyone. But we do ask a little favour of you.'

'This is a very strange way to invite yourself into a person's home, sirrah, and an even stranger way of requesting a favour from a person.' Trying to quell the thumping of her heart, the Countess glanced again at Lettice, Godfrey and Alpiew. They all seemed fit, and she could see no blood anywhere. She held her head high. She had no intention of letting them see she was frightened. 'I prefer good manners in my house-guests, so perhaps you would like to release my friends.'

Kate stamped her foot and raised the guns again.

'Of course I will help you, sir . . .' the Countess continued with as brave a voice as she could muster. 'But you must promise not to hurt those three.' She tried to give a natural smile and straightened her wig. 'What do you want me to do?'

John O'Hara edged nearer to the Countess. 'Do put the guns away, Kate. I told you, we are dealing with a lady. We don't want to scare her, do we?'

'Phough!' huffed the Countess, steadying herself against the wall. 'I am not scared by a dirty slattern like her. Guns or no guns.' She took a deep breath and smiled again, having to lick her teeth first to stop her upper lip sticking. 'Just let me know the task in hand and let me instantly be about it.'

'A simple errand. You must collect something on our behalf, then take it on elsewhere and bring us back the proceeds in coin.' He gave a patronising smirk. 'I'd get my old mum to do it, but you mix in circles she cannot.'

'Circles?' The Countess was hardly famed for dancing at Kensington balls. 'I am afraid you are mistaken. My days of mixing with the high and mighty are long gone.'

'Don't try that game,' sneered Kate Timony. 'We've seen you with 'em.'

'Indeed? Then I am pleased to oblige you. Give me the address and I will get you whatever you like.' She edged towards the door. This was too easy. Of course the moment she turned the corner she would run to the constable and he could round up a posse and . . .

'By the way, don't even think about going to the constable,' said John O'Hara in his low, insinuating voice. 'If I hear anything other than one pair of elderly lady's feet coming up those stairs I shall shoot your friends here. After all, I am already under a death sentence for highway robbery. And if I'm taken again I shall certainly be hanged, whether for that or for three murders.' He threw the casement open and gave a shrill whistle. 'I have provided a companion, to walk with you, just to make sure.' Another whistle came from below. 'He's waiting in the street. His name is Jake. A very dependable fellow.' O'Hara handed the Countess a sealed letter. 'All the instructions are set out in this.'

The candle guttered in the draught.

The Countess caught eyes with Alpiew. She tried silently to say 'don't try anything stupid', but felt that Alpiew's look was saying the same thing to her.

'Get along with you now, lady. This matter must be completed by morning.'

When the Countess emerged into the warm night there seemed to be no one in the street. What a situation. She could see no other way than to follow the instructions. But what if when she returned they shot them all anyhow?

It was dark. She glanced at the night-watchman's box. The door was shut. The old fool would be asleep, as usual.

She tore open the letter. There were two addresses she had to visit. The first was in Southwark, the second was that of Sir Richard Dainty. She waited for her escort to appear, but when after a few minutes no one came, she started walking. It was only as she turned out of the well-lit St James's Square into shadowy Charles Street that she became aware of the soft tread of another pair of feet walking a few yards behind her.

Alpiew lay as still as she could bear. Godfrey was wriggling about on the dusty floor grunting, and Lettice softly wept.

Outside on the landing, their captors were murmuring. John O'Hara's voice was prominent. Alpiew tried to flash her eyes to indicate to the other two to be quiet so that she could listen, maybe even catch the odd phrase.

Alpiew wondered how she had ever let this happen. It was unusual for her to be outwitted, but this pair of ne'er-do-wells had surprised her, and before she knew what was happening she had been pinned down and lined up next to Lettice. Although bound and gagged, she had done her best to warn Godfrey when she heard him coming up the stairs, but to no avail. He had come bumbling in and the two gaol-birds held him fast in a flash.

Alpiew hoped that eventually they would remove her gag, and she could speak to them, make an offer. She hated to think that they were using the Countess for their dirty work. If anything else was required later she would volunteer to take over.

Near the door a floorboard creaked. Then she thought she heard someone going downstairs.

Alpiew wiggled herself up against the wall and managed to get to her feet. She looked out into the night.

The chaperone they had whistled for would have an interest in keeping an eye out for the Countess, making sure she carried out her errand and returned safely with the money.

She heard a horse clopping below, then a coach's wheels rattled past, clattering on the cobbles. More whispering came from the landing. Alpiew wriggled her hands, trying to loosen the bonds. She wondered what the time was. Next time the church bell tolled she must remember to count the hour.

A gang of drunken youths, their bawdy song echoing up to the rooftops, crossed the street further up towards the Hay Market end.

Balancing against the wall, Alpiew inspected the window frame. Godfrey was a liar. No one had been to mend it. The catch was still loose. It would only take a nudge to open. Alpiew realised that if she could pull her pencil from her pocket she could write a note, throw it out and hope that someone would find it in the street below and pass it to the watchman.

Then she recalled the indolent old fool snoring away in his box and her heart sank. Even if she did manage to get a note out, what chance was there that that dotard would do anything? And it was dark outside – would anyone even see a note fall?

While the Countess was at large, Alpiew decided to stay alert and find out as much as she could about her captors. She knew O'Hara was a highwayman, escaped from the gallows only yesterday morning. And the woman, Timony, was a violent house-breaker who had escaped the gallows by claiming to be pregnant. This however did not explain why the woman wasn't banged up back in Newgate now. So at some point yesterday, on the road back perhaps, some-one must have sprung her free.

Alpiew looked to the window again and what she saw made her jump. She looked around to see whether Godfrey or Lettice had also seen it. A shadow fell across the glass, and moved swiftly away.

Someone was on the roof.

Alpiew flashed her eyes towards Godfrey and indicated the window with her head. Godfrey rolled his eyes as though she was mad, but Lettice gaped at the window with a bewildering air of longing.

The familiar red pantaloons pressed against the glass. Then, as a hairy hand rested upon the frame, Lettice let out a muffled cry.

Alpiew hoped the girl wasn't going to ruin any chance they had of making contact with their nocturnal visitor by attracting O'Hara and Timony back into the room.

But when she looked into Lettice's eyes, she realised that her moan was from delight rather than fear.

Slowly four long fingers curled round the window, silently opening it.

Alpiew looked to the door. She could still hear O'Hara and Timony murmuring on the landing.

There followed a breathless pause as Godfrey, Lettice and

Alpiew watched the red satin pantaloons flash past the open casement.

The little fez lowered from the top of the frame, followed by two long arms.

Godfrey stared, open-mouthed. Lettice's eyes were brimming with tears.

Alpiew simply marvelled. With the grace of a dancer, the satin-clad figure, hanging upside down from above the window, tilted his head and stared into the room.

Then with a single bound his little body flipped. He somersaulted through the window and landed silently in the centre of the room.

He dashed across to Lettice, climbed up on to her shoulder, wrapped his wiry arms gently around her neck, and his long agile fingers stroked the girl's tear-streaked cheek.

Suddenly it all made sense. The elegant dwarf burglar of German Street was Lettice's pet monkey. They had found Captain Caruso.

The Countess strode along Pall Mall Street. As she passed Sir Richard's door, she held her letter up to the light of a flaming link which crackled from a post outside the Unicorn.

She had to go to an address in Southwark.

She looked up at the windows of Sir Richard's house. Everything was dark, but that was no indication with a niggardly fellow like him. Probably he was sitting inside in the dark to save on tallow. Whatever, she must prevent him going to German Street to pick up Lettice.

She pulled a scrap of paper and a pencil from her pocket ready to scratch out a note. As she wrote, Jake, her mysterious protector, emerged from the shadows and snatched the paper from her. The fellow had a dusty hat pulled down over his face. He hung on to the Countess's arm while he read her note and then folded it and shoved it under the door.

A small hackney coach rattled past.

Jake whistled and it stopped. He opened the door for the Countess and they both climbed in.

As they slowly jolted through the City to London Bridge the Countess tried to look at the boy. Beneath his broad-brimmed hat he was a dusty, dirty fellow to be sure. His breeches were patched and worn, his buckled shoes scuffed. She noticed too that the grey tips of his fingers protruded from holes at the points of his tattered leather gloves. And the last joint of the forefinger on his left hand was missing.

'It seems an infernal long way.' The Countess tried not to slide along the seat and into Jake's lap as the coach took a hard right turn. 'I don't know that I've ever been to Southwark. Is it nice?'

Jake stayed silent.

'South of the river!' exclaimed the Countess as they clattered past the shuttered-up stalls and shops on London Bridge. 'It's lucky you found a cab that would come here this late at night. Southwark! It doesn't come under the same regulations as London, am I right? Now that we've gone over the Thames, aren't we in Surrey? And it's a rookery, is it not, Southwark? A lawless place? Packed with petty criminals, all fleeing from London justice?' The coach rolled down off the bridge. The Countess took a deep breath and sputtered, unfurling her fan. 'God alive, what is that stink?'

'Tanneries and brew-houses.' Jake had a surprisingly high and cracked voice. To the Countess it sounded as though it belonged to an adolescent and was on the verge of breaking. She glanced again at his gloved hands, inspecting the size of the black fingernails protruding from his gloves. She suspected that this lofty fellow was a mere boy, probably no older than fourteen.

In the flickering light of passing torches she tried to make out whether he had a weapon. His tattered jacket covered his belt, so it was possible he had a knife, but she doubted there was room for a pistol. He shifted along the seat towards her. Frightened he would catch her scrutinising him, she looked away out of the window.

The narrow greasy streets of Southwark were bustling with life. Painted trollops hung round the necks of well-dressed men who seemed the worse for drink. Taverns throbbed with music and chatter. The coach turned another corner into a darker street and the Countess felt sure she glimpsed a man openly having sexual intercourse with a woman leaning against a shop doorway.

The coach stopped only a few yards away from the vertical fornicating couple. Through the open window she could hear the man grunting.

Jake gave her a shove and she climbed down from the coach. The rancid smell of smoke, tanning and overcooked meat made her gag.

'What street is this?' she asked, unfolding her sheet of instructions and trying to read them.

Jake pointed at a dangling road sign at the corner: Dead Man's Place.

'Ah!' The Countess wished she had not asked. She studied her commands again.

Cardinal Blois Alley. Green doorway between the signs of the Four Coffins & Heart and the Golden Pole. Knock four times and announce yourself.

The Countess looked up and down the dismal square courtyard. Behind her a pack of dogs was busily ferreting through a pile of rubbish. With a yelp the rutting man in the doorway climaxed. Panting, he leaned against the doxy, fumbling to tie up his breeches as the Countess swept past. The over-painted female was already straightening her hair, preparing for her next customer.

The Countess knew she must be near the alley when she saw a swinging sign with a tall red mitre. Jake was making no attempt to direct her. He constantly remained a few yards behind, skulking in doorways. She realised it would be possible to make a dash for it. But what would be the point when O'Hara and his crony could kill Alpiew, Godfrey and Lettice?

The entrance to the alley, coming off Dead Man's Place at a sharp angle, was narrow. Too narrow even for a sedan chair to pass through it.

The Countess took a deep breath and ducked into the pitch blackness. The tall walls were so close she could touch them on both sides as she walked. The dank dismal alley-way had obviously been used as a shit-house for years and the stench was overpowering. She looked up, trying to decipher the hanging signs creaking above her head in the dark. A rat scuttled over her feet.

A scraping noise behind her was followed by a spark. Jake had struck a light on a tinder-box. In the brief flash the Countess saw the green door.

She knocked four times.

The door opened. A firm hand hauled her in and the door slammed behind her. Inside, it seemed even darker than out in the moonless alleyway. Without pause a pair of hands was running up and down her sides, checking her clothing for weapons.

'Unhand me,' the Countess snapped, wishing she could see something.

'Name?' inquired a voice. The hot foetid breath seemed to cling to her clammy skin.

'Ashby de la Zouche,' she said, trying to keep her voice

steady. The black was impenetrable. It seemed that if she reached out she could touch it.

Nearby some papers rustled.

There was another noise too, muffled by a door. A clipping sound. Constant and steady, like a dripping tap. Click, click, click.

A footstep and she felt the warmth of a second person standing less than a foot away.

A small leather pocketbook was thrust into her hand.

Before she could react, hands seized her and she was bundled back out into the street. The door slammed behind her.

Jake flashed his tinder-box. Clutching the pocketbook to her breast the Countess trotted towards him. It was not such a hard thing to do, not compared to being gagged and bound by those villains who held Alpiew and the others.

A group of link-boys stood idly chattering on the corner of Dead Man's Place. The Countess paused in the light of their flaming links to re-read her instructions. It would be interesting to look inside the pocketbook too while she had the chance, but she knew that Jake was watching, and she had best leave well enough alone. Plus, she didn't fancy losing whatever it contained to a passing thief.

'Now we must go back to Pall Mall Street,' she said.

Jake let out a piercing whistle and a hackney coach pulled up.

When they arrived at Sir Richard's house, it was past two.

The Countess was relieved to see a light burning in an upstairs room. Clutching the pocketbook, she rapped upon the door. Jake stood in the shadows a few yards away. He had hired a link-boy to stand with the Countess – she presumed to make the whole thing look plausible. What woman would venture out this late with a scruffy type like

Jake, or, and it come to that, on her own without even a link-boy to light the way?

Tentatively the door opened a crack.

'Who's there?' asked a quivering male voice.

'Anastasia Ashby de la Zouche, Countess of Clapham, Baroness . . .'

'What do you want?' The point of a sword appeared in the gap. 'I don't know you.'

'Sir Richard . . .' The Countess was not in the mood for this tease all over again. 'I was at your wedding this afternoon.'

'There's no one in.'

The link crackled in the silence, throwing shadows into the opening. There was a rustling from within.

'Your bride, Lettice . . .'

'Bride?'

Suddenly Jake stepped forward and shoved the Countess. She returned to the official script.

'I bring you some matters of a business nature, Sir Richard.' The Countess put her foot in the door before it was closed on her. 'Items of the utmost urgency.'

'Mm?' The voice within raised an octave. 'Business. Good and well, adod. What is it?'

The Countess glanced down at the instructions and read her part. The link-boy adjusted the light to help her.

'I bring you a promissory note for the sum of a hundred guineas. It has no endorsements. There is also a portfolio of stocks and bonds . . .'

A gloved hand shot out of the door. The Countess handed over the pocketbook.

'I am selling way below the price. But I need the money now. In cash, please.' Having delivered the message in full, the Countess now strayed from the script again, hoping to hurry things along. 'But your bride, Lettice . . .'

Jake poked her in the back.

'Yes, I know. My bride, yes,' said the old man. 'All good and well. A lovely young tit. Which makes it all the more bizarre that you would interrupt an old fellow on his wedding night.'

Creaking of boards upstairs betrayed another presence in the house.

While she was getting to Southwark and back the Countess wondered had Lettice escaped from the house in German Street and was she now returned to her own home? What of Alpiew and Godfrey? Were they shot through the head and lying in a puddle of blood? The Countess took a breath and crossed herself.

Suddenly it flashed through her mind that perhaps Sir Richard also had an intruder at his side, with a gun pointed at his back.

'Sir Richard,' she said as quietly as she could. 'Are you all right. Do you need help?'

'No, no help,' said the voice. 'Please, madam. It is late. I am wanting to get to my bed. I have a young bride, and I am longing to be at her.'

Someone came down the stairs, and the gloved hand thrust a moneybag through the small gap.

Jake moved a pace nearer as the Countess opened it and peeped inside.

'Three hundred guineas in coin,' said the voice as the door slammed. 'Now leave me in peace.'

Jake paid the link-boy and walked beside the Countess. It was only when they turned into a darker street he grabbed the moneybag from her and ran on alone.

Aghast, she called after the boy. What if he was a double dealer, stealing the money from the thieves? And what if she returned to those monsters empty handed? Surely all three of them would be killed by that hateful Timony woman.

Puffing, the Countess scurried along in the boy's wake. She could see him, running on yards ahead.

'Can't you wait for a fat old lady?' The Countess called. 'Or shall I raise the hue and cry against you?'

Jake hesitated, stumbled on a few more steps, then bent down to fasten his shoe.

When she was a few yards behind him he stood up and ran on. She followed.

As the distance grew between them he turned, then at the corner of St James's Market knelt again and adjusted his other shoe.

The Countess turned into German Street. She saw him go into her front door. A few moments later he came out again, paused briefly as he saw her waddling towards him and ran off in the opposite direction.

The Countess pushed open the front door. The hall was in darkness, but a flickering light came from the front room. She could also hear hushed laughter within. She tiptoed past, but only got a few steps before Kate Timony stepped into the hall.

'She's back!' Kate hauled the Countess into the front room.

John O'Hara lounged upon her best easy chair, his feet up on the table.

'That tight-fisted hunks gave you the money? I knew it would work, sending a proper lady to do the business. He'd never have given it to a jackanapes off the street.' He chuckled and swung round to face her. 'Or a villain like me, I suspect, but a superannuated Countess . . . It was a masterstroke of mine. I must remember to make use of your services again. Normally with miserable types like him you might as well get blood from a stone, even if you do have the appropriate paperwork.'

'How are my friends?'

'Your servants, you mean?' He leapt to his feet, and held his face a few inches from hers. 'As well as can be expected.' He took her hand and bowed to kiss it. She could see splashes of blood on his white suit.

In the open doorway Kate Timony was impatiently tapping her foot.

'This unmannerly woman and I will take our leave of you now, Countess.' He took a dark cloak from the back of a chair and threw it over his shoulder. 'Thank you for your hospitality and your efforts tonight.' At the door he turned. 'Oh, yes. Jake is watching the house. Whatever you find upstairs, you will not call the constable for half an hour. If you do, you can be sure I will be making a return visit some day soon.' He gave her a toothy grin and followed Kate Timony out into the street.

The Countess grabbed the chamber light from the table. She came into the hall, shielding the candle from draughts.

What she saw caused her to stop and struggle for breath.

The white walls were spattered red, the balusters smeared with scarlet.

Trying to keep the candle alight, she climbed the stairs, her heart pounding.

On the first landing sprays of blood dripped down the walls.

She hauled herself up the second flight of stairs. Her hand was sticky now from the blood on the banister. As she pushed open the door to the attic room her fingers left a red smear. She held the candle aloft and tiptoed in.

Slumped in one corner lay Godfrey and Alpiew. Lettice was sprawled under the window. Their clothing was drenched in blood.

Hot wax from the candle spilled down on to the Countess's skin. Her hand shook violently. She placed the candle on the mantelpiece.

She stooped over Alpiew, wishing she had a feather or a piece of mirror to test for breath. She realised her eyes were brimming with tears. She blinked. One tear fell and landed on Alpiew's pale cheek.

Alpiew opened one eye, and she squawked.

'Child! Thank God!' The Countess fumbled with the knot on Alpiew's gag. 'I thought you were . . .'

'You certainly took your time,' said Alpiew once her mouth was free. 'You were gone so long I was sure they'd killed you.' She turned and presented her bound wrists, burned and chafed from her attempts to get them free. 'Godfrey and Lettice fell asleep, so when I heard feet on the stairs I decided to lie still too.'

'Everyone's all right? Then what is all that blood?'

'That awful woman shot Captain Caruso.'

'Captain Caruso? The girl's lover? He came here?'

'I'll explain later.' Alpiew scrambled to her feet. 'Let's fetch the constable.'

'Stable doors and bolted horses,' sighed the Countess. 'There is a boy on the lookout until they are far enough away.'

As they picked at Godfrey's bonds the Countess started telling Alpiew of her night's employment.

Godfrey sat up, blinking his eyes. 'Buggered off, have they?' he grumped. 'If I 'adn't got a gammy leg I'd 'ave shown them. Ruddy animals.'

The church clock struck the hour. Three o'clock.

'They have had quite enough time now to make a run for it.' Alpiew marched over to the window and thrust her head out. 'The watchman is there, probably snoring in his box as usual.' She raised her voice. 'Help ho! Charlie! Raise the hue and cry here!'

'Run along, Godfrey.' The Countess wiped her hand clean from the drool from Godfrey's gag. 'Tell him to bring the constable and his men. Then we must get this poor child back home to her guardian or fiancé or whatever that old fool is to her.' As Godfrey shuffled out she glanced at the sleeping Lettice. 'How incredible that the girl can sleep through it all!'

'She exhausted herself crying after they shot the monkey.'

'Captain Caruso is a monkey?'

'I fear, milady, that the sentence may be "Captain Caruso *was* a monkey". That awful Kate shot him. He bolted past them like a thing demented, spraying blood everywhere. They couldn't catch him. The girl was hysterical.'

Lettice sighed in her sleep.

The Countess raised her finger to her lips. 'Let's talk in the next room.' She took the candle and tiptoed into the hall. 'Poor child. How old do you think she is, Alpiew?'

'She seems to me to be about twelve or thirteen.'

'Me too. And I tell you, either her husband-to-be is a senile dotard, or he has some other woman in there with him.' The Countess opened up the tiny storeroom next door. 'I was sent there as part of the job for O'Hara. He even handed over a bag of money, just like that. He talked about being interrupted with his young wife. And as we know, the girl is here, so who on earth was he bedding tonight?' She stopped short, squinting ahead. 'What the . . . ?'

In the far corner of the previously empty room stood a great red, blue and black money chest.

'Identical to Sir Richard's.' The Countess inspected it. '*Identical.*' She inspected the row of locks along the front. 'Alpiew, I think it *is* his box. Why is it here in my house?'

'Let's open it.'

'Impossible. Sir Richard said it had twenty unpickable locks and secret bolts.'

'That locksmith fellow was on about that too, but I tell

you, madam, there is no such thing as an unpickable lock.'
Alpiew pulled a pin from her hair and rolled up her sleeves.
'Let me at 'em.'

'How did Sir Richard's trunk get here?' The Countess
thought about how she had sat on it that morning. 'Do
you think those two reprobates brought it in?'

'I'd have heard them.' Alpiew clicked one lock open. 'I
don't believe they even came into this room. Mind you,
they could have brought it in earlier, while Godfrey snored.'

'That Sir Richard is a queer fish,' said the Countess,
perching on the side of the chest as Alpiew fiddled about
at the front. 'And why has the child agreed to marry him?
What's in it for her? And the boy Robinson – what is he
to her?'

'Some of these rods pass right through the box.' Alpiew
felt her way along the metal braces. 'Help me pull it out
from the wall.'

'But it's too heavy. Sir Richard told me . . .'

'Come on, milady. We can edge it out.'

They shoved together and moved the chest forward
about an inch.

'Did you hear that jangle?' The Countess looked down
at the gap between the box and the wall. She stretched her
arm along the wainscot.

'The keys! It has to be them!' She dangled them in front
of Alpiew. 'The keys to the chest!'

'If he left the keys,' said Alpiew, snatching them and applying them to the keyholes, 'he must mean us to open it.'

'No. It makes no sense.' The Countess sat again. 'But
then tonight nothing makes sense. Where is Godfrey got
to? He is taking an age fetching the constable.'

'Curse this wretched thing.' Alpiew screwed a large key
into another hole.

'I wonder what all those errands tonight were about.

The bill of exchange, or whatever it was. And that strange dark room in Southwark. What were those people up to in there?'

'Eureka!' Alpiew had flicked a number of locks open. 'We're nearly in.'

'That invoice of Godfrey's!' The Countess clapped her hand to her forehead and leapt off the box. 'This trunk must be what he signed for this afternoon. Delivery paid by sender. Sir Richard said yesterday that this room would be the perfect place to keep a money chest.' She stared down at Alpiew. 'Of all the nerve! Pity he didn't think to ask me before sending it over here.'

The front door slammed.

'Oh good. Here are the constables.' The Countess went out on to the landing. 'Now to rouse that poor innocent girl.'

'You'll have to help me lift the top off.' Alpiew tugged at a corner of the lid. 'God help me, madam, but it's heavy. And what is that smell?'

'I don't know.' The Countess took hold of the other corner. 'I cannot believe the impudence of that mean swine, sending this box here without even asking me! What a tight, miserable old hunks he is.'

Feet were tramping up the first staircase.

'Come on, milady. We'll have to concert our efforts if we're to get it open,' said Alpiew. 'One, two, three . . . heave.'

'I wonder how much money is inside,' wheezed the Countess, as she tugged.

Suddenly the lid flew open and a nauseating sweet heavy stench filled the air.

'Alpiew!' The Countess's chubby hands flew to her mouth as she stared down.

There was no money in the trunk.

Curled up inside was a body. Stuck right through the

chest was a Toledo sword. The old man's tongue lolled out of his mouth and his bulging, bloodshot eyes stared accusingly at them.

Curled up inside his own money box lay Sir Richard Dainty, and he was indubitably dead.

FOUR

Teasing — controlling the fire to get just the right amount of heat

Alpiew slammed the lid of the trunk shut. 'But, madam, you saw him less than an hour ago – how did he get here?'

'I didn't *see* him, Alpiew!' The Countess was taking little gulps of air. 'I *heard* him. I saw only a gloved hand, and a sword. And that in darkness.'

The constable and his men were tramping along the first landing.

'So who was that in his house tonight, doling out money to you?'

'And it come to that, where is all the money that he kept in his trunk? And why is the wretched trunk here at all? Oh, Alpiew, what are we to do?'

'Countess?' Lettice's voice drifted in from the next room.

'Oh good lord! The child!' The Countess gasped as the door handle turned. 'Quickly! Lock it, Alpiew! She must not see.' The Countess poised herself in front of the chest. 'One moment, Lettice, dear.'

'Are you all safe, madam?' The constable called up from the stairs.

'Yes, yes,' the Countess called. 'We're all in one piece.'

Alpiew was jamming the keys into keyholes and turning them.

'It's Captain Caruso, isn't it?' Lettice stood in the doorway staring at the trunk, her lower lip trembling. 'He's lying dead in there.'

'No, no, my dear.' The Countess seized Lettice's hand and dragged her out on to the top landing. 'We are trying to add some method to our search for the poor little scamp. We have searched that box and the whole of this room for the Captain. He is not in here, so now it is important to close the door and keep it closed.'

'My dear pigsny has a trunk just like that.' Lettice gripped the Countess's arm.

The constable, John Shaw, with his painted staff of authority, the night-watchman and Godfrey huddled on the landing. A gaggle of armed men in various states of dress, bearing pikes, swords and pistols, lined the stairs behind them.

'Good evening, Constable.' The Countess led Lettice on to the landing and clicked the door shut once Alpiew had emerged behind her, and pocketed the bunch of keys. 'What a night we have had! Murderers, prison birds and thieves descending upon us.'

'They are all gone now, are they?' Constable Shaw looked fiercely at the Countess, who nodded in reply. 'Stand down, men, and wait for me in the street.'

The men turned and ambled down the stairs.

'There's a lot of blood everywhere.' Constable Shaw removed his hat and sniffed the air. 'What's that smell?'

'Godfrey!' The Countess span round and wagged her finger. 'How many times have I told you, not in front of guests . . .'

'Where's the Captain?' Lettice stared at the constable then surveyed the red smears up the stairwell. 'He's dead, isn't he? They killed him. Those criminals. I can tell from your faces.'

'Has there been a murder committed here?' John Shaw turned to call to his gang. 'Stand alert again, men! To your posts.'

The men turned and headed up the stairs.

'You'd better let me see the body, Countess.'

'That's the problem, Constable,' said Lettice, gulping back tears. 'We don't know where he is.'

'Who is this dead "he"?'

'My pet monkey, Captain Caruso.' Lettice waved her arm and let out a painful sob. 'Look at his blood everywhere.'

'Stand easy, men!' shouted John Shaw and the men turned back downstairs again. 'It's a ruddy monkey.' He rubbed his stubbly chin. 'However, there is some compensation, miss. When the dawn breaks you'll have no trouble finding the little blighter's body. You simply follow the trail of blood.'

Lettice let out a wail.

'There, there!' The Countess put her arm around the child's quivering shoulder. How to tell the constable about the corpse in the trunk without revealing the truth to Lettice? 'Please, Constable. Can't you see how upset the poor girl is?'

'Yes, Countess. I apologise, miss.' John Shaw put his hat back on. 'So, let's be escorting you home.'

'No!' The Countess spoke abruptly and the constable looked to her for an explanation. How could she explain about the strange man posing as Sir Richard in the girl's home, while his body lay here in his own trunk in the Countess's house? 'The poor child has been badly shocked. And Sir Richard is an old man. She wouldn't want to rouse him from his bed at this late hour. She will stay here with us, and I myself will take her home first thing in the morning.'

'But what of Captain Caruso . . . ?' Lettice wept into her hands. 'What of my own dear boy?'

'We will look for the poor monkey first thing in the morning, and then take you home. Now, sir . . .' The Countess took the constable by the arm. 'We have all had a long stressful night.' She hoped she could take him off out of earshot and tell him about Sir Richard's corpse.

'I presume you have not had that casement repaired.' John Shaw swung past her into the front room. 'I did warn you . . .'

'Someone from the locksmith's was due to come in today.' The Countess followed him. 'It seems that, by mistake, Godfrey let in the wrong men.'

'Couldn't get wronger than O'Hara.' John Shaw was inspecting the catch on the window. 'He's a villain, all right. Lots of friends on the wrong side of the law.'

'Constable?' The Countess tiptoed across to him and whispered. 'I need to speak to you – but not in front of Miss Dainty. She was due to be married today, but . . .'

'Yes, yes, of course.' He leaned out of the window and shouted down to the men in the street. 'Men of the watch! Disperse and keep a look out for said felons. They've had a ten-minute start.' He pulled the window shut. 'Dead, isn't he?'

'Yes, the wizened old fellow has copped it,' said the Countess, proud of her ability to sound colloquial. 'He's in the money chest. But, for the present, we must keep it from the child.'

'Understood.'

'He's in the chest.'

'Excuse me, Constable.' Lettice stood in the doorway. 'But can you ask your men to look out for Captain Caruso?'

Shaw gave the Countess a surreptitious wink and threw open the window. 'Report all sightings of a monkey.'

He marched past Lettice, then hesitated outside the back room. 'Is it in here?' he asked the Countess, sotto voce.

'Yes.' The Countess nodded. 'Our *money chest* is in there.'

Constable Shaw started down the stairs. 'And now I suggest that you shut all your doors and windows, have a warm drink and retire to your beds. I will make my way out into the street and see if I can apprehend the human vermin who held you tonight.'

'It simply doesn't make sense, Alpiew. If O'Hara and Timony killed Sir Richard, why all the subterfuge sending me to his house at past midnight? And why hold you three hostage while I did it? And who was that in Sir Richard's house anyhow, for we can be certain it was not him?'

The Countess and Alpiew sat huddled in the front room as Godfrey and Lettice slept in the kitchen. A single candle burned in a holder on the table. The first light of dawn was spilling through the window.

'What was it, do you think? Money? Jealousy?' The Countess shuddered. 'It makes me feel quite ill just thinking that we have the body of a man we hardly know lying in a box in our attic store.'

'Madam, you are right. It could not have been the criminals.' Alpiew struck her forehead with the palm of her hand. 'We know they didn't kill him. O'Hara told us so in plain words.'

'How so?'

'Last night when he was threatening you and saying he would kill us if you disobeyed his orders, he said it was as good to swing for highway robbery as for three murders. And he had just escaped the gallows on a charge of highway robbery. If he knew he had since then killed Sir Richard, why did he not say "four"?'

'But they were here waiting for us tonight. Who knows

but they may have been waiting since this afternoon when Godfrey signed for the delivery of the trunk containing Sir Richard's corpse. Perhaps they were the ones who brought it in.'

'They were whispering on the landing till a few minutes before you came up. They went down to answer a rap at the front door.'

'So, we know that Sir Richard's corpse has been lying upstairs since the afternoon. Who could have killed him?'

Alpiew pulled a pencil and scrap of paper from her pocket and started to scribble. 'Who would have wanted to?'

'Robinson Stark; any number of financial people if they are so jealous of their money . . . I don't know. Anyhow, it's all very well, Alpiew, but where and when did Sir Richard *become* a corpse? We saw him at his wedding party at eleven. Godfrey signed for the trunk at what he loosely described as lunchtime.'

'Simple. He must have been killed and brought here while we sat there in his house, waiting with Lettice and Mrs Stark.'

'Yes.' The Countess played a pudgy finger across her pursed lips. 'But you see, Alpiew, that too is impossible.'

'I can't see why.'

'Because we sat in Sir Richard's front room. Would we not have noticed a gang of burly men carrying that trunk down the stairs and out through the hall? You know how heavy it is. Even if they had removed the trunk from Sir Richard's house without its gruesome contents, it would have been too heavy for one person to carry, and surely we would have seen or heard something.'

'Ah!' said Alpiew. 'Perhaps the trunk came from some-where else.'

'Not possible.' The Countess was bemused at the strange conundrum of the money box. 'I saw that trunk only a

116

few minutes before the ceremony started. It was in Sir Richard's bedchamber, directly above the room in which we later sat waiting for him to come home. He sat on it and swung his legs.' She thought back to the conversation she had had with the old man. 'It was full of money, he said. So that's another thing. Where is that money gone?'

'Perhaps it was the chairmen, when that bizarre Van Loon fellow with the sticks up his nose brought his chair into the hallway.' Alpiew thought back, remembering the banging noises coming from the hall. 'Perhaps we should go to the house and look.' Alpiew was happily jotting down notes.

'Why? What is it to do with us?' The Countess realised the whole horrid business could be over with by lunchtime. 'We will inform the constable that the man is dead, then let the child know and plant her on some relative.' She stood and stretched. 'And, most importantly, we need to get that stinking cadaver out of the house.'

'You talking about me?' Godfrey hovered in the doorway. ''Cos if you are, I tell you I ain't goin' nowhere.'

'Of course we were not talking about you, you old mawwallop.' The Countess pondered whether or not to tell him about the body upstairs. 'That note you signed yesterday, Godfrey, what did the man who presented it to you say exactly?'

''E said, "Sign 'ere."'

'Nothing else?'

'Why must you go on so?' Godfrey coughed, showering them with specks of spit, then wiped his mouth with the back of his hand. 'Don't worry yourselves, I'll go round later and get the bugger back 'ere to do the work.'

'It is important you remember exactly what happened, Godfrey. You see, what you actually signed for yesterday was a trunk containing Sir Richard Dainty . . .'

Before she could continue she saw Lettice lurking in the hall behind Godfrey.

She made up her mind to tell her right away.

'My pigsny?' said the child, stepping happily into the room. 'Has he sent a message for me? We will be married today, I suppose. I do hope so.' Lettice looked impatiently towards the front door. 'Can we go now, Godfrey, as you promised? I'd like to find Captain Caruso. If he's not dead, he may be lying injured somewhere. Then I must get home to my wedding.'

Looking at the girl's keen excitement, the Countess found she could not bear to break the news; even worse, to show her the body in the trunk. She peered out of the window. The streets were not yet really light enough to look for a monkey in safety.

The girl stamped her feet and looked as though she would burst into tears.

Maybe it was better to let her go, bring the constables to remove the body and tell her about everything later.

'Go on then, Godfrey. Help the child to find her monkey and then take her home.'

Home! What a situation! What if the strange men from last night were still there? The poor girl was in for enough of a shock today.

The Countess waited till the front door had banged behind Godfrey and Lettice before leaping to her feet. 'Come along, Alpiew. We have no time to lose. We must prepare the way, and have a look round the Dainty home before they get there.'

The Countess banged the knocker of Sir Richard's house. Market traders were trundling into the Hay Market, setting up their pitches. Pall Mall Street was still dark, but as the markets were about to open it was alive and bustling.

'No reply, Alpiew.' She banged again. 'Which is a relief, as I don't altogether relish meeting the impersonating folk who were here last night.'

'Come on.' Alpiew stepped forward and tried the handle. The door opened. 'Let's go inside.'

They glanced about them to see whether they were watched and stepped into the hall.

Alpiew held her finger to her lips. She whispered into the Countess's ear. 'Stay here by the front door, and if I shout, call some burly men from the market.' She made her way upstairs. After a few minutes she called down, 'No one here, milady. Come on up.'

Before going upstairs, the Countess looked into the front room. Lying on the table, where they had left it, was Lettice's note from yesterday saying that she was waiting with the Countess. She tucked it into her pocket and went up to Sir Richard's bedchamber.

Alpiew had struck a light. 'Look, madam! This room has been ransacked.'

The little back office was lined with bookshelves and drawers. Books were in stacks on the floor, the drawers pulled open, and papers scattered everywhere.

'Those fellows I disturbed last night had hours and hours to look for whatever they were after.' The Countess surveyed the mess. 'I wonder if they found it?'

'But, madam, if they hadn't found it, surely they'd still be here.' Alpiew bent down and started picking things up.

'Unless they had exhausted their search and moved on to look elsewhere.' The Countess touched Alpiew's shoulder. 'Leave it all as it is. It will be something to divert the girl and Godfrey while we go about our business of ridding our home of a decomposing body.'

Alpiew winced and said, 'I assume it was money, or something relating to money that they were after.' She felt sick at the thought. 'Poor people spend their lives dreaming of being rich, but what do riches bring but jealousy and greed and all kinds of nasty things?'

'Let's not get obvious, Alpiew.' The Countess sifted through a stack of papers on the desk. 'What infuriates me at the moment is that we have been used. Used by somebody to dispose of a body. Whoever killed the old man and brought that trunk into our house yesterday afternoon chose us. Perhaps wanted us to take the blame for their crime.'

'It could be anyone.' Alpiew had climbed on a chair and was inspecting the higher shelves. 'He had lots of money and people will certainly kill for that.'

'But won't a person also kill from jealousy, or love? Did you not see the way that boy Robinson carried on at the wedding that never was? He was desperate that Lettice would not marry Sir Richard. He was disturbed in his mind the whole time.'

'And Robinson left the wedding with Sir Richard in the exodus to the Exchange.' Alpiew tried to recall how Robinson reacted to the boy who brought the news of the sunken ship. 'If he did kill the old man, it would make perfect sense. Lettice is free now. Free to wed whichever cove she pleases. And the old fellow no longer owns her as his wife, nor rules her as her guardian. With Sir Richard disposed of, Robinson is in a position to get what he wanted: Lettice.'

There was a knock at the front door. Alpiew, who had wandered out on to the landing, darted back into the office and gently pushed the door to. Holding their breath, the two women cringed behind it.

'Surely Godfrey cannot have found the wretched monkey,' whispered the Countess, 'and brought the child back here so soon?'

The front door slammed.

'Good lack, madam, we're trapped!' Alpiew opened the

120

door an inch and applied her eye to the crack. 'Someone's coming up the stairs.' She blew out the candle and pulled back as footsteps marched past the office door.

'Who is it?' the Countess hissed.

'Oh, criminy!' Alpiew ducked back. 'I don't believe it.' She mouthed the name *Robinson*.

They waited in silence. Robinson came out of Sir Richard's chamber and went into Lettice's. They heard a closet door open and close. Then footsteps. Robinson stood on the landing only a few feet away from them.

Alpiew squeezed next to the Countess.

They heard the boy give a long sigh.

Then the office handle rattled and Robinson came slowly into the room.

'My God!' he said, jumping back as he came eye to eye with the Countess and Alpiew. 'What on earth . . . ?'

'What on earth indeed?' The Countess stepped forward, realising attack was the best method of defence. 'Might I ask what you are doing, tiptoeing round Sir Richard's home at this ungodly hour?'

'I'm looking for my . . .' Robinson scratched his forelock. 'One moment! And it come to that, what are *you* doing here?'

'We are waiting upon Miss Dainty.'

'Lettice? Is she all right?' Robinson lowered his voice. 'Where is *he*?' He sneered the pronoun.

'Not here. Now, if you would excuse me . . .' The Countess pushed past the boy. 'I must go into Sir Richard's chamber.'

'Z'wounds, madam.' Robinson grabbed at the Countess's sleeve. 'Do not tell me the old devil has whisked her away?'

The Countess removed the boy's hand from her arm and left the office.

'Who knows?' The Countess realised with the body still

in their attic it would be a good idea to keep things vague. She marched along to Sir Richard's chamber. One glance through the open door gave her the information she wanted. The holes in the floor betrayed the position where only yesterday the money chest had stood. The screws which had secured it lay scattered on the frayed and worn Turkey mat.

'Where are they gone?' said Robinson, stooping in the doorway of Lettice's chamber to pick something up. 'What game is he playing with us now?'

'Game?' The Countess looked hard at Robinson. He had the pocketbook she had carried here last night from the mysterious place in Southwark in his hands. 'Is that your pocketbook?'

He shuffled, looking at the floor. 'Where is Sir Richard? He is not here now, and I know he was not here last night.'

'Really. How is that? Were you here?'

'I watched the house for a while. I wanted to make sure he didn't bundle her into a chariot and speed her off God knows where.'

'And why would he want to do that?'

'Surely you heard of the catastrophe in the City yesterday? Scores of people were ruined.'

'Sir Richard among them?'

'Oh no. He was a winner. As usual. It is his habit to profit from others' loss.'

'So if you know so much, Mister See-all, answer me this . . .' Alpiew had come out into the hall and stood behind the Countess. 'Where is the old man now?'

''Tis that I need you to tell me. My guess is that he spirited himself away. No one has seen him since he left Garraway's yesterday at a quarter to noon.' He eyed the Countess. 'But, Countess, surely *you* must know his whereabouts.'

'I cannot imagine why you think I should know anything. I am a female, and consequently, even if I wanted to spend time in Garraway's, I could not enter that smoky hell-hole.' She glanced down at the pocketbook. She could swear he had just picked it up from the floor. 'I do wonder though, why do you not answer me about that thing you carry?'

'There is no sinister secret.' Robinson tucked it under his arm. 'It is mine. A bearer bond. But you evade my question, Countess. He sent you here to his house last night, did he not? The old man? You came here on his behalf?'

'What gives you that mad idea?'

'I know that at about two o'clock this morning you came to the front door and went away with a bag full of money.'

The Countess swallowed and scrutinised young Robinson's face before replying: 'You were here, in the house?'

'No.'

Alpiew leapt in. 'You just said you were.'

'No. I said I was here earlier.'

'And yet you know I came here at two in the morning.'

'The house was being watched all night.' Robinson smiled and fiddled with his fingernails. 'An interested friend took over when I left. And this friend knows you by sight. And he said you came by, and picked up some money. You were accompanied, he said, by a rough boy.'

'Why are your friends staying up all night, watching people's houses?' The Countess didn't want to be any more implicated than she need be with whatever criminal activities those two gaol-birds had involved her in, and yet needed to know why Robinson had been here.

'I told you, Countess: because I must protect Lettice.'

'Pish, boy! You mean because you desire Lettice and are jealous of Sir Richard!'

'Jealous?' Robinson laughed. 'Something more than that,

I fear.' Robinson faced the Countess. His look was steely. 'You have discovered me. It is true, madam, I will not be happy until I see the old dotard ruined. Or worse.'

'You want to see him dead?'

'In an ideal world.'

'And what would you say if I told you that your wish has come true, and that indeed Sir Richard was already dead?'

'He's not dead?' Robinson blanched. 'Is he?'

'You tell me.'

'Don't joke about such a thing, madam.' Robinson looked down into the Countess's eyes. 'You know something. Do you? Where is the old swindler? And where is his money gone?' The boy looked to the empty space where the money box had previously stood. 'If he is dead, the old man cannot have taken his money box with him. Has he run off somewhere and taken all his money?'

'What is his money to you, sir?'

The front door opened and Lettice called upstairs: 'Pigsny, dear, is that you?'

Lettice ran up to the landing. When she saw Robinson she stopped and glared. 'Oh, you!' She cringed behind the Countess. 'Make him go away and leave me, Countess, please.'

'You heard her.' Hands on her hips, Alpiew faced Robinson. 'Off you go.'

Godfrey was waiting by the front door. The Countess nodded to him and he held it open. Dawn had broken and sunlight flooded the hall.

Robinson clattered down the stairs, pausing briefly for a tender look at Lettice. In reply she only glared.

'Mark my words,' Robinson waved the pocketbook towards the Countess. 'I will find that old cheating skinflint, Sir Richard Dainty, if it is the last thing I do.'

He stepped out into the street.

'Do you have a relative you can call upon, Lettice, dear, to keep you company?' The Countess bustled down in Robinson's wake. 'Alpiew and I have urgent business to see to.'

'Is Sir Richard not back yet?' Lettice seemed utterly dismayed. 'Where can he be? We will be married today, I feel sure. We were unlucky yesterday. As soon as he comes home . . .'

'I think milady is suggesting you should send for a friend or relation.' Alpiew moved towards the stairs. 'Who would you call for if Sir Richard does not come home?'

'But he must come home.' Lettice laughed. 'He is to marry me.'

'Perhaps you could go to your friends Mr and Mrs Stark?' The Countess looked up at the girl, who stood on the top step gripping the banister. She realised she had to start preparing the child for the truth. 'I am sorry, but as he has not returned overnight I fear that Sir Richard may have had an accident . . .'

'My pigsny hurt?' The child lurched down a few steps. 'What do you mean?'

The Countess didn't know how to break the news gently. 'Or worse . . .'

The girl was still smiling, bemused. 'What could be worse?'

The Countess stepped forward and spoke gently. 'It is possible that he is dead.'

'Dead?' Pale as the paint on the wainscot, Lettice staggered down the stairs. When she reached the hall she glared at the Countess, her knuckles white, her mouth set. 'How dare you come into my house and tell me such stuff. Sir Richard *will* marry me, and he will marry me today. If you, madam, want to believe something else, you can get out of his house now. You are worse than Robinson with your prognostications of doom.'

'I must tell you that I am sure he is dead.'

Silently Lettice opened her mouth. Then she started to scream. 'Shut your clack, old frowse-top!' She stepped towards the Countess, gritting her teeth. 'Nothing has happened to him.' She grew suddenly calm, and stepped back, grasping the newel post. 'I know you are lying, for why would anyone tell you Sir Richard was dead before they told me? It would make no sense. I am his ward, and his bride-to-be.'

'It'll be all right, little gal.' Godfrey stepped forward, kneading his hat between his hands. 'Don't worry, milady, I'll sit with her till the old fellah gets back. Then we can 'ave another go at catching that mad monkey of yours, eh, little one?' He tickled Lettice under the chin.

Lettice smiled at Godfrey. 'You can stay with me – but as for you two old crows, you go.' Lettice lunged forward, spitting the words out. 'Go on. Be gone from my house. Get out!'

'I should point out that Godfrey only stays if I say so, miss.' The Countess kept an eye on Lettice. What had stirred this volatile streak in the child? Was it a false bravado? The Countess realised that, if it were not, and was merely an immature reaction, she needed to protect the child. After all, she was very young to be left alone, her guardian/husband-to-be was murdered, and last night this house was full of thieves. 'I must warn you, Lettice, I am asking Godfrey to remain with you because you must take care. Someone, not you or Sir Richard, has been here in the night. Sir Richard's office has been turned upside down. The money chest is gone. Things are not right. You must keep a man here to look after you.'

'Burglars, here?' Lettice glanced up the stairs and her

hands flew to her mouth. 'If they have taken Sir Richard's money, what will he say when he returns?' She shuddered and took Godfrey by the hand. 'You will stay with me, won't you, till Sir Richard comes home?'

When Godfrey nodded Lettice turned and faced Alpiew. 'He's going to catch Captain Caruso for me.'

Godfrey blushed.

'All right.' The Countess gave him a stern look. It was as well to leave someone here to keep an eye on this strange child. 'Look after Lettice and keep an eye out for anything suspicious, Godfrey. Have you any news of the monkey this morning? Is he alive?'

'Someone in the 'ay Market 'ad seen 'im pinching bananas, milady, as they unpacked a cart a few hours ago. The end was off 'is tail, but apart from that he seemed quite nimble, they said.'

'Bananas? Hmmm! He has expensive tastes.' The Countess shrugged and moved out to the street. 'We'll leave you, Godfrey, to the monkey business. Alpiew and I have some removals to do.'

The sun shone brilliantly down on to St James's. Alpiew ran on ahead to rouse the constable. She banged on his front door. He opened up, sweaty, breathless, and clearly in the middle of some kind of early-morning martial gymnastiques. Once she had packed him off to German Street she stepped briskly out into St James's Square. As they had decided to leave the whole mystery alone, while the Countess was busy showing off the corpse to the authorities, Alpiew decided to use the time to make some inquiries of her own, and find somewhere to invest her own share of the money. She hoped to get a job at Garraway's and see what she could pick up from the City merchants, brokers, jobbers and all the motley financial crew who gathered there.

'Well met, Mistress Alpiew. Thank goodness for that!' Blocking Alpiew's path, her face ruddy with sweat, stood Mrs Cue. 'I came over to your house specially to pick up that wedding story the Countess promised me. But you were both out. The engraver has done such a nice picture. See!' Mrs Cue held up a primitive line drawing of a wrinkled old man holding hands with a pretty young girl. 'Shall I come with you now to fetch it? We want to put the report in today.'

'Ah!' Alpiew hesitated. Should she tell Mrs Cue that the wedding had not taken place at all? The complete story, including Sir Richard's death, would make a wonderful column, but until his body was out of the house and Lettice was told, she didn't feel it would be appropriate to place the story with Mrs Cue. 'We have another piece. It is every bit as good, and concerns a burglar who is really a monkey in red pantaloons and a fez.'

'That wouldn't be at all suitable.' Mrs Cue huffed. 'Look at the picture . . .'

Mrs Cue held up the smudgy engraving again.

'Well you could shove a fez and a pair of pantaloons on the old cove and no one would know the difference. He could be a monkey . . .'

'I'll have you know this engraver is costing us a fortune.' Mrs Cue glared. 'And see, the work is lovely. We are streets ahead of all the other papers, having a little picture.'

'Well, I think the burgling monkey is a good story.'

'Hmm!' Mrs Cue was not convinced. 'If you go on at this rate you'll be giving in stories next about comedians eating hamsters, or men arriving in flying machines from Mars. Anyhow, it is a done deed. At this very moment, Mr Cue is setting up the new machinery and leaving a space for your report on the wedding. They have already printed the caption. He's been up all night working on it. He didn't come home till so late last night. It's a tricky business once pictures are involved, you know. So you'd better not let us down.'

'I am so sorry to have wasted your efforts in coming here. The Countess has the finished piece!' Alpiew announced, bare-faced. 'She is at this moment carrying it over to your office.'

'How strange,' said Mrs Cue. 'I felt sure I saw her just now heading the other way.'

'Oh, yes.' Alpiew beamed, wondering how quickly she could write up a fictitious wedding and get it across London by special messenger. 'She has a few other errands to do en route. But really, Mrs Cue, you shouldn't have put yourself to such a labour.'

'It's true I need the story, but I was also coming to you to propose a wonderful new idea that the engraver suggested to my husband. We all feel sure it will be very popular and will bring a few extra pence for you, too, if the job takes your fancy . . .'

'Another job!' Alpiew couldn't believe it. When she had no money it was impossible to come by any, and now she was flush, opportunities for making more money were being thrown at her. 'And the idea is . . . ?'

'Queries.'

'Queries?'

'People write in with questions and you and the Countess answer them.'

'What kind of questions?'

'Oh I don't know . . . Where does fire go, once it is extinguished? What is the cause of titillation?'

'Titillation?'

'Tickling. Why do we laugh?'

'I don't know,' said Alpiew. 'You tell me, why *do* we laugh?'

'You don't actually need to know anything.' Mrs Cue looked vexed. 'Readers will write in with the answers.'

'I thought you said that readers wrote in with the questions.'

'Well, yes.' Mrs Cue looked as puzzled as Alpiew felt. 'But you sift through them and choose the best, and put in your own answers when it takes your fancy. And it's another fifteen shillings a week.'

'And may we put in our own questions too?'

'You can write whatever you like, Mrs Alpiew,' Mrs Cue sighed. 'But just do it. We are running to two pages, and need to fill the space. Competition, you know, from other papers.' Mrs Cue shrugged. 'Times are changing. New papers are springing up like mushrooms overnight. The market isn't growing that much, though more and more people can read. But we need something to catch our reader, to make them need to come back for more. So we hook them in with these questions. So get writing. And get it to the office within the next three days, or you and the Countess are both out of a job.'

'You are telling me that the body lying in a trunk in your house is not the errant monkey burglar?' Constable Shaw huffed as he marched up the stairs. 'Why did you not tell me last night that it was a dead *man*? When you talked of a body, I thought you meant the pantalooned monkey.'

'I believed you understood me, sirrah. And I didn't want to upset the child any more than was necessary. We had had a very nasty experience with those ruffians.'

'She'll have to be told.'

'Yes. You can tell her right after you have taken the body away. Did you have any luck finding the two escapees from the gallows?'

'Not likely.' Shaw was outside the attic room. 'I should

130

think they're on the great road north by now, or on a pacquet boat to France. I'd doubt they'll be hanging around St James's waiting to be apprehended.'

'And you are going to leave it at that?'

'What else can I do?' The constable shrugged. 'We don't have the resources.'

'There you are.' She handed the constable the keys and glared at the chest. 'The old man is inside.'

Shaw fumbled with the locks then applied his strong arms to the lid and pulled the trunk open.

'Are you making a jest of me, madam?' Constable Shaw stood back so that the Countess could see inside.

The Countess gaped down.

'You tell me there is a body in the trunk –' The constable waved his arm over the trunk. 'So, madam, where is it?'

The chest was empty.

'He *was* in here,' said the Countess, looking around the edges of the trunk for some evidence of Sir Richard's body. 'Sir Richard Dainty. He was curled up in this trunk. With a sword through him. Dead. See the stain on the baize. What is that but blood!'

'Blood, indeed! Looks more like ink to me.' The constable laughed. 'I think the events of the evening must have taken their toll upon your senses, madam.' He was using the kind of calm voice people use to idiots and the elderly. 'Now come along with me. You've had a bad shock, and some very nasty types burst into this sacrosanct area that is your home . . .'

'I saw the body.' The Countess realised from his face as he led her towards the stairs that there was no chance of convincing him. 'So did Alpiew!'

'You've had no sleep, dear. These phantasms are not unknown after a sleepless night. If I were you, old sweetheart, I'd have a nice warm caudle cup and curl up on my bed and have a little rest.' He was already on his way down the stairs. 'Oh, and I won't be telling the little girl her old guardian is dead. Not until I have some proof. For all I know, you are a pair of mad old women. If his body turns up, I'll tell her then. Just suppose he walks in tonight, right as rain, and frightens the poor girl into an apoplexy.'

The Countess was appalled by the way the man was suddenly talking to her as though she was a witless dotard. She let him out then rushed up the stairs to investigate the empty trunk. The room seemed the same – the usual lumps of plaster on the floor, the dusty floorboards. Whoever had been here to remove the corpse had left no trace.

She looked behind the trunk and then into it. The only sign anything had been in it was the slight brown stain on the baize lining. She presumed it was blood from the stab wound. But the constable was right to laugh. It could as well be ink or gravy or oil. It had the same glistening sheen as Indian ink. And it was certainly not a sensational enough stain to indicate a murder. The injured monkey's tail seemed to have made much more mess.

The Countess shuddered at the memory of the old man's body curled up inside.

Despite the trunk being a masterpiece of carpentry and ironmongery, the Countess did not fancy keeping it for her own use, not with that blood-stain. But perhaps if she removed the lining . . . She applied her nails to the corners of the baize, hoping the blood-stained lining might come loose. She pulled at a corner and it came up in one go. It was not even glued down.

She held the green cloth up with her fingertips, took it out on to the landing and threw it over the banister, watching it flutter down to the front hall. Then she returned to the trunk.

Inset within the base where the baize had rested was a

thin wooden square. She poked at the edges. A secret compartment perhaps? She tried to pull it out but her nails weren't long enough to get a grip. After running down to the kitchen for a knife she managed to get the slot open, exposing a hollow cavity in which lay two pieces of paper. The Countess fumbled inside and pulled them out.

The first document was a written consent signed by Sir Richard Dainty as legal guardian of Miss Lettice Bride, aged thirteen, to marry Sir Richard Dainty, merchant. How bizarre! But of course as Lettice was under twenty-one and Sir Richard was her legal guardian, he would have had to give written permission before she could marry, even if he himself was to be her husband. How odd too that Lettice's surname was Bride. Perhaps it was a mistake. She remembered that Sir Richard had introduced the girl as Lettice Dainty. Maybe the registrar had had a slip of the pen, and written Bride because she was to be a bride.

The other paper, dirty and well fingered, was a letter, neatly scratched out in an educated hand.

March 15th

My Darling Beloved Lettice

Please, please, please listen to my Entreaties.

You must NOT marry old Man Dainty

today. I LOVE you. He only wants to marry

You to claim the Fortune You have stashed

away in that secret Place of yours. You have in

Me one who loves Only You, and who will love

*You to the End. Do NOT let the old man
wed or bed you. I will come one Day and steal
You away from your Gaol and we can marry, and
You will be free. You know I have loved You.
Always, always, always.*

 Till We are together, my Darling,
 As you surely know,
 *I remain, FOREVER, your devoted and
passionate Slave,*
 Robinson

Well! The Countess folded the letter carefully and slipped it down her cleavage, the safest place she could imagine for the moment. She groped about with the rest of the lining of the box but found no other secret partitions.

She looked again at the two documents. Sir Richard's possession of a love-letter from Robinson to Lettice was fascinating. Had he intercepted it? Had Lettice seen it at all? Or perhaps he had caught her reading it just before the wedding.

And from the timbre of the note it seemed clear that Lettice must at least give Robinson the impression that she reciprocated his love. So, pretty little naive Miss Lettice was not quite the innocent flower she presented herself. And surely her antipathy to Robinson was feigned. Also what of this mysterious fortune of hers – where was that, and where the secret place of theirs?

134

The Countess knew that she should wait for Alpiew to return, but couldn't help herself. She must find out more. Her first instinct was to rush round and talk to Lettice, but on further thought she decided that Cynthia was the person she needed to see. She could easily pump a little background detail out of her, particularly on the subject of her enigmatic young nephew, Robinson.

FIVE

Gather — collection of glass on the end of the iron

It didn't take Alpiew long to concoct a fake description of a wedding between an elderly man and his young ward. She decided to use as many true details as possible but placed the ceremony in a house in 'a street off Cheapside', made Sir Richard a retired admiral, and gave him a new name which implied he was fat. Once she had scrawled the piece she ran to the printer's shop and banged on the back door.

Surprisingly, the door to the printer's workshop was bolted. It was a rare thing to find both Mr and Mrs Cue off the premises, but with the new developments at the paper they must have had business to attend.

On her way back home she cut down into Exchange Alley. She had some inquiries to make.

It was turning into another hot morning, and a group of men were sitting on the bench in the courtyard, smoking their pipes and talking money.

Alpiew perched against a tethering post and listened for a moment.

'Cocoa at twelve! Why, yesterday it was ten. I must unload before the bubble bursts.'

'Sugar, cocoa, rum. All up.'

'I'm selling,' said a youth, causing the chattering to stop. 'Sugar, rum and cocoa. Would you buy? And RAC shares.'

'A strange time to offload.' An elderly man eyed him suspiciously. 'When the market is driving up.'

'I have the bailiffs after me. I need to liquidate.'

The young man was immediately surrounded by men, pulling pocketbooks from their coats, and thrusting bills at him.

'He's a cheat upon the cadge!' A lone voice mumbled into Alpiew's ear. She turned and recognised the man from the stocks, now seated on the bench near the horse trough. 'In the realm of folly the sharper is a monarch.'

'Mr Foe! You are still here.'

'You are back too, wench.' He gave her a weary smile. 'What reason have you to hang about with these blow-flies, as ever hovering over the turds of their precious stocks, shares and projects?'

'I have come into a little money of my own, and want to invest it.'

'Invest!' Mr Foe laughed. 'Put it in your pocket and walk through the Tyburn Fair with it, taking care always to keep near the pick-pockets. 'Twould be a safer bet, if you want to keep hold of it.'

'I suspect, Mr Foe,' Alpiew took a seat beside him, 'that you have had financial dealings and you have been burned.'

'You suspect correctly, madam. I was once a successful journeyman. A wholesale hosier. I dealt in knitted woollen stockings, and fine ladies' hose. Sometimes I bought and sold linen and millinery too. But I was tempted into the world of investment.' He let out a long weary sigh. 'Wealth is a very good servant; but a very bad mistress.'

'And which exact department of the money business were you bitten by?'

'Projects. Needless to say, I lost all.'

'I have been encouraged to try projects . . .'

'If you court ruin, that is the sure way to go. I know all about projects! My first attempt was civet cats. I was told I could make money from their arses.' Foe guffawed. 'Seventy cats for £850. Quite a bargain, apparently. The idea was that I tend to the cats, feed them, keep them happy until their anal glands provided my El Dorado. So I did my duty and waited for them to secrete my own private gold – musk.' Foe ground his heel into the dust. 'Sadly, the creditors moved in and seized the yowling creatures before a drop of the sacred tincture was squeezed from their sphincters.'

Alpiew had to bite her cheek to prevent herself giggling.

'Next I invested in a diving bell. This ingenious contraption was designed to be submerged into the sea, where it would salvage all the lost valuables from a ship which sank off the coast of Cornwall. I laid out £200. I was to get back thousands. I stood on the quay and had the pleasure of watching my machine sink beneath the briny. Alas, it never came back up. That is the world of projects for you.'

'Talking of sunken ships,' said Alpiew. 'Were you here yesterday when the news came in about the sunken ship from the West Indies?'

'I was here all day from breakfast to suppertime. It was rather odd, in fact. A gaggle of investors all arrived at the same time with the news. No one knew about it here, or in the City. They'd been at a wedding, I gathered.' Foe rolled his eyes. 'And don't talk to me about weddings, either.'

'I always thought it might be rather nice to marry.' Alpiew was highly amused by the man, who seemed not to have a good word for anything. 'For a man, anyhow. A wife is much more useful than a husband.'

'Marriage would be fine if you married only the bride,' said Foe with a sigh. 'But it's the whole family you get bound to. My wife and I are reduced to living with my mother-in-law in her home in some god-forsaken village miles away from civilisation.' He raised a fist towards Jonathan's. 'And it is this place and its dreadful world of stock and projects did it to me. I had prospects, and a wife with a good jointure. In my dabbling I lost all my own money and hers too, and then went bankrupt to the tune of £17,000.'

'You lost £17,000!' Alpiew whistled. 'That's a lot of money.'

'Losing the money was not as bad as the *time* I lost, languishing in prison.'

'You were in prison as well?'

'Oh yes. The Fleet first, then the King's Bench.'

'I've been in The Fleet.' Alpiew looked the man up and down, wondering if he was making all this up. 'Filthy place.'

'Mind you, sometimes I think The Fleet was preferable to where I live now. They call it a village, but it is just one muddy street with about thirty houses. All you can hear are cows and crows. So far out, too. Too quiet, too still, too genteel, and reeks of manure. Oh, Stoke Newington is a grim backwater. I detest it. That's why I spend my days here, irritating the people who reduced me to this iniquitous state.' Foe looked at Alpiew intently. 'Do you know what I think you should do with your money? Spend it. Enjoy it while you can: travel, do things you always wanted to do. Or, if you feel you need to hold on to it against a rainy day, buy something you like with it. Something useful like a coach, or a cow. Although, of course, coaches break or get stolen, and cows die.'

'Why were you pilloried the day before yesterday?'

'Some jokers put me in there for my protest here.'

139

'Jokers? You mean it wasn't an official use of the instrument?'

'It most certainly was not.' Foe laughed. 'But any fool who can pick a lock can use them. They thought it funny, I suppose. And came to let me out when they felt I had cooled down.'

Footsteps clattered down the steps behind them and a dirty young urchin arrived waving a piece of paper. 'Urgent message for Hendrick Van Loon.'

'Aptly named,' said Foe, pointing at a sedan chair that had been resting alongside a pile of dead links in the corner of the courtyard. 'The man is quite mad. A butter-box, but even madder than your average Dutchman. He has a mortal fear of wind and catching diseases.'

'Is that his chair?' asked Alpiew.

'Not only the chair, the man himself. He is in there. He rarely ventures out of it. He even makes his bearers carry him inside his own house before he alights.'

'How intriguing. I have seen the man before, all swaddled up, with the sticks in his nose and ears.' Alpiew squinted at the Dutchman's chair – the same one that had arrived so noisily at the wedding that never was. 'Please excuse me, Mr Foe. I am going to take a peek. I have an interest in the eccentrics of London.' She ambled over to the corner, arriving just in time to see the tin window sash open half an inch. The boy presented the letter to the gap and it seemed to be swallowed up into the chair, then the sash snapped up again. After a moment a growl came from within and a banging on the roof.

'De Exchange,' yelled a muffled voice. 'Quickly.'

Alpiew turned to Mr Foe. 'How fascinating.' She gathered her skirts to follow. 'Come on!'

The knocker had barely landed when the door was flung open and Cynthia bustled out.

'Countess! I was just leaving.' Cynthia grabbed the Countess by the arm and marched her along the street. 'Come with me.'

'Why the hurry?' said the Countess, finding it hard to keep up with the woman's frantic strides.

'Husband!' she gasped, glimpsing over her shoulder. 'Shopping!' She shot out her hand and a hackney from the stand across the street pulled over. Cynthia pulled the door open and stepped up inside. 'We're going to buy some of that lace, whether Edward likes it or not. And we might even have time to pop into an India house for a warming cup of chocolate. Come along.' She held out her hand and hauled the Countess inside after her. 'Are you fond of the bean?'

'Chocolate?' said the Countess, licking her lips. 'Why of course.'

'And lace?'

'Lace I can take or leave, Mrs Stark.'

'I adore it. And, as I keep saying to my husband, lace is an investment. How many wills do you hear of where an entire fortune is left in linen and lace?' Cynthia leaned forward and called up to the cabman: 'Laura's Lace Emporium, please. Little Distaff Lane.' She whipped out her fan and flapped. 'So hot again. I fear we are in for a devilish summer if heat like this begins so early.' She turned her back towards the Countess. 'Would you oblige me, madam, and loosen my stays an inch or two.'

'Of course.' The Countess fumbled with the laces to ease open Cynthia's dress, and when there was sufficient gap to work in loosened her corset beneath. 'It was lucky meeting you with my friend Pigalle, then seeing you again at the wedding the next day.' The laces seemed to remain taut as strings on a guitar, no matter how much slack the Countess allowed. 'I was wondering how well you knew

Sir Richard Dainty.' The Countess winced. She had referred to the dead man in the past tense.

'Detestable little freak,' said Cynthia, pulling herself up so that the Countess could tackle the lower part of the bodice. 'My husband makes it his business to keep in with most of the money people. They bore me out of my wits. I have to say, though, I feel mightily sorry for that child, Lettice.' She shuddered, trapping the Countess's finger in a tight bit of cross-gartering. 'Fancy having to copulate with that old cadaver!'

'Hm!' How close to the truth that description was. The Countess was glad Cynthia had her back to her. 'But the child appears genuinely fond of the old man.'

'You think? With his gummy maw and wisp of hair?' Cynthia let out a lewd laugh. 'It's the money, surely. Mind you, then why not marry some young apprentice financier, like Robinson.'

'Robinson?' The Countess was working the loose lace upwards and opening more at the bottom. 'I thought he and Lettice were deadly enemies.'

'They feign that in front of me, but I believe she has thrown her cap at him. She sends letters. He hides them away from me. But then he would.' She gave a grim little laugh. 'Oh yes, indeed. He would. I'd spot it a mile off. I am no stranger to the art of clandestine love.'

'Ay,' said the Countess. 'That little blind boy is not as blind as many would paint him.'

'Blind boy?'

'Why, Cupid!' said the Countess.

'Cupid?' The lace pulled tight over the Countess's fingers as Cynthia took a deep breath. 'What of him?'

'He fires his arrows, but it is rarely a secret when he hits.'

'Oh, Cupid!' Cynthia sighed. 'I see what you mean. Do you have a husband living, Countess?'

'There! Finished!' The Countess tied a knot and sat back. 'Lord only knows where he is, but yes.'

'Ah!' Cynthia turned and gave her a conspiratorial smile. 'So you too know the vicissitudes of married life. There is little love in it after a while, don't you find?'

The Countess shrugged.

'All my husband cares about is money and how to make more. I get lonely in the house all day with no one but a pert little Irish maid for company.' Cynthia grabbed at the leather strap as the coach turned a corner. 'And in my misery I have stumbled across love in rather *different* places. Some would call me a deviant. But I say life is short and love is brief and you must take pleasure where you find it. What harm can there be in it?' She turned and picked up her bag from the floor. 'Look, Countess – we are arrived.'

Laura's Lace Emporium was a mad clutter of white. From every shelf rolls, braids and pieces of net dangled. Boxes labelled 'Bucks Point', 'Bayeux', 'Blonde' and 'Flanders' were stacked high next to drawers marked 'Tippets', 'Lappets', 'Cuffs', 'Ruffs' and 'Muffs'.

'How can I help you, madam?' asked the shop assistant, a supercilious woman in a dark mantua.

'Have you any Flemish?' Cynthia was toying with a length of fancy bobbin lace displayed on the counter-top. 'Or perhaps best Bruges?'

The Countess yawned. She could think of nothing more dull than a rampage through the world of lace. She sat, gazed out into the street and thought about Robinson and Lettice. Robinson had every reason to get rid of the old man. He had also been to the Countess's house and knew that the beds were in the kitchen and therefore the unused bedchambers might be used to hide something away for a while. What if Robinson himself had faked the message about the sunken ship yesterday, then led Sir Richard off and murdered him? And then, with some others, had brought the body to German Street and got Godfrey to sign for it. Why, he could have had the box containing the body taken to a delivery firm and had them do the dirty work.

'Milanese! Why of course. I have it in both flounces and edging.'

The ladies' discussion on lace continued behind her.

And what of Lettice's role in the murder? Perhaps she too was involved. Cynthia seemed to think there was more going on between the two young people than met the eye. But recalling the girl's behaviour yesterday, it seemed unlikely. Lettice had appeared genuinely upset that the wedding had not taken place. Perhaps it was a double deal. Perhaps she played both men for what she could get from them. Maybe Lettice had egged the young boy on, but was still connected affectionately to Sir Richard. That letter from Robinson was dated March, it was now May. Perhaps she had changed her mind since then. She was certainly convincing in her public display of disdain for Robinson and her fondness for the old man. But then, perhaps Lettice was an actress to rival Mrs Bracegirdle and had all the skill of displaying the Passions.

'Would you like to see them?'

The Countess looked doggedly at the passing carriages. She could have sworn she had just heard the shop assistant offering to show Cynthia her nipples.

'Would you like to finger them? Tender nipples. Very special.'

From the corner of her eye the Countess saw the shop assistant lean forward.

'Oh, go on.' With a giggle Cynthia reached forward and groaned. 'How delightful. Made for fondling.'

Was *this* what the woman had meant by deviant? Going into shops to feel the shop-woman's nipples? Good God! The Countess gulped.

'Tender,' added the shop assistant. 'So pretty.'

How embarrassing! The Countess coughed. Perhaps the two women had forgotten she was there.

'Countess! Have a look at these!' Cynthia's voice was insistent. 'They are exquisite. Knobbly, yet soft.'

Reluctantly the Countess turned, blushing.

'They're Danish.' The shop assistant held out a box labelled *Tønder Kniples*. 'Would you like a feel? They're the nicest examples of knipling I think I've ever had here in the shop.'

'Aren't they lovely? At the moment there is so much European stuff available.' Cynthia held up two fancy pieces of knot-work. 'For once, we can buy pieces from *everywhere*. Spain, France, Flanders, Holland, Germany. 'Tis a rare thing that England is not at war with one or other of them. And the result is this wonderful shop.'

'It's an expanding business,' the shop-woman beamed. 'I hope that soon I may have a branch in the City and another one in St James's.'

Cynthia was peering at a display behind the shop-girl's shoulder. 'I'll take the night-gown too.'

The shop-keeper started wrapping a bundle of assorted lace lappets and tippets.

'Would you like to try it on? We do have fitting rooms.'

'If it is large, it'll fit.' Cynthia rubbed her belly, then pulled out her purse. 'What a bargain I have had, miss . . . er, are you Laura?'

'No, madam. I am Belinda. We are partners.'

'Well then, Belinda, can you recommend a good India shop nearby? I am in dire need of a cup of chocolate.'

*   *   *

Following Hendrick's chair into the portico of the Royal Exchange, Alpiew pushed through the stalls selling glass eyes, spectacles and corn cures.

'My ophthalmic secret,' screeched a hawker right into her ear, 'infallibly dissolves suffusion, the seed of cataracts and takes away dimness, mists, flies, gnats, sparks, cobwebs, and other false appearances, all symptoms of approaching blindness if not timely prevented.'

'Ay, after your raucous voice has deafened me,' Alpiew yelled back. 'What cure have you against that?' Rubbing her ears, she swung along the passageway lined with gardeners, mandrake sellers and porters and entered the Exchange.

'This is where you come if ever you have need of a quack, a physick, a wet-nurse, a servant, or want to find a shop which sells anything from sweetmeats to oil.' Foe was at her heels. He pointed to the pillars, pasted all round higgledy-piggledy, one atop another with advertisements. 'The place is divided into walks,' he said, raising his voice against the startling shrill racket of chatter echoing within the huge square. 'Those grave and stately men over there who stink of garlic – they're Spaniards. And the ones flinging their hands around as though they were dancing a minuet, they're Frenchmen.'

'Those men over there,' said Alpiew, pointing at a gaggle of solemn-looking men. 'The ones looking about them, with the sharp countenances. Which country are they from?'

'They are Jamaicans and Barbadians. That corner of the Exchange could as well be called Kidnapper's Walk, for they ply as keenly for servants as a gang of pick-pockets for lace kerchiefs. Many a wench has been bubbled out of her savings and spirited away by them to a world of misery and whoredom on the plantations.'

Van Loon's chair moved through the plantation men and

stopped near a gang of sombre fellows in thrum caps. All wore long whiskers upon their upper lips and stood looking glum, gloves under their arms, hands thrust into their pockets, grunting to one another in a slushy language.

'His own type. Water rats!' said Foe. 'Dutchmen.'

Van Loon's chair was set down amidst the Netherlanders and the metal sash slid open a half-inch. The Dutchmen pushed forward, scribbling notes and thrusting them through the gap.

The muffled sound of Hendrick Van Loon's voice replied. 'RAC – I sell at five shillings; African Adventurers Association – buy if it falls below twelve. How much is the *Cassandra*'s stock valued today?'

A tall thin Dutchman scribbled a note and shoved it into the chair.

'Why do they not simply talk to him through the gap?'

'Germs!' said Foe. 'The mad fellow fears disease so much he avoids all human contact. That's why he has the rue up his nose. He always has a clove of garlic in his mouth too. Strange, isn't it? He is terrified of ordinary safe things, like air, but he braves it out in the much more dangerous world of money. This is where he comes to buy and sell.'

'And where is the actual money? I have seen no one exchange so much as a groat.'

'That's the trick.' Foe shrugged. 'There is no *tangible* money. Yet fortunes are won and lost. Every penny is mere ink on paper.' He pulled a coin from his pocket. 'This, my dear, is the only true money. If you have enough of these to buy a loaf you should count yourself happy. But the thousands of pounds dealt here on the Exchange bear no relation to the humble coin in your pocket. It is all imaginary.'

One of the traders Alpiew recognised from Jonathan's came up to Van Loon's chair and slipped a sealed paper through. 'Presented for Sir Richard half an hour ago.'

Alpiew jolted forward to hear better.

'A fraud.' The sealed paper emerged through the slit. 'Give it back to de bearer and have him apprehended.'

The Dutchmen all turned to listen to a red-haired freckle-faced youth who bawled to the assembly: '*Cassandra* was sighted off the Lizard two nights ago. By now she'll be well past the Isle of Wight.'

'The folk who sold yesterday will be kicking themselves again,' said one Dutchman to another with a snide smirk.

'Yesterday someone said it was sunk. So that information was false?' Alpiew pondered. 'Or perhaps this news is false. A man would have to gallop flat out to carry so many reports from such a distance. They're making it up, surely?'

'That is quite usual,' sneered Foe, 'in this world of cullies and cheats. The whole business of stock is based on speculation and conjecture.'

'You mean rumour.'

'I do. Some rumours send the stock up, others drive it down.'

'You are telling me a man can lose a whole fortune on the back of a rumour which is a lie?'

'Some lose, some win. When we were at war with the Dutch or the French it was easy to say such and such a siege has been lifted, or such a general has been killed and the army routed, instantly sending stock bouncing up and down like a ball.

'Yesterday the news came in of the ship going down, and everyone rushed to sell before the news spread. Others went to buy the commodities that the ship was carrying. If a shipload of sugar was not going to reach London, the London price of sugar would naturally increase.'

'And did you see Sir Richard Dainty? What was he doing?'

'He sat smiling while everyone around him sold. I suspect

he had a runner buying on his behalf. For when he was satisfied, another messenger arrived with news that the ship *Cassandra* was all right and it was another ship, a fishing boat, which had hit the rocks at Fastnet. In a few moments, the old man had doubled his investment.'

'So this is the third report on that same ship?'

Foe nodded. 'But who is to say which reports are the right ones, and which not. No one will really know till the ship starts unloading at Greenwich or Tilbury or wherever it is ultimately bound.'

'Sir Richard got the news that the *Cassandra* was all right? What did he do then?'

'He rubbed his hands in glee, and tottered off.' Mr Foe gave a disdainful leer. 'He was getting wed, he said, and lurched up the stairs, I imagine to find a hackney in Cornhill.'

'Was he alone?'

'Yes. Alone.' Foe rubbed his chin and frowned. 'But there was another fellow here, watching him the whole time. A young fellow. Pale and pleasant-looking. I see him often in the coffee houses of 'Change Alley. And he skipped nimbly up the steps in the old man's wake.'

'Thank you, Mr Foe.' Alpiew had heard enough. It was clear Robinson had followed Sir Richard to Exchange Alley, and Robinson had followed him away. 'Your tale is a sad one, but at least you act as a good warning to others who might get burned in this business. I hope you find better fortune in future. I must get home. I have business of my own to attend.'

'Mistress Alpiew?' Foe looked at her through his heavy brow. 'You are no simple maidservant, are you?'

'I am a writer, Mr Foe,' she replied. 'I write a column for the *Trumpet*.'

'Hmmm! Let's not stand on ceremony any more. Please call me Daniel.' He plucked at his ample, swarthy chin. 'Do you know I have written a few things myself. Pamphlets about the scandalous behaviour of stock-jobbers, mainly. But I have always thought, if I had the time, I should sit down and write a book. A long, long story. About a girl like you, perhaps. Where do you get all your ideas?'

'I look around,' said Alpiew. 'I listen to people, and jot things down.'

'Would you show me your jottings?'

'One day, Mr Foe. But I must go now. Call on me. German Street. Anglesey House. Blue door.'

'I've spent enough time being bitter,' said Foe. 'Perhaps I'll try my hand at writing instead.'

Alpiew started to shove her way back through the foreigners. She smiled to herself, wondering whether there was one time when she had told someone she was a writer and the person didn't reply that they too *would* be a writer, if only they had the time.

Just then she collided with the red-haired boy who had brought the latest news of the *Cassandra*. She turned back to Daniel Foe for one more question.

'The messenger boy yesterday who brought news of the ship being safe,' she called. 'What was he like?'

'Dusty!' said Foe. 'His clothes, his skin, his hands . . . everything. Ingrained with dust. Oh, and another thing I noticed. The tip of his forefinger . . .'

'Yes?'

'It was missing.'

'I could go on drinking chocolate all day and all night. The stuff is essence of paradise, don't you think, Countess?'

'A heavenly concoction.' The Countess was delighted to be treated to a cup in such a cosy shop as this. Although the day had started hot, a steady parade of clouds had slowly filled the sky, blocking the sun, and the rising wind had a positive nip to it. She shivered, crunching into a ratafia biscuit, and gazed at the shelves laden with pretty sweetmeats on glass salvers. 'One does wonder how previous ages managed without it.'

'Trade, you see. My husband's business. We are lucky to live in such an age when the world has opened up. I used to hear him going on about trade and wondered what all those ledgers had to do with me. Till one day Robinson sat down and explained everything so clearly. The economy. Commerce.' She swept her hand indicating the room, with its bamboo stands, beautifully upholstered chairs, the gilt sconces and ornate chandelier, the dainty lace cloths, the glassware, the china and plate. 'This is the result. All these wonderful things we get from Europe, America, Africa, Asia and the Indies – then there's rum, sugar, tobacco, rare fruits, gunpowder, spices, silks and sateens, tea, coffee. Look how our lives are improved since the barbarous days of Queen Elizabeth.'

The Countess ladled more sugar into her cup of chocolate and could not but agree.

'How came the girl Lettice to live with Sir Richard Dainty? Is she a relative of his? Or indeed has she any relatives living?'

'I know nothing of that. He has had her since she was an infant.'

'You don't approve of an old man with such a young girl . . . ?'

'When did I say that?'

'At the wedding. You called Sir Richard perverted.'

'It's more complicated than that.' Cynthia gazed down into her dish of chocolate and sighed. 'I wonder whether I should have said something. But no. Life is hard if you are alone in the world. If Sir Richard cares enough that he will provide for her . . .' She looked up at the Countess and shrugged. 'Though, rather like my husband, I think the only thing he has ever loved is money.' Cynthia stirred the dregs in her dish and signalled to the serving wench to refill. 'Money is a strange thing. Once a person gets a taste for it, they don't seem to be able ever to let go. Even when they have acquired a fortune, they strive for more, wanting to double and treble. I wonder sometimes if Money is not the ultimate Love.' She took a long draught of steaming chocolate, let out a sigh and rubbed her hand across her stomach.

The Countess noticed that, even after loosening her stays, Cynthia wore her mantua too tight, saw how the stitches strained at the seams.

'I hope Robinson doesn't catch the money bug, Countess. He is a good boy. I am very, very fond of him.' She caught the Countess's quizzical glance and added, 'An excellent apprentice. We could not have done better.'

'Apprentice?' The Countess mulled over the word. 'A strange term to use of your own relative.'

'My nephew, yes, of course. Just a figure of speech, you know.' Cynthia pulled herself up in her chair and put another lump of sugar into her cup. 'We are training Robinson into the business. He is the heir, says Edward. After all, we have no children of our own. And he has taken to the work better even than my husband.'

The Countess was beginning to suspect a romance between Cynthia and her own nephew. Perhaps that was the deviance she had referred to earlier.

'You love Mr Stark, I presume?' The Countess observed a definite tremor pass through Cynthia. She saw also that Cynthia had noticed her see it.

'Edward? Fie, Countess!' Cynthia stopped stirring her chocolate. 'Do you think me so ill-bred as to love my own husband?' She laughed, and the laugh had a brittle edge to it. 'Isn't that a line from a play? I used to go to the theatre with my father. Edward doesn't like the theatre. He thinks it is a decadent relic for a snobbish elite. I say it is he who is the snob.'

'Your husband is a successful businessman, though.'

'If you like. The trouble with Edward is that he is a jack of all trades. I always say he has a finger in every public pie and every private tart.' Cynthia threw back her head and gave a bitter laugh. 'Some corners of his business empire revolt me.'

'Really? For example?'

'Knocker-uppers.'

'Knocker-uppers?'

'He helps condemned criminals to evade the gallows. You cannot hang a woman who is with child. He employs men to fornicate with the women in prison. You witnessed one of his triumphs. Staying the execution of that hideous hag at Tyburn the other day.'

The Countess remembered Edward's joy at the escapades of the execution fair and wished now she had turned and hit him. After all, he had been responsible for letting that virago, Kate Timony, escape.

'It appals me that he does these things. Dealing with such criminal types doesn't always pay him the dividends he hopes for. He had a mix-up the other day. But, as he says, once they're dead, who's to care?'

'He takes the money and fails to save them?' The Countess realised the irony of that situation. A promise which might be broken with no consequence. 'I see what you mean – if the job fails, the customer is hardly in a position to demand a refund.'

'Let's talk of something else. I despair sometimes. I feel so alone.' Cynthia took a nibble at a biscuit and laid it down. The Countess thought she looked on the verge of tears. 'I am a City widow, Countess. I should be used to a solitary life. I lived alone with my father . . . Poor old darling . . .' Tears filled her eyes, and her mouth started to tremble. 'He died. Only a few years ago. He was all I had, and . . . Oh, I suppose I believed that marriage would bring me company. Instead it means I spend most of my days yearning for someone, anyone.' Her trembling voice failed her. She pulled out a kerchief and gave her nose a hearty blow.

'Well, we are having a very nice sojourn today, Mrs Stark.' The Countess could see that Cynthia was holding herself together by a thread. 'We can have more jaunts like this one, why not? I am always happy to sit and drink chocolate.'

'I think I might form a club for wives of money-men.' Cynthia looked around the cluttered India shop: at the shelves full of brisée fans, glassware, ivory boxes, silver candlesticks, Malacca canes and Delft jars filled with spices; at the tables crowded with laughing women, chattering away over their steaming dishes of coffee, tea and chocolate. 'We can raid the India houses and spend all our husbands' money on fashionable knick-knackery until they pay us more attention.' She put her handkerchief away and laughed.

'Or perhaps kill you for wasting their fortunes,' said the Countess, thinking how furious she would be if Godfrey or Alpiew took her precious money and wasted it buying this up-to-the-minute trumpery.

'If Edward killed me, what harm would there be in that?' Cynthia sighed from the bottom of her heart. 'I am dead already, and he is dead to me. Once a man is infected with the money bug, for all the company he is he might as well be dead.'

The Countess allowed the briefest of pauses before speaking. 'If Sir Richard Dainty were to die,' she said, seizing the opportunity to ask the unpalatable question, 'who would get his fortune?'

'Why, the girl, I presume. As his widow.'

'But they never married. She is not his wife.'

'A technicality.' Cynthia drained her cup. 'It will happen, today, tomorrow, who knows. But it will happen. Clearly, they both *want* it to happen.' Cynthia gripped the edge of the table. She was gulping and had turned a ghostly shade of green. 'I must get some air.' She threw coins, more than enough to cover the bill, on to the table and staggered towards the door.

In the street she leaned on a tethering post and took a few deep breaths. The Countess was ready to catch her as she slumped down on to the pavement.

'You are laced much too tight, madam.' The Countess helped Cynthia sit back against the post, knelt beside her and went to work again at her laces. 'For a woman in your condition.'

'Condition?' As the corset loosened Cynthia pulled her skirt up to cover the increasingly obvious bulge of her belly. 'Ah, yes. I have a tympany.'

'Of course, a tympany!' The Countess stroked the woman's clammy forehead, sweeping the hair out of her eyes. 'You should go home and rest. Here comes a hackney.'

The Countess helped Cynthia into the cab and climbed up after her. As the coach carried them towards St Martin's Lane she glanced at Cynthia, her head lolling back against the cracked leather of the carriage's upholstery.

A tympany! The Countess looked down at the bulge pushing out the woman's corset. A tympany, indeed! And if it is a tympany, she thought, I'll warrant it's a two-legged one.

Alpiew swung along German Street. She planned to get comfortable in the kitchen and continue her financial jottings. She would clear herself a table-top and try to get

155

some clarity in her thoughts. With Godfrey out of the way looking after Lettice, that would certainly be easier. She could boil up a little broth at the same time. And tear away at a hunk of bread, dipping it as she worked.

'Alpiew, my dear!' The Countess trotted towards her, arriving at Alpiew's side as she pushed open the front door. 'Have I got things to tell you! About Cynthia and Robinson and, oh, so many things . . . See!' The Countess delved into her cleavage and pulled out the papers she had found in the trunk.

They stood just inside the front door as Alpiew read, starting with the letter from Robinson. 'What an insinuating cove.' Alpiew put the letter in her pocket. As she withdrew her hand, one small note fell to the floor – Lettice's to Sir Richard telling him she had gone with the Countess. The Countess picked up the note, and inspected it.

'Ho, Alpiew! What is this? "Pigsny, I am gone with women to German Street, blue door. Hope find Captain. L." And what is this superscription: "Lud – R. Gibb"?'

Alpiew took a look. '". . . German Street, blue door. Hope find Captain"? "Lud – R. Gibb"? The second bit is in another hand, or at least writ with another pen.'

'Lud,' said the Countess, squinting over Alpiew's shoulder. 'What is that? King Lud? Lud's Town is the derivation of the name London. Perhaps it's more baby talk – along with their "pigsny"s.'

'It is not the girl's writing. Perhaps it is Sir Richard's, or whoever was in his house that night. R. Gibb. Is that a person? Whose name starts with an R? Robinson . . . Richard . . .' Alpiew looked up from the scrap of paper. 'Oh, talking of the old fellow, has the constable taken his body away?

'No, Alpiew! But come up and see.' The Countess grabbed Alpiew's hand and they both started up the stairs.

'The significant news about our lifeless visitor is that when I met up with the constable, he was gone.'

'Gone? How, madam? Did the dead carcass get up and walk away?' Alpiew grabbed the poker she had let fall on the landing last night. 'I'll take this up. We can't be too careful, madam. The last few episodes we've had up here.'

They opened the door, and stood on the top landing staring at the trunk.

'I was so embarrassed when I opened it and it was empty. The constable clearly thought I was demented. I pulled up the lid for him and there was nothing inside. Nothing! No body at all. It was quite empty. Look!' The Countess ambled over and grabbed the corner of the trunk lid with both hands. 'Come, Alpiew, help me.'

'I don't understand.' Alpiew pushed back her sleeves and tugged at the top. 'How can a dead body leg it? Unless he wasn't dead? One, two, three. Pull.'

The lid burst open. As though on a spring, with a yowl, a man jumped out. Instantly Alpiew brought the poker down on his head and the man slid slowly to the floor.

'Fie!' The Countess pressed her hand to her thumping heart, and gazed down at the stunned figure of a six-foot-tall negro. 'What on earth . . . ?' Her mouth fell open and she squealed. 'Oh, no, Alpiew! Look who it is!'

'Lawks!' Alpiew fell to her knees and gently stroked the man's hair. 'I hope I have not hurt him too badly, poor, dear little jewel.'

'My long lost boy!' said the Countess, pulling at his grubby cravat and unbuttoning his shirt with one hand while she fanned with the other. 'My darling Cupid!'

'Zooks, madam. Look!'

Around Cupid's neck, hidden by the cravat, was a silver collar. Alpiew fumbled around it, looking for the fastening.

'Don't bother,' groaned Cupid, from the floor, his eyes

slowly opening. 'It is welded on.' He sat up and rubbed his black curly hair, inspecting his fingers for blood. 'I see, Alpiew, that you haven't lost your aim. I shall have a nasty bump.'

'Oh, Cupid, Cupid!' The Countess stooped and kissed the man's forehead. 'My precious baby. How wonderful that you are come back.'

'I came here for your help, my darlings.' Cupid took both women by a hand and kissed them tenderly. 'But from what I have seen here, sweethearts both, I think you are in even more need of help than I am.'

'Cupid! Cupid! Darling little cock-robin. How magical that you are come home. We shall be just as we were all those years ago.' The Countess kissed the top of Cupid's head. 'Together in delightful harmony.'

'I'm not sure about that.' Cupid scrambled to his feet. 'If you give me such a crashing welcome.'

'Lord, but you are shot up, jewel.' The Countess gazed up into his dark eyes. 'But, see, you are still as pretty as ever you were.'

'That's as may be, Cupid,' said Alpiew. 'But can you explain why you are hiding in this trunk?'

'I came to visit you. I came upstairs, looking for you, and then the door slammed downstairs. I heard men prowling about. So I hid. I don't know why.'

'More men in the house? I have had just about enough of this.' Alpiew snatched up the poker and marched on down the stairs. 'Come along, Cupid. Let's see them off, if they dare to be still here.'

'Alpiew,' cried the Countess as she followed them both down the stairs. 'Won't it have been the night-soil men? Weren't they coming today to empty the privy?'

Alpiew pushed the kitchen door open.

Things had been moved. The papers, usually piled in

messy stacks, were laid out neatly. The beds had been made. The chairs were neatly lined up in a row. Any blue-and-white jars which had been on the shelves or floor were all together by the pantry door. Books were shelved in a neat line on the mantel.

'I don't think so, madam. Look! Someone has been here and cleaned up!'

'Perhaps Godfrey did it.' The Countess knew this could not be true. Why would the lazy sloven change the habit of a lifetime? 'The night-soil don't do cleaning, do they?'

'I'd say whoever was here was looking for something, madam. See how everything has been sorted so methodically.'

'The money, Alpiew!' The Countess yelped. 'Where is the money?'

'Oh, no.' Alpiew darted about, peering into the pantry, lifting the bedding and kneeling to look under the beds. 'No! No! It's gone, milady.'

'Even Godfrey's stash?'

'Still buried in the privy, I suppose?' asked Cupid.

'Cupid! You knew Godfrey kept his money in the privy?'

'In the old days, back in the Strand, that's where he always kept his savings. In a jar, beneath the night-soil.'

'Phough!' The Countess tottered towards the yard door. 'The old sod is a grisly hugger-mugger merchant, to be sure. Bring a shovel, Alpiew. And hold your nose.'

The garden showed signs of a recent fray. The creepers, weeds and shrubs which grew up the walls were broken and trodden down, the patches of grass and moss between the tiles torn out.

'Lord, they tidy up the kitchen and mess up the garden! This place looks as though it has been busier than the hackney stand in the Strand during an April shower. What are all these nuts doing here?' The Countess peered down at the weedy ground, which was strewn with nuts. 'Mark my words, that monkey's been here again.' She lifted her leg to step over a straggling stem of bramble. She threw open the privy door and screamed.

Cupid ran up behind her. He took a step back as Alpiew arrived with the shovel.

Lying face down in the privy sludge, covered in a tattered buff coat, was the body of an old man. A still, gnarled hand, fingers filthy from grasping into the excrement, stretched out. The coat covered everything else but a puff of wispy white hair.

'Have we found old man Dainty?'

'No,' said Alpiew. 'Look at the hands. Too big, rough.'

'It's not Godfrey, is it?' whispered the Countess. 'Is he asleep?'

'Lying on the foul soil of the privy, madam?' Alpiew stooped, trying to get a closer look.

'Godfrey?' The Countess tried to yell, but found her voice came out in a feeble croak. 'Godfrey?'

Cupid crept forward and pulled back the coat.

'Who is it?' The Countess peered down at the back of the elderly man. 'Let us see his face.'

With the tip of his boot, Cupid rolled the body over. 'You know who that is, milady?' He stared down at the man. His throat was cut from ear to ear.

'No.' The Countess swallowed and peered at the mutilated body in her privy. 'I never saw the fellow before in my life.'

'I know him, madam,' said Alpiew. 'It's the Charlie.'

'Charlie who?' The Countess couldn't take her eyes off the man's slashed throat.

'The night-watchman.' Alpiew bowed down to take a closer look. 'And see, there – it's not only his throat that's been cut.'

The old man's dark jacket was torn open and his waistcoat ripped. The dark red stain on his grubby shirt framed a cut from his breastbone to his groin.

'His stomach,' whispered Alpiew. 'It is gone.'

Draw — the process of drawing out glass from the bottom of the bowl to make a stem

'What is going on?' cried the Countess, taking another sip of brandy. 'Is there a market in human stomachs? Why would they want to take that from the old fool?'

The Countess huddled with Alpiew and Cupid in a stall at the back of a ninepenny ordinary in Pickadilly. The eating place was packed with stallholders and higglers from St James's and the Hay Market taking lunch.

Better to hide in a crowd, they had decided, and eat while deciding what best to do, than wait in the house, which had clearly become a thoroughfare for every kind of rogue and vagabond.

'Why was he killed at all, and it come to that?' The Countess sighed and took a spoonful of mutton stew. 'And why was he dumped in our privy?'

'The events, once you write them down, make even less sense.' Alpiew chewed on her pencil and gazed at the bizarre list:

1. Witness hangings and escape of a condemned man and woman.

2. Call night-watch Charlie to aid in burglary by monkey.
3. Attend wedding where ancient groom exits mid-ceremony.
4. Get held up by said condemned man and woman in our house.
5. Find body of said groom in a trunk in our house.
6. Body gone. Money too.
7. Find body of said night-watch Charlie in privy of our house.

'So what is it about your house that is attracting all these criminal activities?' Cupid wore a hat pulled low over his eyes, and sat with his back to the room. 'I hope whatever you have about you that invites all this trouble is not catching. I have enough worries of my own.'

'But, Cupid, my dear baby,' cooed the Countess. 'You haven't told us where you have been all these years. And why you never came to find me?'

'It is too long a story. I did look for you for years. And I admit I gave up. Then yesterday I saw Alpiew in the street. And I followed her until she led me to you.'

'Why did you not talk to me?' Alpiew gazed at Cupid. She felt sure that something in his explanation was false. 'I called after you.'

'I could not.' Cupid avoided her look. 'I am in trouble.'

'Too much trouble to talk to me in the street; but not enough to prevent you coming in uninvited and hiding in our house?'

'I am a wanted man, Alpiew. If I am caught I will be hanged.'

'Hanged!' the Countess cried. 'What have you done that they can hang you, my baby? Not murder?'

'I worked for someone and they said I stole from them. Valuable things. I thought I could prove my innocence, then

163

something else happened and I ran away. I know I made it seem worse by doing that, but I was frightened.'

'And do you imagine we can help you?' The Countess thought of Cynthia's revelations about her husband saving women from the gallows, and wondered if he had a ploy that could save men from a similar fate.

'I was certain you could, milady. But now that I see the mess you are in, I am not so sure.'

'The way things are going for us at the moment,' said Alpiew, bouncing her pencil down the list, 'having caught up with us, you will shortly end up dead somewhere in our house.'

'Don't even joke about it, Alpiew.' The Countess wondered what it was about their house that had made it such a rendezvous for ruffians and cadavers. 'Now, what do we do with the Charlie? Killing an officer of the law, however lowly, must surely lead to the gallows. And how on earth can we prove we had nothing to do with it when he lies in our privy?'

'We don't possess his stomach, for one.' Alpiew squeezed lemon juice over her plate.

'Although, Alpiew, an item of that ilk would not be hard to dispose of.' Cupid gazed down at Alpiew's lunch. 'What are you eating?'

'Stewed tripes. Oh, lord.' Alpiew groaned, and pushed her plate aside. 'I can't eat that. Think of it! The poor old cove, lazy with slumber and his lemon drops.'

'Where's Godfrey!' The Countess could just picture him stumbling home and heading for an hour in the privy with a copy of Quarles's *The Virgin Widow*, and instead of repose finding a mutilated corpse. 'We must let him know before he goes back to the house and . . .'

'My lord! Godfrey must be a hundred years old by now.' Cupid was hungrily tucking into Alpiew's leftovers. 'He always seemed old, even when I was as small as your pet marmoset.'

'Godfrey's a rum 'un, that's for sure,' said Alpiew, getting up and brushing down her skirt. 'I shall go and warn the old bugger not to go home quite yet, till we've decided what to do.'

'Like Sir Richard, perhaps the Charlie will up and walk away.' The Countess wished that this would happen. Then, along with losing all their money, and being reduced to penury, things would be almost back to normal. 'Tell Godfrey to go to Pigalle's, Alpiew. I am sure Olympe will let us shelter with her until this affair blows over.'

Alpiew waited outside Sir Richard's house.

Low, dark clouds threatened to burst at any moment.

After a few minutes she knocked again. She listened at the front door. As she tentatively opened it, a scream pierced the silence.

Gathering her skirts, Alpiew raced up the stairs.

'Shut the door!' screamed Lettice, as her agile panta-looned and be-fezzed monkey leapt over the banister and ran past Alpiew down into the street. 'You stupid bitch!' howled the girl, glaring at Alpiew. 'We only got him back a few hours ago.'

Alpiew bowled down the stairs again and chased Captain Caruso out into the street. The monkey scuttled along Pall Mall Street, bounding over all obstacles, scrambling up and over the coaches and carriages. In his wake, women screamed and street hawkers bawled over their upset trays and stalls.

'Stop that monkey!' bellowed Alpiew, panting along in his wake.

Captain Caruso sprang up on to the roof of a coach, grabbed a hanging shop sign, then proceeded to swing along the whole row of signs. At the corner he leapt down, turned into St James's Street and disappeared.

Alpiew cursed as she arrived at the corner. Not a sign of the monkey.

A small crowd had gathered ahead. Alpiew wiped the sweat from her forehead and stepped gingerly forward. 'Oh no!' she cried. 'Please God, don't let a coach have run over the little blighter.' She trotted on, pushing her way through an awed crowd. She was aware of women turning their faces away, men holding kerchiefs over their noses. She jammed through the throng and saw what was causing the commotion. A gang of night-soil men stood gathered around their cart in the middle of the road, shouting and gesticulating up along German Street.

The night-soil men! She had not cancelled them! They would have arrived at the empty house and gone straight about their business. The privy would have been their first stop, and then . . .

It seemed that the night-watch Charlie's body had been found.

'But, Ashby, my darling, *sacrebleu*, I hope no one is going to follow you here and kill us all in our beds. I dispatched my coachman with a flea in his ear, as you know, and my usual man, Jack, is out in ze country on a business errand. Who is here to protect us?' Pigalle kicked a cushion at her feet and three yowling cats leapt up and ran from the room. 'There's only, me, Mustapha and Millicent here. We are flying ducks.'

'Sitting. And anyhow, we have Cupid.' Not having been invited, the Countess took the initiative and sat, gingerly inspecting the sofa first for cat vomit. She waved Cupid to sit beside her. 'Who on earth is Millicent, Olympe, dear? A new lover?'

'Non.' Pigalle let out a squawk of horror. 'Millicent is certainly very fond of ze old jigjig, but not with me. Ooh la la!' She went to the door and called up the stairs. 'Mustapha! Bring my little darling down now.'

'Mustapha?' The Countess looked adoringly at Cupid. 'Olympe has a charming boy, just like you, my sweet.'

'*Oui! D'accord.* I adore ze child.' Pigalle opened her arms as a six-year-old blackamoor boy entered the room. He was neatly turbaned in pink shot satin, his powder-blue damask suit twinkled with glass buttons.

From the boy's shoulders a coffee-coloured monkey hopped up into Pigalle's arms. 'Millicent is my marmoset.' Pigalle kissed the monkey on the mouth, leaving a smear from her own red lips. '*Ma petite belle.*' She sat, the monkey carefully balanced on her shoulder with its arms round her neck, and Mustapha perched upon her lap. 'So, Ashby, you have a dead body in your latrine? What are you going to do with it? It is not so easy to dispose of a corpse, *ma chérie.* They are so heavy, bodies. Much heavier dead, I always think, than they are in life. When the Duc de Limoges . . .'

'Who cares?' The Countess wasn't in the mood for another of Pigalle's wild tales of mayhem from her life at the French court. 'It was probably just a burglary gone wrong.' The Countess shuddered again at the thought of losing a hundred guineas. 'But in case it is connected with the death of Sir Richard, I need to get into Jonathan's or Garraway's. Alpiew said she can get in as a worker, but I want to talk with those men on their own terms. To sit with the dealers as an equal.'

'*Difficile,* darling! Your figure is too womanly. I could stick a moustache on you, but Ashby, look at you! You are too much the *femme*.'

The bell clanged, and the front door shook under a barrage

167

of blows. From the tops of the furniture ornamental birds screeched, and the marmoset joined the chorus.

'*Merde!* What do zey want of me, zese people and their knockers!' Pigalle teetered to her feet, her high heels tilting her at such an angle that she tumbled Mustapha and Millicent on to the floor. The huge Aubusson carpet upon which they landed was dotted with white circles of excrement from her parrots and jackdaws. '*Un moment, mes petits.*' She clattered down the stairs.

The Countess felt agitated. Something was wrong. Cupid started to speak, but she silenced him and listened.

A few words drifted up from the doorstep.

'*Non! Non! Zut! Oui!*'

When Pigalle returned she stood in the doorway, hands on her hips, her red hair standing upright. '*Quel problème*, darling!' She threw her arms up. 'Zey are looking for you. *Il est temps d'employer le système démerde.*'

'You know my French is rusty, Olympe,' sighed the Countess, who barely had a word apart from *bonjour*. 'What is going on?'

'Well, Ashby, my beautiful friend, let us say zat ze night-watchman is not the only person in ze shit!'

Alpiew headed for Pigalle's home to warn the Countess. But when she saw the posse of men on the doorstep she turned briskly away and hovered in a nearby doorway, watching, until Pigalle slammed the door on them and they left. The Countess had Pigalle to protect her, she would be all right.

But for herself she felt the safest thing to do was keep on the move. Hanging her head, she walked briskly along German Street. Outside their house a gang of night-soil men still stood around their rubbish cart in animated conversation with a gaggle of headboroughs. There was a lot of expostulating and arm-waving from all. She could not catch what they were saying, and did not hang around to listen and be spotted.

Spying the constable and his men in the Hay Market, she loitered in the crowds around Pickadilly and took the long way round past the Royal Mews.

When she finally arrived back at the Dainty front door in Pall Mall Street she almost collided with a post-boy as he ran up to the house bearing a letter for Lettice.

Thunder rumbled overhead. It had become as dark as evening.

'I'll take that!' Alpiew gave the boy a penny, grabbed the letter and marched in through the door, happy to be inside before the rain came.

'The monkey got away. I am so sorry.' Alpiew quickly looked down at the writing on the letter. It was unmistakably Robinson's hand. 'Don't monkey's have a homing instinct, like pigeons?' She was about to surreptitiously pocket the letter when Lettice reached out and snatched it from her. She tore open the red wax seal and read.

'How did you find him before?' Alpiew wished she could get a glance at the note. 'I feel sure we can get him back again.'

'He was sitting with the night-watchman in German Street.' Lettice had merely let her eyes fall on the words and then folded the letter again. 'Eating nuts.'

'With the night-watchman in German Street!' exclaimed Alpiew. 'When was this?'

'First thing this morning, of course. Just before the old man finished his rounds. When else would he have been sitting in his box?'

'What time?'

'How do I know? Right after you left us Godfrey and I searched the streets together. We spent about an hour looking: he went along Hay Market and German Street, and I went down Pall Mall Street and up St James's and we met up there. Then we walked back together and passed the Charlie's box and there he was, bouncing my darling Captain upon his knee and feeding him nuts. If it is any concern of yours.'

'What is Robinson Stark to you?' Alpiew tipped the letter with her finger. 'I know he writes you love-letters.'

'Robinson?' Lettice swallowed and a blush worked her way up her cheeks. 'He is nothing but an impertinent coxcomb, if any of this is your business, Mistress Alpiew.'

'Unless he loves you and you encourage him in that love, why does he repeatedly write love-letters to you?' Alpiew stared down at the letter, which Lettice was now folding over and over. 'I know that is from him. I recognise his hand.'

'Go ahead, if you like. Read it to me.' Lettice shoved the letter into Alpiew's hand. 'What care I what he says? Did you watch? I have not even bothered to read it. Believe me, I always hand the letters straight to Sir Richard. For you must understand, it is Sir Richard who is going to marry me, whatever Robinson wants.'

'Robinson wants to marry you, too, does he not?' If Lettice acted like this, swinging back and forth, Alpiew could see that Robinson had every reason to kill Sir Richard. But how far was Lettice involved in the plot? 'Which of them do you *really* want to marry?'

'Read – go on.' Lettice threw down the letter, and marched into the front room, where Godfrey lay snoring on the sofa. 'It is no matter if you read what he writes. It is all so much meaningless stuff. I cannot stop him writing to me. Anyone with a penny can send a letter. I have told you, I do not want Robinson. I want only my pigsny. But where is he got to? I know he would not run away from me. We are to marry as soon as possible. He wants this wedding as much as I do. He is frightened Robinson will try to steal me away abroad or somewhere and marry me first.'

Alpiew picked up the letter from the floor where Lettice had flung it. It was the same sort of stuff as before – formally laid out, written in a very neat hand, the lines meticulously straight, the letters clear and neatly spaced. The content was much the same as the letter the Countess had shown her: he was going to seize Lettice and elope with her before Sir Richard could marry her.

Banging on the front door startled her.

Another post-boy held up two further letters. Alpiew dug into her pocket for another two pennies. The boy thrust the mail into her hand and darted off, clutching his sack closely to protect it from the rain. Alpiew only had time to see that one of them was again written by Robinson before Lettice appeared and took them from her.

'You owe me three pence,' said Alpiew.

'Two. This one's for you!' Lettice passed one back. 'And this other one, which I see you recognise, as it is in Robinson's hand, is an additional proof of how he pesters me.'

Alpiew tore open the letter addressed to her. It was from the Countess. 'Stay away from home! We are wanted.'

So Alpiew was right.

The watchman's body had been discovered.

When she looked up again, Alpiew noticed that Lettice, staring down at Robinson's latest letter, had turned deathly pale. With a small cry, the girl reached out and grabbed on to the wainscoting before sliding to the floor in a faint.

Alpiew roused Godfrey and together they lifted the girl up on to the sofa. As Alpiew bent to lift her legs, something fell out of Lettice's pocket and slid down on to the Turkey rug.

Alpiew glanced down at a silver half-coin – the wedding token Cynthia had given her on the wedding morning. As Godfrey gently rolled her over, to prevent her falling, another half-coin spilled out on to the upholstery.

Two half-coins? Alpiew picked them both up. Why would the girl have two?

Unless . . .

Alpiew remembered Sir Richard putting his own half-coin into his waistcoat pocket before the ceremony. He left his house with that half-coin still about his person, and shortly after that he was dead. Lettice had been nowhere near him, alive or dead, in the intervening time. Or had she? 'Godfrey! Have you seen any hartshorn? She must be revived.'

While Godfrey searched the drawers for a bottle of sal-ammoniac to resuscitate the girl, Alpiew quickly read Robinson's latest letter.

In this one his hand was considerably less tidy. The lines were unmeasured and the script a wild scrawl. Its content was simple: *Catastrophe. Proceed as fast as you can. I am taken. Now on cart on the way to Ludgate. I fear once I am there they will catch up with us and ALL will be known.*

Alpiew thrust the two silver half-coins back into the girl's pocket as Godfrey staggered over, gasping and reeling from the scent of the hartshorn.

'You're not meant to breathe it in yourself, blockhead.' Alpiew snatched the bottle and wafted it under Lettice's nose.

To Alpiew's surprise, when Lettice came round, despite looking pale as snow, rather than take up her offer to go to the prison to see Robinson, the girl simply sobbed louder and begged Godfrey to search the coffee houses for news of Sir Richard.

'I think you had better prepare yourself for bad news.'

The more Lettice cried, the more Alpiew was convinced that she and Robinson were involved in her guardian's murder. 'If Sir Richard is not yet come back, the likelihood is that he has met with some misfortune. It will all come out soon enough. Whatever the plot, you will be found out.' Alpiew waited for a response. 'You and Robinson both.'

Silently, the girl stared into Alpiew's eyes. 'Are you accusing me?' she whispered. 'What do you know? What are you after, you and your prying mistress?'

'Sir Richard is dead.'

'Dead? Hussy, you lie!' Lettice sat up, defiance in her eyes. 'So where is his body? Take me to his corpse, then say things like that.' She pushed Alpiew out of her way. 'Come, Godfrey, *you* will help me find my pigsny. I must marry him immediately.'

'The monkey?' Godfrey shifted about. 'We don't have to go running up and down the street again, do we? I'm too old for all that hurly-burly.'

'I want the Captain back, of course. But now the *only* thing that matters is finding Sir Richard.'

'You can help her find the old boy, can't you?' Godfrey looked to Alpiew. 'I'm going 'ome. I have a household to run.'

'No, Godfrey! You are not to go back to German Street.' Alpiew barred his way. How to prevent him from going home without telling them about the night-watchman's body in the privy? 'The Countess has made it very, very clear. You are to stay at Miss Dainty's side until Sir Richard returns.'

'I thought you said 'e was dead?'

'She is nothing but a lying, trouble-making minx.' Lettice was at the front door. 'You are leaving this house now, Mistress Alpiew. Off you go.'

'Keep your eye on this child.' Alpiew glared at Godfrey.

'And do *not* go back to the house, you understand. Not for *any* reason.'

A May downpour was at its height, bringing with it a smell, fresh yet dusty. Bedraggled shoppers huddled in doorways, and businessmen scurried along, their damp floppy hats pulled low to protect their long flowing wigs. Wiping drips from her forehead and nose, Alpiew ran through the streets. She plunged her hand into her pocket to see how much money she had. Could she afford a cab, especially now? For the moment, time was more important than money, she decided, and hopped into a hackney outside the Royal Mews near Charing Cross.

Once she had found Robinson she would go into a tavern, sit down and write a page of Queries for the *Trumpet*. That at least would bring in some cash.

When she alighted at Ludgate the rain had stopped and the sun had come out. Everyone was steaming as they pressed through the gate into the City.

Alpiew went to the begging grille at the side of the prison.

One girl was there, thrusting her cupped hand through the bars. 'Please relieve a fool whose only fault was to become the orphan of a drunken profligate father when I was too old to be put on the parish.'

'I need to see Robinson Stark,' said Alpiew, trying to ignore the empty hand. 'Can you fetch him? I can pay you.'

'Robinson? There's my luck again!' The girl sighed. 'I was talking to him about half an hour ago. They took him away. An order for debt. A large amount. Quite took my breath away. He'll be all his life paying *that* back.'

'Who was pressing the debt? Did he say?'

'Oh, he was howling and mewling and banging his head like a mad thing. Talked about how he laid a trap for some man who had ruined him, but the ruse had snared him instead.'

174

'Was he brought in by bailiffs?' Alpiew didn't understand. Had Robinson been arrested for debt? It seemed surprising for one who dealt in money for a living.

'No. Some City headboroughs brought him in for passing a forged bond in some place called Fennel's or Nutmeg's. Something spicy.'

'Garraway's?'

'That's it. It made me think how I yearn for a cone of caraway comfits to wash away the taste of this foul place.'

'He was taken for passing a false bond, you said. But what has that to do with debt?'

'The false bond got him brought here, but then some warder here recognised him, pulled out the huge ledger and, hey presto, a whole lot more charges were brought against him. I saw 'em at it, reeling off this long, long list of money and charges.'

'Charges?'

'A great big debt. Huge. Like the National Debt they all talk about what started the Bank of England. And rows and rows of old prison charges. I suppose he'd been inside before. Anyhow, he seemed to know the ropes all right.'

'Really?' A gust of wind blew a spray of rain into Alpiew's face from the ledges above. 'Where did they take him, do you know?'

'I heard them say the Clink. As they threw him into the wagon he was shouting that he would try for transportation rather than spend a life inside that hell-hole. He was frightened about something, I thought. As though worse would come out if he wasn't careful. But that's the way it always is with us debtors.'

Debt indeed! It wouldn't be the debt that brought on the outburst of fear. Alpiew knew Robinson was more likely to be fretting about being discovered for Sir Richard's murder than a tumult of debtors piling in at the kill.

'Poor boy seemed very worried about taking care of his family if he was sent off to America. He said something so pretty: "When you are united by blood, it is a bond no man can break." Isn't that nice?'

Very nice, thought Alpiew, and for 'blood' read 'murder'. The wind, gusting along from St Paul's and funnelling through the City Gate to bowl down Ludgate Hill towards the Fleet River, shook the gibbets overhead. Dripping, they started to creak and sway.

The woman continued. 'He prayed too, and I heard him invoking the spirit of his dead father and mother, poor boy. He was an orphan, of course, like me.'

Alpiew knew she had two urgent visits to make. To Robinson's uncle and aunt, Edward and Cynthia Stark, and thence to Garraway's. 'I'd better go,' said Alpiew, handing the girl a penny. She felt mean and wished she had more to give. But there was only a shilling left now for anything else she might need until she could get something written and delivered to the Cues.

'Oh, thank you, mistress. You are kind. This'll go toward my lodging fee for the night. I wondered what would happen about that boy Robinson. I watched him part with his last pennies for paper and pen to write a letter. I think it was to his sweetheart.'

Edward Stark was out, working at the Exchange, Cynthia told Alpiew. 'But why not come in and share a dish of chocolate with me? I even have some lovely cinnamon cakes.'

Alpiew was only too pleased to be able to eat and make inquiries at the same time.

The Starks' receiving room was beautifully furnished. An expensive gilt mirror on the mantel reflected back the patchy sunlight from St Martin's Lane.

'That's the only problem with being on the better-class side of the road,' Cynthia exclaimed, pulling back the curtain. 'You get the seedy side for your view.'

'It's lovely here.' Alpiew glanced around at the up-to-the-minute carved oak high-backed chairs upholstered in the finest fabrics, lace cloths on all the tables. 'I suppose you will be using some of your savings or investments to relieve your nephew?'

'Robinson? Relieve him from what?'

'He is in prison, Mrs Stark. For debt.'

'Robinson? In prison?' She sank down upon an easy chair. 'How can that be? He was here this morning. I know of no debt. It cannot be true. He is a clever boy, especially with money.'

A pert red-headed maid lurched into the room bearing a tray with two steaming dishes of chocolate and a jug.

'He was taken today, it seems, after trying to pass a false bond. And in prison a huge debt was accounted against him.'

'False bond? Huge debt?' Cynthia whipped out her fan and fluttered it around her face. 'Good lord. Someone must tell Edward. Lord, lord, lord!'

'According to a girl in the prison, his first worry was that his family might get dragged into it.'

'Family? Why should we be his worry?' Cynthia was flushed and flustered by the news. 'We are far from being in debt.'

'Has he any other relatives living, maybe?' Alpiew gulped down a mouthful of chocolate and dipped a sugar knot before sucking it. 'Other uncles or aunts, for instance? Your brothers and sisters?'

'No.'

'Of course, Mrs Stark, as his only living relation, if he should die in prison, or if he absconded, you would become responsible for his debt.'

'But he cannot . . . How has this . . . ?' Cynthia's fan stopped for a moment. Alpiew felt the air grow still. 'Do you know, Mrs Alpiew, I am going to make a confession to you. As well now as ever.' The fan started wafting slowly as Cynthia leaned forward and lowered her voice to a hoarse whisper. 'Robinson is no nephew of mine. I have *no* relatives. And, my father aside, I never did. Except my husband, of course.'

'No brothers or sisters, alive or dead, you mean?'

'No brothers, sisters or nephews. No blood relatives. My mother died giving birth to me, her first, and, obviously, only child.' The fan picked up rhythm again. Cynthia looked down. 'And my father died two years ago. Dear Dad . . .'

'But Robinson says . . . ?'

'He is my husband's apprentice. We *bought* him from the poor house. My husband wanted an heir to train up in the business. So we got an orphan boy.'

'I'm sorry?' Alpiew tried to think back on everything Cynthia and Robinson had said. 'You always both refer to each other as aunt and nephew . . .'

'And if you had listened closely you would have heard that it is almost a game with us. I assure you, we bought him from the parish some six years ago. His name is Robinson George. His father and mother had died, weeks apart, one upon the other, he told us. He had been running wild in the streets for some years before being taken in by the poor house. He kept running away.' Cynthia rested her fan as she slurped down a long draught of chocolate. 'I like a bit of spirit in a child, don't you? That's why I chose Robinson over all the others. He also already seemed to have a good understanding of mathematics and money, or, rather, should I say finance, so Edward was happy to choose him over other, quieter boys.'

'Had Robinson ever been in prison before?'

'Before he came to us, you mean? He was eleven when we took him in. And the poor house said nothing about that to us. And he has certainly never seen the inside of a prison in the years he has been with us.' She sighed, resting her hand on her belly. 'He was always well behaved and polite. Just the sort of boy Edward wanted around him. Things may change rather dramatically soon, though. Perhaps my husband will get what he really wants. Merchants are a strange breed, you know. You cannot predict their behaviour unless it concerns the getting of money, and then they are only too predictable.' She picked up a biscuit and slowly crumbled it into crumbs on her plate. 'Do you know, Mistress Alpiew, things have changed so dramatically since I was a child. In those days a merchant was considered only a short step above the night-soil men and pig-swillers. They were the lowest of the low. Today they practically rule the town. Will you be going back to see Robinson?' Cynthia rose and moved over to a small escritoire on a table in the corner. 'I must write him a note. Could you take it for me?'

'Of course,' said Alpiew. And she could have a jolly good read of it en route, she thought. 'Why do you pretend Robinson is your nephew if he is not?'

'It is nicer to be a family.' Cynthia dipped a quill into her inkhorn. 'My husband was all for the boy being treated like the modern apprentices, to be made to wear a blue apron, paid nothing and forced to sleep in the kitchen or wherever he could find.' She scratched the note, while Alpiew stood beside the desk, fiddling with pens and pencils on the top. 'People say that that is the à la mode way, that it is more genteel to be seen to have an apprentice and treat him like an inferior and display your rising status in the world of trade.' Cynthia folded the letter and lit a candle to warm the sealing wax. 'But I say if you treat a person like an animal, they will behave like one.' She handed Alpiew the note and moved back to the tea-table, where she emptied the dish of chocolate.

Alpiew picked up a piece of pasteboard from the desk. It was the size of an average piece of paper, but scored with a chequer pattern. Some of the chequered squares were cut out, like a maccabean screen.

'What is this?' Alpiew held up the card.

'Oh, that thing.' Cynthia poured another cup of chocolate and sipped at it. 'It's something Robinson was always playing with. I don't know. I always thought it was something embroiderers might use to mark out their frame, but it must be mathematical, I suppose, for all his business dealings.'

'Can I take it?' Alpiew put it with the note. 'To give to him, I mean. Perhaps it will be useful to him in there.'

'Yes. Do.' Cynthia looked down. 'Oh . . . I detest this life of cold business and money, and how it ruins people's lives . . .'

Alpiew thought Cynthia looked as though she was on the verge of tears. But when she saw Alpiew watching her she pulled herself together with a wan smile. 'And I was right to pick him. Robinson has always been a delight to me, and more than a delight . . .'

While Cynthia chattered, Alpiew's mind was running on ahead. Robinson was a parish orphan, and not related to the Starks at all. But he had confessed in Ludgate that there was somebody, somebody with whom he was 'united by blood'. And the blood, rather than familial, presumably was of a more palpable, sanguinary nature, where blood meant blood spilled. That person had to be Lettice Dainty.

'Mrs Stark, you know about Sir Richard Dainty and his ward, Lettice? I was wondering . . . Sir Richard is an old man. He can hope to live about ten years. And, if he lasts that long, Lettice will have only just come of age. If and when Sir Richard dies, as the child's guardian, would his fortune automatically pass to her?'

'It depends upon his will. And with that old pinchpenny, who can say? I always think my husband is the worst hunks in Town, but compared to a skinflint like Sir Richard he is positively munificent. As his ward, the girl would have no rights upon Sir Richard's estate, as she is not a blood relative.'

'Really? How came she to be his ward?'

'My husband had a hand in that. The child had been turned over to the parish. St Bride's as I remember. And for some reason Sir Richard was responsible for all the girl's fees and charges. I don't know how. But anyhow, my husband pointed out to him that the price the parish charges to keep a child, it would be cheaper to keep the girl himself. Sir Richard didn't like the idea at all, but could see that it would save him money. And my husband suggested that he could train the girl up to wait upon him, as a girl apprentice, until she was old enough to be his housekeeper. And, as you see, he is going to make her more than that.'

'When Lettice comes of age and ceases to be his apprentice, he will have to pay her, you mean?' Alpiew was still trying to piece together the motives behind Lettice's dealings with Robinson and Sir Richard. 'By marrying the girl, Sir Richard would get a housekeeper who works for nothing?'

'There have been worse reasons for marriage.' Cynthia gazed out of the window and smiled. 'The old boy seems to have developed quite a fondness for little Lettice. I wouldn't worry about her too much. Not only because she is very young, but remember he is very old, and very, very rich. In return for a little subservience, in no time at all she will be rewarded by inheriting a great fortune.'

Suddenly Alpiew understood everything. Robinson and Lettice were certainly in this together, and it was a very clever game they were playing. 'I am sorry, Mrs Stark. I have just seen the time. I am late for an appointment.'

Once out of the street she bowled along St Martin's Lane, passing a crowd pushing into Old Slaughter's Coffee House. A hand reached out and grabbed her.

'Mistress Alpiew! How are you coming along with that Queries column?' It was Mr Cue, ruddy and sweaty as usual, but rather than the usual inky mess, his clothes were spruce and clean.

'Mr Cue, how strange! I am this minute racing to meet a man at Jonathan's who knows the answer to the eternally intriguing question: "Where do swallows go each winter?"'

'Humph! I thought everyone knew that.' Mr Cue seemed disappointed in Alpiew's proposition. 'It is a well-known fact where swallows go. They dive under water and sleep out the cold season on the bottoms of ponds.'

'Aha! So they say, Mr Cue,' said Alpiew, freeing herself, ready to run on. 'But I believe I have just found a cove with a much more plausible explanation. I shall drop the column into your office tonight.'

'Really?' Mr Cue caught her again. 'But you failed to follow up on the story the Countess told my wife about a certain Captain Caruso.'

'The monkey?'

'Monkey? My wife said he was a dragoon.'

'A dragon?' said a pretty woman at Cue's side. 'That would make a nice engraving.'

'A dragoon,' said Mr Cue. 'You know, in the army.'

'They let monkeys in the army now?' said the woman.

'Ah well, Mr Cue! Whatever the position, the truth will out.' Alpiew was totally baffled, but beamed a smile and tapped her nose.

Mr Cue shot her a puzzled look and took a step away from the pretty woman beside him.

Alpiew used the time bowling along the Strand to run through the facts.

The one thing that seemed clear was that Robinson and Lettice had plotted Sir Richard's death together. But something had disturbed their plan. The wedding had been interrupted a few sentences too early to assure them of the old man's fortune. And, as the plan had misfired, it was important for the conniving twosome that no one should know the old man was dead until the details of his will were known, otherwise they might end up with nothing. After all, as his ward, Lettice could expect her guardian to leave her some money in trust. And that is why Sir Richard's body had disappeared. Lettice and Robinson were depending on the corpse staying quietly in the trunk in the Countess's attic until they were sure. Alpiew remembered that Lettice had been very eager to come back with them to the Countess's house that evening – to check that the body was still there and safely hidden, she supposed. The girl had been exceedingly keen to go upstairs. But the unexpected arrival of O'Hara and Timony had ruined her scheme. She must have dropped the keys down the back when she was surprised by the two criminals.

After the O'Hara incident, Lettice must have realised that Alpiew and the Countess had accidentally stumbled across the old man's body, so Robinson and she had somehow arranged for it to be removed the next day. This would explain the ransacking of the dead man's office too – Robinson must have been there in the house during the night, looking for the will. No doubt when she and the Countess had come into the house he had just gone out for a bit of breakfast.

This also explained why Lettice was constantly drivelling on about wanting to find the miserable churl Sir Richard. She had to *seem* to want him back, in order to make their cover story more plausible.

What an innocent-looking pair of fiends! Now she must find out exactly *when* Robinson had previously been in prison. She would find someone at Ludgate, and if necessary press on across London Bridge to Southwark and try the people at the Clink.

As she approached Ludgate, Alpiew stopped to catch her breath. She pulled out the note Cynthia Stark had written: *I will come to you, love, Aunt.* Ah well. Not much in that then.

She peeked into the prisoners' grille, hoping to find the girl she had spoken to earlier.

No one was there.

She called into the dank void.

No reply. All the prisoners must be at the trough.

What kind of a prison was this Ludgate that no one wanted to beg for pennies?

'Ludgate!' she exclaimed aloud. '*Lud* gate!' The note on the table had said *Lud R. Gibb.* Perhaps Robinson's real name was Gibb? Robinson Gibb. And the note referred to him coming to Ludgate. But could Robinson have predicted that he would be thrown into prison here? Alpiew's own personal experience of arresting officers was that they threw you anywhere, willy-nilly, usually the place nearest to where they had picked you up. Lud? Perhaps by chance he had arranged a meeting here.

Alpiew looked up at the City gate, with its niches and stone statues, its huge oaken door and its swinging gibbets.

A gibbet to her left and a gibbet to her right!

Gibbet . . . right and left. *R. Gibb* . . . Lud.

Alpiew would expect these gibbets to contain the bodies from the recent executions. She looked up, watching the rusty iron cage with its black grisly contents as it slowly turned in the wind.

A man on horseback galloped by, making her leap back from the road. A coach rumbled past in his wake.

Alpiew moved closer. Both gibbets were occupied. The cages dangled so high they were hard to investigate unless you were on horseback.

In the gibbet to her left, Alpiew could see the tarred and quartered corpse of the old coiner they had seen half-hanged at Tyburn.

Darting through the traffic which bowled through the gate, Alpiew tried to see inside the right gibbet, but it had swung round to such an angle she could only see the rear of the pitch-painted cadaver. She clambered up on to a post, stretched out her hand and, with the tips of her fingers, knocked the cage so that it swung and span round. It swayed slightly as it caught in the wind, a trickle of water pouring on to the cobbles below.

But as it revolved Alpiew could quite clearly make out the macabre sight.

The tar-blackened corpse was Sir Richard Dainty.

She gaped up, disbelieving. Through the black lumpy pitch it was clear Sir Richard's stomach had been removed.

Alpiew needed desperately to talk to the Countess, but realised that she would endanger them both if she turned up at Pigalle's front door during the hours of daylight. Once darkness fell she planned to climb in over the wall of St James's Park and enter through the garden. Meanwhile she would spend the evening trying to find out about the bond which had got Robinson arrested, and writing up some Query nonsense for the *Trumpet's* new column.

Maggie, the serving girl for whom Alpiew had previously covered at Garraway's, was only too happy to let Alpiew fill in for an hour while she caught up with a last-minute bit of shopping at the New Exchange.

Alpiew rolled up her sleeves and set to her job, brewing and serving coffee. The damp, worked up into a mist from the heat of the coffee equipment, and the blazing fire, mingled with the smoke from scores of pipes, filled the room with a grey fog.

After a minute or two at the coffee engine Alpiew surveyed the room. A young man sitting alone in the corner, his face buried in today's *Gazette*, waved her over to bring him another dish.

'I hear a young cove by the tag of Robinson was taken earlier,' she said as she placed the steaming bowl on his table. 'Pity! My friend was sweet on him.'

'Really?' said the young man, not looking up from the newspaper and taking a long drag on his pipe. 'I only just came in here.' He blew out.

Engulfed in a low cloud of smoke, Alpiew looked around for another likely fellow to chat with. As she walked over to a crowded table two men burst in and came up to the counter.

'A dish each,' said one, excitedly pulling his jacket off and slinging it over a nearby bench. 'They're on their way here.' Eagerly he rubbed his hands. 'Some prince and his entourage. The Garraway's traders will be the first in London to get in our bids.'

'I heard that the Prince cannot speak English – not a word,' said his friend, '. . . so the man's eunuch does all the interpreting.'

'Oooh! I'm sure we can have a bit of fun tickling up a eunuch for tips!'

Both men guffawed, picked up their coffees and slurped.

'Were you here earlier, gentlemen?' Alpiew proffered a knife for the sugar loaf. 'When that pretty boy, Robinson, was taken?'

'Robinson was taken?' The first man laughed as he started hacking at the sugar loaf. 'That saucy whipper-snapper! What was he taken for? Making too much profit?'

'They say he passed a rogue bond.' Alpiew looked around to see whether anyone else here had anything to add. 'In this very room.'

'I heard Van Loon's man had set the constables upon him.' A man further along the long table leaned forward, eager to tell. 'Robinson was drawing funds against Sir Richard Dainty, but Myn Heer Van Hollander, in the Exchange in his hermetically sealed chair, was presented with the bond, and he said it was definitely a fake and got his chairmen to turn the headboroughs on the boy.'

A rumbling of excited chatter filled Exchange Alley. Both men peered out through the small latticed windows.

'Van Loon?' Alpiew needed to keep them on the subject. 'The strange fellow who has his orifices plugged up with herbal bungs, you mean? Did he see the bond? How did he know it was a forgery?'

'It was brought out to him,' said the man at the table. 'He thrust it back through the sash and yelled his head off. "This is a fake!" he yelled. "Sir Richard could not have sent me this thing. Impossible." Oh, he went on and on. He said Sir Richard was finished, over, out of the picture, something about having his guts. I don't know. Like guts for garters, I suppose. He gibbered on and on like a mad thing till his chairmen carried him off. No more business after that fake bond.'

'Sir Richard finished? In what way finished? Did he say?'

'For letting such a thing happen? I don't know. That

Dutchman is as mad as March butter.' He laughed. 'A Dutchman – butter! Ha ha ha!'

Alpiew tried to smirk at the man's feeble pun as the door burst open and a further gaggle of excited businessmen bundled in, pulling off their cloaks.

'Make room there for His Royal Highness Prince Ajumako of the Kingdom of Kong.'

Everyone turned away from Alpiew. The long table was hastily cleared, and eager businessmen sprang up, ready to talk money with the gracious foreign visitor. Another entourage of men, sweating from their march from the Royal Exchange, pushed into the coffee house.

'Kong, this chap's country, usually only trades with the Americans and the Dutch, I have heard, so we are lucky he is visiting us at all.'

'Where exactly is Kong?' said Alpiew, who couldn't care less.

'Somewhere between Dahomey and the Sahara, I believe. Apparently there is an abundance of gold, silver, ivory, copper, cocoa – hundreds of profitable things.'

'Really?' Alpiew was dismayed. She could not believe the bad timing of this royal visit. Who would talk to her about Robinson now? And she was stuck in this wretched smoky hole till the regular girl came back, another half an hour at least.

'It's a disaster for people holding shares in RAC and AAA.' A blue-coated man rubbed his hands. 'All of the African enterprises will be shaky once we've pulled off decent deals with this new fellow.'

'If he's selling.'

The Prince, fabulously dressed in swathes of opulent silks and satins, a feathered turban adding to his already tall stature, had to stoop to enter the coffee house. A small blackamoor boy carried the train of his cloak, and scurrying along at his side came his eunuch, a fat, bald thing in blue pantaloons and a golden smock.

Sighing, Alpiew pushed the coffee engine over the heat, ready to serve.

With great dignity His Royal Highness lowered himself into the space which had been cleared at the long table. Behind him the eunuch slowly flapped a long-handled fan which occasionally scraped the ceiling, knocking showers of dust from the oak chandelier on to the fawning men below.

Alpiew brought a tray of coffee.

The eunuch coughed. Not surprising with all the smoke, thought Alpiew, pressing forward to lay down the tray and arrange the coffee bowls.

The eunuch rubbed against her. Alpiew groaned in disgust at the sight of the flabby rotund creature.

The eunuch looked up from under long dark painted eyelashes. The plump face bore traces of lip-rouge, and blinked through heavily kohled eyes. Alpiew looked away, revolted.

The eunuch gave her a nudge, and a wink. Alpiew did not ever enjoy being propositioned, but this was the first time she had been flirted with by a real freak. She spun round, ready to let forth a string of invective, and only just stopped herself crying aloud as she came eye to eye with the eunuch.

The bizarre flabby creature that stood before her was none other than her mistress, Lady Anastasia Ashby de la Zouche, the Countess. Her un-wigged, nearly bald head was shaved quite bare.

The Prince of Kong was Cupid, the waiting boy was Pigalle's Mustapha.

Looking more closely, she recognised most of their clothing too. It was a melange of Pigalle's bedcovers and curtains.

'Bambara ndongo mpumbu coffee,' said Cupid.

'He'd like a cup of coffee,' said the Countess, in a weird accent somewhere between French and Irish. 'And for me a dish of chocolate, very sweet.'

Mustapha pulled at the Countess's smock.

'And the same for the pretty child, of course.'

A gaggle of men pulled out money and offered it to Alpiew to cover the cost of the royal cup of coffee.

Cupid had told the Countess that to pass for the language of Kong he would reel off a list of every town and country he knew in Africa. It seemed to be working.

'Igbo asante teke,' he said in a sonorous tone. 'Sir Richard Dainty?'

'His Royal Highness wonders if any of you have done dealings with Sir Richard Dainty?' translated the Countess. 'Who once cheated him.'

A short hiatus followed as the businessmen looked around. Then as one they all raised their voices, trying to offer their own personal stories of swindles perpetrated against them.

'Sir Richard would have been in contact with the Prince, I suppose,' said a grovelling little man in a buff suit, 'when he served as governor out there in Bambara all those years ago.'

The Countess sighed. This was not what she needed. Some know-it-all shoving the conversation in the wrong direction. She gave Cupid a kick under the table.

'Kakongo ovambo ghat,' he said quickly.

'His Royal Highness would like to meet with Sir Richard's enemies, if there are any you know of here in London.'

The babble which arose named almost everyone who frequented the Royal Exchange.

During a brief hiatus the man reading the paper, who had until this moment kept out of the skirmish for Cupid's attention, raised his head and said, 'Don't forget Van Loon.'

'Sir Hendrick Van Loon?' asked Alpiew. 'The fellow with the plugs up his nose?'

'Yes.

'But he is Sir Richard's partner . . .'

'Hmm!' The man raised his brows in an inscrutable way and lifted his paper.

'Come along now. Order!' The man in buff tapped a great ledger with the end of a long battered quill. 'Is His Royal Highness selling?'

'Sahara congo?' said the Countess to Cupid, suddenly realising that in order for this translating idea to work, the language had to go both ways. Her knowledge of geography was not the best. 'Madagascar?' she added quietly.

Cupid suppressed a smile.

The Countess had not planned on doing business here. She was only in Garraway's to ask a few questions, but now realised she had to go ahead with the charade of a sale or they would soon be discovered for the impostors they were.

Trading started.

While the men round the table bid and outbid each other for shares in gold, silver, copper and stashes of ivory, the man in buff scratched all the details into the ledger.

Within half an hour Cupid and the Countess had sold a huge portfolio of non-existent stock in an imaginary business and gathered running credit notes totalling almost £800.

'Company name?' asked the man in buff, as he prepared to fill in the title page.

'African . . . Royal . . .' The Countess looked down at the bills of exchange. 'Selling . . .' She rooted around for a business-like word to round it all off. '. . . Enterprises,' she said.

'*ARSE*,' wrote the man in buff.

The Prince of Kong went into a coughing fit, and Alpiew dived behind the counter.

'His Royal Highness is tired.' The Countess stepped forward and handed the long fan to Mustapha. 'We must go back to his quarters in St James's. He thanks you all for your kindness and enthusiasm, and should he need to know, erm, *sell* anything else he will come back tomorrow.'

'One more thing,' called Maggie, the serving girl, returned from her shopping trip. 'I'll set myself down for some shares too.' She turned and winked at Alpiew. 'Always fancied a spin myself.'

'Don't.' Alpiew tried to grab Maggie's arm before she handed the cash over, but she was too late. The man in buff took the girl's money, handed it to the Countess and wrote down 'half per cent' in his great ledger.

'I don't know that we understand enough about all this stuff,' said Alpiew. 'Don't gamble it.'

'Why not?' Maggie looked alarmed. 'Is there something wrong with the company?'

The Countess was glaring at Alpiew. Was she trying to get them arrested for fraud?

'I just don't think women should . . .'

'Harrumph,' said Maggie. 'You are one of those women who live in the Dark Ages, to be sure.' She took her certificate and pocketed it.

Cupid had risen and stooped again to leave the coffee house. Mustapha scampered behind him, struggling to hold both the satin train and the long fan in his small hands. The Countess, bowing and grovelling, was the last out of the door.

The breeze whipped their clothing as they paraded along Exchange Alley.

'That wind gets to parts others cannot reach,' Cupid

murmured, hoicking the fabric of his gown into a manageable bunch around his groin as he started up the steps to Cornhill.

'Kalahari!' warned the Countess. 'Timbuktu!'

'My Moroccos!' replied Cupid. 'Oyo.'

At the top of the steps their way was barred by a chair positioned sideways across the road.

'Make way there!' The Countess raised her voice and held up a chubby hand. 'His Royal Highness must pass.'

The chairmen were nowhere to be seen. The Countess knocked on the tin sash. It opened an inch. Van Loon's voice oozed out.

'I need to speak with de Prince of Kong. I have an offer he cannot refuse.'

Cupid and the Countess exchanged a look.

'He does not speaka di English,' said the Countess, getting her continents muddled. 'But I canna relay your weeshes to heem.'

'I have a big order. An export to America, to my lands in Virginia.' Van Loon's oily tone was tinged with excitement. 'Twenty thousand. Twenty thousand, do you hear? I can pay the prince in glass beads and guns.'

'Ujiji?' asked Cupid.

'He's Sir Richard Dainty's partner,' said the Countess. 'Hendrick Van Loon.' She bent in to speak through the small gap. 'Twenty thousand of what exactly?' she asked.

Cupid raised his long fingers, pulled down his lace collar and stroked the silver band around his neck.

'Blacks,' growled Hendrick Van Loon. 'Twenty thousand men for de plantations.'

Gently, Cupid moved the Countess aside, stepped forward and pulled down the tin sash.

Inside the confines of his chair the Dutchman flapped, shoving the plugs further into his nostrils and pressing the handkerchief tight to his gaping mouth. He struggled to push the sash up, but Cupid held it fast.

'The answer is no,' said Cupid.

Then slowly and with tremendous force he smashed his fist into Van Loon's face.

SEVEN

Wrythening — moulding with a twist

Alpiew used up the rest of her time in Garraway's washing up the many dishes used by the men who had mobbed Cupid. Once the gaggle of men had left, proudly clutching their portfolios, the only customer remaining was the quiet man with the newspaper.

'Interesting what you said earlier about Van Loon,' said Alpiew with a casual air. 'It's a dog-eat-dog world, isn't it? Hating his own partner.'

'Frequently the way of things. I don't know that he *hates* him, but it's certain he don't trust him. They seem to be friends, as far as either could be friends with anyone. But Van Loon suspects Sir Richard. That I know.'

'Suspects him of what?'

'Who knows, but why else does he pay some boy to spy upon him?'

'Really! A spying boy?'

'One of the dusty boys. The City Black-Guard they call themselves. Ragamuffins one and all. You must have seen them about. Cutpurses and pick-pockets by trade, they pride themselves upon not taking public money from living on the parish. They roam around in small gangs, always grey with dirt. They do anything for money, and are well known for their linguistic party tricks.'

'How do you know about this boy?' Alpiew wondered if this was anything to do with the messages regarding the *Cassandra* and her cargo. 'When did it start?'

'A few days ago. I saw one of the Black-Guard boys talking through the sash of Van Loon's chair. I was surprised because the Dutch fellow is so crazy he thinks the merest whiff of someone's breath will kill him, and yet he let a filthy urchin stick his head right into the chair. I witnessed the boy take money too.'

'But how do you know what Van Loon was paying the boy for?'

'My interest got the better of me. I was out walking to take the air. It was one of those balmy nights last week. I had nothing better to do, so, out of mere curiosity I followed the boy. And the boy followed old man Dainty home from the Exchange. And whenever Sir Richard went inside anywhere, the boy set up camp outside until Sir Richard came out.'

'When did you last see the boy – or Sir Richard, and it come to that?'

'I saw them both yesterday afternoon. The boy followed him out of here after the false news of the *Cassandra* sinking. Naturally Sir Richard has kept a low profile since then. He made a lot of money out of that bogus intelligence. I have to wonder whether he had any part in issuing the information about the ship going down.'

'Where would I find this boy?'

'I don't even know that I'd recognise him again. Except for the dust. And look at how many dusty boys there are. You'll see them roaming the streets at holidays and wherever a crowd gathers. And every night, after the taverns spill out the last rob-able drunks, they slink away to their night quarters, one presumes to share out their booty and plan their next attacks.'

'And where are the Black-Guard quarters?'

'Somewhere warm, sheltered and very dusty.'

When Alpiew entered St James's Park it was dark. As she emerged from behind a bush a cow lowed and flapping ducks spattered about on the water. She pressed herself tight to the wall, hoping she had counted the right number of houses to Pigalle's. It would be very embarrassing if she found herself in the wrong garden. Which of the dukes, earls and viscounts who were Pigalle's neighbours would believe she was not a night-budge, coming to burgle them?

Alpiew dug her fingers into the cement pointing and started to climb the wall.

The cow gave another loud moo.

As she got a grip, Alpiew heard the feathery sound of footsteps on wet grass behind her. She was glad there was no moon tonight. Grabbing the top of the wall, she hauled herself up, and sat astride, legs dangling.

She looked down, but could see nothing moving in the park. She turned and faced the Duchesse's house. Pigalle was still up. Through the curtains the glow of candles in the first-floor room painted shimmering yellow vertical lines on the velvet black wall.

Alpiew swung both legs over and dropped softly down on to the grass below. She arrived at the kitchen door and gave a quiet tap. After a while she heard someone inside.

'It's me,' she hissed, her face right up to the panelling. 'Alpiew!'

Cupid opened up, let her in and locked up after her.

'What a day!' they said in unison and laughed.

'It's very good to see you again, Alpiew.' Cupid put his arm round her shoulder as they trudged up the staircase.

'And you too.' Alpiew looked up. She could see that his dark eyes were brimming with tears.

'There's never a dull day with the Countess, is there?' he said. 'I really have missed you both.'

As they came into the room Pigalle was pouring spumante into a row of elegant drinking glasses. 'I have a man who brings me this stuff all ze way from Piedmont on a horse. But ze cost of zat is as nothing to these glasses. Are they not ze most beautiful?' Pigalle lifted one and gazed at a candle through it. 'Flint glass. Ze latest in glassware.' She flicked it with her fingernail. 'It sings to you.'

'Which song?' The Countess seized a glass and sipped the sweet sparkling wine. '"Blowzabella My Bouncing Doxy"?'

Pigalle handed a fizzing glass to Cupid.

'Look at that for a big knop!'

'Olympe, please!' wailed the Countess. 'Don't embarrass the poor boy.'

'What are you talking about? *Zut*, Ashby, you have a mind from ze *égout*.' Pigalle pointed her taloned finger at the stem of the wine glass. 'You see this nice round bauble in ze stem? Zat is a knop. In this case it is a quatrefoil knop. Very expensive, I assure you.' She handed Alpiew a glass, and returned to sip at her own. 'And you may also notice zat my own glass is diamond-point engraved with my name.'

The Countess stooped forward to take a closer look. 'Not written by the steadiest of hands, dear. It looks like "Piss all" from here.'

'You always had bad eyes, darling. If I were you, I would invest in some spectacles.' She snatched the glass away from the Countess's view and raised it high. 'A toast to us all.'

Pigalle took a great slurp of champaign and looked narrowly at her friend. 'Now you must sort out how to get yourselves out of zis mish-mosh.' She took a step back, tripped over a guitar which lay on the floor and tumbled into an easy chair. 'You don't want to stay here forever in hiding.' She sipped, not having spilled a drop of her drink.

'I'm feeling cold, Olympe.' The Countess rubbed her bald pate. 'Where is my wig?'

'Ah! Ze wig!' Pigalle quaffed her drink in one and rose to top it up. 'A little accident . . .'

'Accident?'

'Ze sexy monkey ran off with it.'

'Sexy monkey? You mean Millicent? Then let us get Mustapha to fetch it off her.'

'Not *my* monkey. A smartly dressed boy monkey. He comes here for . . . *baiser* with my little Millicent.' Pigalle grimaced and puckered her wrinkled, scarlet lips. 'Ooh, Olympe, but he is some stud, zat monkey. At it *so* many time a day. It is like living in ze house of a Roman emperor when he is here. A constant orgy of monkeys fucking.'

'And this fucking monkey took my wig?' The Countess slammed her glass down. 'So tell me, does this sartorially gifted satyr of a monkey by any chance wear pantaloons and a fez?'

'Don't worry, Ashby. I will treat you to a new wig tomorrow. I know a good shop with lovely second-hand ones, some of them real human hair . . .'

The Countess gave Pigalle a withering look. 'If you don't mind, Duchesse, my woman, Alpiew, and I need to talk privately. So I am retiring to my bedchamber. And in the morning I expect you to satisfy me.'

Before Pigalle could make the obvious quip, the Countess had left the room.

Before the sun was up the Countess and Alpiew decided to sneak into their home and pick up some of their things.

They each wore a long black cloak with the hood up,

and slipped in without disturbing the new watchman, who was dozing happily in his box.

While Pigalle looked for a replacement, the Countess was wearing a wig usually used by the Duchesse for amateur theatricals. It was threaded through with filaments of gold yarn and flowers and dyed a startling shade of pink. 'At least after yesterday's visitors we are returning to a nice tidy kitchen.' She put down the hood and marched along the hall.

Alpiew strode ahead and fumbled about in the darkness till she found a candle and lit it. 'Ahem!' she coughed, holding up the light. 'Not any more.'

The place was a mess. Papers were strewn everywhere, the bedclothes lay in tousled piles on the table. The mattresses and pillows had been ripped open. Down and feathers settled like snow on every surface.

'Pshaw, Alpiew, our house is become like Cheapside on Lord Mayor's Day so many people come through it. Who has been here this time?'

'More to the point, what do they all *want* here?' Alpiew pulled open a drawer and rooted about. 'Robinson is already locked up. But I think we'd better question his little friend Lettice and turn her in. There's no doubt she and Robinson between them dispatched Sir Richard to lay hands on his fortune.' She shoved a couple of pencils into her pocket. 'Aha! I had forgot about this!' She pulled out the chequer-holed pasteboard square and held it up. 'Do you know what this is?'

The Countess peered at it. 'A sort of strainer made of bandbox?'

'It's a key!'

'A key?' The Countess grabbed it and took a closer look. 'Must be a very big lock.'

'It is the key to their correspondence. I *knew* they meant more. Do you have that letter?'

The Countess delved into her cleavage and pulled out the letter she had discovered at the bottom of Sir Richard's money box.

'Watch this! I know it will work.' Alpiew grabbed the letter, laid it on the table and smoothed it out. She waved the holed piece of pasteboard in the air. 'It's a card counter-cipher, an ingenious contrivance favoured by cryptographists.'

'Speak in English, please, Alpiew.'

'A code-maker's key.' She placed the pasteboard card upon the letter. 'Look!' She pointed at a line drawn under Robinson's signature. This is where you line it up. Here is another line at the side. So now it sits pat.' Alpiew's fingers ran along the line, reading out the letters left exposed by the cut-out squares: 'N-O-T-L-O-N-G-T-I . . .'

'Wait a moment.' The Countess snatched one of Alpiew's pencils. 'Let us write it down.'

'N,O,T,L,O,NG,T,I . . .' Alpiew raced through these, anxious to decode the rest of the message. 'L-L-W-E-A-R-E-F-R-E-E.'

They both gazed down at the row of letters. The Countess put slashes between the words. 'Not . . . long . . . till . . . we . . . are . . . free.'

They both gasped.

'Wormwood! Wormwood!' The Countess removed the pasteboard and gazed down at the full text of the letter. 'So they write of love, but beneath the code it is murder they are at.'

'I wonder what the other letter says. Lettice didn't even look at it when she received it. But why should she need to, when the *intended* content was only perceptible with her de-coder?'

'They planned to kill the old man. Brought him here. Took him away again. And . . . tell me, Alpiew, how did they get his body into that gibbet?'

'Rolled him there on a cart and shoved him up. Who would question a person doing that if they looked business-like about it?'

'It would be Robinson alone or with another. We know where Lettice was throughout it all. But how did the boy get access to the gibbet? They must surely be locked.'

'It's like the pillory where we first saw Mr Foe. Anyone who can pick a lock could make use of it.'

'But why did they kill the watchman too?' mused the Countess.

'Perhaps he caught them red-handed?'

The Countess looked to the yard. 'I wonder whether, after the night-soil men found the body, they still cleaned out the privy?'

'One way to find out,' said Alpiew, holding up the candle and marching outside.

Rather than be left alone in the dark, the Countess followed her.

Alpiew pulled open the privy door. 'Good lack!' She stooped to make sure she was not mistaken in what she saw. 'You know the night-watch Charlie, madam? He's still here.'

'The dead body of the watchman? Still in our privy?'

'Yes. Look!'

'So what were the night-soil men making such a racket about . . . ?'

'And why were the constable's men looking for me?'

Inside the house a door slammed.

'Quickly!' Alpiew grabbed the Countess's hand. 'We don't want to be found hovering over a corpse.'

They arrived back in the kitchen just as the hall door slowly opened.

'Lady Ashby de la Zouche?' The constable, John Shaw, stood before them. 'My sentry on the watch saw you come in.' He stood, feet splayed, hands on his hips. 'Old bugger who usually does this patch didn't turn up for duty last night. And, though we'd usually let such a thing pass and the people of German Street would go for a night without a watchman, in light of the recent manoeuvres in this house, I took the precaution of putting one of my head-boroughs on duty in his place.'

The Countess and Alpiew waited in silence. Using her heel, the Countess clicked the door to the yard shut.

'At your ease, ladies,' said the constable, sifting through a mound of feathers on the end of Alpiew's bed to clear a place for them to sit. 'You'll be in shock, I should think. And no wonder. It's like the day after the battle of Agincourt in here. But you should have seen the place yesterday . . . My word!'

'Yesterday?' The Countess raised her eyebrows, hoping her face took on an innocent air. 'We were not here. We were away . . . visiting friends.'

'So I gathered. And lucky for you. A pair of house-break-ers were found here, going about their illicit business. Anyhow, the upshot is that these nasty miscreants were caught going through your stuff. As cool as a pair of Arctic hares they were. Well, as you can imagine, a skirmish ensued and the crooks were routed, but would you believe the nerve, one of them came back here. There was a nasty scene when the night-soil men surprised him in the act of burgling you. A brawl ensued and this lad put up quite a fight.'

'My lord!' The Countess sat. 'Here in my kitchen?'

'The night-soil men mustered in the street and called for pillicoddy here, and I put a guard on the place. Naturally we needed to warn you.'

'Who were they, these burglars? Where are you hold-ing them?'

'Ah!' The constable shifted from foot to foot. 'That's why we needed to warn you. The night-soil men didn't *exactly* catch either of them, you see. They saw the one off, all right. But I was afeared he or his partner might make a return trip, so I put a patrol out to watch the house, and went off in search of you. I paid a call on someone up the road, some Frenchy going by the name Pig-All, to warn you. She claimed she hadn't seen you in weeks. Keeps a house full of freaks, I gather, so I can see why you'd steer clear of a strange-'un like her. These foreign types, you know what I mean.' He grimaced. 'Perverts all!' He leaned forward in an intimate manner and lowered his voice. 'You know, this Madame Pig-All was seen on her doorstep yesterday, kissing good-bye to some fat, bald monstrosity. What they call a "Mophrodite", I believe.' He indicated his genital area. 'You know . . . A fellow with no nuts.'

'Eunuch!' snapped the Countess.

'Exactly,' retorted the constable. 'I agree. Euch! Anyhow, ladies. I told my man out there to let me know when you returned to your abode so as I could warn you about the mess, and all.'

'In fact, Constable, you saw us come in a mere moment ago, and having seen what we have seen, we are going right out again.' The Countess realised that they now had the perfect alibi for when the night-watchman's body was found. 'Are we not, Alpiew? Thank goodness you came in to warn us about the break-ins. We will stay away until my man Godfrey is back here to guard us.'

'That dribbling nincompoop!' The constable held the door open and followed both women out. 'I wouldn't think he could protect a piece of rancid meat from a blow-fly. Do you have a friend you can stay with for a day or two, or until you've had decent locks fitted throughout the house? As it stands, I suspect you would be a temptation to any marauder from those murdering swine the night before last to any passing petty pilferer who fancied an easy prey. London is not what it was a few years ago, Countess. You can't trust anybody these days.'

Chattering about the state of affairs, and how merely walking on the streets was become a danger, and how it was too easy for the criminal to escape the consequences of their actions, the constable walked the Countess and Alpiew down to Pall Mall Street.

He gave them a salute and returned to his beat.

The Countess rapped on Sir Richard's door.

Although it was still dark, the sky was brightening and the street was busy with stallholders unloading their carts for the Hay Market.

Rubbing her eyes, a bleary Lettice let them in.

'Oh! The harpies are back.' She moved into the front room and flopped down on to the sofa. 'What do you want now?'

'We have some very bad news for you, Lettice.' The Countess perched at the end of the sofa. 'Your precious Robinson is locked up.'

'And Queen Elizabeth is dead. Tell me news.'

'Talking of dead, so is your guardian, Sir Richard. But you'd know all about that . . .'

Lettice started to speak but the Countess pressed on: '. . . and his death was brought about by you and this boy, your lover, Robinson, in order to get Sir Richard's fortune.'

'How can you? How dare you!' Lettice sprang up and grabbed at the Countess, showering her with little slaps. 'You vile old bawd, you lie! You lie! You lie!'

Alpiew surreptitiously opened a drawer and peeked inside. She was looking for any other of Robinson's letters she could decode.

'But there was a mistake in the timing of the old man's

murder, was there not? The way things should have gone are thus: he should have wed you first, then been killed. But you were not reckoning on the boy interrupting the ceremony with news about that ship before the vows were taken.'

'He is not dead. Sir Richard is alive.'

'We both know that is not true, Lettice, dear,' cooed the Countess. 'But before you let the world know where his body hangs, I realise you need to find his will.'

'You lie! You lie!' Sobbing, Lettice beat her fists against the Countess's arm. 'I tell you, Sir Richard is not dead. He is alive.'

'So where is he, Lettice? Why has he not come back here? He was about to marry you, a pretty little girl. What wrinkled old man could resist that?'

Behind them, Alpiew's hands slid gracefully through drawer after drawer.

'Once you had dispatched Sir Richard and got hold of his money, you were going to marry Robinson, I presume, and set up in splendour: a pair of City magnificos living on the dead man's wealth.'

'Do you mean it?' The girl stopped beating the Countess, gasping for breath. She lay on the sofa, her head thrown back. Her face was white, washed out. She wiped tears from her cheek with the palm of her hand. 'Is Sir Richard really dead?'

'Yes.' The Countess looked into the girl's eyes and nodded. 'He is.'

'Then all is lost.' A sob tore through the girl and she collapsed into the cushions.

'What are we to do? What are we to do?' She lifted her head again, struggling for breath. 'I need Robinson. I must speak to him. How can we find him? Oh God!'

The Countess sat still, watching her.

'I implore you, Countess. I beg you.' The girl reached out, pleading. 'Help me! Help me! What can I do?'

The Countess thought Lettice's distress seemed very convincing, but she remembered a similar moment on the wedding day, when the girl had turned and dramatically whispered, 'Save me!' Who was to say she had not all the arts of the best players at Drury Lane?

'Help you to do what, exactly?' asked the Countess.

Quietly Alpiew moved over to the window and sat, facing out, her back to the drama taking place on the sofa.

'I am frightened, Countess. Frightened in case you are *not* lying to me, and Sir Richard is indeed dead.' Lettice swallowed and ran her tongue round her lips to wet them.

'I heard you arrive.' Godfrey chose this moment to enter with a tray of hot chocolate. 'And here I am with victuals for all.'

The Countess turned and silenced him. He put the tray down and left the room.

'Do you know why I think you could be right and he might be dead?' Lettice was wiping tears from her lashes with her fingers. 'Not because he has not come back for me. But he would never run off without his money.'

'You forget, Lettice, that I have seen the bedchamber.' The Countess laughed. 'I know that his money box is gone.'

'He didn't keep any money in that box.' Wearily Lettice pushed her hair back off her tear-stained face. 'That was a bluff. He kept a few hundred guineas in a vase full of dried flowers. The bulk of his money was in paper bonds hidden all over the house. Bonds and bills of exchange. He also had something he said was so valuable it made him rival the King in wealth. He called it the Eye.'

'His glass eye? That was worth money?' The Countess was wondering whether it had still been in his eye socket when they had first found the body in her attic.

'No,' said Lettice, blowing her nose into a fine lace kerchief. 'He didn't have a glass eye.'

'He told me he was blind in one eye.'

'Yes. He was wounded when he was in the army. But *that* eye was just blind. The Eye was something else. And he always kept it around the house.'

'Whereabouts?'

'Oh, he never told me that. But he'd smile sometimes and pat his nose, and say things like, "I spy with my little eye," then cackle.'

'And what is this Eye, that it is worth so much?'

'I don't know. He talked about it, but never showed it to me. I think it must be a brooch. On our wedding day he wandered round the house singing, "I spy with my little eye" and laughing. "The Eye, the Eye! I spy the Eye!" Perhaps he was finding a new hiding place. I don't know. But when he was called away to that ship thing, he didn't have the opportunity to return and fetch the Eye, did he? He didn't come back here.' The girl looked around the room. 'And I am sure Sir Richard would not have gone away without the Eye, or without all the bills of exchange and certificates.' She walked over to the chest, pulled out a drawer and plunged her hand inside. 'I found this one the other day, crammed behind the woodwork.' She handed the Countess a bill of exchange for a hundred pounds. It was payable only to Sir Richard Dainty.

'So what was all the hubbleshow about the money chest?'

'It was his plan.' Lettice sighed. 'He must have thought you would tell people about it. It was full of books and bricks, to make it very heavy. He wanted people to think that it was full of money, so that if thieves were to come here they would take it and not bother to look for the rest. They did take it, after all, the same day that he vanished.'

The girl cocked her head and took a step back from the Countess. 'Oh no! It was *you*, wasn't it? You took his money box. I know he took you upstairs and showed it to you on our wedding day. And you insisted on hanging about here in the house all that day. And then the thing was taken from here and it was taken *there*, wasn't it, to your house? I saw it. I saw it in that room you were so hasty to lock. It wasn't just a trunk the same as his, it *was* his trunk. You stole it!' She backed away, holding her hands up. 'What do you want from me? Who are you? What have you done to Sir Richard? What?'

'Believe me, we are concerned for you and were not responsible for the old man's death.' The Countess stepped forward, appeasing. 'What benefit would it be to us to kill him? And why would we come here to you? But we are all involved now, and none of us want to end up swinging from a rope for something we did not do.'

'Eris!' said Alpiew suddenly, rising from the window seat. 'What does it mean?'

Lettice spun round, grabbing on to a chair-back, and stared at Alpiew.

'Why does Robinson write you a letter in code where the message is just two words? The first is "Remember", the second just those four letters: ERIS.' Alpiew held up the letter and her code-card, and pointed at the window pane. 'The same four letters which are scratched here on the window. The window where you so frequently sit, staring out at the street.'

The girl stared at the scratched window, then at the letter and Alpiew, then back at the Countess. She looked like a wounded, cornered animal.

'Take me to Robinson,' she said quietly. 'Now!' she screamed. 'Now!'

*   *   *

Having demanded to be brought to the prison where Robinson was held, she sat in the corner of the cab and resolutely refused to speak.

As the coach passed along the Strand, Alpiew whispered to the Countess to look out as they passed through Ludgate, to see the gibbet.

'Where is Sir Richard's body?' Lettice asked. 'It is somewhere near here, isn't it? Is that what you are whispering about? I need to see it, then I will really believe you, and know that my nightmare has come true.'

'But didn't you write the note? You know where to find him.' Alpiew pulled the paper from her pocket. 'Look at the bottom of your note! Did you not write "Lud R. Gibb"?'

'Any fool can see that is writ in quite another hand to mine. I wrote the rest of the note, you watched me write it, and I left it behind in the house. It was to say that I was going with you to German Street. I left it on the table so that when Sir Richard came home he would know where to find me. But that inscription at the bottom must have been added after I had left with you. Oh, fatal night. What is to become of me?'

The Countess thought the child wore such a weary air of dejection she seemed more than twice her age.

'It ain't pretty, the old man's body,' said Alpiew. 'It is tarred.'

'Show it to me, then I will believe he is dead. Not until then.' She clutched tight to the leather strap, her knuckles showing white through the fragile young skin.

Alpiew called to the hackney-driver to stop at Ludgate.

'Lud – R. Gibb,' said Alpiew. 'So whoever wrote that note knew about the old man's death, we can presume. Ludgate, you see. R. Gibb, right gibbet.'

The Countess and the girl looked up, their eyes following Alpiew's gesture. As the gibbet slowly turned and Sir Richard's blackened face came into view, Lettice put her own face into her hands and wailed like a banshee.

In the Countess's opinion Southwark by day was not much of an improvement on Southwark by night. The prostitutes were still plying their trade, and the vile smell from stalls selling cooked meats and the nearby brew-houses and tanneries was, if anything, worse when the sun was up, warming everything. The river bank was busy with craft crossing and barges loading and unloading. Nearby a public cesspit on the bankside steamed, adding its own tincture to the general stink.

The coach rattled along Pepper Alley and Montague Close. The Countess put her handkerchief to her nose. 'Don't tell me people really live in this malodorous place.' She flapped her fan.

Lettice groaned. When the coach pulled to a stop in Clink Street she was still sobbing.

Alpiew paid the driver and they alighted at the entry to St Saviour's Stairs. A gang of wherrymen sat laughing on the steps, their boats bobbing away behind them on the glistening river. They were tucking into a shared breakfast, a huge meat pie and tankards of small beer. The mutton fat gleamed from their chins. One of the men lifted his head to joke at the crying girl, but the Countess shot him such a look he simply bit into his portion of pie and looked out to the river.

The Countess presented herself to the gatekeeper, who led them all into the chief turnkey's office. The Countess explained that she was acting as Robinson's financial advisor and was come here upon business which might lead to the payment of the boy's debtors, therefore she needed to consult with him. She needed Alpiew to be with her as scrivener, and Lettice's father, she said, was one of the bondholders who might provide funds.

It was arranged for Robinson to be taken to one of the condemned cells where they could talk in privacy.

The three women were led down some steps and along a long damp stone-flagged corridor lined with cells. Prisoners rattled their chains as the entourage passed. Cupped hands were thrust through the wicket gates. 'Spare a farthing, madam? Spare a groat?'

The turnkey opened a cell door. The place was dark, lit only by a grille in the ceiling which led directly to the street above.

Huddled on a stone bench, Robinson darted a look from the Countess and Alpiew to Lettice.

'Why are you here? What conspiracy are you cooking up against me?' He turned his head away from Lettice. 'Has that old devil of a guardian been at you again?'

'No, Robinson. Sshhh!' Lettice put her finger to his lips and sank down beside him. 'The time has come to tell.'

'Tell what, Miss Dainty?' He jumped to his feet and strode away from her. 'Just because a boy has a month's mind to you, miss, do you have to bring more suffering to my already perilous plight?'

'Robinson, stop! Stop!' The child was crying, her voice shaken with tears. 'The old man is dead. Dead! I have seen his body.'

Robinson looked at her in silence. Their eyes held contact for a few seconds, then he lurched backwards, his legs giving way. He leaned against the dank wall, gasping for breath. 'And you did not marry him first?'

Lettice shook her head.

'You did *not* marry him?' Robinson repeated.

Lettice's reply was little more than a sigh. 'No.'

'And he is dead?'

'Yes.'

Robinson howled. 'Then truly we are ruined.' He flopped down on to the wet flagstones and thrust his face into his hands. 'Oh, sister! Sister!'

Lettice rushed to him. They clung tight to one another, crying into each other's shoulders.

'I know, Brother, I know.'

'You are brother and sister?' The Countess edged nearer, running her mind back through all she had seen and heard pass between them.

'Yes.' Robinson gently wiped a tear from Lettice's cheek. 'Lettice is my baby sister.'

'But you are a parish orphan . . .' Alpiew was trying to recall what Cynthia had told her. 'With the surname George.'

'Ay.' Robinson smiled. 'St George's Parish, Southwark. Hard by this place. Our mother died here. In this prison. Perhaps in this very cell.'

'But Lettice's name is . . .'

'Bride,' said Lettice. 'St Bride's, over the river.'

'She was a baby when I took her from this prison, and I kept her safe until the day I left her for the parish, hiding in an alley over the road and peeping and peeping to make sure no harm came to her. As long as she did not seem to be related to me, I hoped my plan would work, and that one day the old man would pay us.'

'What has the old man to do with this?'

'Everything,' said Robinson. 'Sir Richard Dainty killed my parents.'

'He murdered them, you mean?' The Countess was bewildered. 'You just said your mother died in this prison, so how . . . ?'

'He ruined my father, then my mother, and now, see, even in death he has caught up with me.'

Alpiew and the Countess helped Lettice and Robinson up and sat with them on the bench, while Robinson told his tale.

'Our father was a goldsmith. A man of means. He had

a successful business in the City. He loaned and kept money before there were banks to do it. He also provided insurance for ships, and in return he took a good share of the profit of those ships which came safely home. Until, one day, he undertook to insure a ship for Sir Richard Dainty. The merchantman was sailing from Virginia, laden with all kinds of goods: tobacco, sugar, rum, ivory, gold. Sir Richard saw the ship off from America and accounted for a cargo worth thousands, even millions of pounds. But the ship went down in the Atlantic. All hands were lost. And the cargo lies deep in an ocean trench, well out of reach of human hands forever.

'When Sir Richard arrived back in London some weeks later, he put in a claim against my father: unlimited liability. The figure was more than the sum of all my father's possessions. When he could not pay, Sir Richard took out a charge against him on mesne process, and had him thrown into debtors' prison with a writ of capias ad satisfaciendum. Once inside the debt went up and up, with interest, prison charges and gaoler's fees. The law ruled that he should stay inside until the debt was paid in full. And so Sir Richard could keep him in gaol for life, and it was perfectly legal. My mother was reduced to living upon the parish. I was seven and she was with child – Lettice. She had to walk about the streets wearing the red P of poverty upon her outer garments. My father cried when he saw that because of his miserable dealings with Sir Richard she was all but branded.'

'To claim a debt against someone is not to kill him,' said the Countess. 'I have had debts taken against me more times than I care to mention, and yet, as you see, I live.'

Robinson continued in a flat voice. 'My father hanged himself. He believed by dying he would end the whole business; he would expunge the debt, and we, at least –

his wife, son and unborn child – would be free to live a decent life. But he had not reckoned with Sir Richard Dainty's greed. The old man continued to press for recovery of the debt from my mother. She was taken up by the bailiffs and thrown into Ludgate. You see, as she discovered that day, just as a widow might inherit her husband's fortune, so she does his debt.'

Marching feet echoed along the corridor outside Robinson's cell. There was a jangle of keys and the Countess feared it was gaolers coming to tell them their time was up.

'While my mother was inside, I slept in doorways, foraging for food on the streets after market days and fairs, begging from strangers, scavenging among the waste-tips in Tottenham Court Road, and every day I came to the prison to see her, and brought her any tid-bits I could. Tortured with the horror of leaving me, a boy of seven, to roam the streets while she languished in prison, she went into early labour. It was snowing outside, I remember, that evening as I spoke to my mother through the prison grille, but she was in a sweat, whether it was the pangs of childbirth or fever from this filthy place I know not. But when I returned to see her the next day, she was dead.'

The clatter of boots in the corridor resumed. A man called out, setting other prisoners jibbering and catcalling. Robinson had to raise his voice to be heard.

'The gaoler greeted me when I arrived. "Your mother's dead," he said roughly, and handed me my baby sister. Then he said, "Here is your brat. Your father's child, I presume." And he winked in a lewd sort of way. And that wink gave me an idea. I worked on it for five years while I lived rough, begging for prog to keep us alive, sleeping in the glass-houses, running from parish to parish with the other street children. I took care of the baby as my mother would have expected me to. Then, when Lettice was old enough to walk and talk, I left her on a doorstep in the St Bride's parish with a note around her neck. And that note was to start the game with Sir Richard.

'In it I wrote that I was a poor shamed woman, the child's mother, and that the villain who had got me with child was one Sir Richard Dainty, and wrote down his address for good measure. Mothers do this all the time. I'd watched them. When they can cope no longer they leave their children with the parish, and name the father. And under the law, the woman's word is enough. Once the man's name is down on the ledger the father *has* to pay the parish charges to support his own offspring. I gave myself up to the parish at the same time, and submitted myself as a possible apprentice.'

Alpiew looked from Robinson to Lettice. Both were fair-haired and pale in complexion. Could she perceive a slight likeness about their eyes, or was it only a shared secret sadness?

'Edward Stark took me on and we started to win again,' Robinson continued. 'Either Sir Richard would be forced to pay the parish for Lettice's upkeep, or the parish would make him take her in. He protested, but the parish has power to enforce the law, and it didn't look so good for a businessman, having them hovering round his front door like blow-flies round a dog turd. I talked quietly to Mrs Stark, and she talked to her husband, and he advised Sir Richard to take the child himself. He probably would have done so without my intervention. He was too mean to pay the parish their charges, so he took her to his house in Pall Mall Street, and, at that tender age, she became ward of Sir Richard Dainty.'

'That is what she meant by perverted!' exclaimed the

Countess. 'Cynthia thinks Sir Richard was planning to marry his own daughter.'

'But Sir Richard knew as well as we do that she was no relation of his.' Robinson stroked his sister's hair. 'You have only to see how fair she is. He was a swarthy man. And too mean to pay even the meanest of prostitutes. According to my father, his only delight was taking advantage of the poor African women he shipped to their doom. They cost nothing, you see. He thought he was going to get Lettice for free, too.' He held his sister close. 'But he didn't know it was a serpent he was nurturing to his bosom; didn't realise that the sweet little girl, Lettice Bride, was the daughter of his old business partner, the man whom he had ruined.'

'And you didn't worry that you had simply sacrificed the child to his whim?'

'She had been in the poor house,' sneered Robinson. 'Do you have any idea how that is? At least at Sir Richard's she had a warm bed to sleep in and food without maggots. And I was there watching. I took care to keep my eye on his house. And we wrote to each other. Together we had already planned that, once Lettice was old enough, twelve, she would wed him. Once she became his wife our debt became his! As a dowry from his bride, he himself would inherit those prison charges he had brought against our parents, and the cost of the sunken ship and its cargo. He would inherit his own unlimited liability, and, finally, we would be free.'

'A very pretty story,' said Alpiew. 'And, if it is true, a very sad one. But it still don't explain one very incriminating thing. As far as I can see, Sir Richard behaved very wrongly to you, and your parents. But murder is still murder. And nothing can excuse the fact that you murdered him.'

'I did not. I could not. It was not in either of our interests for him to die.'

'Aha! But you see, in your pocket, Lettice, there is some solid evidence against you.' Alpiew slipped her hand into Lettice's pocket and pulled out the two wedding tokens. 'How come you have both pieces of the wedding coin upon you? Before the ceremony I saw Mrs Stark give you one half of the coin and Sir Richard the other, and yet, though the old man never returned, you now seem to have both halves.'

'Not both, Mistress Alpiew. I have two half-coins, but see – they do not match.'

Alpiew pieced them together. The girl was right. The heads were askew and the cut edge not a perfect match.

Robinson pulled off his shoe and upended it. With a clink another half-coin hit the stone flags. Robinson handed it to Alpiew. 'See if that matches one of hers.'

Alpiew slid it together with Lettice's to make a perfect match.

'You are brother and sister,' said the Countess, 'yet you are wed?'

'No. The tokens belonged to our parents. From *their* wedding. We kept them as a symbol of how we are united, even though apart.'

The Countess looked up. Through the grating in the ceiling she could see a wagon's wheels, hear the sound of a gang of men alighting in some excitement.

'What was the point of the letters you wrote to Lettice?' asked Alpiew. 'Apart from your secret coded messages within them?'

'I knew he would sneak looks at them, intercept them maybe,' said Robinson. 'I wrote them to make him want her more. Even if he didn't want a thing, the fact someone else was after it made him desperate to have it.'

218

'Ah, yes!' said the Countess, thinking back to the evening Sir Richard had stood in their kitchen. 'The cup of posset I offered to you.'

'By making him think I was going to try and run off with Lettice, I made him propose and arrange the wedding. Whenever he slacked I would send a new letter, and Lettice would make sure Sir Richard saw it. But I needed to make him think she feared me too, so he wouldn't associate us too closely and work out the truth. So she played her part.'

'"Save me"?' The Countess looked at Lettice, who nodded her reply.

Robinson shuddered and clutched again at his sister.

'But surely, if Sir Richard is dead, it must be good news for you?' The Countess felt sorry for the siblings, their lives eaten up by Sir Richard's treatment of their parents. 'The debt is gone. There is no one left to press it.'

Robinson lifted his head and looked the Countess in the eye. 'Oh yes there is: an even more formidable reptile than Sir Richard. And as Lettice did not marry Sir Richard, this man inherits everything of a business nature. He has left a jointure for Lettice, but the debt will still wipe that out. We are talking about a whole merchant ship and its cargo, and the interest the debt has accrued over the years, and the prison charges . . .' Robinson put his head in his hands. 'We are ruined.'

'You know about the will? How is that?'

'I was worried when Sir Richard had not returned after the *Cassandra* episode – even though I paid a Black-Guard boy to deliver a message to him saying the ship was safe. I was worried because the wedding had not taken place. Frightened he might have got cold feet about it. For all I knew, someone had talked him out of it. I needed to know how things stood for Lettice. Just before dawn when I heard he had *still* not come back I returned to Pall Mall Street, and I let myself in and searched the house. I saw the money box was gone, and I was desperate. I rummaged through the drawers in his office till I found his will.'

'So?' The Countess gazed at him, this intense pale boy. 'Who is Sir Richard's heir?'

'A monster who will pursue that debt even more vigorously than Sir Richard. Once it is known that the old man is dead, Sir Richard's house and all his possessions, including the debt against us, belong to Hendrick Van Loon.'

At the end of the row of cells a door slammed with a jarring echo. A clamorous noise of chatter grew nearer, until a key turned in the cell door.

The room filled with officers of the law.

'Robinson Stark?'

A gang of men in workmen's clothes stood behind the prison governor.

Robinson rose.

The governor turned to the men behind him.

'Is this the guilty party?'

The workmen nodded.

'Robinson Stark, as representative of His Royal Highness King William III,' said the governor. 'I am here to press a serious charge against you. If found guilty there is no mitigation of the sentence, which is always death. I am here, Robinson Stark, to charge you with murder.'

Robinson blanched. Lettice clung to him, weeping.

'Countess Ashby de la Zouche?' said the governor. 'You see before you the very man who was discovered burgling your home yesterday. But it seems that while he was in your house he also murdered an officer of the law, a nightwatchman, and dumped the corpse in your privy.'

The Countess, Alpiew and Lettice clambered up the steep incline of Pig Hill.

'We must find that uncle of his,' said the Countess. 'Edward Stark.'

'Not uncle,' corrected Alpiew. 'His master, or whatever he calls himself.'

Lettice wailed.

'As Mr Stark is seen by all the world to be Robinson's uncle, I cannot see why he won't help him,' said the Countess, elbowing Alpiew into a hot-sausage seller's brazier to make her keep quiet. 'If he doesn't help, it would look very bad for him. Phough!' she exclaimed, looking at the hill ahead, crammed with shops and stalls offering pork in all its forms. 'Roasting pig, pig on a spit, pig pie, pig sausages – enough pig to satisfy the largest appetite. Where do they find all these pigs to cook?'

'I was told, madam,' said Alpiew, 'that they breed them out in the back yards, and they have spaniel bitches who suckle the piglets, which adds sweetness to the flesh.'

Lettice wailed again. 'If Robinson is hanged,' she cried, 'what will become of me?'

'Something will be done in time.' The Countess put her arm round the child and tried to reassure her. 'Mrs Stark told me herself that her husband has a business which saves people from the gallows. And we are speaking about saving the *guilty* and condemned ones, so he must have some tricks to save the innocent.'

The Countess's mind was racing, for of course there was no saying that Robinson *was* innocent. To be identified by six night-soil men was a pretty convincing argument that he had been in the Countess's house at about the time the night-watchman had been killed. And though the story he had told was compelling and upsetting, it still did not clear him of murdering Sir Richard either. The Countess longed for some time to think it all through, as there seemed to be glaring holes. 'I wonder if it is called Pig Hill because of the pork shops?' said the Countess, striding past a great hog roasting on a spit. 'Or did the pork shops come here because it is called Pig Hill?'

'What's ahead?' said Alpiew warily. 'Thieves? Hold on to your pockets, my friends.'

Towards the entrance into Thames Street a crowd blocked their way.

'Make way there,' cried Alpiew, shoving through the tattered throng.

The men, some ragged ragamuffinly fellows with despair etched on their countenances, others wild striplings who wore the air of runaway apprentices, queued before a makeshift desk manned by four well-dressed blades with the sharp features of hawks.

'Might I ask,' inquired the Countess of a meek-looking man in a worn suit and frayed breeches, 'what is the attraction here that you feel free to block up the entire passage to perambulatory traffic?'

'There's a ship leaving for America,' replied the poor fellow. 'Those are the masters' agents there at the desk. They're offering jobs, jobs for those like me who have none. I've had enough of this country. There's nothing to hold me here. My wife ran off with the talleyman, and there's no chance any more to go for a soldier now there's no war.'

'And is whatever they offer here good enough to make it worth your while standing about in the middle of the street, hindering people's movement?'

'Oh yes.' The man licked his dry scaly lips. 'A voyage to America for free.'

'For free?' The Countess's ears pricked up. She had always wanted to do a bit of travelling.

'That's the bargain in't, you see, madam. Once we arrive in the New World we are given a job on the plantations, a four-year contract which pays the cost of our passage. We are given food and lodging, and at the end of the four years we are free men in a wonderful new land, to set ourselves up as we please.'

'And what was your job here, sirrah, that you cannot find another?'

'I was a runner for a jeweller. He went bankrupt like so many did a few years back when the new banks came into being. And if a gentleman like him couldn't cope, what chance for me? Now that we have the penny post, there's no use even trying to get a job as a runner, so I'm giving the New World a go.'

The three women peered into the window of Jonathan's. The tobacco smoke had not had time yet to work up into a thick fog, and they scoured the faces of the men within. At one table the men wore expressions of such malice, horror, anger and despair it looked as though they had heard of a new plague sweeping London, or that all their wives had run off with their journeymen. At the other table sat a gaggle of merry blades laughing and pointing at the others with abundance of satisfaction.

'Money is the lord of man and beast,' cooed a man's voice behind them. 'See what fools and monsters it makes of them.'

'Pox, man!' snapped the Countess, spinning round to face Daniel Foe. 'I believe I was never so frighted since I popped out of the parsley bed.'

'We need a male to go inside, Mr Foe,' said Alpiew, 'to fetch out Edward Stark.'

'I'll do it.' Foe had an impish air about him. 'For a fee.'

'Fee, Foe?' said the Countess.

'Fie, Foe!' said Alpiew.

'Fum!' Foe pushed the door open with a flourish. 'I smell

the blood of a true-born Englishman.' He turned and laughed. 'Only jesting. But as I always say, "It is not the longest sword, but the longest purse that conquers."'

Foe disappeared into the coffee house, returning to the small courtyard of Exchange Alley a few moments later.

'Gone,' said Foe. 'Believe it or not, to an establishment called Laura's Lace Emporium.' He pointed to an advertisement posted to the wall: '"Chantilly lace and a pretty . . ." The next word is missing, it seems. But they provide "Bucks, Beds . . . Milanese. Private fitting rooms, and any number of bobbins."'

'No,' said the woman behind the counter. 'Edward Stark has not been here. I wonder why you think he might have been?'

Behind a screen, in a corner of the shop, a couple of ladies were bent over, fussing and giggling. The Countess could see their heads bobbing up and down.

'Now there's a nice-sized bott!' said one. 'Nice and plump and squishy.'

'I prefer a tighter bott myself,' said the other. 'You can get a better grip.'

'I shop here a lot.' The Countess gulped and stared ahead. 'But I usually deal with Belinda.'

'She's busy out at the back.'

'Are you Laura?' The Countess was increasingly aware of the titters emanating from the corner.

'Yes.' The serving woman gave a curt nod. 'How can I help you?'

'Easier, too, when they're softer like that . . .' said one of the women behind the screen. 'Mmm! All the better when you're after a bit of pricking.'

'Anyway, er, Laura,' the Countess pressed on, trying to ignore the women behind her. 'If Mr Stark does come in, could you please say that I was looking for him upon a matter of some urgency . . .' She lowered her voice. 'What kind of things do people get up to in this place?'

Laura gave her a haughty look and watched as the women emerged from the corner.

'I promised myself I'd be the proud possessor of a new bott today and so here I am.' One woman presented herself at the counter, beside the Countess. 'I'll take this big bott,' she said, plopping down a lace-maker's cushion. 'My friend will have the smaller one.'

'So, Laura . . .' With a knowing sniff, the Countess continued. 'My name is Lady Ashby de la Zouche, Countess of Clapham, Baroness Penge . . .'

'I have customers to attend to, madam,' snapped Laura. 'What do you want?'

'Please tell Mr Stark, if he does come here, that I am just now going to pay a visit on his wife.' The Countess tapped the side of her nose. 'And I am bringing her news that concerns him more than it does her.'

Huddled in the street outside, the Countess and Alpiew put all their coins together and, appalled at the meagre sum they accrued, decided against a hackney.

'Phough,' sputtered the Countess, sifting through the money. 'Clipped! Look here, Alpiew, someone has given me a clipped coin in my change. I'm not going to pass that. What if they suspect me of having clipped the thing!'

'Bundle it in with a handful of good coins.'

'I don't want anything to do with it now that I know what they do to coiners! Why it's a worse death than if you've committed a murder.'

'Give it to me.' Alpiew held out her hand. 'I'll find a way to offload it. These wretched people. They surely can't make that much melting down the stuff they clip off.'

'Unless they have a huge network, a factory, all clip, clip, clipping away,' said the Countess.

'Can we go home now?' Lettice sighed.

'Come along,' said Alpiew, with a wary glance at the wan child. Lettice certainly looked as though she might at any moment burst again into sobs. 'It's not so far to walk.'

They turned up the alleyway at the side of Laura's shop in Little Distaff Lane.

Bustling towards them was Mr Cue. A woman swung along at his side.

'Oh lord! The *Trumpet*!' hissed Alpiew. 'The new column! I had forgot all about it.' She put on a wide smile as Cue came into earshot. 'Oh my, Mr Cue, we are so busy today following up a wonderful scandalous story. Prepare to be shocked!'

'Really?' Mr Cue gave a wan smile. 'I was just going to the er . . . er . . .'

'Ink supplier,' said the woman at his side.

'And we will have that Queries column for you by tonight.' Alpiew wished she had given it even a moment's thought.

'Yes. Ah well!' Mr Cue shuffled. 'This engraving business is taking its toll on the supplies.'

'Oh, you!' said the woman, elbowing him in the well-padded ribs. 'But look at the new readers it has brought in. Sales figures are looking magnificent this week.'

'This is Sally, by the way.' Mr Cue looked down at the woman by his side. 'Sal is the new engraver. My wife told you . . . ?'

'Yes, yes,' said the Countess, eager to get on with the business at hand. 'I'm sure you will forgive us, Mr Cue. A story will not wait upon us, as you know.' She smiled at Sally. 'Lovely to meet you, finally.'

She marched on, whispering to Alpiew. 'Didn't you say the engraver was a man?'

'I think Mrs Cue thinks it is,' said Alpiew, glancing back.

They had barely taken a few more steps when footsteps pounded along the alleyway behind them.

A heavy hand fell on the Countess's shoulder.

'You were looking for me, Countess?' Edward Stark was flushed from running, his face covered in a light sweat. 'I just popped into the lace shop for a few gifts for my wife, and the lady there told me that you had been in. You are going to St Martin's Lane to bring Cynthia some news?'

'It was you, in fact, Mr Stark, that we want to see.'

A flock of barking geese, driven along by a boy in a white smock, blocked the path.

'Me?' Mr Stark blanched. 'What on earth have I done?'

'Alpiew, do you walk along with Miss Dainty. I will catch you up.'

Once Lettice had gone, the Countess told Edward Stark about Robinson's situation. 'If the worst comes to the worst and the boy is found guilty and charged, I simply ask is there anything you can do?'

Clutching the parcel of lace in one hand, Stark rubbed his chin with the other. 'I can hardly arrange to get the boy pregnant. Even my most effective knocker-upper wouldn't be able to accomplish that one, but I shall put my head to the problem. How much are you prepared to pay?'

'Pox, man!' cried the Countess. 'The boy is your nephew!'

'I may remind you, Countess, the boy is in fact no relation of mine. He is my apprentice. It is only by some maggot of my wife's that I carry on the pretence of his being my relative. And, talking of maggots, if the worm is in trouble, what is it to me? I have trained him up in this business to make money, not get thrown into prison for adultery, robbery and murder.'

227

'Pshaw, Mr Stark!' The Countess could not believe the attitude of the man. 'Whoever said anything about adultery?'

'The saucy jackanapes has been playing at all sorts of games,' said Edward Stark. 'My wife insisted I took him into the family. Indeed 'tis my belief that she has been wantonly dawdling with him. So you see, Countess, if the impudent coxcomb does hang, between you and me, I will not be sad to see the back of him.' He rubbed his hands together. 'But, as we say in trade, business is business, and if I can come up with an idea and you can come up with the price, then the deal is on.'

Edward Stark held out his hand, a handsel to cement the bargain.

'We will shake on it, sirrah –' the Countess looked down with disdain at the proffered hand – 'only when you can tell me your plan, and give me the quotation. Good morning to you.' She walked on, turning to call after him. 'And do, please, give my best wishes to your dear wife.'

Godfrey had prepared lunch. Or rather he had been out to the market and bought in a lot of goodies for himself and Lettice. When they all arrived at Sir Richard's house the front table was nicely laid out for two.

Whimpering, Lettice rushed straight up the stairs and threw herself upon her bed, letting the door slam behind her.

'What 'ave you pair o' gorgons done to my little girl?' snarled Godfrey, holding up a toasting fork to Alpiew. 'I heard you going at her earlier.'

'Her brother is in prison, Godfrey. Her guardian is dead. One way or another she has had a bad morning.'

'I didn't like to comment before . . .' Godfrey was staring

at the Countess's pink-and-gold headgear. 'But what's that on your head?'

Ignoring him, the Countess speared a sausage on the end of her knife. 'Are you joining us to eat or not?' She took a bite. 'You have become quite the housekeeper, Godfrey. If you can regularly whip up such a wonderful spread, I shall have to up your wages.'

'What wages?' Godfrey piled hunks of greasy beef on to his plate. 'Last time I got paid was twenty years ago.'

'It was a joke, Godfrey.' The Countess munched. 'As you know, we share everything between the three of us.'

'While I do all the dog's work,' Godfrey mumbled as he chomped. 'Meanwhile you two laze around, sucking on the end of your pens, and laughing merrily together with your so-called "authoring".'

'It's not quite how it seems, you know, writing.'

'Oh no?' Godfrey guffawed. 'Any fool could write. All you need is pen and ink and leisure.'

'Godfrey,' said Alpiew, suddenly inspired with a wild idea. 'Now that you have suggested it, I realise we do have a little writing job you could do. But first you have to answer me this question: "Where do swallows go during the winter months?"'

'Is this a trick?' Godfrey chewed, then, while he thought, he held his mouth open, exposing a melange of chewed bread and meat.

'Yes?' Alpiew took a sip of small beer from a pewter tankard. 'Do you know?'

'Where do swallows go in winter, indeed. Ha! Everyone knows that one.' Godfrey wiped his mouth with his sleeve. 'They fly to Africa, of course.'

'Africa!' The Countess guffawed. 'Oh, Godfrey, occasionally you are so humorous.'

'Well, I like a joke. Here's a little riddle for you then, Alpiew:

"What is greater than God; more evil than the devil; the poor have it; the rich want it, and if you eat it you will die?"'

'No more, Godfrey.' Alpiew broke open a roll and crammed it with a lump of cheese. 'You have got the job. You too can write a column for the *Trumpet*. What do you say to that?'

'Nothing,' Godfrey said triumphantly.

'That's nice,' said Alpiew. 'I get you a job and all you can say is "nothing"?'

'No. That's the answer to the riddle,' said Godfrey. '"Nothing". Here's another one: 'ow did you ever get a job writing?' He laughed, firing a lump of chewed meat from his gaping mouth on to the Countess's plate.

The Countess failed to see the projectile land, so busy was she gazing at the letters scratched upon the window pane. 'Eris. Eris.' She muttered, plunging her fork into Godfrey's pre-masticated meatball and popping it into her mouth. 'Mmm! Delicious.' She swallowed. 'It's very tender, this beef.'

'How are a jeweller and a gaoler alike?' said Godfrey, diverting the subject from the meat. 'Answer: the jeweller sells watches and the gaoler watches cells. Here's another, though I 'as to say I don't know the answer to it: If the whole earth was covered in water during the forty-day flood of Noah, tell me . . . where did it all vanish to?'

'How did Hendrick Van Loon know that Robinson's bill of exchange was a forgery?' mused the Countess.

'Got me there,' said Godfrey. 'How *did* Hendrick Van Loon know that Robinson's bill of exchange was a forgery?'

'And that writing on the window – "Eris",' the Countess continued. 'Who put it there? She never did answer the question. We must ask her when she comes down. And what did they use to etch those letters upon the glass window pane?'

'Well, if I'm not wrong,' said Godfrey, scratching his stubbly chin, 'I think I know the answer to that one. There's only one thing guaranteed to cut glass and that's a diamond.'

EIGHT

Annealing – relieving the strains in glass so that it does not shatter with changes in temperature

The Countess decided to take advantage of the spring sunshine. She and Alpiew sat on a bench in St James's Park. Some sheep nearby baaed prettily and then saw off a gaggle of geese who blocked their way.

'My word, but they have the patience of Job, those two youngsters, to wait so long to effect their plan. Still, Robinson's story seems to make sense.'

'A pretty story, as I said, and yet, madam, there are more holes in it than in a colander.' Alpiew kicked a pebble into the canal. 'Why was he burgling our house? Did he kill the night-watchman? And who was he with? The constable said there were two men there. And, of course, who did kill Sir Richard Dainty, if not him?'

'Do you know, Alpiew, on days like this I realise that I could happily live in the countryside.' The Countess stretched, basking happily in the idea of herself dolled up like a shepherdess, doing embroidery while sipping warm milk (fresh from a nearby beribboned cow) at the side of a rippling lake. 'I'd gambol happily through purling brooks, my milk pails over my shoulders, and gather garlands of honeysuckle, cowslips, woodbine and er . . . er . . . hollyhocks for my hair.'

'Hollyhocks, madam?' Alpiew took a peek at the Countess: a plump elderly woman with a double chin, her make-up crazed and melted in parts, her décolletage plump but withered, the whole lot topped off with a ridiculously tall pink wig that sparkled as the gold and silver tinsel braid caught the sunshine. 'Marsh-mallow? In my opinion 'twould be too much. A simple daisy chain would suit you better.'

'Are you calling me simple, you impudent hussy?'

'On the contrary, madam. Your face is very pretty and doesn't need such garish adornment.' Alpiew was mightily glad there was no looking glass near. The Countess would swoon if she saw what a figure she cut in this pantomime top-knot. 'And what of Hendrick Van Loon?'

The Countess kicked a pebble and watched it plop into the canal. 'I suppose we had best pay him a visit.'

'Will we have to dress up like Eskimaux, milady, with plugs up our noses, to gain admittance?'

'Oh, we will gain entrance to that madman's presence. If Sir Richard has left his estate to Van Loon, I wonder if the mad Dutchman knows about it? And, more importantly, if he knows that Sir Richard is dead?'

'If he did know, surely he would already be in his house by now, claiming his assets?'

'Not if he killed him, Alpiew, for who knows Sir Richard is dead apart from us, those two orphans and the guilty party?' The Countess stopped to pick up a ball which had rolled to her feet. She threw it back to the boys playing a few yards away. 'I wonder whether Sir Richard and Van Loon were partners back in the days when the *Eris* went down?'

233

'Eris! That's a strange name, madam. Robinson was a child at the time. Might he not have misheard? Perhaps the ship was called the *Eros*?'

'Eros! Greek for Cupid. Dear Cupid. What a surprise! How lovely to see the boy after all this time. He is mightily troubled, too. And whoever has put that silver band about his neck? You do know what that means, don't you? It means someone for whom he worked believed he owned him, like parcel, body and soul. The collars are there to give you instructions on how to return him should he be lost.'

'It's an upcoming fashion now in London. It wasn't the same a few years ago.' Alpiew sighed, surprising herself as she realised that she too felt nostalgic for past times, usually the Countess's domain. 'I didn't read the collar, madam. Did you?'

'He doesn't want us to read it either. Have you seen the swathes of cravat wrapped over it? No doubt his "owner" is advertising for his return. Once these villains get it into their silly heads that something belongs to them, it takes an earthquake to shake the idea out of them. So whoever has lost him will be wanting him back, or his money's worth.'

'Poor Cupid.' Alpiew longed to sit up into the night talking with him, as they had done all those years ago at the Countess's old house. 'I wonder if there's a ship called Cupid.'

'I see no reason why the ship wasn't called Eris. All these trade ships have mighty fine names to be sure: Cassandra, the purveyor of doom, and Eris, the daughter of Night, goddess of Discord. Eris was the one who threw that apple down at the banquet, you know.'

'The Lord Mayor's Banquet?'

'No, some wedding feast for ancient Greeks. Then afterwards a shepherd boy had to choose between three women and naturally gave the wretched apple to Aphrodite, goddess of sexual desire. And look what a mess that led to.'

'Apples always seem to lead to trouble, madam. Look at Adam and Eve.'

'And talking of that sort of business, *is* young Robinson fornicating with Aunty Cynthia? The woman is certainly with child. I have as good as felt the baby kicking.'

'She has cravings too. While I was with her she must have downed a gallon of chocolate.'

'What kind of partnership was it that Sir Richard would leave everything to Van Loon? Van Loon was there to witness the wedding which would effectively disinherit him. If he knew Sir Richard was leaving him everything it would definitely have given him a reason to knock off Sir Richard before the wedding was finalised. Meanwhile Van Loon was paying boys to spy on Sir Richard and both of them somehow seem to be involved in a plot using those same boys to spread a network of false rumour and speculation, thereby increasing their fortunes.'

'I was just thinking, madam. What are we going to do with all those bills of exchange drawn against the fictitious company you and Cupid invented?'

'Oh!' The Countess paused. She had not considered the bills to be real money, any more than the shares were real shares. 'What can we do? Will we be arrested for owning them . . . if we never cash them? I don't understand this new way of dealing. I do understand cash. And someone has stolen all of ours.'

'Augh!' Alpiew deflated. 'Who on earth . . . ? But when you think of the turmoil that has been going on in that house . . .'

'I agree with you, Alpiew, there is nothing to be said

about it. Back to the matter of that investment company.'

'Those men spent good money buying those shares. I suppose they will notice the fact they have squandered it. Perhaps I should burn the bills of exchange.' Alpiew was convinced someone would recognise Cupid or the Countess and they would be charged with a crime even worse than coining. 'Oh, madam, I fear this whole world of money. I shall go into the coffee houses and use the bills to buy all the stock back, then no one can be hurt by it, and there will be no stock any more nor any bills of exchange to incriminate us.'

'Pshaw, Alpiew, fie upon paper money. In comparison a battlefield seems as quiet and pleasant as this sunny park.'

A gang of well-dressed children firing pop-guns stampeded past, kicking up a cloud of dust.

'Pox!' Alpiew tried to fan the dust away, only making it worse.

'Fie! These children nowadays.' The Countess shook her skirt and rose to her feet. 'No respect.' She spat out a mouthful of dust. 'That boy, Jake, with the tip of his finger off – his hat was as dusty as the top of a slut's cupboard.'

'Remember the business with that chair in the hallway when Van Loon arrived at the wedding, milady?' Alpiew sucked on the inside of her cheek, and bit her lower lip. 'Might not that have had some bearing on the matter? Perhaps the noise was a cover. Perhaps the chairmen were busy stealing the money box while the priest started the marriage ceremony.'

'Do you know, you may well have hit it, my girl. Come along, Alpiew, let us leave this bucolic scene and track down the old Dutchman. We should at least feel safe being alone with such a squeamish old duffer, for if he threatens us we can simply open our mouths and blow.'

*   *   *

Hendrick Van Loon lived in a wide house in Tobacco Roll Court, just off Gracechurch Street.

His chair was outside the front door, the tin sashes up.

'He's inside. Listen.' Alpiew stood close to the rear, between the two lifting shafts.

There was a hum of low conversation coming from inside the chair.

'Is he talking to himself?'

Stealthily the Countess approached the side of the chair.

'I've seen enough knobs for one day, my little rose . . .' murmured a male voice within.

With a sudden swoop, she slammed down the tin sash.

Two astonished chairmen looked out, one of them hastily doing up his buttons.

'Can I help you?'

'I am looking for Hendrick Van Loon.'

'He is inside the house, madam.' One of the chairmen stepped out, looking her up and down, taking great interest in the pink-and-gold wig. 'Have you a message for me to take to him?'

'No message required. I would like to speak to the gentleman in person, please.'

'Impossible,' said the second chairman, a spotty youth, lazing inside the chair. 'He wouldn't see you.'

'Not see me? And who are you to decide? His own personal Cerberus, with one head missing?'

Mystified, the two men scowled by way of reply.

Alpiew strode towards the front door, but the tall chairman blocked her path.

'Perhaps you had better go in and tell Myn Heer Van Loon that he has some visitors,' said Alpiew.

'He's had enough visitors,' the lanky boy sneered. 'You should have seen his face after he got a packet in the penny post. Don't want to see no one today. He said so.'

'But I am Anastasia Ashby de la Zouche, Baroness Penge, Countess of Clapham . . .'

'He doesn't speak to women. Ever.' The spotty chairman sniggered. 'Even when they've come in costume, direct from the City Pageant.' He stared at the Countess and smirked.

The tall chairman gripped Alpiew by the hand as she tried to raise the knocker. 'No, wench. I assure you he will not see you.' Alpiew pointed back towards the Countess as she tried to struggle free from his grip. 'Nor Grannum there in the fancy frizzle.'

'It is all right, Alpiew. Let the man be.' She smiled sweetly, baring her brown teeth. 'I promise you, you impudent dog, I *will* have a meeting with Herr Van Loon, and I will have it this afternoon.' She turned on her heel, catching her shoe on a cracked cobble, and, wobbling slightly, steadied herself on an adjacent tethering post. 'Come along, Alpiew. Before that we have business with an African Prince.'

'I will not do it,' said Cupid. He sat, his head in his hands. He was dressed in the simple livery of a footman (as simple as the Duchesse de Pigalle permitted, at any rate). 'The man is a monster.'

The Countess watched Cupid carefully. There was more on his mind than he was letting out, of that she was sure.

'You are on the run,' she said softly. 'From whom?'

Instinctively Cupid's hand moved up to his neck. His collar was well covered by a lace cravat, wound about covering the silver, and flowing down, one end hitched up to his lapel with a fancy brooch. 'Don't worry about the collar. That isn't the thing which upsets me most.'

'Then tell me what is.'

'I cannot.'

The Countess moved over to Pigalle's drinks table and

poured them both a glass of claret. 'Why did you come back to me?' She took a sip as she sat. 'I should rather ask why did you not come back sooner?'

'I had big ideas.' Cupid sat up and looked the Countess in the eye. 'I'm not proud of it. After your husband left you, Alpiew too, I watched you go down and down. There was no money, people shunned you as you fell, and as the money went. Then came that terrible day when you were carted away and thrown in prison. The other servants ran off. Not Godfrey, of course. But I was a young, pretty boy. I thought I had a future. I didn't go on the parish. I looked after myself. I took to performing. I played drums with some musicians in the pleasure gardens, I worked as a swordsman for a while at the Bear Garden. Then the Bear Garden was closed. I was a hairdresser in Covent Garden for a while. Finally I became a masseur.' He chuckled. 'I was very successful at that. All the ladies wanted me. I made lots of money and dressed myself like a real finical beau. I didn't really think about you, by then. And when I went back to your old house to show myself off to you, swaggering with my own success, the place was demolished. No one there knew what had become of you. I thought you must have died in prison, and then, too late, felt sorry that I hadn't come to visit you.'

'Don't worry. I understand. You were a child.' The Countess laid her hand gently on Cupid's leg. 'It was a long time ago. And how came it you went from a successful masseur to a bought slave?'

'Times change. Ladies who liked to have me suddenly decided they needed to wear a mask if they employed me, and eventually did not want me at all.' He raised a finger and pointed at his cheek. 'Black skin. Suddenly it meant something different. Then, when I was reduced to touting for trade in the piazza, I was seized by some louts who put me up for sale, swearing I was a black who had escaped from their ship that morning. They chained me to the stones at Queen's Hythe Dock and sold me to the man who put this round my neck.' He closed his eyes and groaned. 'He traded me on in some big deal. I was happy – well, as happy as you can be wearing one of these.' He pointed to his collar. 'Then something happened and I made my escape. The other day I saw you in the street. You were pushing through the crowd at the Tyburn Fair. I was taking refuge in a crowd. Always the best place to hide.'

'You should have come and said hello, my baby. I was yearning to be rescued from the dreadful people I was with.'

Cupid flinched. 'I didn't think you would want to see me.' He rose and stood looking out of the window at the street below. 'Everything here in London is changing day by day. You've seen how it is become for people with black skin these last couple of years.'

'But surely, Cupid, there are still enough people about like me, like Pigalle . . .'

'I am probably more English than he is, the man who owns me. I can trace my parentage on these shores back to the time of Henry VII. But now someone here in London believes that I am a chattel of his. A stolen chattel, what is more. The final insult being that I stole myself by running away! I worked for him, and he accused me of all sorts of things, the worst of which was stealing!'

'*Did* you steal from him?'

'No.' Cupid turned and looked the Countess in the eye. 'But I do know where the things and the money went.'

'And did you have anything to do with it?'

'Of course not. But I cannot accuse the person.'

'Because of your position?'

'Something like that.' He stretched back his head and

sighed. The top of the silver collar glinted briefly in the light. 'I was very happy there, in that household, despite the collar and the man. But suddenly I realised that everything which kept me there and which made me so happy would be my ruin. It was a kind of theft, I suppose, the happiness I had. And so I ran away.'

'Well, you are safe now, with us.' The Countess could see that Cupid had tears in his eyes. 'If only we can get that wretched thing off your neck.'

'I know people who have died in the attempt to remove theirs. The saw slips, goes that fraction of an inch too far, and the vein is cut, or the neck broken. They are purposely made thick and indestructible. Mine was soldered on. And it sits tight.' He ran his finger round the inside of the collar. 'By running away, in fact I *have* done a bit of serious thieving, for this symbol of my slavery is forged of solid silver.'

'And won't you tell us the name of this wretched man who imagines you are one of his chattels?'

He hung his head and tightened his lips. 'I cannot. I owe it to another to keep silent.'

'Please come with me, Cupid, to this dreadful man, Van Loon.' The Countess leaned forward and placed a chubby hand on his knee. 'Remember, we can sell him what he wants, and he will get nothing. After all, you are not an African Prince, you are a Londoner, a Briton.'

'Why do you want to pretend to trade with him? Is it a game?'

'Much worse. I rather suspect, Cupid, that this man is a killer. That would be bad enough, but someone else is languishing in gaol for the killing and like to be convicted.'

Alpiew spent half an hour chatting to various men outside Jonathan's until one seemed willing to go inside and trade on her behalf.

'African Royal Selling Enterprises?' The young man, prinked up in a foppish yellow suit with silver buttons, scratched his full-bottomed periwig. 'Only been on sale a day, but it's slow at the moment. There's been no word on it, and no sighting of that Prince at the Royal Exchange or anywhere since his visit to the coffee house, so people are rather wary. You'll get a good deal, I think. How much does your lady want to spend?'

Alpiew presented a couple of the bearer bonds and bills of exchange.

'Phew!' said the man. 'Quite a lot, then. Is she a gambler, your mistress?'

'Oh yes.' Alpiew thought of all the slow, ponderous games of basset the Countess played with Pigalle and her friends, using counters and pennies. 'A high player at lansquenet and hazard.'

The young man disappeared into Garraway's and returned a few minutes later with some certificates. Alpiew thanked him profusely, then cramming them into her pocket she ran up the steps and across Cornhill to the Royal Exchange, where she traded more of the bonds and bills for stock in Cupid's fictitious company.

When she had finished, she sat down on a bench in St Paul's Churchyard and started to add up the total number of shares she had managed to buy back.

All around her bookstall-holders were packing up for the day. Men were hauling tarpaulins over the supplies delivered that day for the new cathedral, while the builders, sprawled out on the grass around the bench, were rousing themselves from an afternoon basking in the sun.

Alpiew fiddled about with the box of Napier's rods until she arrived at a final figure. She had at first bought much cheaper than the Countess sold for, but in the Exchange people started asking more for their stock. She realised there was only half per cent of the company left for her to track and buy. The half per cent they had sold to Maggie, the serving girl at Garraway's.

'That's what I always say – once you get to meet a person you keep on bumping into them.' Cynthia flopped down on the bench beside her and looked at the list of figures on Alpiew's lap. 'What is that? A puzzle, like the ones you get in *The Ladies' Mercury*?'

'Something like.' Alpiew crammed the paperwork back into her pocket. 'I enjoy puzzles of a mathematical nature.'

'So does dear Robinson. Poor boy.' Cynthia wrung her hands. 'I've been down to that dreadful prison, but they told me I could not see him. Do you know, they have charged him with the murder of a night-watchman! Robinson! It is astonishing. I cannot believe it could ever be in his nature to do such a thing, but they told me there are witnesses. I am so shocked. I came up to the Exchange looking for my husband, but they told me he had dashed off half an hour ago to some business meeting.' She unfurled her fan and started flapping. 'Oh, dear Robinson! What is to be done to save the poor boy, Mistress Alpiew? Answer me that.'

Alpiew didn't know what to say.

'A poor orphan. He has only us in the world.' She leaned in to Alpiew and lowered her voice. 'The tragic thing is, I inquired at the prison to pay off his debt, but you cannot believe how huge it is. Thousands and thousands of pounds. I don't know what kind of business he has got involved in, but even if we sold everything – the house, the carriage, everything – we would never be able to pay it. And do you know who is pressing the charge? None other than that miserable clunchfist Sir Richard Dainty!' Cynthia huffed. 'And to think I tried to cheer the man up and brought him lucky tokens for his wedding.' Cynthia was breathing heavily, flapping the fan faster and faster. 'That'll be why he's doing it, of course. I think the girl had a bit of a crush on Robinson. And who wouldn't love him? He is a polite boy . . . Good looking, kind . . .' She sat forward and sobbed. 'What is to become of everyone at this rate? Oh lord! I am so unhappy.'

Van Loon sat in a corner of his oak-panelled room. Despite the fact that it was a warm evening, all the windows were closed and shuttered and a fire crackled in the grate.

The Dutchman was wrapped in his overcoat, the usual sticks of rue in his nose and ears, a thick cotton mask covering his mouth. He had a nasty black eye.

Sticks of incense smoked all around the room.

Without rising he waved a gloved hand. 'Your Royal Highness, please sit.'

Cupid took his place in an easy chair opposite the Dutchman.

The Countess, in her eunuch costume, stood behind Cupid's chair.

'I am glad dat you changed your mind, Prince. I find dat most of your people are usually very amenable. Trade is trade, after all, and I am sure we can strike a good bargain.' He gently wiped his injured eye. The Countess chose not to refer to the punch Cupid had given him.

'Tangier,' said the Countess to Cupid. 'Elephant dido camel carthage good hope.'

Cupid nodded.

'So twenty-thousand heads. Can de Prince do dat?'

'He can,' said the Countess. 'But before we sign any agreements, His Royal Highness would like to make contact with your partner, Sir Richard Dainty.'

'Impossible,' said Van Loon. 'De man is indisposed.'

'You had a young man arrested, I believe, for passing a note drawn upon Sir Richard's name.' As she stepped into the centre of the room the Countess watched Van Loon's eyes. 'Why was that? Do you not honour your own partner's bills of exchange?'

'I knew de note could not be drawn upon Sir Richard.'

'Really, Myn Heer? Why was that?'

'There was something wrong with de bond.' Van Loon shifted in his chair, and pulled his scarf tighter round his jaw. 'I mean . . . Sir Richard is . . . very unwell. Since yesterday he has been completely indisposed.'

'I do hope he gets better soon,' wheedled the Countess in her best eunuch voice. Indisposed and unwell, indeed. On the day in question Sir Richard was about as indisposed as a man could be. Dead as a doornail, in fact, and whilst the note was being passed to Van Loon his body was lying inside a trunk in the Countess's house. She realised the Dutchman needed to be cornered. She moved closer to him, watching keenly. She could see that the nearer she came, the further he pressed himself back into his chair. 'Sir Richard is an important and busy man, I know, but the Prince has an interest of his own in Sir Richard's business.'

'Really? Dat is no concern of mine. What connection could dey possibly have? De prince has only been here two days.' He hesitated. 'And during dose days Sir Richard, has, as I said, been unavailable.'

'Ah yes, of course, but . . .' The Countess recalled something somebody had said in Jonathan's. 'I was told Sir Richard was once in Africa, in, er, where was it?'

'Bambara,' snapped Van Loon. 'He was governor. But dat was years ago. Fifteen or so years.'

'Of course. Bambara. I believe he had a connection with the Prince's father back then.' Inspiration hit. The Countess decided to put a challenge to Van Loon that ought, one way or another, to flush him out. 'And because of that connection, Myn Heer, His Royal Highness is very keen to meet him. I am afraid, you see, that without Sir Richard being present, there is no deal.'

'Tell him Sir Richard is gone back to Africa. He can meet wid him dere.'

'I will tell him no such thing, Myn Heer Van Loon.' The Countess took another step forward. 'You see, I know that Sir Richard is no more in Africa than you are. In fact I have seen him here in London this very afternoon.'

The sticks fell out of Van Loon's nostrils and landed on his lap. With gloved hands he fumbled frantically, trying to poke them back in place.

'Alive?'

'Of course.' Fascinated, the Countess regarded Van Loon's total astonishment. 'You seem startled by that information, sir. Why is that?'

Van Loon blinked a few times and started plucking at the arms of his chair. 'Are you here for de business or are we playing a game of cross-questions and crooked answers?'

'I was simply hoping you could produce the man – in the flesh, as it were.'

Van Loon started making gibbering noises. The Countess moved away to the table and sifted her hand through a large bowl full of glass beads. 'And these delightful baubles are what you propose to trade for black men?' She rolled a bead across the table, then watched it fall off the edge and land with a click on the polished floorboards. 'His Royal Highness will be pleased. How many beads per head?'

'A sackful of beads for every hundred men?'

'You have two hundred sacks of these pretty things ready for dispatch?'

'Indeed. Guns too, if de Prince would like . . .'

The Countess stopped, stooping over the table to look past the beads at an easy chair in the corner. There, splayed on a cushion, lay something hairy and inert.

The Countess sidled round the table, fingering the beads all the while.

'May I sit, Myn Heer?' The Countess eyed the cushion. 'The Prince and I have had a busy day at the Royal Exchange.'

'De Exchange?' Van Loon seemed even more agitated. 'Is dat where you have seen Sir Richard?'

'No.' The Countess had edged round to the cushion. 'Sir Richard was not at the Exchange.'

'Of course he wasn't! Because de man has been kidnapped or worse by two women in a house in German Street. They have had him there in their house, and unless he shows up alive by tomorrow morning I will have dem both apprehended for his murder.'

The Countess suppressed a gasp. How did Van Loon know Sir Richard's body had turned up at their house?

'Women are de snares of Satan, Prince. It is in de Bible. Never have dealings wid women if you value your life.'

'Might I ask you something, Myn Heer?' The Countess sat, grabbing the fuzzy item and putting it on her lap to inspect it closer. 'If you detest women so much, why do you have a woman's wig lying upon a cushion in your home?'

Van Loon's nose-plugs shot out of his nostrils again. He pushed himself back into his chair as, pinched between two fingers, the Countess held up her own wig and waved it in his direction. It was as though she was proffering a live tarantula.

'What is dat?'

'A wig, sir. A wig which I happen to know belongs to a celebrated aristocrat, the mistress of a king of England.' She toyed with saying the woman was from German Street, but feared his reaction, given what he had just said about Sir Richard.

As it was, Van Loon's eyes were darting all over the room, as though he expected an army of such wigs to come marching from the wainscot to attack him.

'I could remove it for you, Myn Heer, if you so pleased?' She stuffed it into the pocket of her satin pantaloons. 'Now . . . back to business. Sir Richard Dainty? You say he is at a house in German Street? And you imply that he is dead. Why would anyone want to kill a harmless old man like Sir Richard Dainty?'

'The money, of course. It is because . . .' Van Loon, still squeezing into the chair-back, nodded. 'I wish I had kept hold of that forged bond now. Sir Richard is careless – keeping that silly girl in the house – when he . . .' He dropped a stick of rue and stooped to pick it up. 'At least he has not married her. I sent my men to try to bribe her away before the wedding but . . .'

'But . . .'

'But' – he was urgently stuffing the sticks back into his nose – 'she was too busy doing de sewing to listen to dem.'

'Sewing?'

Van Loon looked at the Countess as though she was an imbecile and mimed a needle and thread. 'Sewing!'

'Dongola massawa chinguetti?' said Cupid, indicating his nostrils with two fingers splayed in a V.

'I should . . . er . . . cocoa, Your Royal Highness. Tripoli!' The Countess turned to Van Loon. 'The Prince is desirous to know why you are so swaddled up, with plugs stuck up your snurls?'

'De draughts!' wheezed the Dutchman. 'I always avoid de draughts.'

'Draughts!' exclaimed the Countess.

248

'Yes, draughts.' Van Loon leaned forward. 'Look at de facts. Why do de fish live so long?' He threw up his gloved hands. 'Simple: no draughts!'

'Canaries banana cairo bonkers,' said the Countess to Cupid, who nodded sagely as she rose and moved towards the door. 'His Royal Highness is delighted to have struck up a deal with you. He will be overjoyed to take the offer of two hundred bags of glass beads, and looks forward hugely to his meeting with Sir Richard.'

Alpiew agreed to walk with Cynthia to Laura's Lace Emporium.

'I don't know if you feel the same,' Cynthia had said, 'but when I am overwhelmed with powerlessness or misery I feel a pressing need to go shopping. Do you?'

Alpiew couldn't say that she did, but was happy enough to tag along.

The lace shop was busy.

Cynthia fingered some cravats displayed on a table near the door. 'They would suit my husband, don't you think? What about this blonde? Or this Bruges Steinkirk?' She held up the flounce of lace under her chin, demonstrating to Alpiew. 'And I could buy him these lovely matching guipure cuffs, too. What do you think?'

'Won't he mind you spending all that money without asking first?' Alpiew had seen the price tag, and the very thought of losing that amount of money made her shiver.

'I'll use my pin money and tell him I picked it up cheap in one of the markets.' She rifled through the rest of the box of gentleman's lace. 'Best Flanders too. Look at these Arras love-knots.' She turned to go to pay, but the gaggle of women at the counter was still chattering away with Belinda.

Cynthia dived behind the screen and looked at the boxful

of sale goods. Alpiew went with her and sat on a three-legged stool near the window while silently Cynthia picked out the good bargains from the pieces too badly damaged or soiled to be worth even the lower price.

'I need a night-gown, but, oh,' sighed Cynthia digging deeper into the box, 'look at these beautiful shifts and undershirts.'

'Lovely!' Alpiew flicked through the pile of sales leaflets on a small side-table as Cynthia plunged back into the bargain box.

Laura's Lace Emporium! Flanders, Battenberg, Bucks, Beds. Private fitting rooms. Chantilly lace and a pretty ... Alpiew turned the page ... *selection of Bruges tippets and lappets.*

The shop door slammed a couple of times and when they emerged from behind the screen, Cynthia clutching a chemise and a long night-gown, no one was left in the shop. Even Belinda had gone from behind the counter.

'She cannot have seen us there behind the screen. She must have gone to the privy.' Cynthia tiptoed behind the counter. 'I want to try these things on before I buy. Come along, Mistress Alpiew. I am going to a fitting room and you can tell me if the chemise suits me or no.'

Reluctantly Alpiew followed her into the back of the shop.

'It is a marvellous innovation, having these private fitting rooms in shops.' Cynthia marched briskly up the stairs. 'It is so much better than taking the wretched clothes home to try on and having to trudge back to the shop when they don't fit.'

On the landing was a row of five narrow doors. Cynthia pushed one open and popped her head inside.

'Lovely. It's free.' She put down the clothes on a large bed in the corner and started to undress. 'Could you help me unlace, Mistress Alpiew?'

Alpiew hastily worked her fingers along the eyelets on Mrs Stark's mantua until the long cord was almost loose enough for her to remove the dress. Alpiew had no doubt she would soon see for herself the evidence of Mrs Stark's so-called tympany. She tried to keep the conversation casual. 'It's odd having these beds in here, isn't it?' Alpiew took a final tug at the long lace. 'I suppose it is a means of displaying more of the stock.'

'I think it's a lovely touch.' Cynthia glanced down. 'Somewhere for your friends to sit while you change, and, as you say, another way of seeing their gorgeous sheets and pillow cases.' Cynthia stooped and fingered the pillow. 'I mean! Look at the *dentelle de la vierge* on that bolster cover. My word, how lovely is that?'

'Lovely,' echoed Alpiew, to whom she might as well have been speaking Chinese.

'Oh dear,' said Cynthia, wiggling her way out of the mantua, but still clutching the dress's fabric up to her chest. 'Could you run downstairs and pick up the other chemise? I believe I have taken one too small for my figure.'

Evading tactics, thought Alpiew. Frustrated that she could not verify the Countess's surmise that Cynthia was pregnant, Alpiew nodded politely and headed downstairs to the shop.

Belinda was back behind the counter. 'Oh!' she exclaimed, spilling some drops from a dish of coffee she was sipping. 'You startled me! I didn't realise anyone was here.'

'I am helping a friend who is upstairs trying on a chemise.' Alpiew rummaged in the box. She wanted to get back as quickly as possible. 'She fears she needs a larger size.'

'I thought you might be Laura's customer?' Belinda pointed a finger up. 'Private rooms? Bucks and Beds?'

'Just aiding a friend.' Alpiew didn't care for any more

fancy lace talk. She snatched up a bigger chemise and darted up the stairs, shoving open the door and running straight into the fitting room, hoping to catch Cynthia before she covered up again.

But Alpiew had picked the wrong door.

The room had the same layout as the one she had been in with Cynthia, but in this one the bed was being used. Not only that, the people in the bed, for there were surely two, were neither trying on clothes nor taking a nap.

'I'm sorry,' Alpiew retreated, stumbling backwards as the linen-covered couple stopped humping. 'I . . . er . . .'

Astonished, a male head reared up from beneath the sheet and turned back to glare.

Alpiew gasped and dropped the chemise.

The fornicating man was Edward Stark.

'Alpiew?' cried Cynthia Stark, from the landing. 'Are you lost?'

'I . . . I . . .' Alpiew tried to get out and shut the door but was not quick enough to prevent Cynthia, dressed now in the long loose night-gown, from peeking over her shoulder into the fitting room.

'Husband?' Cynthia stopped stock-still. 'What are you . . . ?'

'Oh God, no!' grunted Edward, reaching for his breeches which lay discarded at the foot of the bed. 'My wife!'

As Edward leaned forward the sheet pulled back with him, revealing the naked sweaty body of Cynthia's red-headed Irish maid.

Footsteps clattered sharply up the stairs.

'What is going on up there?' Laura pushed forward, shoving Alpiew out of the way, her face ruddy with mock horror. 'Good heavens, Mr Stark! How came you in this *fitting* room?' Emphasising the word 'fitting', she turned back to face Cynthia. 'Bless me! Sure this man and woman have mistaken the apartments. Nobody ever comes into this room, but for . . .'

'Private purposes!' cried Cynthia in a voice hoarse with passion. 'I see the meaning now, Mistress Laura, of your "private rooms" – you infamous woman. I understand your "Bucks" and "Beds".' Slowly she turned, then suddenly flew at her husband, railing, shrieking and scratching. 'But he is no buck in bed when he is at home with me.'

The Irish maid slid to the floor behind the bed and started frantically throwing on her clothes.

'If you must treat me thus, why not let me go?' Cynthia paused in her beating. She sobbed and walked away from the bed, wiping the tears from her eyes. 'You have had everything from me now.'

Edward Stark's sword lay on a side-table. Cynthia reached out and wrapped her fingers around the handle. Then with one swift movement she drew it, rushing towards him. 'You use me and abuse me, Husband. I will be free of you!'

Her husband, still naked, leapt from the bed and grabbed out for the sword.

'Calm down, woman. Calm!' He grabbed at the blade, cutting his own hands in the struggle. Blood from his injured hands dripped down on to the white linen. 'Remember what I did for your father?'

Cynthia stopped where she stood and burst into tears. Backed up against the shuttered window she leaned against the glass, weeping and shivering with rage and misery.

The red-headed maid took this opportunity of slyly slipping from the room and running away down the stairs, with Belinda, half-way up the staircase, howling profanities after her.

The rays of the sun beat through the lace curtain, and

displayed Cynthia's outline through the white lace of her gown. She was undeniably pregnant.

'I am in a maze!' Edward did not move. He gazed at his wife's body. 'You have a great belly on you, wife. Are you with child?'

Flinging up her hands to cover her face, Cynthia burst into heart-wrenching sobs.

'I . . . I . . .' Edward took a step towards her. 'I didn't realise.'

'I am astonished, madam, at this Bacchanalian spectacle,' said Laura, turning to face Alpiew, clutching the soiled sheets to her bosom. 'That red-headed bog-reared wench came in to try on a night-gown, and this man must have followed her up without me noticing.'

'Quiet!' Edward turned and growled. 'You have had your money for an hour's private use of this room, Mistress Laura. Now please leave us in private for the remainder of the time.' He looked at Alpiew. 'And you can go, too, you insinuating smut-monger.'

Suppressing a grin, Alpiew bit her lip and left the room. What a story! She could not wait to jot it down and take it to Mrs Cue. And what a lovely spectacle for an engraving!

'So the wretched monkey has been in Van Loon's house. How else did that madman have my wig?' The Countess fiddled with the belt of her pantaloons. 'Though whether Van Loon caught the monkey or the mischievous little devil merely paid him a visit, it is impossible to know.'

'He didn't seem a happy man.' Cupid relaxed in the back of the hackney carriage which carried them along Gracechurch Street, heading back towards St James's. 'I am glad of that, at least.'

The Countess was trying to work out how Van Loon knew Sir Richard was in their house, unless he had been somehow involved in the old man's death. She was aware that time was against them. She didn't fancy being thrown into a condemned cell next morning. But Van Loon of course would run into the same problem that the Countess had had when she first tried to present the corpse to the constable. And though she now knew where the old man's body was, unless Van Loon had had something to do with his death, how would he?

Her eunuch costume was beginning to pinch. 'Pshaw, this belt is so ornate it is like wearing a full corset on top of my clothes. I can barely move once I am sat down.' She writhed about, trying to loosen the jewelled clasp on the satin cummerbund which held up her pantaloons. 'I don't know where Pigalle gets most of these masquerade outfits of hers.' She leaned forward, pressing her face against the side of the carriage, trying to edge a little material free. 'Hey dey, what have we here? Look, Cupid! Those chairmen of Van Loon must have legs like leopards. How can they have overtaken us, and we riding in a horse-drawn hackney?'

Ahead of them, coming out of an alley with a chairman's cry of 'Have care!' was Sir Hendrick Van Loon's sedan. The chair turned, heading down towards the river.

'Hack-man!' The Countess leaned forward and yelled up to the cab-driver. 'Follow that chair!'

The chair bobbed swiftly down hill and over London Bridge into Southwark. The Countess's cab rolled along behind it.

The entourage turned into Pepper Alley and continued along Montague Close into Clink Street, where the chair stopped.

'Is the mad fellow going to the prison?' The Countess stuck her eunuch-bald head out of the window, and watched the chairmen shaking their arms, then swapping ends. 'Have care!' cried the lanky boy and the chair continued, turning into Stoney Street.

Making sure she was not seen as the chair veered round, the Countess pulled back into the coach.

With a cry of 'By your leave, sir!' the chairmen rested. The coach drew up outside a tavern some yards behind the stationary chair.

The tin sash on the chair opened an inch and the end of a letter appeared through the gap.

The tall chairman strolled back, took it and walked a few steps along the road. He knocked at a door and, without waiting for anyone to answer, he stepped inside.

'Where is he going?'

'As it happens I know this area very well.' Cupid peered out behind the Countess's shoulder. 'From my Bear Garden days. That is Jackson's glass-house. He is heading into the foreman's office.'

'To order the sacks of beads, perhaps?' The Countess felt such a rising disgust with the man, she didn't mind having lied to him. 'In one way at least, we have him on a hook.'

'I wonder which is the door for beads, my darling?' said Cupid softly. 'There are two adjacent glass-houses. Along the way, you see? There – the brown door. That is the green glass-house, where they make bottles and so on. But this is the building where they make fine crystal glass. It's called the flint glass-house. A speciality kind of place. They produce only expensive stuff, like the wine glasses the Duchesse was showing off last night.'

'With the big knops!'

'Those are the ones.' Cupid smiled.

The chairman returned.

Van Loon's tin sash came down an inch. The chairman slipped a tiny canvas bag through the gap. After a second

Van Loon growled and passed the bag out again. The chairman handed him a second bag.

The window slammed up and the chair rocked about for a minute or two, while the two chairmen rolled their eyes and made yawning gestures to one another. The tall chairman emptied the small bag into a vest pocket.

A bang from inside and the two chairmen moved to their positions and picked up the chair rods, ready to move off again. They strolled along for a few yards then turned another corner into Dead Man's Place. There they picked up speed for a while, then slowed again, finally stopping at the entrance to Cardinal Blois Alley. The tall chairman walked back to the chair and held open the door.

'Lord Almighty! I know this place.' The Countess pulled back inside. 'And fan me, ye winds – look, Cupid, the man is going for a walk!'

Hendrick Van Loon emerged, wrapped in a long coat, with half a dozen scarves wound round his neck, a tall beaver hat pulled down over his eyes, and a mask covering his nose and chin. He turned to address his chairmen. The lanky chairman patted his vest pocket, and handed something to Van Loon.

'How strange! It looks as though the chairman just tipped his master. He passed him a small coin or something.' The Countess was kneeling on the floor of the carriage, peeking up through the window. 'I wonder . . .' She looked at Cupid, then down at herself, inspected their clothing. 'Oh, phough, 'tis impossible!' The colourful satins and silks they wore were far too exotic. 'Pish to any hope of either of us following him on foot. Dressed in this fantastical garb we would barely blend in with the crowd.'

'Do you think not?' Cupid removed his feathered and jewelled turban, gold satin mantle, silver jacket and silk shirt. He then slung his sequinned slippers into the corner of the coach. Bare-chested, in plain cream breeches, with his silver collar on full display, he rose. 'Now, see! I look like any other black in London.'

'You cannot go out there, darling Cupid.' The Countess clutched at him, staring at the dull gleam of his collar. 'What if someone catches you?'

'What care I?' said Cupid, pushing open the door and jumping down into the street. 'If they try to pick me up I will run. Remember, if they want to know to whom I belong, they will have to get near enough to read the collar.' He raised his fists and winked. 'And the odds are I shall be bigger than them!' He looked slyly over his shoulder and watched the swaddled figure of Hendrick Van Loon disappear into Cardinal Blois Alley. 'Bye bye, Countess. Wait for me here. If I am not back within an hour, go back to St James's. Somehow I will make my way to the Duchesse's house.'

As she watched Cupid go off after Van Loon, the Countess's heart felt heavy. She rested her head against the upholstered side of the carriage and closed her eyes. How had it come to this? she wondered. How had the little sweet boy, who she had dandled on her lap, who had made her laugh with his kisses and winks and teasing, grown so big, and so troubled?

She breathed in, instantly regretting it. The rancid stench of tanning and rotten fish flooded her head. She could almost understand why Van Loon went round shrouded in scarves and masks, like some winter highwayman. Given half a chance, during this brief sojourn in Southwark, she would dearly like to borrow his rue sticks.

For a while she idled away the time looking out of the coach window, watching the ruddy rays of the setting sun cast long shadows on the dirty walls. A shrill chattering interrupted her thoughts.

A crew of diminutive vagabonds marched past the coach

in rank and file like a miniature battalion of foot soldiers. Their clothing was filthy with dust.

They spied her and stopped, bustling in a crowd round the window.

'Give us a halfpenny, mister,' yelled their leader, 'and you shall hear what you like. We can recite the Lord's Prayer backwards, swear the compass round, and call a whore as many proper names as a peer has titles. What trick are you after?'

'You are a parcel of hopeful sprouts,' said the Countess.

'We can follow your wife to see what she gets up to, we can carry letters for you. You say what you want doing, and the Black-Guard boys will be pleased to oblige.'

She was about to get out her purse and give them a penny when the hackney-driver bent down from his seat and cracked his whip.

'Be off with you, you parcel of varmints,' he yelled. 'Get your dusty fingers off my coachwork. Decamp! Go on. Shog off!'

He snapped his whip again.

The miniature army marched away, jeering at him over their shoulders.

The Countess sat back in the seat.

How on earth did those children get so dusty, she wondered? It was an odd fact. You could tell just by looking at them that if you caught one at any time of day and beat their clothing it would generate clouds of the pinkish grey dust which seemed ingrained in the cloth.

Briefly she drifted in and out of sleep. She heard the clock of St Mary Overie's chime the half-hour. She stared at Van Loon's chair and hoped Cupid would return quickly.

Alpiew bowled along Fleet Street. She had dropped a note off for Mrs Cue, telling her about the lace shop with its 'private' rooms. She suggested Mrs Cue might like to get a sketch of the room for the story she would provide.

She had decided to write the story first thing tomorrow morning.

Tonight she wanted to go home to German Street and put the house back into habitable shape. She looked forward to a return to normality after such a rantum-scantum couple of days.

She crossed the road at Charing Cross, just before the statue of King Charles the martyr. She lifted her skirts and darted between apparently suicidal horse riders, who delighted in taking the corner leading down into Whitehall at breakneck speed.

It would be just her luck, she thought, to survive the perils of the last few days and then get killed by a young man too excited at the prospect of getting the best speed out of his horse to heed people in his path.

She hoped the old watchman was finally gone out of the privy. Surely, if the authorities had charged Robinson with his murder, the watchman's body must have been taken away? Alpiew crossed the end of St Martin's Lane and bowled along past the entrance to Dung Hill Mews.

A conjuror had set up his stall on the open space. Alpiew recognised him as the man from the Tyburn Fair.

'A ho-bee bo-pee! Jacko cracko! Felto! Swift, fly, begone!' He threw a card into the air amid a puff of coloured smoke. 'Quick presto, passa, largo mento hi cocolorum! The card is flown.' He looked around the small audience and picked a victim, out of whose ear he pulled the vanished card.

While the crowd applauded, he turned and opened his gaily painted trunk.

The card, Alpiew realised, had been up his sleeve all along, even while the spectators watched the puff of smoke.

The magician pulled a tray from his trunk. He turned

towards the audience and flicked it. Four legs sprang out, turning it into a table, which he set down in the centre of his stage.

The secret of all this magic, Alpiew knew, relied on two things. Preparation beforehand and diverting the audience's attention at the critical moment.

The magician collected a stack of golden cups from the trunk and lay them on the table, lifting them one by one to show they were all empty.

Then he swirled and lifted, swirled and lifted, swirled and lifted in a dizzying motion, as a small ball seemed to appear and disappear before their eyes.

Of course he had two, if not three, balls in position, managed with such speed as to deceive the eye.

While his hands whirled and whizzed about the table, and he dextrously juggled cards and balls, making them appear and vanish with a startling and nimble flamboyance, Alpiew watched the transfixed crowd. She quite fancied working as a magician's assistant, just to be able to find out the tricks of the trade. You never knew when such legerdemain might come in useful.

She wandered on, pausing briefly to buy a hot pie from a higgler in the Hay Market.

Pity she wasn't a conjuror and so didn't know how to make one pie into two. She had a hunger that could easily have devoured four pies in a row, but only a few pennies left in her pocket.

She kicked open the front door, sucking the gravy up from her chin.

The kitchen was still a mess of paper and feathers.

Could this burglar really have been Robinson?

She knew she would have to go to the Clink and question the boy again.

Perched on the side of the Countess's bed and resting

her feet on the mattress, which lay on the floor, she tried to work back through the events here in the house. The Countess was right. It seemed that their German Street house had become busier than any London fairground on a public holiday.

First monkeys, financial advisors and burglars, then money boxes and corpses.

She popped the last morsel of pie into her mouth and stood up again. She wandered about, making a path through the feathers wherever she wandered. A sneeze shook her. She opened the back door for some air.

The night-soil men seemed to have been very eager in their cleaning out of the privy. What green there had been in the garden was gone. Certainly there was no grass left, and the weeds and brambles were all broken and down-trodden into the dusty, dug-up soil.

'A ho-bee bo-pee! Jacko cracko! Felto! Swift, fly, be tidy!' Alpiew tried a bit of hocus-pocus, but to no avail. Neither the garden nor the kitchen seemed in the mood to tidy themselves.

She hauled the Countess's ripped mattress back on to the bedframe, and pulled a number of pots and pans from beneath the bed.

She spent half an hour on the room, her mind flinging back through the recent events while she swept up feathers and crammed them back into pillowcases, hung the pots over the fire, stacked the logs in the fireplace, put the books into neat piles or back under the wobbly tables and chairs which they usually propped up.

Finally, when the room looked almost as it had done before all this bother, she looked about her. All that remained was to sort out the vast stack of loose papers.

She couldn't face that long and static task, so instead wandered out to the hall.

Perhaps she should look upstairs. She had climbed five steps when the sight of the blood sprays from the monkey's tail overwhelmed her with fear. She went back and fetched a poker and a carving knife. Then slowly she climbed up to the top of the house.

She kicked the door open as she passed every room, checking for interlopers.

She found no one, but someone had been there and had left evidence: floorboards had been pulled up and merely thrown back, exposing joists and crossbeams. Broken pieces of lathe wattle from the plastered ceilings below were tossed about in the dust.

Alpiew opened the attic storeroom door, expecting to find Sir Richard's money box. But someone had been in here too. And by the look of things they had brought an axe.

The chest was now simply a pile of painted wooden strips, like so much kindling.

Alpiew checked the main attic next door. The window was shut. The floorboard where they kept their money was ripped out and of course the pot of money was gone.

She went back to the remains of the trunk and knelt on the floor beside it. She spent some time attempting to arrange the wood back into shape, hoping that by putting it together she might see if any part of it was missing. Perhaps then she might know why it had been so roughly dismantled.

First she laid out the metal crossbars, and the locks, many of which were fakes, blind fronts with a keyhole and no lock behind it. She laid out the base and three sides. A long piece seemed to be part of the base but she couldn't fit it in. She placed it to one side. There seemed to be a great many pieces left.

'Quick presto,' she cried. 'Passa, largo mento hi cocolorum!'

The pieces of Sir Richard's coffer lay immobile on the floor.

She worked for a few minutes assembling the top.

What on earth could a shattered box tell her? If Sir Richard had hidden something inside, it was clear that it must now have been found.

The pile of splintered wood seemed as large now as when she started.

She swept her hand through the mound of dusty shards and splinters.

The wooden boards which had been covered by the trunk were dark brown. She cleared more of the wood-chips away. In the centre of the space where the trunk had stood was a small hole. The hole was the size of the tip of a Toledo sword. And round it in ever-decreasing density was more stain. Alpiew licked her finger and scraped some of the brown with her nail. This was blood. It was here Sir Richard was killed, pinned to the board with his own blade, his body thrown inside the trunk and the trunk locked.

And yet how could that be? She and her lady had seen the trunk here in German Street before it could have ever been taken from Sir Richard's house.

She ran downstairs and flopped on her bed. After a moment she started sorting through the stacks of papers. Pages from the manuscript of *Love's Last Wind*, the Countess's once-performed verse tragedy, were mixed up with old bills from the coal man, notes on scandals for the *Trumpet*, recipes for meat hash, biscuits and fricassees, as well as receipts for pots, pans and furniture.

Alpiew thought of all the papers they had encountered in this recent ghastly business. Love-letters which were really coded messages of encouragement; wedding licences; the note Lettice left in her house to let Sir Richard know she had come here, and the superscription with the location of his corpse; torn bills of exchange; false bonds. Such quires of paperwork. Perhaps she should get it all together and look at everything and see if it added up. Perhaps seeing it all together would make some sense of this chaos. Yes. That was what she would do, once she had sorted this lot out and had a bit of space.

A knock at the front door jolted her out of her thoughts.

She brought the poker with her, stood behind the door and called out. 'Who's there?'

'Night-soil,' said a rough man's voice.

'You've been already,' said Alpiew through the door.

'I know we have,' the man replied. 'That's why I'm here, to present you with my bill for labour finalised.'

Alpiew opened the door a crack. The smell of the man's clothing immediately betrayed his occupation.

With a sniff he thrust a grubby piece of paper at her. 'Cheap at the price,' he said. 'What a lot of bother to collect a pile of shit. Burglars, bodies! God almighty, give me a wheelbarrow full of tantadlin tart any time. Turds is easy to deal with, you see, wench, in comparison with the leavings in this house. And turds don't hit you on the 'ead neither when they runs out into the street, like that black fellow done. I can still see stars when I move me noddle.'

'Black fellow? I thought you caught a white man in the house.'

'Oh yes, when we come back after lunch, we did. But earlier we were about to come in the house to do the job, like, and while we were getting our equipment off the wagon a black fellow and a white fellow came running out of the front door – not looking too innocent, I have to add. They ran off like the devil. The black fellow got all agitated when we ran at him; lashed out like a wild thing. Gave me quite a thump to the block. We chased them up the street, but they got away. Then we didn't think it was much point going back to the job for a bit after all that running about, so we had lunch, like. When we went back the second time it was just the one fellow inside the house. White chap. He got away too. But they caught up with him . . .' He made a gesture of pulling a rope up from his neck. 'He's for a jig with Mr Roper, I expect.'

'Can you describe the black fellow?'

'Tall. Quite well-spoken. Must have been a lady's moor, I'd say, back in the old days. Had a thick white cravat wound tight round his neck. I'd lay a bet he was hiding one of those new-fangled silver collar things under all that lace.'

'And did you clean out the privy the second time you came?'

'No, of course not. That would have been the fourth time.'

'You came here four times?' Alpiew was dizzied with all their comings and goings.

'Oh yes. After all that running up and down the street after robbers yesterday we were late for the next job. So we went on with that and came back this morning for the third time. And, good lord, what a shock that was, finding that body. We had to wait for them to cart the cadaver away till we could start on the privy, so we went off for a quart of ale to steady our nerves and then we came back just before lunchtime and did the privy job.' He stood with his hands on his hips, waiting. 'So, you going to pay me?'

'Oh!' Alpiew knew there was no money in the house. 'Can you give us a week or so? We won't let you down. You can imagine, with all this disturbance, it's a real mess inside. Call back when my lady is here.'

The night-soil man grunted and moved off, riffling through a handful of further invoices to dispense.

Alpiew shut the front door and returned to the kitchen. She sat idly fingering the papers on the bed.

Robinson and Cupid had been found together burgling their house. How could it be? What was going on?

She picked up a bill for coal and laid it on the bill pile.

'Rissoles of capon.' Alpiew flicked through the recipes, sorting them into categories. 'Potages of turnip with duck', 'broiled sheep's tongues', 'farced tripes, after the Swiss mode, with a cherry sauce', 'cow's udder in a daube with apricocks' – Alpiew gulped at the thought. She was amazed that the Countess had collected so many of the damned things, considering she never ever cooked anything, let alone a leg of faun, or ragoo of chicken-livers with mushrooms and gammon. The Countess even had a recipe here for fritters of cod! Cod, indeed! Who could afford to eat *cod* in this household? The stuff was more expensive than best prime steak!

Alpiew put the recipes down and ran back through the events of yesterday. The important thing was to follow the day here in the house. She and the Countess had left just before dawn and gone to Sir Richard's, with Godfrey and Lettice following shortly afterwards. The Countess had returned an hour or so later to show the constable the corpse of Sir Richard, but it had vanished.

Alpiew found another page of the verse tragedy and inserted it into its place. And here was a page of strange balderdash. French, Alpiew supposed. Something illegible and weird-looking, anyhow. She put it back among the recipes.

She realised that after they had taken the constable up to see the vanished body, the house was again empty for some hours while she and the Countess were around the town at the Exchange and in the lace shop.

When they came back at lunchtime they found Cupid

in the trunk and the body in the privy. After that she and the Countess were with Cupid all the time. So Cupid and Robinson must have been to the house shortly before they came in and found Cupid hiding in the trunk. Cupid must have come back almost at once, and Robinson must have come back while the three of them were eating at the ninepenny ordinary in Pickadilly. So perhaps together Robinson and Cupid had robbed them and been seen off by the night-watchman. Perhaps they were coming back to dispose of the body and then she and the Countess had found Cupid and shortly afterwards the night-soil men found Robinson.

A duplicate recipe here for fritters of cod. 'A ho-bee bo-pee! Jacko cracko!' she sighed and put it to one side. 'Hi cocolorum!'

Duplicates? Should she make a second pile for them? No. She crumpled up the second cod and tossed it into the fireplace. No need for duplicates.

Another paper went on to the unpaid stack.

Wait! A ho-bee bo-pee!

Duplicates! That was the clue! Wasn't that how the magician made the cards and balls appear and disappear?

She clutched a bill to her stomacher as she thought. Duplicates? Rhythmically she tapped the hard front of her corset with her fingernail and sucked the inside of her cheek. But how could that work? Even if the wedding did prove the most marvellous eye-catching distraction for the main event – a murder – there were hardly two Sir Richard Daintys!

Alpiew looked down at the bill she held. It was crossed with the words *Paid with thanks*. She moved it over to the paid-invoice pile.

Prepaid by sender was scrawled over the next one. Alpiew looked again. Jacko cracko! This was the invoice for the delivery of the fatal money chest which Godfrey had so carelessly signed for.

Alpiew ran her fingers along the lines.

Divers items of carpentry, as per order, prepaid by sender. I hereby accept delivery, signed this day of Our Lord ... and Godfrey's signature.

Items of carpentry! It was not a *delivery* note for Sir Richard's trunk. The bill came from a carpenter.

Duplicates indeed! That was it. It wasn't that there were two Sir Richards, but there must have been two money boxes.

Someone had had a replica trunk made up and delivered here to this house during the time they were out at the wedding that never was. But what had happened to the original? Yet this *had* to *be* the original, for the Countess had found the letter and certificate here.

Still, one way or other, Alpiew felt sure there had been two trunks. If she could find out whether she was right, and, if she was, who had had the trunk made up, surely that person would be the guilty party, the person who had killed and spirited away the old miserable hunks, Sir Richard Dainty?

Alpiew gazed down at the address on the carpenter's invoice. The address of a carpenter's shop in Southwark.

A painted female, face smeared with white lead ceruse, lips an unlikely shade of vermilion and her cheeks spotted with fraying taffeta patches, thrust her head into the carriage.

'Looking for a bit of poop-noddy, fine sir?'

'Fine sir?' The Countess gaped, then suddenly realised how this strumpet saw her: a bald plump creature in exotic but decidedly male clothing. A hairless old man in fine clothing. Somehow it seemed more honourable to be what she intended to be: a eunuch. 'Sorry, I'm one of the castrati.' The Countess pursed her lips and winked. 'Don't have the equipment, dear.'

'Oh lord, one of them uniques!' The prostitute called back to a colleague further up the street. 'Look here, love, I am sorry, but do you mind movin' on. You see, you're queerin' my pitch.' The woman frowned and looked the Countess up and down, her pocked face etched with disdain. 'Literally, I mean.' The prostitute screeched with laughter and reeled back. 'One of those perverts 'ere again, Moll. You should get a gander. What a freak!'

The Countess slammed down the blinds and thanked heaven she was not really what she seemed. She bent down and fiddled with her fancy satin slippers, wishing Cupid would hurry back.

Realising that she must be able to continue watching Van Loon's chair, she slowly edged the blind up a couple of inches.

The hour rang out.

Then, while the echo of the bells was still resonating against the tall dark buildings, Hendrick Van Loon, heavily swaddled and hat pulled low, returned to his chair and, with a cry of 'Have care!' from the lanky chairman, was whisked away.

The Countess contemplated getting the hackney-driver to follow him again, but decided, as agreed, to wait for Cupid.

The half-hour chimed again.

Cupid did not return.

The Countess did not want to go, leaving the boy behind in this stinking place. She sat back and closed her eyes as the darkness started to fall. She could hear the streets livening up, the drunken gangs reeling along towards taverns and stews, the carousing of youths on the run, grunts of men huddled up along the tall narrow dark alleys with seedy, cheap prostitutes.

There was a rap on the window. The Countess pulled up the blind.

'Are we staying here all night, mada— . . . er . . . sir . . . ?'

'Perhaps if we could just have another five minutes?'

'Look here, have you got the money to pay for all this?' The cab-driver scratched his arse. 'I reckon you've run up about ten shillings already.'

'Ten shillings!' The Countess suddenly realised that she had no money. Nothing. Not a penny. She had given Cupid her purse before they went into Van Loon's. Cupid's breeches had real pockets.

She wondered whether she could get the cab-driver to take her to Pigalle's, where she could borrow the money. But Pigalle, she knew, was out dancing this evening at one of Princess Anne's balls in Kensington Palace.

'You've got no money, 'ave you, you grotesque malkin?' The driver opened the door and hauled the Countess out of his carriage. He stooped, reaching back into his cab, and picked up Cupid's discarded clothing. 'Nice bit of lace there, and the fancy clothes . . . Mmm, well, I suppose they'll cover costs, so far. Now off you go.' He slammed the door and, hugging the pieces of clothing Pigalle had loaned to Cupid, climbed back up on to his perch. With a crack of the whip the horses jolted into motion and the coach lurched off.

The Countess gazed after him, unsure what to do next.

'You can't set up pitch here, you tawdry piece of goods,' sneered a trollop whose painted and patched bosom seemed way too big for her already scanty bodice. 'Brush your grig. Go on. Shove along, you rum punk.'

Alpiew found the carpenter's workshop easily enough. The entrance was set up Rochester Yard. She couldn't believe how warm the lane was. It seemed to be heated by gusts of hot air.

She listened at the door. She could hear the tap-tapping of someone at work within, so, although it was after hours, she knocked and walked in.

A wizened man in a dirty leather apron looked up from his workbench. He was clutching a small hammer and had a mouthful of tacks. 'Yes?'

In the corner a cauldron bubbled. The stink gave away the contents. Hides and hooves boiling up to make glue.

The carpenter swiped the tacks from between his lips and put them to one side. 'I'm closed.'

'I know,' said Alpiew. 'I am very, very sorry to bother you, but I need to ask you about this invoice.'

'Is it paid?' The man's eyes rested on her cleavage.

'Oh yes,' Alpiew smiled, deliberately tripping as she moved forward to set her bosom a-wobble.

The man sniffed and put the hammer back into a pocket on the front of his apron. 'Let's 'ave a look at them, er, I mean, then. Let's 'ave a look then.'

Alpiew handed him the invoice. He rubbed his chin. His eyes darted from the bill and back to her breasts. 'Mmm. Yes. Lovely jobs, er, I mean, yes, I remember that job. Very precise instructions. He gave me a drawing and everything. It was a weird 'un, I remember.'

'Why weird?'

'Top heavy. Lid oak with iron bands, bottom made from the thinnest cheapest wood you could lay your hands on. Couldn't have carried anything in it, that's for sure.'

'Did you make up a chest or simply deliver one?'

'Chest?' The man's voice quivered. 'That's right. Lovely big chest . . .' he tapered off and his gaze settled again on Alpiew's cleavage.

'So you made a new chest to the specifications of a man,

a cove who gave you the drawing. Which fellow was that?'

'Fellow?' His eyes had a misty look, and his lips were moist. 'Mmmm.'

'Who was the fellow who gave you the drawing?' Alpiew lay the invoice across her bosom.

'Fellow who ordered it, o' course,' snapped the carpenter, plucking up the tacks from the worktop.

'And who was he, the fellow that ordered it?'

'I don't know.'

'A big fancy chest like that and you don't remember . . . ?'

'I never forget a big chest.' He was staring down at her breasts again.

'You said yourself it was a precise job making that . . .' Alpiew emphasised the next word, trying to get him back on track: '. . . *coffer*, and yet you don't remember who ordered it?' Alpiew wanted to shake information out of the man, but realised honey was better than vinegar when it came to dealing with a reluctant witness. 'Do you still have the drawings?'

'No.' He waved an arm. 'Look 'ow small the place is. And with the fire I have to keep going 'cos of the glue, and all the wood about, well, I don't like to tempt fate with hanging on to too much paperwork. Highly inflammable, paper, you know.'

'So, sir, do you remember when the order was placed?'

'When the order was placed?' He scratched his head with a nut-brown hand. 'Can't say as I do. It was a week or so ago now.'

'But the trunk was only delivered this week.'

'Well, o' course. I 'ad to 'ave time to make the thing up, didn't I? Day before yesterday, I delivered it. German Street wasn't it? Blue Door?'

'You delivered it yourself?'

'Of course. I do all me own deliveries. Got an 'orse, see,

and I like to let it 'ave a bit of a clop into town now and then, you know, with the old cart.'

'But it was very heavy. How did you carry it?'

He laughed. 'Oh, I don't do the carrying. Got two boys for that. Strong lads. They got the thing up all those stairs, where they was instructed to leave it.'

'Instructed by whom? The old man in the house?'

'That dribbling lazy bag o' bones!' The carpenter guffawed. 'You'd be lucky if you got him 'elping a blind man over the street. Oh, sorry – 'e's not your 'usband or anything, is he?'

'Certainly not!' Outraged by the mere suggestion, Alpiew tugged the front of her bodice right up again. 'He is my lady's steward.'

'Well, stranger things 'ave happened at sea!' The carpenter edged over to the cauldron and gave it a good stir. 'Look at that old lecher who got married this week. 'Im and that little tit, young enough to be 'is grand-daughter, I gather. Lord 'elp us, there's a chance for us all.'

Alpiew held her breath. Was he about to link the trunk with its dead owner?

'Read about it in the *Trumpet*,' chortled the carpenter. 'But Lord, there's a scurrilous rag for you. Only saw it 'cos I bought a pie wrapped in the thing.'

Alpiew deflated. He was talking about her own invented article, written to fit the previously drawn engraving!

'So you don't remember who brought you these fabulously precise instructions for making the trunk, you don't remember who paid you, and you don't have the drawings.'

'I didn't say I didn't remember who brought me the instructions.'

'You did,' spluttered Alpiew. 'You said quite distinctly that you didn't know him.'

'I don't know 'im.'

Alpiew threw her arms in the air and gave an exasperated cry. 'Do you or don't you remember the man who brought you the instructions?'

'I remember him perfectly well, but I don't *know* 'im.' The carpenter sighed, implying that Alpiew was the exasperating one. 'The fellow was one of the Black-Guard.'

'A soldier?'

'No, the Black-Guard. You'll 'ave seen 'em. They march around chanting, and live underground round the corner here, over in the Tower Hamlets, and Wapping, Salisbury Court, White Friars . . . You know, wherever they make glass. Clever kids, really. You 'ave to take your 'ats off to 'em. Get their money which way they can. The dusty boys.'

Alpiew couldn't believe it. 'You're saying that the order for the trunk was brought by a dusty boy? And you made it up for him, just like that?'

'He paid cash,' he grunted.

'And who gave him the cash?'

'How am I supposed to know that? I told you all I know.' The carpenter looked her up and down. 'Anyhow, what are you after, coming here after hours, a-bothering me with your queries and your ruddy fancy chest?'

The Countess held her head down and trotted along in the shadows, trying to keep as near to the walls as possible. It was dark, the only illumination in the streets came from potato braziers and links.

How to find the way home? She had only the vaguest idea where she was. Southwark in Surrey, south of the River Thames. And there were two ways to get across: London Bridge or the Horse Ferry at Westminster. London Bridge was far longer a route, but she wasn't sure whether the ferry charged foot passengers to cross, or even if it ran after dark.

She dived into an alleyway, hoping it would take her back up towards the bridge. The alley was a dead end. She stumbled back into Dead Man's Place. Ahead of her a group of rowdy apprentices from the City staggered along, singing. They were drunk. Jeering and cat-calling, they manhandled her as she pushed her way through them.

'Look here!' cried one. 'It's one of those nig-me-nogs with no nutmegs.'

One by one they grabbed at her, flinging her about as though she was a ball.

'Still got his pud but lost his nick-nacks!' One man lurched forward, hand out, trying to grab at the Countess's crutch. 'Look at the trim-tram trull!'

The Countess side-stepped him but lifted her knee and gave the boy a good thump in the groin.

'There are advantages,' she cried, 'to lacking certain parts of anatomy.'

As the boy bent over in a spasm of pain, she darted away, flinging herself along Dead Man's Place with the rest of the gang in pursuit.

She darted down a narrow black alley. They came behind her. She plunged onwards into the black, running until she had no breath.

She stopped, pushing herself back into a recessed doorway, gasping. Only when she had stopped did she realise that the boys had given up the chase. She also knew she was now stuck in this passage with no light, and no way of seeing her way out. She had no inclination to go back the way she had come and bump into them again at the exit. But if she pressed on into the dark, who knows what might await her?

For a moment or two she stood, hands on her knees,

panting and trying to work out what to do. The rancid stench of rotting meat and urine made her gag.

She let out a sob and sank down on to her heels, running her hand across her bald pate.

How would she ever get safely home?

A few minutes passed. She was breathing more naturally now, and slowly calmed herself. Certainly she was lost, alone in Southwark, a wild district outside the laws of London, where criminals walked freely in the streets and famously ruled the place through violence and bribery.

London, or should she say civilisation, was only a bridge away, she knew. It might feel like a million miles, but it was a mere river away. She simply had to get herself as far as London Bridge and instantly she would be in a safer place. Then she must walk over the bridge.

And once she was back in London, yes, there was a hefty walk in the dark through city streets, and no money to pay for a link-boy to light her way, but at least she'd be out of this appalling area.

Good lack! Was she such a coward? It was only a walk. The people here had other things on their mind than attacking a lone old woman. They were here for sex, and dividing out the spoils of their burglaries and so many other things. She would be all right.

She stood upright again. First, she considered what she must look like. She knew her bizarre eunuch make-up must be smudged and smeared after the fray. She would do better to wipe it all off. That would make it an easier journey home. Without the make-up she would draw less attention to herself.

She plunged her hand into her pocket looking for a kerchief. She jumped. There was some hairy animal in there. Gingerly she pulled out the fuzzy limp thing and peered at it in the dark.

'Phough!' She had forgotten having picked up her wig at Van Loon's! She dusted it off and slid it on to her head.

She brushed her clothing down and stood silently, sharpening her resolve.

She took a couple of deep breaths and started walking.

Then she heard it.

Below the now familiar distant sound of carousing youths in nearby taverns came a more worrying series of noises: a cobble-stone carelessly stumbled upon, a rubbing of clothing, someone steadying themselves after almost falling. And these sounds were much nearer, mere yards away.

Barely daring to breathe, she looked back the way she had come.

After a moment her eyes seemed able to penetrate the black. Someone was there. She could see him, silhouetted against the entrance to the alley. Jutting out from a doorway, some fifteen feet from where she stood, there was the clear definition of a man's profile.

She sidled slowly away from him.

Then she heard another footfall behind her. She glanced back. The man was coming towards her.

Perhaps he was just a drunk using the alley to urinate. It was obvious from the smell that many did.

She walked on.

So did he.

She stopped.

So did he.

She listened again, and realised he too was holding his breath. There was no doubt about it. Whoever this shadowy figure was, he was pursuing her.

With damp hands she staggered onward, feeling her way along the slimy walls, eventually breaking into a run.

The footsteps behind her became louder, no longer uncertain.

The man was now loping in her direction.

Heart thumping, she bolted away from her pursuer, running towards the flickering lights ahead.

NINE

Paraison — a rounded lump of red-hot glass gathered on the iron

A lpiew had to find these Black-Guard boys. Round the corner, the man had said, where they make the glass. She came out of Rochester Yard.

A gang of nasty-looking link-boys were lolling against the railings.

'Where's the glass-house?' asked Alpiew.

One of the link-boys cocked a thumb over his shoulder. 'Stoney Street.' He thrust out his hand for a tip.

Alpiew ignored him and turned back to look for the street.

Stoney Street ran parallel to Rochester Yard. Alpiew hurried along. A swinging sign with a drinking glass indicated the glass-house. The door was shut. Alpiew banged.

No reply.

She walked briskly up the street. Another swinging sign depicting a golden bottle. Two glass-houses in one street! Alpiew banged again.

No reply here either.

What had the carpenter meant when he said the Black-Guard lived here? How could anyone live in a glass factory? Factories shut at night.

She stamped her foot and regretted her handling of the carpenter. Surely she had addled the man's brain by tempting him with glimpses of her bosom.

Alpiew turned on her heel and looked up and down the street. There were no gates or doors which could possibly be alternative entrances to the glass-houses. She walked the length of the street and back a couple of times before giving up and deciding on another line of inquiry.

She was only around the corner from the Clink.

And with the news that the night-soil men had given her she wanted to quiz Robinson further about the reasons he had been twice discovered in the Countess's house, even if, first time, he was apparently there on the strange mission of tidying up. Why had he run off? Had he seen the body of the night-watch Charlie? Was Cupid the cravated Moor with him? And, if so, why were they there together? And on top of all that, how on earth did Robinson know Cupid?

Alpiew rounded the corner into Dead Man's Place. Strumpets tramped up and down under the flickering light of a solitary link stuck in a hanging iron basket.

No doubt the link belonged to one of the clients, who was at this moment up the nearest alley playing a vertical game of hide the sausage.

''Ere! Miss Forebuttocks!' screeched a painted trull. 'Shove off!'

Alpiew gathered she was being addressed. She smiled, giving the woman the two-fingered gesture originally used by archers at Agincourt. Then she walked on, head held high. She made a point too of thrusting her chest out that extra inch to annoy the woman.

She turned the corner into Clink Street. The street was full of the usual drunken male rowdies, so she carefully pulled her bodice up again. There was a time and a place to expose your spare flesh, and this was not it.

As she got nearer the prison, Alpiew realised that there was some disturbance around the gates. Men were yelling in the street. A couple of wardens dashed down the steps to the waiting boats.

She increased her step.

'A woman's been stabbed!' called a boy running towards her. 'Where is there a chirurgeon?'

'Where is the lad gone?' A gaoler was running backwards and forwards, waving his arms about. 'In all the confusion he's got away.'

Alpiew arrived at the prison door, which was flung open.

'Escape! Murderer on the loose!' Men holding flambeaux were marching up and down shouting. 'Catch the malefactor! Block the bridge!' No one seemed to be going after the runaway.

Alpiew marched through the commotion and right into the gaol. Once inside, she darted along the stone corridors, pushing through the crowd in the prison bar, peering into all the grilles of the condemned cells, looking for Robinson. The solitary prisoners shrieked and rattled their wrist chains. In the resonant vaulted stone corridor the din was deafening.

Alpiew reached the cell where she had last seen Robinson. It was empty. But Alpiew knew these gaolers. They moved you about from day to day.

She ran onwards. Moisture was seeping into the hem of her skirt as it brushed the floor. If the damp was this bad when just passing along, she pitied the poor wretches who were condemned to stay in here, lying on the bare stone all day and night breathing the foetid air.

Ahead of her, a prisoner thrust his aquiline nose through the bars on his door.

Alpiew ran up to him. 'Have you seen Robinson? He's young, handsome, brought in yesterday . . . ?'

'He's done the vanishing trick,' said the prisoner. 'Just now. He asked for a meeting with the governor, and as he came out of his office, whoo, you should have seen him go!'

'He's the one who escaped?' Alpiew marvelled. 'How long ago?'

'Four, five minutes.'

Alpiew gathered her skirts and ran.

'He'll swing if they catch him. Stabbed some poor woman, see,' the hawk-nosed prisoner called after her. 'She's lying in the governor's room. Right to-do, I tell you!'

Alpiew sprinted along the dank hall. The door to the governor's office was open. Alpiew glimpsed the blood-stained clothing of a woman who lay sprawled out on his desk.

It was only once she had run past the door that she realised who the woman was.

She turned back.

'Mrs Stark?' Alpiew whispered as she entered.

The prison parson was sitting in the room holding Cynthia's hand.

Cynthia Stark was dove-pale. Her loose mantua bore a spreading brown stain.

'Mistress Alpiew?'

Alpiew took Cynthia's hand.

'Please, Alpiew, help them find him . . .'

'But . . . ?'

'Not the boy's fault,' she whispered. 'Really. Find him before they do. He has done everything for me . . .'

'But . . .'

'Best leave her,' said the priest. 'Delirious, no doubt. She ought to be quiet and keep up her strength.'

'Listen!' Alpiew advanced on him and gripped his shoulders. 'I am trusting you. Take care of this woman. Save her life, for the lord's sake. Do *not* let her die.'

'That's not up to me, dear.' The priest shrugged his shoulders.

'Yes, yes,' snapped Alpiew. 'It's God's will, I know . . .'

'No. In fact I was going to say it's up to the surgeon.' The chaplain sat smugly back in his chair. 'And surgeons don't come cheap. So tell me, if you want a surgeon, who is going to pay him?'

'I will,' shouted Alpiew, glaring at the priest. 'Do you hear me? *I* will pay. Now, make sure he does a good job. And don't worry, Mrs Stark, I will be back.'

The Countess didn't bother to check the road behind her. She emerged into the flickering light of a narrow street lined with taverns and brothels. Link-boys leant in small gangs against a railing. Their extinguished torches stood, ready to light, in a great basket in the road. Before them, in an iron cresset, a coal fire flamed, throwing shadows along the street and brightly lighting their impudent faces.

'Wanna boy to light you 'ome?' screeched one.

The Countess pushed past the children.

'She's a bit too bloody old for this game,' muttered a gangly boy in blue as she passed by. 'No wonder she's going 'ome so early.'

'What a get-up!' sneered another. 'Did you ever see the like?'

'I suppose she 'as to 'ave some gimmick to bring in the punters.'

The Countess dived into a mob pressing to get into a rowdy tavern. She pushed and shoved till she was lost in their midst. She hoped that whoever was following her would pass by now, and then she could double back and give them the slip.

The tavern exuded the aroma of grilled chops. The

Countess realised that she was terribly hungry. If only she had a few pence about her person, she would have happily gone inside one of these rough hostelries and treated herself to a bowl of soup and a nipperkin of warm ale and brandy.

She let people press tight against her, happy to be hidden within the crowd for a few more minutes.

Why would anyone be following her? Oh lord! She wrung her hands. Perhaps the whole episode was a figment of her imagination. Of course any person entering that tight alley at one end would be heading for the other. They were just using the alleyway for its true purpose – a way of getting briskly from one street to another. It was a perfectly innocent explanation. She tutted at herself, wondering how she had worked herself into such a state about it. Slowly she jostled her way out of the crush and wandered into the less urgent bustle of Southwark Borough Road.

Pshaw! It was just a busy street filled with rowdies who had set out to get drunk – what was so frightening about that? Covent Garden was the same, and she was never frightened there.

The Countess brushed herself down and, although she was dressed in a gold tunic and blue pantaloons, held her head up. She beat time with her hand against her thigh and marched forward, singing silently to herself.

Only a few hundred yards to the bridge. She could see it ahead.

'Watch your way, you hell-bound hag,' yelled a young spark, staggering across her path. 'Are you a whore, or a blue post?'

'You! Wrinkled slut!' cried another drunken chap, pressing his face close to hers, and wrapping his arm round her rump. 'How much for a squeeze and a squirt?'

The Countess knocked his hand off and marched on, staring ahead, ignoring them all.

It must be a mere twenty yards to the river. She could almost smell the fishy, foul water.

She skirted a sedan chair pulled up outside a whorehouse, waiting for its owner. The chairmen were taking turns gulping beer from a pewter tankard, wiping their mouths with dirty lace cuffs, while they munched their way through great slabs of larded bread and charred sausage.

How she wished she dared to ask them for a bite. But she knew that asking anyone for a bite of their sausage in these parts could lead to a most unfortunate episode.

Ten yards to go to the bridge.

The bridge's shops would be closed now, their windows shuttered for the night. A cold breeze blew off the water.

She looked up. Although the sky was moonless, a sprinkle of stars shimmered against the black. She shivered. It was cold, and here she was walking out dressed in only a silk blouse and satin pantaloons.

What a fuss she had made for herself! The cold was a worse problem than any imaginary man with sex or robbery on his mind.

She wrapped her arms around her belly for warmth and took the last few steps uphill towards the bridge.

To her left towards the Clink a great commotion filled the street as people ran up and down shouting, waving great flambeaux over the water.

She stepped back into the shadows of St Olave's Street. The roar of black water racing through the arches under the bridge was deafening.

A few desultory revellers came lurching towards her. To her right she could hear the retching of a pair of men, standing side by side on Pepper's Alley Stairs, vomiting in unison on to the pebbled beach below.

A gull shrieked as it dived down into the swirling river.

A posse of drunken revellers ran past, pushing her rudely aside.

She looked back towards the hubbub in Pepper Alley, and it was with a sigh of relief the Countess took the last few steps along the dark road leading to London Bridge.

'Got you!' A leather-clad arm gripped her neck and she was dragged rapidly to the side of the street. She staggered, pulling against the arm which held her, but she was gripped tight, a knife to her throat.

'Not a sound now, Countess. Do you hear me? Not a sound.'

Once she was off the main highway she was thrown roughly into a dark shop-doorway. The blade glinted in the distant light from the taverns in Borough Road.

'You recognise me, I am sure, your ladyship.' The gloved hand grabbed her chin and held her face steady. 'You know who I am, don't you?'

Alpiew ran out into Clink Street. Looking from side to side, she tried to think what she would do if she was running away from this prison. Which way would she turn? Not into the river. Everyone knew the Thames was lethal, with its eddies and swirls, and nowhere in the Thames was worse than the flow through the arches beneath London Bridge, which boiled like a raging cataract. Nor would she head for London Bridge. That would be too obvious a route, and, anyhow, if you were cornered on a bridge your exit could be too easily blocked. What choice then but to leap over the side and into the river?

So the choice had to be between going left into the heart of Southwark or south along Stoney Street whence she had just come.

At night time, south was a fairly good prospect. If you could edge your way on to St Margaret's Hill how easy it would be to make for the heath of Newington, and then trudge through the wasteland, which was a highwaymen's favourite wilderness, with plenty of stubble and gorse to shelter beneath till morning. Or you could walk on until you reached the sleepy hamlets of Stokewell and Clapham.

Alpiew looked both ways and decided the path she would take was into the busy, throbbing centre of Southwark. The place was a honeycomb of lanes, alleys and yards. Any route you took there would lead to plenty of dingy unlit dives, and there were scores of hidden entrances leading up narrow alleyways in which to hide.

She turned left and loped back into Dead Man's Place, running past the pox-ridden patched bawds who marched, pouting, up and down the road.

Alpiew could see that along the length of this street there were a handful of nooks and slits in walls, all unlit, perfect hidey-holes for a fugitive.

'Here, you!' Alpiew grabbed hold of a ragged whore who looked down on her luck. 'A young man, running? Did you see him go past?'

'Not surprised he'd run away from you, you tart-tongued maux.' The whore leered, attempting to shake off Alpiew's hand.

'He stabbed a woman.' Alpiew squeezed her fingernails into the woman's shoulders and thrust her face right up to the woman's pock-marked nose. 'Did – you – see – him?'

'I see lots of men . . .'

Alpiew let go and moved along the row of prostitutes.

'Where is the young boy gone? Tall. Dark hair. Thin. About twenty years old?'

The woman all thrust up their shoulders and looked blank. It was clear to Alpiew that some of them had seen something, but they wanted paying for the information.

Alpiew, however, had no money to give them.

She darted into the first lane and ran along, trying to keep quiet, to listen for breathing.

There were at least three couples along here fornicating. With the grunts and groans Alpiew realised that Robinson must either take shelter, curled up in a doorway, or risk being stumbled over by the brisk sex traders who came in and out of the place at regular intervals. She ran back and tried the next lane. It was a short dead end, and occupied by another couple.

'This is my patch, you filthy maw-wallop!' snarled a woman kneeling before a flustered sweating man. 'Get out.'

Alpiew made a quick exit and dived down the next alley. It was hot here, as it had been across in Stoney Street. What was the cause of this strangely temperate corner amid the streets of Southwark? One alleyway was cold as any winter night, the next was warmer than the hottest summer day.

Alpiew ran on, emerging at the far end of the warm passageway into New Rents. She turned down the street and came into the next narrow lane. It was marked with the sign of the Cardinal's mitre and crown. Had not the Countess talked of this place? She had been brought here by the dusty boy with the snipped-off finger the night they were held up by the highwayman and his doxy. Alpiew stumbled along into the lane. It seemed to be darker than the others, too many twists kept out the light from the links and flambeaux parading along the main roads either end.

She snapped open her tinder-box.

In the brief flicker she saw a row of three doorways to her left. She could hear signs swinging overhead.

One of these must be the door the Countess had gone into for those crooks to pick up the bond which she had brought to Sir Richard's house and which Robinson had then attempted to cash at Garraway's.

She tried the doors, one by one. In this darkness if she surprised anyone inside she could always say she had mistaken the door colour – like cats, in this darkness all doors were grey.

She pushed open the first door and flicked her tinderbox. It was another carpenter's shop. The remains of a dinner were on the table. But no one was about.

The next door led to a small printing workshop. The printing machine was set up and the floor piled high with stacks of leaflets and papers.

Alpiew listened at the next door in the row. A strange clicking sound came from within. She tiptoed inside.

It was black.

She struck up a spark.

In the brief flash she beheld a half-dozen startled faces gazing at her. The clicking sound stopped.

She lit the tinder-box again, aware in its lightning flash of people scurrying away, of sparks of light glinting upon the floor.

She struck again.

Then with a dull thud a cosh landed on her head. She briefly saw bright light, then slumped to the floor, unconscious.

The Countess was looking into the steely eyes of Kate Timony.

'You remember no doubt that I brook no fuss or dithering. I am not afraid of using the knife to open your vile gizzard. I could throw you over the side into the river. Who would miss a fat, furrowed old bawd like you?'

'What do you want?' The Countess heard her own voice come out like a stranger's, shaking and thin.

'You know what I want.'

'I don't. Truly, I don't.' The Countess put her fingers up

to her neck. She could feel the edge of the blade. It was newly sharpened. 'Tell me what you want and I will see what I can do to help. Did I not help you last time?'

Kate Timony gripped the Countess harder, pressing her back into the shadow with her own lean, leather-clad body.

'Where have you hidden it?'

'Hidden what?'

'The Eye.'

'What eye?'

'Don't mess with me, you ancient bitch.' Timony pressed the knife harder against the soft flab of the Countess's chin. 'Where is the Eye?'

'I do not know about any eye.' The Countess suppressed a sob. How was she to deal with this hard creature? She swallowed. As she gulped, the blade nicked her skin. She felt a warm trickle of blood dribble down into her cleavage. 'Really. I have no idea what eye you mean.'

'The Eye of the Idol. The diamond. Sir Richard Dainty's priceless piece of thievery.' Kate Timony lifted her arm ready to strike the Countess. 'Where is it? Where have you hidden it?' But as her arm swung back, Timony let out a sound somewhere between a howl and a screech and staggered backwards, clutching at her side.

'Out of my way, you vile slut!' John O'Hara loomed over Kate Timony's shoulder. His dagger was stained with red. Kate Timony slumped back against the wall, gasping and rubbing at her wounded side. 'You bastard bully,' she whimpered. 'You have cut me.'

'A mere warning nick, Countess. The tiniest prick of the skin. Mistress Timony always made a lot of fuss about nothing. She'll be all right.' He smiled his soft patronising smile. 'We wouldn't want that uncouth woman harming you in any way, now, would we?' He edged nearer. The Countess could feel the warmth of his breath on her face. 'I do know,

Countess, that you are an amenable person, willing to go about our business, when we are, shall we say, indisposed.' He ran his finger over her cheek. 'Look at that! Nasty Kate has made you cry. This roughness is no way to get a person to help us, Kate. How often have I told you?'

He slipped his dagger back into the sheath strapped to his leg.

The Countess had a moment to look at him. His customary white clothing discarded in favour of a dark brown stuff suit. His golden locks were covered by a similarly dull brown peruke. It was the type of attire worn by poor journeymen. He looked like hundreds of other people walking the streets of London.

'So, Countess, I trust you not to try running away. You know I would catch you, do you not? And as for screaming, well, that wouldn't be very pleasant of you, would it? And if you caused a commotion I should have to silence you before anyone got here. It would only take the flash of my blade and you would be plunged into an eternal silence.'

'I don't know what you are after, sir.' The Countess spoke slowly. 'Perhaps if you would explain to me, I might be able to help you.'

'You must have known there have been a number of people passing through your house over the last couple of days and yet you have not remarked upon it, not realised what they are after?' O'Hara laughed. 'Why do you think they have been there, sorting and searching and lifting your boards, opening your mattress, killing ludicrous interfering old men? Would you not think they must be after something that you have?'

'If they are, sirrah, I assure you not one of them has had the politeness to let me know what that thing is, for I have nothing of any value.' Though her mouth was dry, the Countess tried to have a conversation with him in the same tone, as if this was a perfectly civilised meeting over a cup of chocolate in a City India house. 'I swear to you, if someone would tell me exactly what it is they are looking for – apart from the hundred guineas in gold coin which they have already taken – I would surely help them find it. Anything to put an end to this chaos.'

'You had a hundred guineas there? I should have liked to have laid my hands upon that.' He sighed, putting on a mock tragic face. 'What a pity. Perhaps you will have noticed when the interest in your house began?'

The Countess thought back. As far as she could remember it had started with a visit from the two escapees from Tyburn's Tree who held her now.

'I cannot say. It began around the time you and I first met, I suppose. Did you hide something in my house that night, perhaps while I was here in Southwark, running your errands for you?'

'You're a plucky one, milady.' O'Hara laughed in her face. 'Full of humour. I like that in a woman. That is why my dear partner in crime will never be a lady to suit my taste. She is too much the man; she has too few pretty tricks in her conduct. With you I can talk civilly and know you understand me.'

The Countess was mentally running through the rooms of her house, scouring them for anything out of the ordinary on that night. 'Was it you that brought in Sir Richard's money box?'

'I know nothing of his money box.' John O'Hara thrust his face forward again, gripping the Countess's elbows, pinning her back against the filthy wall. 'The question is, did he bring you his Eye?'

'I have already told you, I know nothing of Sir Richard's Eye. I can tell you where his body is now, though . . .'

'Very droll.' O'Hara did not move. 'He is dead? How fascinating. But his corpse is of no interest to me.'

'Perhaps, Mr O'Hara, you might tell me what it is that you left in my house?'

'We hid something there, yes.' He let go of the Countess, pulling back a few feet then turning to smile at Kate Timony, who was dabbing at her side with a huge handkerchief. 'We left something behind, for safe-keeping, you understand. It was a sort of instrument of torture, intended for someone else, of course, not you, milady. We felt it was a safe place to leave the thing, seeing your house provided such a good disguise for it. Sadly we little realised how popular you were suddenly become, and what a nasty sort of company you keep.'

'I saw no instruments of torture left in my house, otherwise I am sure I would go and get it for you, right now.'

O'Hara laughed again. 'Dear Countess, you are such a pretty comical wench. The instrument is really of no great matter to us now. It provided us with a means to an end, that is all. And whether we have our hands on it or no, it still has some effect. Where there is a cully and a cross-biter, the cross-biter can keep that cully dancing to his tune for as long as he wants.' O'Hara ran his finger down the side of the Countess's face and let his hand rest gently on her shoulder, his fingertip tickling her throat. 'No. No. The thing Kate and I want from you is something quite other. Something which we only discovered through sheer chance, but something worth so much more to us than our feeble instrument. And do you know, we so nearly had hold of it. But then we didn't realise what it was.'

'And this is the eye? What eye? Whose eye? It would help if I had half an inkling to what you are referring.'

'The Idol's Eye.'

The Countess tried look as though she knew nothing.

'It was Sir Richard Dainty's great fortune. No doubt you remember now?'

'The money box, you mean?' The Countess went on playing for time. 'That was a blind. His money was all in bonds and shares and paperwork.'

'Ay, ay. The *working* part of his fortune. But the man was a miserable cheese-parer. He enjoyed sitting on a fortune while making no use of it. Now, if it was me who owned the Idol's Eye, I would have parted with the thing in a twinkling and lived off the proceeds for the rest of my life, lived as though I was a prince.'

Lettice had mentioned it, thinking it might be a brooch. The Countess was now mentally going through the old man's home, trying to picture anything that could be the Eye. 'Is it something to do with those little wooden statuettes on his mantelpiece?'

'It may once have been. I know that the name was given to it because it was the eye of an idol. A statue in Africa. The Eye is a great diamond. A diamond bigger than the ones in the King's crown. As big as a golden guinea. A diamond worth a fortune. And Sir Richard owned it.'

He said the word 'owned' in a strangely double-edged way.

'You mean he did *not* own it?' asked the Countess, thinking back to the letters etched upon the window in Sir Richard's house. Even Godfrey had realised that a diamond had been used to make that mark. 'Did the Eye belong to someone else?'

'The Eye was stolen. Twice stolen, when you think about it: first time from the Idol in Africa, and then from the people who stole it. But all that is immaterial, as I am sure you realise. The only important thing is to find the Eye.'

'Get on with it, for God's sake, man!' Kate Timony blew through her lips like a horse at a trough. 'We haven't got all night.'

'Ah dear, my partner is becoming a little restive. She always was a stubborn mare.' He laughed again, displaying a line of perfect square white teeth. 'So, Countess, tell me what you know about the wicked man.'

'Which wicked man do you mean? Sir Richard Dainty?'

'Ay, a conundrum. He is seen entering your house, and next thing the man is vanished. And on his wedding day too.'

'Entering my house? Sir Richard Dainty? On his wedding day? I'm sure I don't know what you mean.'

'I saw him.' Kate Timony leant forward, thrusting her face between O'Hara and the Countess. 'We had been hiding in the bushes at St James's Park. In the daylight we split up. I mixed with the crowds in the Hay Market. We were looking for somewhere and someone to use that night. And those big houses round St James's are famous for well-connected old crones.' Timony laughed. O'Hara grabbed her by the chin.

'Less of your lip, madam. The Countess is our friend.' He let go of her. 'So, continue . . .'

'The old man was looking flustered. He scuttled along the street, feeling at his pockets, rubbing the sweat from his forehead, pushing back his tattered wig. And he went into your front door. I saw him.'

'What time was this?' The Countess was putting a picture together. Sir Richard had left the wedding just before eleven, and went to 'Change Alley and the Exchange but only stayed a short time. He could have got back to his house just in time for canonicals. But if by accident or design he had got to within a few steps of his home, it would not be difficult still to make that small diversion up to German Street. 'What time did he go in?'

'Just before noon. I remember I was sweltering hot, and hungry too. I had decided on your place because the only servant seemed to be some toothless old fool rubbing his eyes as though he had just been disturbed from a long sleep every time he opened the door.'

'Opened the door? To whom?'

'How should I know? Ask him.'

The Countess could see what had happened. Not only had the trunk been brought to her house that lunchtime, but someone had lured Sir Richard to German Street. And he had been killed right there in her top room.

'What time did he come out?'

'How would I know that?' sneered Kate Timony. 'I watched him go in, then I moved off. Constables and watchmen everywhere these days.'

'Later that evening, as you may remember, Countess, Mrs Timony and I entered your home. And you were so kind as to perform a service for us. A service which brought you round to these parts.'

The Countess wished the picture would become clearer, but the more she was discovering the more puzzling it all seemed. Who was to say that these two criminals were telling her the truth?

'What do you know of the man Edward Stark? And was it you who set him after us?'

'Mr Stark is a businessman. He lives in St Martin's Lane. And I believe he arranged for you two to escape the gallows.'

'No. You have got it wrong. I managed the business myself by untying my own rope. But the man at my side who swung that day had paid his fee to be saved. And somehow or other the service he paid for was not provided. For it was in Edward Stark's interest to let him die.'

'I don't understand.'

'The man beside me, the old fellow charged with coining, was meant to escape. He had paid, but Stark did nothing to effect it. But when I managed to free myself, our friend Stark must have been pretty frightened. He must have known that the old man would have talked to his cell mate . . .'

With a sudden jerk O'Hara unsheathed his knife and pressed it to the Countess's throat. 'Did you get that diamond from the monkey, or is our little simian friend still cavorting about your house wearing it?'

'Captain Caruso?'

'Who?'

'The monkey! You are telling me the monkey has the Eye?'

Timony lunged forward and grasped the Countess by both arms, pulling her back and presenting her bare neck the better to O'Hara's blade.

'The Eye is worked into the buckle on the monkey's belt. Jake told us. In not so many words. So . . .' O'Hara slightly changed the angle of the knife. The Countess was aware of its sharpness against her skin. 'Where is the monkey?'

'I cannot tell you where the monkey is, but I know where he has been today . . .'

'Yes?'

Unconsciously the Countess reached up and touched her wig. 'The monkey was at the house of Hendrick Van Loon, Sir Richard Dainty's partner. And Van Loon has been hereabouts an hour or so ago.'

'Here?' O'Hara pulled her roughly from the wall. 'Where was he?'

'I saw him go to Cardinal Blois Alley.'

'Stark! I knew it. Van Loon has brought the diamond to Edward Stark.'

When Alpiew opened her eyes the tiny room was lit by a wall sconce.

Her face was pressed into a Turkey carpet. She could

see the legs of two chairs, and near the front door a small side-table.

Alpiew wondered how long she had been unconscious. Time enough for the people who had filled the room to disappear, and for the coin clippings to be swept up from the floor.

She raised her head. To her side a small wooden door led into another interior room. Alpiew felt sure everyone must be hiding through there, clutching their clippers and bags of coins.

The picture which had greeted her in that short spark of light was of a coiner's workshop. A cunye house. A room full of treason.

'How's the head?' Edward Stark leaned down to meet her eye-line. 'You took a nasty blow.'

'I should have known you'd have been involved in this mischief,' said Alpiew, sitting up and rubbing her scalp. 'All I have to say is you had better go to your wife, sir.'

'I cannot imagine what business my wife is of yours,' said Edward.

'She is lying in a pool of blood in the governor's office at the Clink.'

'You live in a world of fantasies, do you not, Mistress Alpiew? You and your fanciful dreamer of a mistress. You imagine you see things.'

'It was no fantasy when I caught you at the lace shop in bed with the red-haired maid.'

'You can say you saw such a thing, but I will deny it.'

'Your wife saw it too.'

'Ay, but she too is prone to fantasies. It is that time of life.'

'As you so keenly noticed, Mr Stark, she is carrying a child.'

'Rather late in the day for that sort of gesture, don't you

299

think? And I would have thought it was the surest way to get out of your husband's affections, having a baby sired by another man.'

'It could be yours.'

'Oh no, it could not. I haven't touched the bitch for years. Even when I am drunk the thought of her naked body does not tempt me. Everything about her revolts me. Everything. From her simpering while she hovers around people like your Countess to her constant chomping away at sweetmeats, and her obsession with spending my money.' He crammed a plug of tobacco into the bowl of a clay pipe and struck a light. 'You work hard all your life, and what do you get for it? You know the answer, madam, I am sure.' He took a draught from his pipe, and puffed a blue swirl of smoke into the room. 'What did I get, then? A wife and an apprentice working in a league of malice against me.'

Alpiew had heard quite enough of this. 'Where am I?' She lifted her aching head. 'What is this place?'

'What does it look like?' Edward looked around at the chairs, the table, a large oak coffer, the small captain's chest of drawers, lined with inkhorns, and stacks of papers. 'It is my front parlour. My private office. This is where I sit and think, away from my wife. This is where I smoke my pipe in peace, an area guaranteed free from nagging, where I decide how I can best manage my investments.'

'Do you organise your knocker-uppers from here?'

'Do you mind your own business?' He jumped up and paced the room, glancing back at her. 'I wonder what I should do with you? Shall I kill you now, or later?'

Alpiew slid herself backwards up the side of the wooden trunk. A tiny sliver of silver glistened beside her hand. Trying not to look at it, to keep Mr Stark's attention elsewhere, using her little finger, she swept it under her palm.

300

'Killing a person seems a desperate remedy for her stumbling accidentally into the wrong door. After all, what is here but an office?' Alpiew hoped if she played along he might let her go. If Edward Stark thought she had seen the clippings, of course, he would want to get rid of her. Coining was a capital offence. Worse than that, coining was treason. And she had stumbled into an organised forger's den. She had witnessed coiners at work. If he let her go, who was to say she wouldn't bring the constables back and point the finger and send him straight to the gallows? Unless she could convince him ... 'I opened a door. Do I deserve killing for that? I walked into your office, Mr Stark, and found you smoking a pipe. Where is the harm?'

'Don't play the simpleton with me, wench. I know that you know what this place is. Your lady Countess was here before you. She came here in the dark and took delivery of a forged bond. I handed it to her myself.'

Clutching the sliver of silver in her palm, Alpiew slowly got to her feet. 'I think, Mr Stark, that you should let me go. Your apprentice Robinson is on the run, your wife is stabbed. There are other more pressing things you should be seeing to.'

'I assure you, minx,' Edward Stark moved over to the street door, barring her exit, 'you are going nowhere.'

As he flicked his finger, shooting a bolt into its socket, the door shook.

A heavy fist hammered away on the outer side. 'Open up! Open up!' The battering continued. 'Open up, in the name of the law.'

'The constables!' Edward Stark blanched, stepping gingerly away from the door. 'They will not catch me here. You let them in, pray, Mistress Alpiew.' He plunged his hand into his pocket, pulled out a fistful of coin shavings

301

and flung them on to the carpet. 'See how they will catch you red-handed.'

He shoved Alpiew roughly to one side and threw himself into the back room.

Alpiew followed him to the door and saw a commotion, a gaggle of people in chaos, struggling to climb out of a tiny window set high in the wall.

Edward Stark was first out.

The banging on the street door rose to a crescendo. 'Knock it in,' ordered a stern voice from the street.

After a few hefty blows the door sprang open. A gang of men lit by four huge flambeaux stood in the tiny alley.

'Seize her!' cried a tall well-dressed man as he strode into the room.

As two officers grabbed hold of her, Alpiew guessed this man was no simple constable. This was a Justice or an Excise officer.

'Definitely a cunye house, a mint,' he called to his men. 'Arrest everyone here. We have caught 'em in the act. The cells of Newgate will be busy tonight. For everyone in this house is guilty of treason.'

'You cannot arrest us,' screamed a man from the other room. 'This is a Liberty.'

'Liberty! Once you're in the wagon and over the bridge I will show you what liberty means. You will cry for liberty until the day you dance the hempen jig. You are a traitor, sir. A traitor to the Kingdom of England. We have been watching this place for days. We know all the comings and goings.' He marched over to the large wooden chest in the corner. It was secured with a heavy padlock. 'No doubt this is where you stash your store of clippings of silver and gold, ready to be carted away and melted down.'

The Justice waved to one of his men who duly applied

an axe to the lock, splitting it open and chipping the wood behind it.

'Open it,' he barked.

The man lifted the lid.

But they did not find a stash of clippings from His Majesty's currency.

There was a man inside.

He was wearing nothing but his underwear. His face was blue. His mouth wide open.

He did not move.

Sticks of rue still firmly in place up each nostril, Hendrick Van Loon stared out into the crowded room.

There was a simple explanation for his immobility.

Hendrick Van Loon was dead.

A knife to her back, and both Timony and O'Hara's arms tight round her waist, the Countess staggered into Borough Road. They were walking her fast, both their heads lolling down. They sang in slurred voices, like drunks. What better disguise in a squalid purlieu like this?

'*A lusty young smith at his vice stood a-filling,*' yelled O'Hara, as they lurched in time with his song:

> '*Rub, rub, rub, rub, rub, rub, in and out, in and out, ho!*
> *When to him his buxom young damsel came smiling . . .*'

They rolled past the busy taverns and stews, where cheap prostitutes leered out of upstairs windows, catcalling to men below who might want their services.

> '*And asked if to work at her forge he would go,*
> "*A match," quoth the smith, so away they went thither,*
> *With a rub, rub, rub, rub, rub, rub, in and out, in and out,*
> *ho!*'

The Countess felt the rough hands tighten around her waist as they turned into Foul Lane.

They reeled past a gang of sober-looking men, maybe law officers. O'Hara sang the louder for it.

> *'They stripped to go to it – t'was hot work, and hot weather –*
> *She kindled a fire, and soon made him blow,*
> *With a rub, rub, rub . . .'*

They turned again. New Rents, the signboard said. A few yards ahead, the Countess caught sight of a familiar hanging sign. A sign bearing the picture of a Cardinal's Hat.

> *'Red-hot grew his iron, as both did desire,*
> *And he was too wise not to strike while t'was so,*
> *Quoth she: "I am hot, I am hot with this fire,*
> *Oh, prithee, strike home and redouble the blow . . ."'*

The Countess knew now where they were taking her.

They bowled along, turning suddenly into the alleyway. Heads still down, they marched the Countess briskly into the dark passage.

O'Hara stopped singing.

The Countess was aware of something different about the place. She was coming in from the opposite end to when she came into this alley before, of course, but whereas before it had been impenetrably dark, the place now seemed to glow. There was also a burble of voices, some kind of commotion ahead.

'What the . . . ?' O'Hara stopped, staring towards the glimmering light before them.

They edged forward a few steps, trying to look round the kink in the wall.

O'Hara pressed himself against the corner and peered ahead.

'Law officers!' He ground his heel into the dirt. 'They got to the monster too soon, damn their eyes.'

The flickering light faded, and the alley grew black again. The footsteps receded and were gone.

'They've carted off a whole batch of his workers too,' hissed O'Hara. 'I doubt there will be any pickings left for us.'

The Countess watched O'Hara's eyes in the dying light. They glinted, cold and hard. He stiffened, and turned to face her.

'Do you know, Countess,' he murmured, 'in the last few moments your value has decreased significantly.'

The Countess watched his hand slide down and his fingers wrap slowly around the hilt of his dagger.

He was going to kill her.

'I can lead you to the Eye!' she whimpered, wishing her voice had more strength.

'Don't make me laugh,' snapped O'Hara. 'You didn't even know what the Eye was.'

The Countess swallowed, holding her breath, preparing to dive to the floor, to run, anything rather than die alone here in this stinking black lane.

The blade glinted as it flashed through the air.

TEN

Wetting off — using a wet tool deliberately to crack the glass, separating it from the iron

Alpiew sat crammed on the back of the wagon among the captured coiners. The officers had under-estimated the size of their catch, and were never going to make it all the way to Newgate with a cartload of people crushed up like this.

The wagon pulled in at the Clink to offload the over-flow.

Alpiew edged herself near to the front corner. This was rather easy to do as all the coiners were busily edging the other way. Everybody knew the Clink was a filthy, damp hell-hole, and Newgate, for all its squalor, was nowhere near such a horrible place. No one on the cart but Alpiew wanted to be chosen.

'You!' An officer seized Alpiew and yanked her down.

The gatekeeper unlocked the great door as the officer gave Alpiew a rough shove through it.

The other prisoners put up an energetic resistance. Officers from the Clink came out into the street to help the Justice's men drag them into the prison.

Alpiew meanwhile marched briskly forward, her hands still bound with rope. It all seemed too easy. But her name had not been taken, and, if Cynthia was still conscious, she could see a way of getting herself out of this mess and back on to the streets a free woman.

She looked neither to left nor right. As she encountered nobody, it was without interference that she walked straight to the governor's office. If there was any question she would call for the prison chaplain, who must surely remember her from before.

Cynthia Stark lay on the table, still pale as a ghost, but alive.

Alpiew hurriedly sat, her back to the door. She presented her tethered hands to Cynthia. 'Your husband is a no-good, wicked, double-dealing, murderous villain,' she said as Cynthia's fingers started to pick at the rope. 'He has just escaped justice and landed me in here.'

'I will help you,' whispered Cynthia, wincing as she deftly worked at the knot. 'The surgeon has staunched my wound. I owe you for that.'

'Why did you not tell us Mr Stark had no business but crime?'

'He does mix with some criminal types, I admit, Mistress Alpiew, but he also has a healthy financial business.'

The door opened. Alpiew snatched her hands down on to her lap and wrapped her fingers around the rope, trying to hide it. She turned and smiled at the governor.

'I am come back to visit Mrs Stark, as I said I would. If you could arrange a hackney cab, sir, perhaps I can take her home, where she will be looked after in comfort.'

'Ah!' The governor rocked back and forth apologetically. 'There is a bit of a crisis inside the prison at the moment, I am sorry to say, but if you go and fetch the cab yourself I am sure, by the time you find one, things will have calmed a little and my men can assist Mrs Stark out into the street.'

He held the door open and waved his arm towards Alpiew.

Alpiew glanced at Cynthia Stark, who understood, and reached out, grabbing Alpiew's wrists. 'Please don't leave me again, Alpiew,' she implored. 'We can wait a few moments longer, until the governor and his men can help us.'

'As you wish, madam.' The governor strode across the room towards the table. Alpiew dropped her hands to one side to prevent him seeing her bonds.

'Excuse me.' He pulled open a drawer in his desk. 'I need the register. We have rather a large number of new inmates to record tonight.'

The ledger was huge. As he pulled it from the drawer it slipped from his grasp. Instinctively Alpiew reached out to catch it.

Cynthia let out a loud groan, attracting his eyes away from the rope binding Alpiew's wrists.

'I do apologise, madam.' The governor bent over Cynthia and whispered. 'That was my fault for dropping the damned thing. I think the sooner we get you home the better.' He picked the prison register up from the floor and tiptoed out of the office.

Once he was gone, Alpiew spoke quietly. 'Your husband's healthy financial business is hard by this place, Mrs Stark, did you know that?'

'No, Alpiew, you are mistaken. My husband works from the Exchange and in the coffee houses.'

Alpiew looked at the poor injured woman and felt very sorry for her. She had seen this before: women who protected their husbands, even when they knew them to be nasty cheating rogues and as guilty as sin.

'Why do you stay with him, madam? And more to the point, why do you protect him?'

Cynthia turned her face away. Her eyes brimmed with tears.

'I have to. He once did me a great favour.'

'And might this favour have something to do with your father?'

'How do you know that?' Cynthia scrutinised Alpiew's face.

'Because I have noticed that whenever you talk of your father you start to cry.' Alpiew held up her bound hands. Cynthia continued unpicking the knots.

'My husband saved my father's life.'

'I thought you said your father was two years dead.'

'He is. He died.' Cynthia gasped, suppressing a sob. 'But at least it was a natural death, not like the one he would have faced if . . .' Her voice trailed off.

Alpiew pulled one hand free of the tether, loosened the remaining cord circle, freed herself and hastily stuffed the rope into the governor's desk drawer.

'What crime had your father committed? It must have been something serious.' Alpiew worked her way through the possibilities, the methods Edward Stark might have used to save his father-in-law from dancing the Tyburn frisk in a hempen cravat. 'Murder, perhaps?'

'No. No. My father was a good man really. It was a surprise to me what he was doing. I suppose it was greed.' Cynthia bit her lip, trying not to cry. 'But my husband petitioned the King on his behalf. It was a success. He managed to get the sentence commuted from execution to transportation.'

'Your father was sent to the plantations?'

Cynthia squeezed her lips tight, and shook her head. 'He didn't make it. He died of an apoplexy, in Portsmouth, on his way to the convict ship. Some would say he died of shame, appalled at the ignominy of his own misdeeds.' Cynthia cried now as though a dammed-up deluge had finally been released. 'Poor Dad.'

'I am sorry.' Alpiew took the woman's hand and squeezed it. 'Why did Robinson wound you?'

'Oh God! It was not Robinson who cut me.' Through her tears, Cynthia looked to Alpiew, terror in her eyes. 'It was my husband. He stabbed me in the street near that fateful lace shop. He was in a fury at my making a fool of him. It was all over in a moment. He left me in a small court and ran off. I lay for a few minutes, while people stepped over me. I suppose they thought I was drunk. Finally I got to my feet and dragged myself to a cab. I came here with the wound covered but still bleeding. I had to warn Robinson that next Edward would come for him.'

'Because of the baby?'

'Baby?' Cynthia gave a wan smile and placed her palm on her belly. 'Oh no! This is not Robinson's baby! But Edward thinks it is. If he knew the truth he would be even more horrified. How he hates to look a dupe.'

The door swung open.

'Mesdames!' The governor stood in the doorway, clutching the register to his chest. 'My men have found you a hackney. Let me help you to it.'

He marched over to the desk and reached for the drawer.

'Allow me,' said Alpiew, snatching the book from him. 'If you could please assist Mrs Stark from the table.'

Cynthia staggered to her feet while Alpiew shoved the register into the desk, pushing the incriminating piece of rope as far to the back of the drawer as it would go.

Once settled inside the cold of the cab, Cynthia turned to Alpiew.

'You do realise I cannot go home. Will the Countess mind if we turn up at her house so late at night?'

'Of course not. She never retires early.' Alpiew was tired, and longing to lie down. But Cynthia Stark was going to talk, she felt sure. And what she had to say would illuminate so much, Alpiew felt certain. 'My lady will be glad of the company. She will no doubt be sitting up by the fire, reading.'

In the blind darkness of Cardinal Blois Alley, the Countess saw the knife shoot up in the air ready to strike her.

By instinct she ducked. But at the same moment she was pushed by a forceful hand, thrust out of the path of the lethal blade.

The next moment arms were wrapped around her waist and she was dragged back along the alley. She limped along, not knowing who had hold of her or where they were heading. She could hear the pounding feet of O'Hara and Timony yards behind.

Suddenly the arms which supported her thrust her to the ground, forcing her body into a small hole in the wall. A gush of dry dusty heat wafted into her face as two hands shoved her roughly from behind. She put out her hands ready to fall, feeling the ground beneath her descending in a sharp slope.

Nimble feet behind her dashed away as she continued rolling, rolling down the slope, until she came to rest, sprawled out on a soft bed of warm ashes.

She lay on her back, spluttering, sucking in fine dust with the hot dry air.

After a moment or two she sat up, coughing, and crawled forward along the long tunnel towards an orange light. As she approached the light it seemed to be getting warmer and warmer. There were cavities in the brickwork all along the tunnel, presumably air vents like the one she had just tumbled down.

She listened. She could hear the faint murmur of low voices ahead. From the dancing shadows, it seemed there were candles lit. Then she heard laughter. Not the scornful laughter of O'Hara and Timony, but the easy, relaxed laughter of friends.

She got to her feet and, crouching, padded forward. The tunnel widened. Ahead of her was an arched space, easily high enough to stand in. In the centre of the ceiling was a huge grating which radiated heat. The floor was a thick carpet of pink ash.

All around the edges of the room, chatting quietly, leaning up against the arches and walls, were small gangs of men and children.

In the centre of the tunnel directly below the grating there was a tray full of candles.

The men turned to her, unsurprised at her sudden appearance in their midst.

'Like a sup of ale, love?' said one, thrusting a tankard in her direction.

The Countess smiled and took a sip of the man's beer.

'I suppose this is the glass-house?'

'*That* is the glass-house.' The man pointed a finger skyward. '*This* is our home. Well appointed, don't you think? And did anyone ever encounter such an efficient heating system since the Romans built their famous baths?'

The Countess was amazed to have been plucked from such danger and thrust into such apparent safety.

'It's lovely,' said the Countess, taking a position squatting on the floor beside the man. 'I am sorry if I am intruding, sir, but I didn't have much choice in the matter.'

'All new inhabitants welcome,' said the man. 'They neal the glass up there. The fire is always hot, for the glass-making.' He ruffled the cinders around him and plucked up a small teardrop of glass. 'And we are even rewarded with our own jewels. We might get a little bit dusty down here, rolling in the ash, but it is comfortable as a down pillow, and the warmth makes full amends for such a dirty way of life.' He nudged her in the side. 'Especially when it is cold out.'

'Do you all have to roll down through that hole every night to get in?'

The man guffawed. 'There are easier routes, once you know them. There are two great man-sized entrances, and with a little reconnaissance you can easily manoeuvre yourself inside once the upstairs work-force has gone home. This place is purposely big. The glaziers come down here to clear out the ashes each morning. And the glassmakers need an up-draught to feed the furnace and a space below the fire to catch the ash. And here we live. The subterranean tunnel beneath a glass-house.'

'It is very dusty.' The Countess could see that no one had avoided collecting a new powdery white skin.

'Oh yes. No chance of clean clothing after a night down here!' The man ran his hands through his hair, creating a small cloud round his head. 'The advantages though are, as you see: the place is perfectly close, and consequently it is as warm as the dressing room of a bagnio.'

'I wouldn't know,' said the Countess, rather disgruntled that the man must think her familiar with the insides of a whore house. Then she remembered she was dressed in a silk tunic and satin pantaloons. By no means everyday wear for a respectable London lady.

'The fact is, madam, that once inside this place it is impossible to feel any cold, were we in Greenland or Nova Zembla. The only inconvenience, as I said, is the wretched dust.' He sifted some through his fingers. 'It makes it a little difficult to look spruce and ready for parade during the day time.'

'You are a military man?'

'Alas, madam, there are no military men any more. The late peace has seen to that. And the government with their absurd budgeting.' He rested his head against the wall, and sipped at his beer. 'We are all gentlemen of leisure. We, the warriors who once fought on the fields of Flanders, Holland, Ireland, Scotland and France.'

'So many conflicts during our lifetime!' The Countess had been brought up during the Civil War, and it seemed that, till now, there had never been a time when England was not at war with someone or other.

'We worked the ships too, fought the Dutch on the Thames and the French in the Channel.' He pointed down along the row of powdery men, grey with dust, ragged with poverty. 'Some of these boys have spent their lives fighting on ships. They've protected the fleets of merchantmen from Barbary pirates. Some of them even worked in garrisons stationed as far away as America and Africa. And what do they give us in return for a lifetime of patriotic endeavour?'

He looked as though he was waiting for the Countess to reply, so she obliged. 'I'm sure I don't know. What did they give you?'

'The precious Treaty of Ryswick, that's what! Curses on the infernal place, wherever it may be, that produced such devil of a treaty, for it put most all of us out of a job. And tell me what we got by way of compensation? The National Debt, the Lotteries, the Bank of England, recoinage . . .' He spat.

'Are there no jobs at all?'

'Some of my colleagues were lucky. They landed work in the area of security: gaolers, constables, headboroughs, watchmen – you know the stuff. A few got into the trained bands. But there are only so many of those occupations. We came home in our squadrons, battalions, regiments.

And where could you find so many jobs for so many men and all at once?'

'And none of these new-found business establishments in the City would have you?'

'We are trained warriors, madam. We are fighting machines, not smug prick-me-dainties in full-bottomed wigs, chewing on clay pipes and throwing so much coffee down our maws till our skins turn brown from it.'

The Countess tutted. She felt sorry for the man, but also saw that it was rather fortunate she had landed up sitting next to someone who might be able to put up a decent fight against John O'Hara and his partner Kate Timony should they find their way into this strange and wonderful place.

'You look all in, madam,' said the ex-soldier. 'Would you like a little peace from my prating?'

'Not really.' The Countess knew she needed to stay here for a while, perhaps till day-break. 'But maybe I will shut my eyes for a minute or two.'

The man gave her a smart inclination of the head and turned away to talk with his companions.

The Countess closed her eyes and sank back into the soft warm cinders. She needed to go through everything she knew and try to make some sense of it all.

Africa!

Africa had to hold the key to the whole horrible business.

Sir Richard's ugly little wooden statuettes; his governorship in Bambara; the monkey; the Eye of the Idol. All Africa.

She tried to picture Captain Caruso on her roof when he flashed past the window that night. 'Twinkling' Alpiew had said he was. 'Twinkling.'

The Countess cast her mind through all the other

events: the interrupted wedding, the hold-up by O'Hara and his friend; the old man's body hidden inside his own garish trunk in her attic store; the other body in the privy, the poor ineffectual watchman with the lemon drops and no stomach; and Cupid, suddenly appearing from nowhere with his revolting silver collar; the tarred old body in the gibbet, its stomach gone; Robinson, his arrest for passing the very bond that the Countess had brought to Sir Richard's house, and his tale of an orphaned childhood on the parish with his baby sister, Lettice . . .

The vaulted ceiling suddenly resounded with chatter like a chamber full of trapped starlings. It was a vaguely disturbing commotion.

The Countess tapped the army man on the sleeve. 'Who is come here now with such a shrill clamour?'

'Ah, those little fellows are regulars here. They are an army all of their own making.' The soldier bent to whisper into the Countess's ear. 'Some among them are no better than they could be.'

The Countess was aware of a resentment in his voice.

'They are only children, I suppose. Just little tatter-medallions who manage to keep themselves whichsoever way they can, be it through ventures innocent or criminal. If a penny is offered they care not from whom, 'tis a penny.'

'They must be the dusty boys.' The Countess sifted some of the cinders through her fingers.

'Dusty boys, indeed, madam. But they term themselves the City Black-Guard.'

A gang of the children entered the part of the cavern where the Countess sat. They were looking around, trying to find somewhere to lie down.

As she watched them, the Countess came eye to eye with a face she knew.

The boy looked at her. Quickly she darted a look at his hand, just to be sure. Yes. The tip of one finger was missing. It was Jake.

Suddenly, raising a cloud of dust in his wake, the boy turned on his heels and ran.

Alpiew flung the front door open for the hackney man to carry Cynthia into the Countess's kitchen. It was past midnight. The new German Street watchman was snoozing in his box.

She was glad the cab-man was with them.

The house was cold, dark and quiet.

Alpiew wondered if the Countess had gone to Pigalle's for the night.

'Would you just come around and check the house with me, sir?' Alpiew asked as the coachman helped her lay Cynthia upon the Countess's bed. 'Only there has been a lot of nasty crooks passing through in the week, and I'd like to be sure we are alone.'

The cab-driver, having had his fare and a hefty tip from Cynthia, was happy to oblige.

'Now there's a strange house,' he whispered to Alpiew as they descended the stairs, the job done. 'All show and no substance. Surprising, really.' He rubbed his fingers together. 'Your mistress doesn't look short of the old chinkers.'

'Yes. Eccentric.' Alpiew decided not to disabuse him either of the fact that Cynthia was not her mistress or that her real mistress was currently penniless. Thanking him profusely, she waved him off and shut the door.

She hurried through to the front room and dragged a chair out into the hall. She wedged this under the lock. Although there was a lock, it could not be applied as Godfrey had lost the key. But the chair would serve a similar purpose. At least if anyone tried to barge in now they'd have to use force and make quite a noise into the bargain.

'It's cold.' Cynthia was stooping over the grate, trying to kindle the fire as Alpiew came back into the kitchen. 'I hope you don't mind.'

Alpiew knelt beside her and broke some long sticks into kindling wood and started piling them up in the iron fire basket over some crumpled-up paper.

While Cynthia took a flame from the candle with a taper, Alpiew checked the pots swinging in the fireplace.

'Full of feathers! I will take one into the yard and wash it. But first I'll see if I can find any food or drink. No point getting cold washing a pot if we've nothing to put inside it.' Alpiew put the iron cauldron by the back door, crossed the kitchen and stood outside the door to the pantry. She hesitated, holding the handle. She had not checked the pantry. What if someone were in there, hiding?

'What is wrong?' Cynthia was standing, facing her. 'Why do you not open . . . ?' She lowered her voice. 'Is someone hiding in there?' She stooped and picked up the poker, then tiptoed across the room and stood at Alpiew's side. She nodded and raised the poker.

With an abrupt jerk Alpiew pulled open the door.

In a blur of sudden movement a man leapt out, his hands waving, and Cynthia brought the poker crashing down on his head.

The fact that the boy Jake had taken to his heels once he caught sight of her confirmed the Countess's decision to stay in the warm tunnel beneath the glass-house, surrounded by these soldiers who seemed none too fond of the City Black-Guard.

Black-Guard! What a name for a raggle-taggle bunch of

children on the run from the poor house. She looked along the row of grey soldiers. There were two or more Moors amongst them. They in all fairness might call themselves the black-guard.

The Countess thought of Cupid. What on earth had become of him? She hoped he was safe. She thought of his grim silver collar and wondered how they could remove it without beheading him or severing his vital arteries. Which devious mind had thought up such a wicked contrivance?

And that vile, mad Van Loon who thought you could buy people for a bag of glass beads. The monkey had been in his house, that was certain. How else had her wig made its way there? And if the monkey was there, and what O'Hara said was true, she presumed the Eye had been there too. If Jake had told them about the Eye, she hoped he was not on his way to fetch them to her now. Perhaps she should run for it while she had a chance. She looked around. There were a lot of burly-looking men here. No. She was safer to stay.

She settled back into the ash and thought.

Van Loon had seemed so horrified by the sight of her wig that it was clear the Dutchman had not brought it in himself. As Captain Caruso had taken it from Pigalle's house, it must be supposed it was the monkey who dropped it at Van Loon's.

She wondered whether the Dutchman had perhaps killed the monkey to get at the stone. Though if it was on his belt, he could have got the gem easier by simply undressing the creature. He obviously knew Sir Richard was dead. His reactions to the name were too intense. And what was it that had driven the man out of the house so soon after she and the pretend Prince had visited? Why had Van Loon come to the glass-house? Here! She supposed he had sent his man into the room above them to pick up whatever it was he picked up in the two tiny bags.

'Excuse me –' the Countess touched the ex-soldier on the arm – 'could you tell me, sir, is this the flint glass-house or the green glass-house?'

'The flint,' said the man. 'I decided upon the superior works!' He sieved some ash through his fingers and held out a few pebbles of glass. 'Look at it! Bright and clear. As pretty as a jewel on any lady's necklace from Versailles to Vera Cruz.'

The Countess took the small bauble of glass and rubbed it clean of all ash. She held it up to the candle and gazed through it towards the candles' dancing flames.

This was why Van Loon was here. He had bought a piece of glass. A piece of glass small enough to slip into a vest pocket.

True, this flint glass did not burn and shoot fire like a diamond, but even a diamond, until it was cut, lacked that famous flaming lustre.

The gem everyone was after had been the eye of an African idol. Would it have been cut out in Africa? It would have come from India, as all diamonds did. The Dutch were the ones who did all the cutting and shaping of diamonds. Van Loon would know all the connections in Amsterdam, he would have known where to get the Eye cut, perhaps even reducing it to a score of different gems. And there were many Dutch in Africa too, of course. Perhaps Van Loon had been there himself.

There was certainly a connection between the Dutchman and the Eye. He must have taken the diamond from the monkey's buckle. And placed an order for a glass replica. Then, this evening, she had witnessed him picking up that exact reproduction of the Eye, a copy made of flint glass. A big knop! She chuckled to herself.

And wherever it was that Van Loon had gone when, uniquely, he left his chair to walk alone down Cardinal Blois Alley, he had taken the fake diamond with him.

And whichever person in this deadly chain he had given it to would not realise the cheat until they had it refaceted and shaped by an expert, or tried to use the diamond to cut letters into glass.

The Eye, the real diamond, had been used to carve a word into that window in Pall Mall Street.

Eris!

Eris – Strife. What a fateful name to give a ship. Like Cassandra – Doom. As though being at sea wasn't a dangerous enough occupation without risking the superstitious connotations of their namesakes. No doubt some fool was out there launching a boat today and calling it Pandora, Chaos, Night.

Eris – daughter of Night.

Eris. The start of it all.

The Countess turned to the soldier.

'Excuse me, sir, but may I ask you one question? You said your friends there worked on ships.' The Countess edged the inquiry forward, fearful of its consequences. 'Do you know anything of a ship called *Eris*?'

Cupid lay sprawled out on the floor.

'Oh no! It's Cupid!' sighed Alpiew. 'Not again.'

'Do you know him?' asked Cynthia, dropping the poker and kneeling at Cupid's side.

'Oh yes, madam. He is as good as my baby brother,' said Alpiew. 'He was the Countess's Moorish boy, back in the good old days.' She sighed. 'And this is the second time this week he has been knocked out by a poker blow to the head while secreting himself about my lady's house.'

'Do you have any hartshorn?' Cynthia loosened the belt round his breeches while Alpiew rooted through the shelves in the pantry.

'Some Nantes brandy is all I can find.' Alpiew pulled the stopper out of the bottle and poured a little into a leather beaker. When she returned to the kitchen Cynthia was rocking back and forth, cradling Cupid's head on her lap. 'I am so sorry.' She bent low and kissed him on the lips. 'Darling Cupid.'

Alpiew stopped where she stood. 'Are you feeling quite well, madam?'

'I hope you are not shocked, Mistress Alpiew?' Cynthia looked her square in the eye. 'I took you for a person with old-fashioned values, like your mistress. She was one of the belles of the sixties, was she not? A creature from the time of free love? Well, you see, I may as well confess to you now, Cupid is the love I spoke of. My husband bought him in some strange crooked deal from Van Loon. He was my husband's slave. But, in this brave new world of business and affairs, husbands go out to work and wives stay at home.' She gave a scornful laugh. 'Affairs! If ever there was a love affair it was between me and pretty Cupid. I love him with all my heart.' She was smoothing Cupid's brow, gently caressing his black curly hair. '"The heart is a small thing, but desireth great matters. It is not sufficient for a kite's dinner, yet the whole world is not sufficient for it . . ." Quarles. My father used to quote that, all the time.' She bent forward and kissed Cupid again. 'Please, darling boy . . .' She looked up to Alpiew. 'He will be all right, won't he?' She ran her fingers round the inside of his collar. 'I swear we will find a way to get this thing off his neck. Would you like to read, Alpiew?'

Alpiew knelt and read the inscription carved into the

silver band. *Property of Ed Stark, St Martin's La. Return to legal owner*. If he loved you, Mrs Stark, why did he run away from you . . . ?'

'I told him to run.' Cynthia gripped his hair, clearly upset. 'My husband had got it into his head that Cupid was stealing from him. I am certain he wasn't, and told my husband so. But he was about to bring a charge against him. And you do know that, as a slave, my husband could have called for Cupid to be executed, simply on a whim? The irony is that there was thieving going on in the house and I knew who it was, and I felt sorry for the creature.' She gave a sound of disgust. 'It was Molly, that wretched maid with the red hair, who was the thief in our house. She took pieces of lace, Flanders lace. Very expensive stuff. I don't know whether she just sold it for cash, or gave it to someone, but she took it all right.'

'And you let your husband blame Cupid?'

'Of course not. I told him in definite terms that I was certain it was not Cupid, but I tried to cover for the wretched girl. The more I did so, the more Edward became convinced that the thief was Cupid.' She laughed and gazed down at his immobile face. 'Can you imagine this big milksop sneaking around stealing my lace, when, if he'd wanted lace, I'd have given it to him by the box-load, over and over, as much lace as he ever wanted, and more.' She stooped and kissed his forehead again.

'And your baby?' Alpiew looked at Cupid.

'Yes.' Cynthia nodded. 'Cupid is the father of my child. I thought I might get away with it. My plan was to drink so much chocolate that people would think it was the same as that lady at Versailles a few years ago who drank so much of the stuff when she was pregnant that she was brought to bed of a little black baby.'

'You jest?' Alpiew laughed. 'People believed her?'

'Apparently so! Chocolate is such a novelty, no one could be quite sure about it.'

Cupid's eyes started to flicker.

'Sweetheart!' Cynthia stroked his cheek as he slowly opened his eyes. 'Lie still.'

'There was a bit of an accident,' said Alpiew, applying the cup of brandy to his lips. 'How were we to know it was you?'

'I'm afraid I struck you, Cupid.' Cynthia seemed terribly upset.

'The last nasty bump I got from Alpiew is not recovered yet.' He smiled, rubbing the top of his head. 'And here you are giving me a fellow to keep it company.'

Alpiew wanted to question him, to find out why he had been in the house on the day the night-watch Charlie had been murdered, and why he was back now, hiding in the pantry.

Cupid saw the blood-stains on the side of Cynthia's mantua, and she in turn was fussing over the bump on his head. Alpiew helped them both up and smoothed a place for them on the Countess's bed.

Pshaw! The two love-birds were all over each other.

'I am sorry to interrupt you,' Alpiew coughed. 'But I would please ask, Cupid, if you might answer a few of my queries before you drift off to sleep.' She glanced back to the pot by the door. 'And then I will try to cook up some beans and dried meat, which is all I can find in the pantry.'

Wrapped in each other's arms on the bed, Cupid and Cynthia nodded. Alpiew wasn't sure she trusted either of them. But at least their injuries meant that their joint strength did not add up to much, for the moment, at least.

'Cupid, why were you here with Robinson tidying up our kitchen on the day the watchman was murdered?'

Cupid cast his eyes down.

'Will you not answer me?'

'I was looking for something.' His voice was quiet. 'Something important.'

'In my lady's house? Could you not have asked us first?'

'We didn't want to . . . inconvenience anyone. In case that thing was not here.'

'And did one of you take the hundred guineas which went missing from the house that day?'

'Of course not. We would never steal from you.'

'And yet you came secretly tiptoeing round this house and when you were caught you ran away, and came back later only to be disturbed by me and the Countess.'

'Phough! Am I mistaken in you, Cupid?' Cynthia had pulled herself away from him. 'What exactly was this thing that turns you and Robinson into house-breakers and burglars?'

'I cannot say, until . . .'

'Until . . . ?'

'I cannot.' He shook his head and looked down.

Alpiew realised that he was not going to speak.

'Perhaps while we wait for your memory to come back you might help me fetch some water from the butt in the yard.'

Alpiew swung across the kitchen and picked up the iron pot with both hands. Cupid loped over and unbolted the door. As he pulled at the handle the door burst open, knocking him to the floor.

Edward Stark smashed his way in. He was holding a gun.

'What a moving scene of domestic harmony! My slave tupping my wife. And there was I thinking she'd been given a rollocking by my apprentice.' He pointed his gun towards the prostrate figure of Cupid. 'If I killed you both, you know they could not accuse me.'

'They could accuse you of murder, I think, Husband.' Cynthia raised herself to a sitting position.

'But what justification! It is petit treason for the wife to betray the husband, and treason for the slave to steal his goods. And what a theft! To be screwing at my wife. You are both stealing what belongs to me.' He raised the barrel of the gun and aimed it at his wife, who cowered back against the headboard of the Countess's bed.

'You told me, sir, you did not care for your wife.' Alpiew dropped the pan to the flagged floor. The crash made Mr Stark spin round. The gun was now pointing at Alpiew.

'Might I ask you, sir, what business you have here, marching into a lady's house in the middle of the night and thrusting the muzzle of a gun in our faces?'

'It was your mistress I came to see, wench.' Edward Stark advanced on Alpiew. 'But meanwhile, you will do.'

'The tales are plentiful about the *Eris*. Never has a ship been so whispered about. Never was a ship so aptly named. But no one knows what really happened.' The seaman was brown as a nut, and his skin looked as tough. 'It left Virginia. The supercargo was a gentleman, a colonel from His Majesty's service. He signed for the stock and, my word, what a stock it was. The ship must have been laden from the bilboes to the poop-deck. 'Twas rumoured by many that the cause of the disaster was greed. They said the ship was over-laden.' He licked his dry wrinkled lips then continued chewing on the stem of his pipe. 'And yet there are others who said that was so much piffle, for the ship had barely a cargo on board at all, lest you count the price of the men.'

'Slaves?'

'No, not slaves.' The sea-dog spat a piece of tobacco on to the ashes. 'Unless you include a ship's company under that term. For the crew are slaves to the captain and the captain is a slave to the master and the super-cargo carries the word of the master.' The sailor sniffed. 'The ship left on a calm day, and sailed out into the Atlantic Ocean. Now, as everyone knows, that ocean is a big 'un, and bleak, with no sight of land for weeks. There's a heavy swell out there too. But when the *Eris* left, never to be seen again, a number of other ships left at the same time. And they all made it home safe. And none of 'em reported anything more than the usual weather. In fact most of 'em said the sea was smoother than a mill pond. *Eris* was a hermaphrodite brig. An ideal ship for that crossing, with an experienced crew. And yet she went down to the bottom of the ocean. Now here's the mystery: all the cargo, all the crew, and the ship plunged down to the bottom of the sea, out there, thousands of miles from land. And yet one single person on that ship made it safely home. And that person was none other than our aforesaid supercargo.'

'But how could it be,' asked the Countess, 'that one man could survive if the ship was so far from land?'

'He had got away all alone in the *Eris*'s yaugh, and that yaugh was picked up by another ship. A ship in the same line, as it happens. And the man came home with tales of mutiny and fighting amongst the crew, and a fire which ravaged the ship and took her down to the bottom of Davy Jones's locker.'

'The man got a reward from the company, I suppose?'

'Oh, the man *was* the company. Him and another fellow, a Dutchman. He's a rum cove, by all accounts, the Dutchman. And the other one 'as a queer lamp.'

'Lamp?'

'He's blind in one eye. But that didn't seem to hold him back. To this day he is one of the richest men in London.'

'And his name?'

'His name is Sir Richard Dainty. Now it turned out that these crewmen had brought something very valuable with them on to this ship, the *Eris*. It was a little idol they'd got hold of in Africa. They traded it with some tribe for their guns as they were leaving for America. And they always carried it around with them. They took turns to care for it. It was their pension, so they said. But they took it on to that ship, and everyone who knew about it presumed it had gone down with the ship.

'But then a whisper went round – someone 'ad seen it, in a house right here in London. And it seems that house belonged to this same Richard Dainty. So he now 'ad this idol, or a part of it at any rate.'

'I see,' said the Countess. 'Might that part be called the Eye?'

''Twas you tipped off the Justice about my house in the Cardinal Blois Alley, wasn't it, wench?' snapped Edward Stark. 'That was my business you threw in the bin. Oh, I know I can find somewhere else and more people to work for me, but these things take time, and who is going to pay for the time and money lost?'

'They will pick you up again, Mr Stark,' said Alpiew. 'Running a workshop for clipping coins is one thing, murder is another.'

'Murder? What are you talking about now?'

'Clipping coins?' Cynthia rose from the bed. 'Who is clipping coins?'

'Shut up!' yelled Edward Stark, moving towards Alpiew, thrusting the muzzle of the gun into her ribs. 'Shut up!'

Alpiew backed away. But Stark followed her, prodding at her with the gun, until she was lined up next to Cynthia, by the Countess's bed.

From the floor behind the door Cupid groaned and raised his head.

'As for you, you thieving, fornicating animal –' Edward Stark swung round, lowered the gun, and took aim at Cupid – 'prepare to die.'

'Hold it where you are!' With an explosion of glass, Kate Timony arrived in the kitchen by way of the window. At the same moment John O'Hara slammed in through the back door. Both held a cocked pistol in each hand. Everyone in the room now found a weapon aimed at them.

'It might help if you had primed your gun before raising it,' sneered O'Hara with a gesture towards Edward Stark. 'You are at half-cock, sir!'

'The story of my life,' muttered Cynthia.

Stark's hands flew to pull back the lock mechanism.

'No, you don't!' O'Hara fired, blasting the gun out of Stark's hand, and filling the room with sparks and smoke. 'Nobody move.'

Alpiew looked at the guns O'Hara and Timony carried. One ball was fired. Three more to go before they would need to reload.

O'Hara and Timony strode forward, all guns now pointing towards Edward Stark. 'Hand it over.'

'What are you talking about?'

'Don't play the singleton with me, Stark. You are no jack-fool.'

'Arsehole!' screeched Kate Timony. 'Let's have it.'

'We want it, Stark, and we want it now.' O'Hara spoke gently, as though addressing a child or an idiot. 'We know you have it, and, if you are not willing to give it to us, we will simply shoot your brains out and take it from you.'

Like a snake Cupid edged across the floor out of the firing line.

Timony rounded on him, pointing one gun in his direction. 'No clever tricks now, eh, blackbird.' She waved the gun back towards the bed where Cynthia and Alpiew were lined up. 'Keep out of this, you three, and all will be well.'

Alpiew sensed that the wisest course of action at this moment was to do nothing but obey them and keep quiet. How could she judge how to handle these mad people until she knew what was going on and why they were here? She pulled at Cynthia and Cupid. Together they lowered themselves and sat lined up in a row on the Countess's bed, watching.

'Don't shoot me.' Stark held his hands up. 'Tell me what you want, O'Hara. I obliged you before, did I not?'

'I was not one of your gallows clients, remember? I saved myself.' The highwayman leaped forward and slammed the muzzle of one pistol against Stark's head, the other into his abdomen. 'Not a good day for you, was it, the day I made a break for it? Knowing where I had been, who I had shared a cell with. What a big secret I know about you! It would have been so much more convenient for you had I not helped myself to freedom that day, would it not, you piece of excrement?'

'You are none of my concern, Mr O'Hara, as you yourself have just now pointed out.'

'There was another man hanged that day, remember? A coiner.' O'Hara twisted the barrel of the gun against Stark's peruke. 'He was a friend of yours, he thought, your partner. You promised *him* an escape. But he ended up not only being hanged but quartered and tarred into the bargain. I wonder why? I wonder what he knew about you?'

'It was a mistake.' Edward Stark was shaking, his mouth so dry his lips caught on his teeth as he tried to speak. 'The hangman was drunk. He should have seen to it.'

'Liar!' O'Hara rammed the guns into him, forcing him back against the wall. Stark's eyes were flicking from O'Hara to Timony.

'He broke the law, and that is why he was hanged.'

'Oh my, Mr Stark, you are turned comedian!' O'Hara chuckled. 'In prison, you see, you've nothing to do but have long, long chats. And in your friend the forger's case he did more than chat. It was more a like a swan singing his heart out before he dies.'

Stark shrugged. 'So? I produced a bond for you, did I not? You got your three hundred guineas.'

'Shall I tell your wife what we know? Would you like *her* to know the truth about you?'

'I care not what she knows about me.' Stark never took his eyes from O'Hara's face. 'So I ran a business in Southwark and you kindly informed the Excise about it today. Am I right?'

'We wanted you flushed out, right enough. But I am talking about something else. The Master of the Mint will be glad to hear the news, and the Lord Chief Justice. No one likes the law to be made a total mockery.'

'Phough!' Stark gave a sardonic sneer. '*You*, a highway-man, lecture *me* about Law and Justice? That's amusing.'

'You know the saying, Stark: Honour among thieves. But there is no honour in the soul of a double-crossing, lying, cheating sharper like you.' O'Hara ran his thumb across the pistol's lock. 'To trepan a convicted forger out of a bit of money, which was only paid to help evade the law, is one thing. But to let your own wife's father go to his death . . .'

'I didn't. The man died of natural causes. Everyone knows that.'

O'Hara twisted the gun from side to side, hooking Stark's periwig on the barrel and flicking it away, pushing the gun now into his close-cropped temples.

'What *I* know is that there was a royal pardon.'

Alpiew noticed Cupid's hands form into fists on his lap.

'Of course. Everyone knows that. The old man's sentence was commuted . . .'

'Not commuted, Stark. He was *pardoned*. Pardoned because he did *not* do any coining. But you took that document of pardon, did you not, sir, and prevented it from reaching the governor at Newgate? Instead you replaced it with one of your pretty forgeries by which he was sentenced instead to live as a convict, working the rest of his poor innocent old life, slaving on the American plantations.'

Alpiew glanced at Cynthia, who was grown ever paler.

'Why did you do that, sir? Why did you let Mrs Stark's father, an innocent old fellow who never did you any harm, go to his certain death – for we both know the plantations are a killer, even among the young and healthy?'

Edward Stark drew his lips into a tight line.

'Perhaps it is because the old man never did any coining in his life. But when the authorities got near to finding you out and discovering the forging plant you have run for years and years, you artfully concealed the tools of the trade around his home, and then informed against him.'

'What care I for your tales of royal pardons? The stuck-up old fool is dead, and so what?'

Alpiew knew Cynthia was crying, could see the silent tears falling on to her clasped hands.

'Shoot me. Go on. Shoot me.' Edward Stark jerked his head away from the pistol with an insolent jeer. 'And then go hang for it. And I will not be able to save you from the gallows this time.'

Alpiew gave a quiet cough. She didn't want to surprise either O'Hara or his partner by suddenly speaking, especially as, although she was watching the two men, Kate Timony had a pistol pointing back towards the three people seated on the bed. 'Might I suggest, Mr O'Hara, that you let us go,' she said softly. 'If your business is solely with Mr Stark?'

'Shut your hole!' screeched Kate Timony, lurching forward. 'And don't you move or I'll blow your block off.'

'Sssshh, Kate, think of your baby!' O'Hara gave Kate Timony a patronising smile. 'Mistress Alpiew is quite right. It is very tiresome of Mr Stark to keep us all here when we might be going about our business. You know what we want, Stark. All you need is to hand it over, and then we can all get away from here.'

'More bearer bonds? Tell me what you want. What? A running cash note?'

'Nothing so trivial,' said O'Hara. 'We want something worth lots of money. We want the Eye.'

'But that's not the end of the story of the *Eris*,' said the sea-dog. 'Far from it. You see, some years after this – and remember the ship went down, oh, let's see, fourteen, fifteen years ago, it must be, well, some years after that, these rumours started going round the town that Sir Richard had scuttled the ship himself, 'cos he had an insurance claim on it, see.'

'But if he was the only one to survive,' the Countess said, puzzling it through, 'who can have started such a rumour with any kind of credibility?'

'Exactly.' The old sailor waved his pipe around, stabbing the air to emphasise his point. 'That's what everyone said. But the rumours went around all the same. And they said the same thing, over and over. That Sir Richard had scuttled the ship because there was *no* cargo, no tobacco, no rum, no ivory, none of the things listed at such length in the manifest. And the only things of value that went down were the ship and the men. A few people in New York were of the opinion that Sir Richard came from Africa with no money, and here in London 'tis well known it was only thanks to the *Eris* and its cargo that he became a rich man.'

'But if this second rumour had any truth about it,' said the Countess, 'it has to be true that some of those men must have survived, just as Sir Richard did.'

'I see you're getting my point. There is a tale about that a gang of these crewmen, soldiers they were, the ones who had come up from the garrison in Africa . . .'

'With Sir Richard?'

'I don't know about that. But they were asleep in their hammocks when the fire took. When they saw the flames, they jumped overboard, into the ocean. They saw the yaugh go off. They called after it. But it didn't hang around. They saw, too, the other, bigger ship on the horizon. But no one heard their cries, or should we say no one bothered to listen. So there they are, these crewmen, bobbing up and down in the water with bits of charred timber and lengths of rope shooting up alongside 'em. Treading water all the while, they made a makeshift raft from the flotsam of the burnt-up ship. They clung to this thing for days, the sun burning down on them by day, at night shivering in each other's arms, cold as fish. There was no food but bits of sodden biscuit left in their pockets, nothing to drink but the rain. One by one the men died. And to live, the remaining men had no option but to drink the blood of their companions and eat their raw flesh. After some weeks drifting out there in the Atlantic, with nary a passing ship in sight, there was only two of 'em left. And when they were as near death as a man who doesn't find himself next day in a shroud can be, they was picked up by a French merchant ship on its way to the West Indies. These Froggies took the men to the nearest land, went out of their way to do it, so, if it's true, hats off to them Froggies, I say. They

dropped these two forlorn ragged fellows in some godforsaken place called Newfoundland, and, from what I've 'eard
tell, it might have been better if the land hadn't been found
at all. Some Puritans live there. Fishermen mainly, and fish
curers. These Puritans took 'em in, two starved coves with
scarce a lump of flesh hanging off their bones, and they
made 'em work to earn their keep, the way Puritans do.
Nothing for nothing, you know 'ow they like it. So these
two men worked, helped them drying out and curing cod
in this godforsaken place. Plaisance, the town was called.
Pleasant place in French. Pleasant enough for Puritans, but
for normal folk it was more like purgatory, nothing but
work, work, work. Laying fishes out in slow ovens, or with
salt, the *morue seche* and *morue verte*. It wasn't work like
they knew it – one was an army engineer, mended the
guns and so on, and the other in the infantry – so spending years drying fish wasn't much to their taste. Anyhow,
after some time stuck here in this Puritanical place they
finally got their strength back and had earned enough
money to get them back to America, and in America they
got work, crewing on board another, luckier ship and, years
later, finally they made their way home to London.'

'What an incredible tale,' said the Countess. 'If indeed
it is true.'

'Ay. 'Tis that.' The sailor refilled his pipe and gave a long
pull before blowing out a thin blue line of smoke. 'So,
anyhow, they'd been here in London a year or so, telling
their story, and o' course no one believed 'em. It was too
long since the *Eris* had gone down, see. No one cared about
that ship any more. No one remembered her, really. Why
should they? Ships go down all over the place, don't they?
Then, one day, one of these two castaways spied this 'ere
Dainty fellow in the street and challenged him. They
wanted to know, if there *had* been a fire on board, what

he thought he was doing jumping on to the yaugh all on his own and cutting it loose without even stopping to save his fellow ship-mates, not even calling out to see if anyone was alive or in the water.

'Next thing, the Dainty fellow had some charge brought against the soldier, and the other man went on the run. And this here friend and him made a pact together.'

'And?'

'Well, that's the rub, you see. All the rumours stopped about that time, and these fellows, the two survivors, disappeared into thin air.' The seaman sucked hard on his pipe, then flicked his tongue round the front of his brown teeth. 'If they ever survived at all, that is, and it wasn't all just some tall sea story.'

'Thank you so much for that tale, my old friend.' The Countess clambered to her feet. 'But I really have to go.' She bent down and whispered into his ear: 'You know what they say, Captain.' She winked. '*Dead* men tell no tales.'

ELEVEN

Sandiver — the dross or scum on the pot that must be removed or it will spoil the glass

Kate Timony shoved Edward Stark hard against the wall, while O'Hara, a pistol balanced under one arm, pulled open his jacket and rummaged through his pockets. With a yelp he pulled his hand out of Stark's breeches pocket. He was clutching a small envelope.

'Keep him covered, Kate.' O'Hara backed up to the table and laid one of his guns down. He tipped the envelope and emptied out the contents: a large rose-cut gem.

'So *this* is the famous Eye.' He gave a low whistle. 'Now there's one big diamond!'

He held the jewel up to the light.

A banging came from the front door.

'Who's that?' O'Hara pocketed the gemstone and aimed his pistol at Alpiew.

'It sounds like someone at the front door,' said Alpiew. 'But I am on the wrong side of it and so can't tell you who it might be.'

'It'll be the watch!' hissed Kate Timony. 'You fool, John, you shouldn't have fired that shot.'

'We've got what we wanted. Let's discamp, gal.' Snatching his second pistol from the table, he turned and with a great leap made his escape out of the window.

While the banging from the front door continued, Timony stooped to pick up Stark's gun. In the second she was down, Stark kicked her in the head, sending her sprawling over the flagstones. She lay inert in front of the Countess's bed.

'Cupid!' Alpiew dived forward. 'Come on.'

Before Stark had time to retrieve his own weapon, Alpiew and Cupid had seized a pistol each from Timony's limp hands.

'Back, Mr Stark.' Alpiew raised the gun to eye-level. 'Unlike you, I have used a firearm before, and would not be afraid to use one again.' She marched towards him. 'Now that you have lost the thing everyone is after, perhaps you might take a hint from the highwayman and make your way out of here before the watchman breaks down the door.'

Stark had a smug smirk on his face. He raised his hands in mock fright. 'Ooh, how you bold women frighten me.' He strode towards Alpiew, stepping over Kate Timony. 'We both know the truth, Madam Alpiew, do we not? O'Hara has not just now removed the gemstone called the Eye from my pocket, because said gemstone never made its way into my pocket in the first place. True, I paid a great deal of money to buy the thing from that hideous Hollander, but you and your lady double-crossed me with him, did you not? You beat me to it, and before I could get back to my place of business, you replaced the real Eye with a fake.'

'I'm sure I cannot comment on what you think my lady and I have been up to.' Alpiew gave a serene smirk. She had not a notion what he was babbling about. 'I do know, however, that you killed the grisly Dutchman in your Southwark front parlour and locked up his naked body in the trunk.'

Stark threw his head back and laughed. 'Oh, but there

is a good comical plot for you. I thought it was your mistress who wrote for the stage.'

Brushing herself down, the Countess followed the exit route described by the sea-dog, arriving in a small court-yard piled high with cases and barrels.

'Like some help?' asked a soft voice in the darkness.

'How kind.' The Countess held out her hand. A young man took it and sprang up on to the barrels, pulling her swiftly behind him. He lifted her to the top of the wall and vaulted up after her. Then, wrapping his arms tightly round her waist, he jumped with her to the ground, letting his own body break her fall. The second she had regained her equilibrium his arms wrapped tightly round her waist again.

'You are not to run, Countess.' The boy tipped his dusty hat back upon his head with an incomplete finger. 'You recognise me, do you not?'

'Jake!' But before she could finish pronouncing his name they were running helter-skelter along Stoney Street.

'Where are you taking me? I am in a hurry. Unhand me, you unmannerly brute.' The Countess tried to beat at him but her hands were pinned to her side.

The boy hustled her across the busy Dead Man's Place, where rowdy taverns still bulged with people.

'Listen, you rude rapscallion, I shall cry out a rape if you do not let me go.'

'Round here that is quite the order of the day.' Jake tightened his grip round her waist. 'Men pay good money for a woman to cry those words at him. People would think you had a good happy client. And certainly no one round here would run to your aid like I have done today.'

Aid? Could this boy be the one who had been follow-ing her in the alleyways of Southwark, and had snatched her from the arms of those two criminals, and thrust her into the air vent of the glass-house tunnels? But why? She knew he was in communication with O'Hara, so why should he save her from him?

Jake propelled her forward into a tiny courtyard, taking his arms from her waist but grasping her firmly by the hand. 'You are no coward about horses, I presume.'

A sturdy mare stood tethered to a railing. She was saddled and ready to go.

Before the Countess could run for it, Jake grabbed her slippered foot and crammed it into a stirrup. He then pushed her up, both hands on her rump. 'Lucky you are wearing that Turkish rig-me-role,' he cried when she was safely mounted astride the horse. He leapt up behind her, shot his arms forward to snatch the reins and jerked his heels into the horse's side. 'Giddy-up now, gal.'

There was not much she could do but see how events unfolded. And at least this would get her out of Southwark. She prayed it would not be to a worse place. The horse trotted out of the courtyard, cantered along Clink Street, and by the time they reached London Bridge she flew along at a full gallop.

As the dusty boy sped her along Watling Street the Countess thought hard. Two soldiers, survivors of the *Eris* were at large. Surely between them they had killed Sir Richard and the poor night-watch Charlie. And all for a jewel. The Countess had heard tales before of men swallowing jewels whole in order to smuggle them away. That way they could be secure in the knowledge that they would get the thing back sooner or later and meanwhile it was as well hidden as a thing could be.

As they ducked under Ludgate the Countess crossed herself, thinking of the wretched old man swinging in the gibbet, lacking his stomach. Though much good a stomach was to a dead man.

Eureka!

That was why the two men had been slit open and their stomachs taken. Either they had swallowed, or the thieves *believed* they had swallowed the gem.

Jake's arms tightened around her as the horse sped through the narrow Temple Bar and into the Strand.

She thought of the foolish old watchman, constantly popping his lemon drops into his mouth. To a desperate man, would a hastily swallowed lemon drop be distinguishable from a diamond? If the watchman had come in, perhaps to tell about the monkey he had been holding that morning, and surprised those two men as they went about removing Sir Richard's body from the trunk . . .

They galloped past the miraculous statue of King Charles the martyr.

The horse slowed to a canter as they turned up into the Hay Market.

'Why is this happening, Jake?' the Countess yelled to the boy as soon as the horse was travelling slowly enough for her to be heard. 'What is this unmannerly kidnapping all about?'

'I am certainly not catching you for the plantation men. I got you safely away from those ruffians, and once I was sure you were inside and they had not followed you I had to let my colleague know.' Jake called into her ear. 'He wanted you brought away from Southwark. As you see from our route, I want nothing but to get you safe and quickly to Pall Mall Street, madam, as I have been ordered to.'

'Ordered?' Now there was a strange way to go on. 'Ordered by whom, if I may inquire?'

'Whoa!' cried Jake once they were outside Sir Richard Dainty's front door.

Jake dismounted and helped the Countess down, then pushed her forward.

'In you go,' he murmured as he shoved her into the dark house. 'I will be waiting out here.'

The door slammed behind her. The house was dark and silent.

The Countess felt her way along the hall. There was no light at all.

'Lettice?' she called tremulously. 'Godfrey?' She prayed she was not about to be reunited with O'Hara and his cohort.

There was no reply.

She tiptoed into the front parlour. The shutters must have been drawn as the room was utterly dark.

She fumbled her way to the mantel, feeling along the surface for the candlestick.

It was not there.

'You need a light?' Robinson's voice. 'Can't we talk in the dark?'

'We can talk whichsoever way you please, sirrah, but I would appreciate it if you left me to choose to whom I talk and not have me transported here willy-nilly like a pig to market.' She felt her way to one of the fixed chairs round the table. 'Why can't we have a candle to light us?'

'Because we cannot find it.'

'Where is Godfrey?'

'I sent him away, about fifteen minutes ago, when I knew you were safely on your way to me. Why all these questions, Countess? Did I not aid your escape from those criminals who had held you?'

'I know all about the *Eris*. You are not the only one with a grievance against Sir Richard.'

The Countess moved her foot and felt it touch something small which rolled away.

'Tell me, Robinson, why did you take that bond from Sir Richard's room yesterday morning?'

'How do you know I did?'

'I saw it in your hand. I recognised it as I myself had brought it here the night before.'

'I wish I had never seen the thing. It was a ploy which backfired. The old man vanished before wedding my sister. I thought if I stole one of his own bonds and passed it round, it would flush him out of hiding.' Robinson let out a long sigh. 'I'd like to know why Van Loon thought it was a forgery.'

'Perhaps simply because it *was* a forgery.' The Countess stooped, feeling across the Turkey mat for the object she had just kicked. 'Tell me, Robinson, was it you who etched the word Eris upon the window pane there?'

'I did it one day when my guardian was out.' Lettice's voice drifted over from the sofa.

'Lettice!' The Countess turned towards the voice. 'What did you use?'

'A piece of glass.'

'Do you still have that glass?'

'I could probably lay my hands on it if there was some light.'

The Countess picked up the object from the floor and held it to her nose. Tallow. It was a candle. 'Do you have a tinder-box, Robinson? I believe I have a candle here.'

In the dark Robinson reached out and took it. 'Don't be startled by what you see.' He struck a few sparks and lit the tallow.

The Countess tried not to display the shock she felt when she saw that his untied lace ruff was smeared with blood.

'Where is the candlestick?' Lettice bobbed up from the sofa and started to search the room. 'We must find the candlestick, then I will show you the glass I used to scratch on the window.'

The Countess dripped wax on the table so that she could stand the candle upright.

'I have the bond here. It was used for my arrest, and I got it back before I ran. I need to know how Hendrick Van Loon knew it was a fake, if he had not done away with Sir Richard.' Robinson pulled the crumpled paper from his pocket and laid it on the table. 'Look! It is no different from any bond I have seen before.'

The Countess looked at the inscription on the outer paper: *Bearer bond – Sir Richard Dainty, Pall Mall Street*. It was certainly the same bond she had fetched from Southwark and brought here for O'Hara. She flicked it over and read. 'Good lord!' She smoothed the bond out, squinting down in the flickering light. 'Who'd have thought it? It is writ here as clear as if it was an arrest warrant.'

'What is?'

The Countess chuckled. 'No wonder Van Loon had you picked up. I am lucky they did not take me. Did you not read it?'

'Yes. It is the usual form for a bond.'

'But how about the Latin inscription?'

'Many bonds have a Latin inscription. Who bothers with those? The mottos of the drawer or the company. Remember, Countess, I did not have an education. I know no Latin.'

'I have never seen anything like this. Most humorous!' The Countess now realised why O'Hara had used her as a courier. He knew not to trust the forger, and he had been right. If the real Sir Richard had received this document, he would have scrutinised it well before handing over any money, and she would certainly have been exposed carrying a false bond. As it was, whoever it was impersonating the old man at the front door that night did not speak Latin, or they would have noticed that the inscription read: *Syngraphae corruptae. Apprehendite eum qui illas in manibus habet.* 'This bond is false. Seize the bearer.'

*   *   *

Edward Stark rested the palm of his hand on the mouth of the gun Alpiew pointed at him and pressed the barrel downwards. 'If we are going to talk, we should concentrate on the subject in hand. I will tell you what I know and it is this: you and your mistress conspired against me to get the Eye. I know you and your lady were up at Van Loon's house this afternoon, and his chairmen sent you away. I know that later you and my wife staged that embarrassing scene at the lace shop in order to delay me getting to my meeting with Van Loon. My faithless wife stayed on to fight with me in the street, till all I could do to get away was stick my pen-knife in her side to shut her mouth. When finally I arrived at Cardinal Blois Alley, Van Loon had come and gone. He had left me the goods, as he had promised. But meanwhile this colourful character here had joined the charade.' Stark tossed his head in Cupid's direction. 'I believe he followed Van Loon into my place in Southwark, and he substituted the real Eye for the cheap piece of cut-glass that Mr O'Hara has just so happily run off with. Then he came here, bringing the real diamond for the Countess.'

'I never went *into* any place down in Cardinal Blois Alley. I stood outside in the shadows. I followed Van Loon as he went down the alley, I saw him go through a door and a few minutes later I watched him come out again. I was all set to follow him, when I saw you bustling towards me.' Cupid pointed to his silver collar. 'The clever thing about these possessive collars is that they instil fear in the person unlucky enough to wear them. I saw you and I was afraid. As you came towards me down that lane, Mr Stark, I am ashamed to say I ran from you. I ran for my life.' He raised the pistol. 'I wish I had had this weapon with me then, because I would have used it. There must be someone who will put an end to you and your evil ways.'

Stark spat in Cupid's direction.

Alpiew wanted to kick herself for having earlier put the chair under the handle of the front door. The knocking had stopped.

'Peace at last!' sighed Edward Stark. 'Thank goodness for that. The racket was giving me a headache.' He flopped down into Godfrey's chair and sat back, smiling at Alpiew all the while. 'I am in no hurry, Mistress Pert. I am happy to sit here and wait for your lady to come back. A diamond as big as the Idol's Eye is worth the wait.'

Edward Stark seemed to pay no attention to Cupid, sitting only a few yards away glaring at him, his gun raised.

The calm was broken by another loud smash from above, followed by the sound of footsteps rapidly descending the stairs.

Edward Stark leapt to his feet.

Then three things happened in rapid succession:

The kitchen door slammed open. A gust of wind extinguished the solitary candle, and a gunshot rang out.

Lettice was still wandering around the room searching for the candlestick.

'Sit down, Sister. What does it matter if there is wax left on the table?'

'I must find it. Did you not want to see what I used to write on the window?'

'You used a candlestick?' The Countess thought back. She remembered that the candlestick on the mantel in this room had been a strange affair of wood, brass and glass droplets, placed before a reflecting mirror. A cheap crinkum-crankum affair she had assumed Sir Richard had bought as it would make the best use of the light.

'Come, Robinson, help us look for the candlestick.' The Countess got down on her knees and crawled under the table. 'When did you last see it here?'

'This afternoon. When Godfrey brought Captain Caruso back, the little darling flew all over the place and knocked it down and it broke. Godfrey was mending it when Robinson arrived. He is gone out now to look again for the Captain.'

'Harrumph!' growled the Countess. She knew all about Godfrey and his efforts at home husbandry. The candle-stick could be anywhere.

'I have it,' cried Robinson from the corner of the fireplace.

'So show me, Lettice –' the Countess clambered back on to the fixed seat – 'what part it was you used.'

Lettice sat beside her and pointed to one of twenty sparkling square-cut gems which studded the base and dangled from little arms around the tin reflector.

The Countess ran her finger along the circle of twinkling glass droplets. She chuckled. An old trick: the safest place to hide is in a crowd. To conceal something you value, how better to effect its disappearance than to place it among a crowd of something very similar, and keep it in full view.

She tugged a piece free and moved to the window.

'But, milady . . .' Lettice gasped.

'Hold!' Robinson held the Countess's wrist. 'You cannot open the shutters. Don't forget I am a wanted man.'

'Blow out the candle, Lettice dear, and, Robinson, go hide upstairs.'

While Robinson left the room, the Countess hauled open the shutters and placed the bauble against the window. Firmly she slid it across the glass and felt the pane.

Nothing.

'Are you sure it was this piece?'

'No.' Lettice stood at her side, holding the rest of the stick. 'It could be any of them.'

'Start breaking it up. We must find the right one.'

Methodically the Countess swiped each gem across the glass until there were none left.

'None of these pieces cut glass.' The Countess rose and held Lettice's wrists. 'You must have used something else.'

'I swear I used a piece of the candlestick.' Lettice gulped. 'Have I done wrong?'

'So where is it?' The Countess peered into the grate, searching for any pieces which may have gone astray. 'Where is the exact piece?'

'Oh dear. I couldn't actually get it back on to the stick, so I . . .'

'Yes?'

'I . . . swapped it.'

'Swapped it?' exclaimed the Countess, rising so abruptly she banged her head on the mantelpiece. 'For what?'

'Another one.'

'Another . . . ?'

'Candlestick.'

'There was a pair?'

'No. But when I couldn't get the little piece back on I rushed out to the market and bought a replacement before Sir Richard would notice I had broken it.'

'You bought another from one of the stalls in Six Bell Alley.' The Countess could see exactly what had happened. 'And I suppose you used that missing shilling to buy it?'

Lettice shrunk back, nodding. 'It was where he bought the other. It was exactly the same.'

'Hmmm.' The Countess resisted the urge to shake the child. 'And what did you do with the original candlestick?'

Lettice stepped into the fireplace and clambered up into the chimney. A flurry of soot fell into the grate as she reached up into the void and came out with another dusty stick.

The Countess took it to the window and examined it in the shimmering glow of passing links.

'There is a piece missing.'

'I didn't mean anything by it,' said Lettice. 'I was so frightened Sir Richard would be cross with me for breaking it, and I didn't know what to do with the loose piece of glass, so I put it the only place I could think of that he would never find it.'

'Yes?' The Countess looked up at her, waiting for what she knew would be a fantastic reply. 'So where is it?'

'Not here.' Lettice hung her head and spoke quietly. 'It's sewn into the clasp on Captain Caruso's belt.'

It seemed to Alpiew that in the darkness there was an unaccountable amount of screeching. Gripping her pistol she leapt from the bed and backed up towards the door. Perhaps she could get out into the hall, unhook the front door and make it out into the street where she could raise the hue and cry, bring in the constables and wait for the Countess, leaving the others to fight it out between themselves.

She had just reached the threshold, ready to bolt, when a light was struck.

Kate Timony still lay dazed on the floor.

Cynthia was standing near the fireplace, gripping a lit candle in one hand, a smoking pistol in the other. Cupid was standing stock-still, holding a tinder-box and staring down at Godfrey's chair, where Edward Stark was slumped, blood flooding across the front of his shirt.

Flying around from top to top, hanging from the wooden chandelier, then swooping down to cling to the hangings atop the Countess's bed, gibbering and shrieking all the while, was Lettice's pet monkey, Captain Caruso.

'A real diamond!' Jake staggered back. 'I thought that by telling them the piece of glass I had helped you sew on was valuable I was sending them off on a wild chase.'

When Robinson had explained the whole story to Jake, the dusty boy offered his services at once to help find the monkey and Godfrey – not an easy job in the dark empty streets of St James's.

Robinson and Lettice had taken one half of the square of streets, the Countess and Jake the other. The Countess, sitting astride Jake's horse, had circled St James's Market and now they were trotting along Charles Street heading for St James's Square.

All this mayhem for a jewel! Something so small it could be pocketed in the smallest slot of a hidden pocket, in the toe of a person's shoe, under a wig, anywhere! And the wretched thing had been sewn on to a monkey's belt.

And two soldiers, survivors of the *Eris* were at large, killing anyone who stood between them and the jewel which they believed was theirs. Surely between them they had killed Sir Richard and the poor night-watch Charlie?

And who might they be, these two soldiers, thought the Countess, one a plain infantryman, the other an engineer?

'Nothing here, Countess,' said Jake, directing the horse up York Street and into German Street.

'Halt!' As they cantered past her own front door the Countess saw that there were two people bending low, peering at the door furniture.

'Eureka!' she cried. 'Look, there is Godfrey. Set me down here, please, Jake. Godfrey!' the Countess called as Jake helped her down from the saddle. 'What is going on?'

'We're locked out!' Godfrey shrugged. 'I'm trying to get in, chasing after that ballocking monkey. I just saw the little blighter running along the rooftops and swinging in through our attic window.'

'I will go round and tell the others,' yelled Jake, turning the horse and galloping away.

'But we have no lock, Godfrey. Or rather we have no key for that lock, so how can it be functioning?'

'Don't ask me. That's why I roused this 'ere locksmith fellow from his bed to get me in.'

The Countess froze as the swarthy little man looked up from his work.

The locksmith! The man who designed the trunk for Sir Richard Dainty, who sang paeans of praise for him, who . . .

'Godfrey!' The Countess spun round, hoping she could call Jake back. 'Run!'

Bob Gaunt, the locksmith, lashed out at Godfrey and then, pressing his fist against the Countess's mouth, he flung her against the wall and pulled a lump hammer from his bag.

Godfrey staggered backwards, gathered himself and limped off.

Another man stepped from the shadows and gripped the Countess from behind. In the briefest of glimpses she saw he was swaddled up under a low hat, scarves covering his mouth. It looked like Hendrick Van Loon.

A glint of cold metal caught the Countess's eye as the swaddled man shoved her forward. He had a knife.

The locksmith meanwhile applied the lump hammer to the front door.

The Countess was bundled inside.

They were met in the dark hall by Alpiew. She held a pistol.

'Drop it,' said the man holding the Countess.

Alpiew stared at him. It could not be Van Loon. She had seen his corpse only a few hours since. Whoever this was holding the Countess, it was clear to Alpiew that he was wearing a murdered man's clothing, a murdered man who had been left naked. The man holding the Countess was a killer.

'Drop it!'

Alpiew was in two minds. The gun was their only defence. But with one certain murderer holding a knife to the Countess's neck, and his accomplice wielding a huge hammer above her head, Alpiew realised she had no option but to do as she was told.

The two men marched the Countess forward while Alpiew backed into the kitchen with her hands up.

Once they reached the kitchen the locksmith kicked the door shut behind them. Alpiew noticed he had retrieved the gun from the hall floor.

Edward Stark was still slumped in the chair, and Kate Timony lay unconscious in the middle of the floor, but Cupid and Cynthia were gone. Alpiew heard them making their escape over the back wall. The other pistol was gone with them.

'Aha!' The man holding the Countess shoved her forward. 'Look who you have as a guest. Did he try to take de diamond from you? Mr Stark wouldn't like being left wid a fake. Not when he had paid for de real thing. But, you see, I know where it is, de Eye. It is here with you in dis house, or upon de person of de Countess. But it is mine.'

'Who are you?' Slowly Alpiew edged away from the men. 'You are not Van Loon.'

'Step away from the fireplace, woman.' Swinging the hammer, the locksmith jumped towards Alpiew. 'No clever ideas like pokers, please. Let's just keep it quiet and sensible. You have something which belongs to us, and we will get it back, whichever way we have to.'

The Countess was flung into her easy chair, a large rope tossed round her and tightened. 'You have forgot one thing.' The Countess struggled against her bonds, realising that by fighting she was only tightening the knots. 'My man Godfrey is on his way to fetch the constable and you will be taken.'

The swaddled man strolled over to the fireplace.

'Now there's a jester for you! The watchman is fast asleep.'

'I didn't say the watchman – I said the constable.'

The swaddled man pulled off the scarves and hat, and dropped the Dutch woollen greatcoat to the floor. 'And I *am* the constable, madam. Constable John Shaw, formerly Captain William Ferguson of His Royal Highness's 2nd Foot. An infantryman. Stationed in Bambara for a while under the governorship of the late Colonel Richard Dainty, along with my colleague, *Sergeant* Bob Gaunt.'

'I know the rest,' said the Countess with a sigh. 'Your story is indeed a tragic one, Captain. Being left for dead on a raft upon the ocean with neither food nor water through another man's greed is a woeful thing. But you have no grudge against us. How have Alpiew and I harmed you?'

'Right from the start you have interfered.' The constable, now down to his breeches and shirt, inspected Edward Stark. 'You are apparently not above a spot of murder yourselves. This man looks at death's door.' He touched Kate Timony with the toe of his boot. 'And she is out.' He surveyed the rest of the room, noting the smashed window. 'You've had a few visitors already, I see.' He span round to face the Countess. 'Now, before they come back, hand it over.'

'The Eye is gone,' said Alpiew. 'Along with the crooks who took it from Mr Stark.'

'Don't mess with me!' screamed the constable, rushing forward and pushing Alpiew to the floor. 'I know it is here.'

Alpiew hit the flagstones and sprawled out alongside Kate Timony. From this angle she suddenly realised the floor under all the beds was a carpet of feathers.

Bob Gaunt handed John Shaw his hammer.

'Stark's gem was a fake.' Shaw held the hammer above

Alpiew's head. 'I sent a message this afternoon to Van Loon. I knew he had just taken possession of the thing. He was aware Sir Richard had gone to meet his maker as we had sent him a little souvenir. He didn't like that, Mr Fastidious, not at all, receiving a stomach in a box in the penny post, but it made him appreciate that we were serious about getting our jewel back. He couldn't wait to sell the thing on, to be rid of it, and, as he thought, us.'

'So he sold it to Stark,' said Alpiew into the floor, sneezing from the dust and a feather tickling her nose. 'And as I have just told you, Mr Stark's jewel was taken by John O'Hara, the highwayman partner of this woman lying unconscious beside me.'

'O'Hara! We're not that simple.' The locksmith sniggered. 'Van Loon was a double crossing swine, just like his friend Dainty. Who do you think was waiting out there in the middle of the Atlantic to pick him up in his stolen yaugh? They were together right from the start.'

'Calm yourself, Bob, you always were the impetuous one. I've had enough of your mistakes, knocking off that old watchman, 'cos he found you here that day.' Constable Shaw shook his head and tutted. 'Bodies are hard things to get rid of.' He made himself comfortable, straddling Alpiew, pressing her shoulder down, holding the hammer up.

'Perhaps you might like to continue your story about the Eye,' said the Countess, who, whenever the men weren't watching, was patiently working at the ropes which bound her.

'We knew this fellow Edward Stark here was after the diamond too, and Van Loon was very keen to sell, so we made sure Van Loon believed that Stark had changed his meeting so that we could take possession of the diamond before he got there. And I went to Stark's hideout and lay in wait for the mad Dutchman to come and bring me the Eye.'

Alpiew turned her head slightly. She saw Kate Timony's eyelids flicker. She could also see, tucked under Godfrey's bed, the handle of a gun. Stark's pistol, which O'Hara had shot out of his hand.

'So Van Loon arrived, gibbering away in his usual foreign fashion, and then fetched the gem out of his pocket so easily that I knew it was a set-up. Even when I pulled the sticks out of his nose and puffed my breath all over his fat face, he went on and on about it being the genuine jewel. I had to slam my hands across his mouth to shut him up. He was squealing like a pig. Then I just hit him and hit him and he squealed more. I knew he wouldn't trust leaving the real gem alone in his home with those nosy chair-boys of his around the place; it had to be on his person. So I stripped the clothes off him. I then noticed how keenly he protected a certain part of his anatomy. Not so squeam-ish when it comes to keeping a gemstone for himself, it seems. Do you know where the miserable sod was keep-ing the Eye?'

'No.' Alpiew lay still, watching Kate Timony. 'Where?'

'Up his arse!' The constable and the locksmith both guffawed. 'He hid the diamond up his porthole! Now there's a Dutchman for you. But once we'd killed him it wasn't so hard to get it out, was it?'

'Piece of cake,' sniggered Bob Gaunt.

'If you have the gem, Constable, why are you still here?' The Countess wished he would get up and away from Alpiew. Her knots were sufficiently loose now for her to attempt an escape if only she could be sure Alpiew would be safe. 'Spit it out, man. What do you want from us?'

'You are a pair of lying thieves,' yelled the locksmith, waving the gun about and striding towards the Countess.

'The one up his bum was a fake and all. We only knew this once we got it back to my workshop.'

'So tell me who was in there visiting the Dutchman just before he came to see Stark?' The constable jumped up and turned on the Countess. 'You can't fool me with your disguises. You've got the real Eye. It has to be you.'

From the pantry, the monkey, which had been busy up till now raiding the jars for biscuits, gave a loud screech and sprang back into the kitchen to perform a series of somersaults.

'What the hell?' yelled John Shaw, spinning round. 'Shut that thing up, Bob!'

Bob Gaunt was holding the gun with both hands, trying to get the monkey into view as it pirouetted across the various pieces of furniture.

The Countess watched the creature flying through the air like a dancer at the French ballet. She squinted at the monkey's belt and could see no twinkle, only a dull glint.

With a yelp, Bob Gaunt pulled the trigger.

The Countess was not sure whether the shot had propelled him or he had jumped nimbly away out of sheer fright at the noise but, in the puff of smoke, the monkey disappeared through the window at great speed.

When he was gone, silence reigned.

On the floor Alpiew caught eyes with Kate Timony and the two women moved simultaneously, Alpiew grabbing Stark's gun, Kate jumping to her feet, seizing the hammer from John Shaw and flinging him forcefully against the wall.

The Countess wiggled her arms free and slid out of the bonds, pulling the rope away from the chair and throwing it over Bob Gaunt. She tugged at the end till the rope was tight.

Alpiew aimed the gun at the two men.

In the same instant the front door flung open and in marched Robinson, Jake and the Black-Guard boys. Godfrey and Lettice hovered in their midst.

Behind them all came the Justice and a corps of men from the trained bands.

TWELVE

Lear — the special furnace used to cool and anneal the glass

Pigalle poured champaign into her flint glasses.

'*Zut!* You two. Always in an adventure.' Pigalle passed a glass each to the Countess and Alpiew. 'And zey are a pretty pair of love-birds, your little Cupid and Cynthia.' Pigalle quaffed a glass in one gulp.

'It is very kind of you to let them stay here, Duchesse,' said Robinson, perched on the end of a chair covered in four sleeping cats.

'I have known ze boy since he was zis big,' she said, holding her thumb and forefinger a few inches apart, and flopping down on to the settee next to the Countess. 'I know too of a French jeweller with ze finest tools for removing zat horrible thing from his neck.'

The sun was up but no one in the house wanted to sleep. There was still too much to talk about.

Lettice sat in a corner playing with Captain Caruso and Millicent.

Alpiew moved over to a desk in the corner. There was barely a space on it, but somewhere between a stuffed alligator, a brass azimuth, a stack of plays by Molière and a human skull, Alpiew found enough room to rest a piece of paper.

She dipped her pen and started making notes.

Dribbling gently into his champaign, Godfrey dozed in a chair near the fire.

'So it was you paid the boy Jake to follow us?' The Countess smiled at Robinson. 'But how did you know to trust him?'

'He was at the poor house with Lettice. We have always tried to help one another out, Jake and I. He told me about those two crooks who paid him to accompany you that night on your journey to Southwark, and helped me watch out for Lettice. On my behalf he brought the news of the *Cassandra* being all right, in a desperate bid to get Sir Richard back to the wedding.'

'You did not really plan to kill the old man once the wedding was over?'

'Of course not, Countess. Once Sir Richard was wed to Lettice, we planned to present him with the whole story. He would see that he was hoist upon his own petard, for by marrying Lettice the debt would be his. We wanted nothing from him but freedom.'

'But of course –' having quaffed her champaign, the Countess presented her glass to Pigalle for a refill – 'you realise that because the cargo on *Eris* was non-existent and because Sir Richard scuttled the ship with an intent to defraud, your father's liability is nil.'

'There is another thing you haven't explained,' said Alpiew, sucking on the end of her pen and looking up from her writing. 'Why did you rob us?'

'I didn't.'

'All our money went missing at about the same time you and Cupid were discovered tidying the Countess's house on the day the poor watchman was killed.'

'We were searching for the legal document of Cynthia's father's pardon which O'Hara had placed in your house.

As far as I saw, there was nothing there to rob. Not a farthing in the house.'

'But how did you know about the pardon, and why were you looking for it in my kitchen?' The Countess took a long swig of champaign and loosened her belt.

'I knew Stark was in mortal fear of O'Hara from the moment he escaped the gallows.' Robinson put his hand out to move one of the cats sprawled across the easy chair so that he could sit. The cat bared its fangs, hissed and lashed out. 'I knew also that O'Hara was *not* one of his clients. If he had been, why would Mr Stark be scared of him? I saw the note O'Hara sent him, in which he claimed to have the incriminating pardon, and demanding money – and I vowed to find it. Without the document I doubt Cynthia would have believed it *could* have been the truth. Anyway, I also knew from Jake that O'Hara and Timony were sleeping rough, and the only house they had been in was yours, so it seemed to me a logical place for him to have hidden something like that. The best hiding place for anything is among more of the same. To hide a bit of paper – where better than among pieces of paper? Cupid and I went there to look for it. And, pardon me, Countess, for saying this, but it is easier to search through papers when they are in some kind of order.'

'This pardon . . .' Alpiew peered over her shoulder. 'Was it in some foreign language?'

'All English legal documents are in Latin, are zey not?' said Pigalle, rolling her eyes.

'Then I have seen it. It is with a pile of my lady's recipes, lying in the front hall,' said Alpiew, dipping her pen and making another note.

'You have seen it! Please forgive me, Countess.' Robinson leapt up. 'I must go and collect it now. It is a painful thing for her, but its existence is not only more evidence for any trial of Edward Stark, but also means freedom for Cynthia. No number of Lords would refuse to grant her a divorce from a man who had flouted their laws to that extent.'

Robinson grabbed his hat and ran out of the house.

'I still don't understand, Ashby darling.' Pigalle sat back and a cat leapt out from behind her with a growl. 'How many people have you had in your house zis week? And how did two men come to be killed zere?'

'Well, Olympe, Sir Richard was lured away from the wedding by a fake rumour of his own arranging. He knew he would be able to make hundreds even thousands of pounds in a few minutes, particularly since no one would expect him to leave his own wedding. Then the other nice boy, prompted by Robinson, contradicted the rumour, trying to chase the old man back to the ceremony.

'What Robinson hadn't bargained for, though, was that, as Sir Richard hurried back to continue the wedding before the end of canonicals pushed up the price, he bumped into, or rather, was intercepted by Bob Gaunt, the locksmith.'

'Why was he in such a hurry anyhow?' said Pigalle. 'Ze old *raclure* could have had her ze next day, ze next week . . .'

The Countess raised her fingers to her lips. They watched Lettice play for a moment before continuing in a whisper.

'That was the point of the love-letters Robinson kept writing. Very clever of the boy. The letters inspired the old man to think he would lose her, worked him up into a frenzy of fear about it, in fact. With misers like him, even when they don't want a thing they don't want anyone else to get it. Besides, the old fellow had got rather taken with the idea of a young wife.'

'Ze way these senile *patapoufs* all do.'

'So the locksmith intercepts him in the Hay Market and says, "Do you know, Sir Richard, while you were away just now, I saw some people running off out of your house and along the street with the money box I made for you." And drags him up to German Street. A constable is waiting outside the door with his staff of office (having just over-seen the delivery of the fake box), and the locksmith yells ahead, "Oh, did you see which way they took the big colourful box?" And naturally the constable says, "Through that door –" pointing to my front door. Sir Richard, now agitated beyond belief, enters my house. The locksmith follows him in and talks briefly to Godfrey, just to make sure the real business is not interrupted, while the con-stable marches the old man up the stairs to the top land-ing, where Sir Richard is so astonished at the sight of his box that he fails to see the constable raise his staff. The constable pushes the old man into the attic, he then pulls out the old fool's rusty sword from his scabbard and threat-ens him with a thousand deaths if he doesn't hand over the Eye. Of course the old fellow babbles away, saying he knows of no such item, and he's swallowing away out of fear. So our friend the constable concludes that the old man has just eaten the diamond, and puts an end to him. He then searches his clothing to make sure, and finds nothing but the two pieces of paper I later discovered. He crams these under the base of the trunk, and bundles the body in after them, then locks it and leaves my house.'

'Why use your house at all?'

'He'd been up there when the monkey first came in, saw how we rarely use the upstairs rooms, and thought what a perfect place it would be to hide something. And on a normal day it would have been. But that night, in came the crooks and sent me off to fetch their money, arranged for them by Stark.'

'And all hell broke loose,' sighed Alpiew from the desk. 'Lord, madam, but we have so many stories here. I am

362

jotting down the headings: Captain Caruso; Cynthia and the lost Flanders lace, and the lace shop; Mr Stark and that girl, Moll; Robinson and his sister; Jake and the Black-Guard boys; Sir Richard, the colonel, governor of Bambara and the theft of the Eye . . .' She laid down her pen. 'You realise, Countess, you almost caught them when you went to pick up the bond O'Hara had got out of Stark? The two murderers were in Sir Richard's house, searching high and low still for the wretched diamond. But we almost upset their game.'

'Really?'

'Yes. After O'Hara left us, we raised the hue and cry. Hearing it, the constable had to put in an appearance. So he had to rush off, leaving Gaunt alone in Dainty's house. That must explain why Gaunt wrote that note. He had made the key to the Ludgate gibbet, but had not had time to discuss the details with the constable. So he left it on the table, next to the hastily scratched directions.'

'I told you I did not write that inscription "R. Gibb's Lud", or whatever it was,' said Lettice quietly from the corner.

''Ave some more to drink, *petite*,' squawked Pigalle, wielding a great silver pot. 'Go on, Ashby, *chérie*. Continue . . .' Pigalle poured Lettice a steaming dish of chocolate, then flopped down beside the Countess. 'I want to know about all these corpses you kept finding.'

'Well, the next day, as Godfrey said, my house was busier than a harlot's bed. We left home before dawn and went to Sir Richard's. The two *Eris* survivors had gone from there, taking the real trunk with them. But not having found the wretched jewel they came back to my house to search the old man again. When they didn't find the Eye upon his clothing, they took him out into the yard and removed his stomach. But they were disturbed at their work by Godfrey, who came home looking for the monkey. So they clambered over the back wall, and hurriedly dragged Sir Richard's corpse along the alley and into the back door of the constable's house.'

'That's when I arrived at the constable's front door,' said Alpiew. 'He was all sweaty and tousled. I sent him back round to German Street, where of course he and the Countess found the body gone.'

'I suppose it must have been around this time that Godfrey found the monkey in the watchman's hut,' said the Countess. 'Anyhow, after I left, Bob Gaunt came back to the yard. They'd left Sir Richard's stomach in the privy, and while Gaunt was fetching it, out comes the watchman with a bag of nuts for the monkey. "Oops!" he cries, stooping to pick up a nut, then has the misfortune to pop a lemon drop into his mouth just as Gaunt is wondering where the jewel has got to. And that was the end of him. But Robinson and Cupid pick this moment to arrive in the kitchen to search for the royal pardon. So Gaunt hauls the old Charlie into the privy until the coast is clear and he and the constable can come back for him.

'But the constable decided on a better way to flush them out. So minutes later he arrived at the front door and frightened them away,' added Alpiew, still scratching away at her notes.

'And a short while later Cupid came back and hid in the trunk, where we found him.'

'While we were at lunch, Robinson came back looking for Cupid and the pardon, but was discovered in the house by the night-soil men, who chased him round the house and almost caught him . . .'

'Enough history!' screeched Pigalle, leaping to her feet and hovering on her six-inch heels. She teetered to the table and returned dangling a bottle of champaign over the Countess's glass.

'But, Olympe, darling, the real mystery is still unsolved.' The Countess stretched and yawned while Pigalle topped her up. 'Whatever did happen to the real jewel?'

'Ze one from ze monkey's belt?' Pigalle flopped down again, glass in one hand, bottle in the other. 'Why, Ashby, you are wearing it.'

The Countess jumped to her feet with a screech. 'What!'

'I looked at zat belt on ze monkey and thought it far too garish a clasp for an animal's belt. And so I swapped it for another jewelled clasp of my own.' Pigalle inclined her head. 'Mine had a similar cut-glass *bijou* sewn in, but mine was rose-cut, so much prettier.'

'This is no glass, Olympe.' The Countess was staring in awe at the jewel in the centre of the belt holding up her Turkish pantaloons. She lurched forward, beating at Pigalle with both fists. 'Do you know that by putting this on me you could have had me killed?'

'I think you are very good at getting yourself killed, Ashby darling, without any help from me. More champaign?'

Lettice gasped. 'The piece of the chandelier I got Jake to help me sew on to the Captain's belt was a diamond?'

'Ze Eye!' wailed Pigalle with a wink in her direction.

'Why did you get Jake to help you?' Alpiew's pen was poised.

'Have you ever tried to get a needle through leather?' Lettice adjusted the monkey's belt.

'That explains it . . .' Alpiew rose and presented a complicated drawing like a family tree. 'I began to wonder whether there was a real diamond at all. So this is it –' She pointed at the Countess's midriff. 'The Duchesse's *bijou* went off in Captain Caruso's belt. When Van Loon was told Sir Richard was dead he got his men to catch the monkey, took the bijou out and sent it to the glass-house to be copied. While the Countess watched from the hackney cab, he picked up the fake and what he thought was the real thing. The bijou disappeared up his own fundament, the copy of the bijou he presented to Stark.'

'Who cares about the copies?' The Countess was screaming and bouncing up and down, trying to pull the buckle off as though her clothing was aflame. 'Get this thing off me.'

As she flung the belt away, a thundering on the street door followed by feet bounding up the stairs brought her to a halt.

'Quickly, Countess —' Robinson, blanched of all colour and covered with smuts, ran into the room. 'Run fast. Everyone!' He darted out and clattered down the stairs again.

With no belt to hold them up, the Countess's pantaloons fell silently to the floor.

'What on earth is the hurry?' Alpiew called down the stairs.

'Fire!' shouted Robinson from the street. 'Fire is the hurry!'

THIRTEEN

flammiform — glass in the resemblance of a flame

The Countess, wrapped in a Chinese gown of Pigalle's, stood beside Godfrey while her home in German Street burned to the ground.

Alpiew had tried to join Robinson and others pulling charred pieces of furniture from the debris, but once the upper rafters and the roof started tumbling in, they all gave up.

As the men tugged away their fire-engine and sealed up the wooden water pipes in the street, Robinson was sifting through the pile of papers he had rescued from the hall. 'Your recipes are saved, Countess. And your play.'

'*Love's Last Wind*,' sighed the Countess, resting on a tethering post. 'That just about sums it up.'

'Perhaps that fire that Cynthia was trying to set finally caught,' said Alpiew, handing the Countess two spokes from the back of her easy chair. 'And all those feathers everywhere, and the draught from the broken window . . .'

'Who cares what started it?' said the Countess gazing at the ruins. 'What difference can that make now? We are all washed up, Alpiew. Things couldn't get any worse for us.'

'You're dismissed!' cried Mrs Cue, red-faced as ever, as

she bustled towards them, fanning herself with a sheaf of papers. 'Dispatched, relieved of your services. That's it. End of the joke. Very funny. Ha, ha, ha. Phough, what is that acrid smell? Your contract with the *Trumpet* is terminated.'

'Kiss my cooler, Missus Cue!' Alpiew loomed over Mrs Cue, a fist raised ready to strike her. 'What's your game? Can't you see how upset we are?'

'Upset! *You're* upset? What about me!' Mrs Cue was so red now she looked as though she was about to keel over in an apoplexy. 'How upset do you think I am? There I was, on your orders, first thing this morning in that wretched lace shop, with my footboy ready to take notes for a drawing as you suggested, and whom do I surprise, naked and sweating, playing at the old rumpy-pumpy in the private rooms, but my new engraver, Sal, and my husband, Mr Cue. Oh, and the Queries column is out, too. Whoever heard such nonsense? Swallows flying to Africa every winter, indeed! Where did you dream that one up? Everybody knows they fly to the Moon.'

'I'm sorry,' said Alpiew, 'but you can't punish *us* if your husband lets you down.'

'Can I not?' said Mrs Cue, brushing down her apron and marching away. 'Just watch me! Phough!' She wiped her cheeks with her ink-stained apron. 'All these smuts! I will never get my face clean.'

'No house,' said the Countess.

'No job,' said Alpiew.

''Ere, you!' A blowsy girl in a very low-cut dress was crossing the road, waving at Alpiew.

'Oh lord, madam. The shares! That woman still has shares in your company.'

'I need a word, wench.' The woman stood before Alpiew. 'You know those shares you were going around buying up the day after the African prince came . . . ?'

'Did I?' stammered Alpiew. 'I don't remember.'

The Countess tilted her head away, scared the girl would recognise her as the Prince of Kong's castrated translator.

'You only bought half a per cent though, be fair.' Alpiew was waiting for a fist in the face.

'Do you know, I spent the last of my wages buying those things.' The wench stood with her hands on her hips, her head thrown back. 'All the men who bought that day managed to sell theirs, but I didn't realise I was meant to.'

'I'm sorry.' Alpiew was gathering her skirts together, ready to run for it. 'But I'll buy them back from you. How much do you want?'

'Are you joking?' She stepped towards Alpiew.

Alpiew flinched.

'One of the young fellows in Jonathan's saw my certificate and his eyes popped out on stalks. Next thing I know he gave me ninety-five pounds. It was a great day for ARSE. Ninety-five pounds! I chucked in the job, and I'm buying my own tavern now out in Hackney.'

The woman grabbed Alpiew and gave her a kiss. 'So thank you deary. If ever you need a job drawing ale, or pouring strong waters to the guests, pop up to the White Swan and I'll see you right.'

Smiling, the ex-coffee house, now tavern-keeping wench swung off down the street.

'I suppose, Alpiew, you don't have any of those shares you bought back?'

Alpiew shook her head and sank down against a tethering post. 'I threw them all into the night-soil wagon.'

'No hope of a windfall then.' The Countess let out a long sigh, gazing in disbelief at the smoking timbers. 'Well, at least no one was hurt.'

'Yes,' said Alpiew. 'We still have each other.'

'And we've still got all our money,' sighed Godfrey.

'Yes.' Alpiew and the Countess sighed in unison. 'We still have all our money.'

Alpiew gave a start.

'No, we don't, you senile old fool,' barked Alpiew. 'Someone took all our money, remember!'

'Mistress Alpiew! Mistress Alpiew!' Mr Foe was scurrying towards them, waving his arms in the air. 'You said to visit you, if I was passing, and here I am on my way up to St James's Palace. Got a new job. Supervising the Lottery, of all things. Very exciting.'

Alpiew wondered how it was that people's timing was always so skew. 'You remember Mr Foe, Countess?'

'Mr Foe!' The Countess looked up at him. 'Yes. I'll never forget that mole.'

'Are these all your jottings?' Foe eagerly surveyed the stacks of singed papers piled up round the Countess. 'My word, what a lot of work. Could I take a peek?'

Alpiew handed him a sheet from the top of the pile, the cleanest piece of paper she could find.

'It's not a good time to call at the moment. We have had a disaster. But I'll come and see you another day.'

'Lotteries Office, that's where I'll be. A good, official, paid job, for the government.' Foe groaned. 'Oh, I know what you're thinking. Yes. I'll never get down to writing that book now. After all, I'll be forty years old in a few months.' He moved off. 'Oh, and by the way, I'm not called Foe any more. I took your advice and changed my name. I added a De. My full name is now Daniel Defoe.'

As he walked away, Defoe glanced down at the notes Alpiew had given him. He crumpled up the paper and dropped it in the gutter.

'Ludicrous pomposity,' said the Countess as she watched him turn down into Duke Street. 'Whoever adds a De to their name nowadays? And whoever heard of anyone over forty successfully taking up writing?'

Alpiew picked up the crumpled paper: *Colonel? Jake? Robinson? Caruso? Molly? Flanders?* No wonder he had discarded it. It was meaningless.

'Oh, Godfrey, about that money . . . ?' The Countess turned back to Godfrey.

'There was no thief,' grunted Godfrey. 'That's what I was trying to say. I took the money for safekeeping, but . . .'

'*You* took it?' The Countess squinted at Godfrey. It was clear that even if he had taken the money he no longer had possession of it. 'Have you spent it all on drink?'

'Well,' said Godfrey, brushing himself down. 'If you're going to be like that . . .' He snorted, a long harmonic sniff with a rattling sound to it. 'I did take our money, and I still have it, but, well, it's not exactly *all* our money.'

'Godfrey,' barked the Countess, 'what are you prattling about? Spit it out, man.'

'I went in to the house when I was searching for the ruddy monkey, and I got all the money from our hidey-holes and took it to Sir Richard's house. All hundred guineas of it.'

'And *then* what did you do?' Alpiew loomed over him.

'The thing is, I only did it 'cos this fellow was putting pressure on me and I couldn't get rid of him.'

'What . . . ?' said the Countess. 'What happened to it? How much is gone?'

'We have forty-nine pounds left.' Godfrey flinched, expecting Alpiew to hit him.

'Forty-nine pounds!' The Countess smiled, and rested her hand on Godfrey's. 'It was good that you took it, Godfrey. If you hadn't, no doubt one of those ruffians would have had it all. Oh, forty-nine pounds is a good sizable amount. We can live on that for a while.'

371

'And the rest?' Alpiew was not feeling so forgiving.

'This thing –' Godfrey plunged his hand into his jacket pocket and pulled out a sheet of foolscap paper – 'I don't even know what it means. But it cost me fifty pounds.'

The Countess and Alpiew glanced at the document.

'Certificate of insurance? Really?' The Countess gazed ahead at the rubble of her home. 'And what does a certificate of insurance entail exactly, Alpiew?'

But Alpiew was too busy kissing Godfrey, her arms thrown around him, her bosom pressed close to his.

Godfrey was so astonished he didn't even have the leisure to enjoy the embrace.

'You wonderful, wonderful creature, Godfrey.' Alpiew turned and put her other arm around the Countess. 'Godfrey has insured the house against fire. They will pay us to build a new one.'

'Really? Someone will pay us to have a new house? How wonderful!' The Countess had perked up. 'So what about the other pound, Godfrey? What became of the other pound?'

'I knew you'd ask that.' Godfrey looked sheepish. 'We'll know on Monday . . .'

'Monday?' The Countess pursed her lips and screwed up her eyes. 'All right, Godfrey, what exactly happens on Monday?'

'I put the other pound on the lottery.'

'Ah well.' The Countess laughed, getting up from her post. 'No point sitting round here moping. We have forty-nine pounds, we have each other, we have a pound on the lottery . . .'

'We have hope,' added Alpiew, as they swung arm in arm along the smoky street.

'And, God willing,' said the Countess, 'we have tomorrow.'

HISTORY

I have received lots of e-mails and many people have approached me to discuss the veracity of events in the Countess series. When I ask them which are the fictitious bits that worry them they inevitably mention something that I have stolen hook, line and sinker from history.

So here is a little post-script:

I am always astonished to see how many Restoration words, lost now in England, are still to be found going strong in America. Although I have used the word jacket throughout, the correct Restoration usage would be the American 'vest'. 'Pocketbooks' were larger than a wallet and smaller than a suitcase. Yet again the Americans have it right. 'Pud' is another word I have used which is still current in the States. Over there it is not an abbreviation of pudding.

Turnpikes were introduced in London to solve traffic problems and to generate finance to pay for roadworks. Again the Americans still have it. The New Jersey Turnpike is one of the major gateways to New York City.

There was an efficient penny post service in London at this time. Collections were made from postal stations within shops and taverns every hour, and there were up to fifteen deliveries a day. Most letters posted before 9 p.m. reached their recipient on the day of posting.

The people who write in to criticise me for talking about the penny post 'over a century before it existed' should note that Rowland Hill only improved on the existing service, made the cost of a letter payable by the sender rather than the recipient, and introduced adhesive penny stamps.

The Bank of England was founded in 1694 to solve the National Debt problem. Over a hundred women were among the primary investors. In 1699 the bank operated from Grocer's Hall.

Though ships had been insured by Lloyds for many years, insuring houses against fire was new, and life insurance was an idea being talked about. Ship insurance was based on the principle of unlimited liability – the same rule which bankrupted so many Lloyds underwriters in recent years.

Stocks and shares were new ways of using money, but all dealing was done in the coffee houses and on the Royal Exchange. In 1699 the Stocks Market was a square where vegetables were sold.

The laws of debt, along with ever-escalating prison charges, meant that a debtor could be arrested and kept in prison for life by his creditors. Dickens later expounded on this problem in *Little Dorrit*, *David Copperfield*, etc.

The Poor House was a newish invention. The first was opened in Bristol in 1696 and was a going concern with profits to be made. Poor Houses had not yet earned the scandalous reputation they had by the time Dickens wrote *Oliver Twist*.

Pregnant women with no visible husbands were discouraged from settling, because bastards born within the parish boundaries had the right to support from that parish. An act of 1576 had made it an offence to beget illegitimate children likely to be chargeable to the parish. Any suspected father was forced to give security to 'save the Parish harmless'. A woman's word was considered proof enough to make a man liable for the child's Parish expenses.

Any person in receipt of Parish relief was obliged to wear a large red or blue P on their outer garments.

Inheritance and marriage laws made widowhood the most highly sought state. While young, a woman's wealth generally belonged to her parent; once married, it belonged to her husband; but once he had turned up his shoes . . .

Although on marriage a woman was deemed free of debt, the debts of dead parents and husbands were inherited by their children and wives.

When peace broke out all over Europe, the British Army was all but laid off. The Tangerines, 2nd foot, were used to support colonial interests in Africa, and there is a true tale of a diamond taken from an idol. Throughout the history of diamonds there are stories of people having their stomachs cut out to make sure they haven't swallowed a jewel.

All the events concerning the *Eris*, from the sinking by fire down to the crew members drinking their ship-mates' blood and finally washing up at Newfoundland courtesy of a French merchantman where they were made by the Puritans to pay their way home working in the cod farms, are from the true account of the slave galley *Luxborough*.

Cod was a rarity, more expensive and sought after than prime beef.

Hot chocolate was something of a craze. In France a duchess was brought to bed of a black baby. This was believed to be the result of imbibing too much chocolate. The infant died when only a few days old.

Southwark was and was not part of London. Although for some purposes it passed as a London ward, it was technically in Surrey and still passed as a Liberty where the law could be openly flouted. The liberties had been made illegal a few years before 1699, but in Southwark no one seemed to notice. Although the theatres and bear gardens were long gone, there were plenty of brothels and taverns, also the notorious Clink prison. Both the prison and the brothels were founded by Cardinal Blois, a relative of William the Conqueror's son Stephen Blois.

Forgers were more likely to hang than highway robbers; forgery and coin clipping were considered treason. Isaac Newton was busily regulating the currency at the Royal Mint, but coining cases still popped up. The actress Susannah Percival's father was taken for a coiner and, after much pleading by famed actors and writers, his death sentence was transmuted to deportation to the American plantations. He died on the way to Portsmouth.

America served as a dumping ground for undesirables, as Australia was later to do. Young men with no prospects subscribed for the free passage to America in exchange for four years' work on the plantations, and their eventual freedom. Few lasted the course. Other Englishmen paid their way out, tried the plantations for a while, and moved on to establish themselves all over the new continent. Oliver Cromwell had already deported many Irish and English Catholics to a life of slavery on the plantations. Like their black African co-workers, the white Catholics were not offered the option of eventual freedom.

The African slave trade was in its very early days. Up till this point black servants in Britain lived on similar terms to white servants. In many cases the lot of a black servant was easier, as their beauty was hugely admired, and they were frequently dressed in sumptuous clothes and treated more like a pampered child than a servant. Many 'Moors' chose to stay on with their ladies even after the women had lost their money or prestige. There were many black musicians, swordsmen, soldiers, masseurs and entertainers in London from Tudor times through to the start of the eighteenth century. Most of them were descended from black families who had been in England for centuries. These people were nothing to do with the slave trade.

Boys, many of whom had escaped from the Parish or were runaway apprentices, together with ex-army personnel used the nealing arches under glass-houses for free accommodation. Much of this, along with the ways of the dusty boys, the 'City Blackguard' is described by Defoe in his novel *Colonel Jack*.

Daniel Defoe was thirty-nine in 1699 and went by the name Daniel Foe. His only literary offerings up to this point were pamphlets, mainly diatribes against stock-broking. He was officially put in the pillory a few years later, but by 1699 had lost the amazing amount of £17,000 and been declared bankrupt. Among his investments were a diving bell which never came back up and civet cats which were seized by creditors before they produced any musk. Around this time he took an advisory job at the Lotteries Office. He had worked in wholesale hosiery and poultry, and lived with his wife at his mother-in-law's house in Stoke Newington. Jonathan Swift called him 'an illiterate fellow'. He was also known as 'the Hackney Turnip'. Defoe's first novel, *Robinson Crusoe*, was not published till Defoe was fifty-nine, in 1719, twenty years after this book is set.

ACKNOWLEDGEMENTS

I would like to thank:

Peter Bennet at J. M. Finn for explaining stockbroking and the principles of white-collar crime;

Colin Brain for information on glass-making and glass-houses – and for his wonderful website on seventeenth-century glass: http://www.interalpha.net/customer/cbrain/home.htm;

Delphine Cingal for assistance with French swear-words, and Claude Amoz for the Latin bond translation;

KS for explaining bonds of every variety and pounding the streets of Southwark with me, while encountering every diabolical waiter and waitress that London has to offer;

Philip Prowse for luring me back to the stage after ten years off. I adored playing in *Chéri*;

Jill Benedict and Celia Imrie for so many things, especially looking after my cats while I was in America;

All the fans I have met along the road, and in particular to the RAMmers. Thank you for your enthusiasm and generosity when I was touring in the States;

And of course Julia Wisdom and her amazing crew at HarperCollins.